*Of Flesh and Blood*

BY DANIEL KALLA
FROM TOM DOHERTY ASSOCIATES

DANIEL KALLA

# *Of Flesh and Blood*

A TOM DOHERTY ASSOCIATES BOOK

NEW YORK

OF FLESH AND BLOOD

Copyright © 2010 by Daniel Kalla

A Forge Book
Published by Tom Doherty Associates, LLC
175 Fifth Avenue
New York, NY 10010

www.tor-forge.com

Forge® is a registered trademark of Tom Doherty Associates, LLC.

ISBN 978-0-7653-2141-1

First Edition: April 2010

Printed in the United States of America

0  9  8  7  6  5  4  3  2  1

*For my girls: Cheryl, Chelsea, and Ashley*

# *Acknowledgments*

Stripped down to its studs, this is a story of family. And I am forever grateful for the love and encouragement I receive from mine.

I wouldn't be in print without the support of the friends and colleagues who read the early drafts and provide pivotal feedback. I'm especially indebted to the wonderful Kit Schindell, a freelance editor (somervillebook works@shaw.ca) whose insights, suggestions, and advice are essential to my work. I would also like to acknowledge Nancy Stairs for her razor-sharp critique and feedback. And thanks to Dal Schindell for so carefully proofing my pages.

I am so grateful to my agent, Henry Morrison, who inspired this novel by suggesting that I spread my wings and tackle the genre of the epic "industry" saga that, to use his words, "has lain fallow for too long." I would also like to thank my foreign rights agent, Danny Baror. And I am fortunate to work with a terrific marketing consultant, Kristin Andress.

I am lucky to have found a home in New York with Tor/Forge, a publisher with true heart and soul. And my editor, Natalia Aponte, epitomizes the "triple threat" of the publishing world: friend, collaborator, and advocate.

*Of Flesh and Blood*

# 1

*Where the hell is my heart?* Erin McGrath wondered as she burst through the swinging door and into the operating room.

Inside OR 22, the usual controlled chaos reigned. The staff buzzed with activity. The anesthesiologist, a taciturn South African named Peter Proust, hovered beside a bank of high-tech monitors as he mixed the cocktail of drugs required to achieve the delicate balance between putting the patient to sleep and keeping her brain and other organs viable during the three-hour transplant surgery.

Wearing green hospital scrubs, but not yet gowned, Erin strode up to the stretcher beside the operating table. Her patient, Kristen Hill, lay still on the gurney. Kristen's pale face was covered with a bulky breathing mask to optimize the oxygen delivered to her fluid-logged lungs. On the right side of her neck, several intravenous lines converged at the plastic hub connecting to a central line that tunneled through the skin and into her jugular vein.

Erin felt a deep affinity for the young woman who, like her, was a mother of fraternal twins. Life had dealt Kristen one blow after another. Abandoned by her husband when her twins were only toddlers, forced to support the family on a minimum-wage income, and now incapacitated by a failing heart, somehow the twenty-six-year-old remained perpetually hopeful. Underneath the clear plastic mask, Kristen wore the same accepting expression as usual. But despite the oxygen, her lips were bluer than ever. She appeared to deteriorate by the minute.

*Where's the damn chopper with my heart?* Erin thought again as she reached the bedside.

Kristen's own heart was shot. The once-powerful pump had turned into a mass of engorged useless tissue after a virus had suddenly attacked it. The illness had begun innocuously enough, as little more than the same cold that had hit her children. But the virus unexpectedly turned on Kristen's heart, causing myocarditis. Within days, it had destroyed the muscle that constituted the cardiac wall. Despite the maximal medication and all other interventions Erin had tried, Kristen's shattered heart couldn't keep up with the circulatory demands of her body.

Erin rubbed her patient's elbow. "How are you holding up, Kristen?"

"Okay." She mustered a grin through her mask. "Dr. McGrath, I thought I'd be asleep by now."

"Not much longer," Erin said, hoping she was speaking the truth.

The call from the national organ donor registry had woken Erin at five A.M. from a very light sleep. The day before, because of Kristen's drastic deterioration, the heart surgeon had put out a plea through the transplant network for any viable heart within a thousand-mile radius of the Alfredson Medical Center. That evening, on a rainy highway outside of Billings, Montana, a twenty-two-year-old biker hit an oil slick and lost control of his motorcycle. Slamming into the guardrail, the biker was thrown thirty feet and smashed headfirst into the mountainside. His helmet was no match for the wall of rock. Brain-dead at the hospital, he turned out to be a close enough tissue match to Kristen Hill for organ donation. By seven A.M., the transplant team had harvested the biker's heart, finding it in healthy condition and miraculously unscathed from the accident.

As soon as Erin heard the news, she had ordered Kristen transferred into the operating room to prep for the imminent transplant. Everything looked promising. And then a sudden storm blew in from the east and grounded the Alfredson's transport helicopter.

Erin viewed her patient with an apologetic smile. "Kristen, the heart is still not here."

Panting heavily, Kristen nodded. "It'll get here soon, huh?"

"Very." The chopper was in flight and expected to arrive at any moment, but Erin knew that wasn't the problem. "The donor organ has been outside the body—or 'on ice'—for almost four hours now."

"That's too long?"

Erin squeezed Kristen's hand. "Generally, we accept five hours as the upper limit of cold ischemia, the time a nonbeating heart can be outside of a body and still usable in transplant."

"So you still have an hour," Kristen encouraged.

"But it will take longer than that to open your chest and implant the new heart."

The first flicker of despair crept into Kristen's features. "What happens after five hours?"

Erin frowned. "It gets dicey. The donor heart can become irreversibly damaged from lack of blood and oxygen. It often doesn't pump well after transplant. Sometimes, we can't even get it restarted once we've implanted it."

Kristen's face tensed with resolve. "Dr. McGrath, you don't know when another heart will become available, do you?"

Erin shook her head grimly. "No."

"Look at me." Kristen sputtered a moist cough, as if for effect. "We both know I can't wait much longer."

Erin nodded.

"I am willing to take my chances on this heart. Today. Right now."

Erin leaned closer. "Kristen, you do understand that once we begin, there's no turning back? If the new heart doesn't take . . ."

Kristen swallowed. "I understand, Dr. McGrath. I still want you to try."

Erin let go of her patient's hand. "Okay, Kristen. As long as the heart arrives in the next fifteen minutes, we'll go for it."

Erin looked over and saw that the anesthesiologist was eyeing her dubiously. "Fifteen minutes, Peter," she said. "Not a second more."

With a minimal shrug of his shoulders, Proust turned back to the syringes and vials laid out in front of him.

Erin looked over at the charge nurse. "Joanne, let's get Kristen on the table and prepped for surgery."

The heavyset nurse turned and nodded to another nurse. Together, they headed for Kristen's stretcher. The wall phone behind Proust rang shrilly. The anesthesiologist grabbed it. "OR twenty-two," he said in his terse Afrikaner inflection. He hung the phone up without saying another word into the receiver. "It's here," he announced matter-of-factly.

Erin turned back to her patient. "Kristen, this is the point of no return, you understand?"

Her lips broke into a brave smile. "I just want to see Katie and Alex through grade school. That's all."

"Fair enough." Erin swallowed, thinking of her own twins, who were in their last year of grade school. "I'm going to go scrub now."

Even before reaching the swinging door, Erin felt the first twinges in her belly. *No!* She wanted to scream. *Not now, of all times.*

Erin stood at the metallic sink outside the OR, scrubbing her hands as she struggled to hold back the surging anxiety. *It's not real, Erin, it's not real . . .* , she repeated over and over in her head. But the mantra didn't deter the sense of suffocation from growing, as though a pair of strong hands was squeezing her throat. Her fingers began to tingle with needles and pins—a telltale sign of hyperventilation.

The first panic attack had struck out of the blue three months earlier. Late one night, Erin was wheeling her garbage can down her driveway when she was overcome by a horrible sensation, as though someone had suddenly tightened a bag over her head. She wanted to run, but she couldn't breathe well enough to move. So she stood beside the garbage can, gripping its handle and trembling like a leaf. Though vaguely aware that she was suffering a panic attack, Erin still expected to die at any moment. Nauseous from anxiety and the smell of decaying fruit and vegetables, she spent ten of the most distressing minutes of her life frozen in the driveway before she was able to pull herself together enough to even go inside.

Since the first panic attack, Erin had experienced six or seven more. None of them came with any warning. She had not told anyone about the attacks, not even her husband. Instead, she had started herself on an antidepressant that was supposed to suppress the episodes. It hadn't. And today, for the first time, she was experiencing what she had dreaded most: a panic attack at work.

Fingers shaking under the warm soapy suds, Erin fought to slow her breathing and focus her racing thoughts. Thanks to the storm in Montana, too much time had already been lost. Every second she wasted at the sink trying to calm herself would lessen the chance of the donor heart working. She considered calling a colleague in to take over the operation, but the only other cardiac surgeons in the building were already scrubbed into surgery. By the time one of them could respond, the donor heart would be as useless as ice cream that had been left out of the freezer too long.

Erin turned off the tap with her knee. Her chest thudding, she studied her fingers and noticed that the shake had lessened to a subtle tremor. The needles-and-pins sensation had dissipated, too. She took a few controlled breaths and then, holding her sterile hands in the air, backed through the swinging door and into the operating room.

Erin was relieved that her mask shielded her face from the others, but she avoided all eye contact, not wanting them to see the remnants of panic in her eyes.

"She's under," Proust said with his typical economy of words.

Erin glanced over to see Kristen Hill unconscious on the table with an endotracheal breathing tube poking between her lips and connecting to a respirator. One of the surgical assistants had already sterilized and draped her chest, exposing a ten-by-ten-inch surgical field centered on the sternum, or breastbone. Kristen looked peaceful, which helped calm Erin slightly, but she still started at the sudden noisy whir of the bone saw when her assistant tested its blade.

Erin slipped her arms through the gown held open for her. The same nurse held out sterile gloves. Erin had breezed through this step innumerable times without a second thought, but now she concentrated on getting her fingers safely into the gloves as though it were as delicate an undertaking as sewing in a new heart valve. She breathed a small sigh of relief when she slipped into the gloves without complication.

Erin walked over to join the assistant on the near side of the OR table. She had a quick glimpse of Kristen's exposed chest. *Get it together, woman!* she commanded herself. She turned to the tall surgical resident, Dr. David Robards, who had prepared the bone saw. "Okay, David," she said, testing her voice. "Open the chest."

He nodded enthusiastically. The scrub nurse passed him a large scalpel that he immediately applied to the skin overlying the sternum. He drew down like an engraver, splitting the skin from the base of Kristen's throat to her belly. Dr. Karen Woo, the elfin second surgical assistant standing on a step across from him, followed the separating skin wound with a sponge to dab at the blood. She used a handheld electric coagulator, which resembled a high-tech pen, to burn the bleeding vessels closed.

Satisfied with the incision, Erin nodded to Robards. He raised the saw and it buzzed to life in his hand. Robards applied it to the incision, cutting through the sternum that he had just exposed. The acrid smell of burning bone, a vivid reminder that her hands-on role was rapidly approaching, launched Erin's heart racing anew.

Robards traded the saw for bone spreaders, which looked like giant tweezers. He inserted the teeth of the tool into the gap he had created in the sternum and spread the handles. The chest cracked open with a familiar crunch.

Erin took a deep breath and stole a glimpse at her hands, which were no longer trembling. *No room for error now.*

Without a word, Robards moved out of the way and Erin stepped into his spot. Everyone understood it was her surgery from now until the time came to close the chest again. She shut her eyes for only a moment and then plunged her hand through the open chest wound. Her fingers slid underneath the thin-layered pericardium, the fibrous tissue that covers and protects the heart. Enveloping the organ, she squeezed the heart gently and felt it beat sluggishly in her hand. With the tips of her fingers, she explored the anatomy of the great vessels—the aorta, pulmonary artery, and vena cava veins that connect the heart to all of the other blood vessels in the body—as she mentally walked through the next steps of the surgery. "Forceps and scalpel," she said to the OR nurse, who was already holding them out for her.

Erin withdrew her hand from inside Kristen's chest and reached for the tools. "Headlight," she said, and someone switched on her fiber-optic headlamp. She looked down and shone the bright beam inside the wound to better illuminate the chest cavity. Her own heart thudded in her ears, but her hand was steady as she reached out with the forceps and grasped the pericardium with the metallic teeth. She raised the tissue, tenting it away from the heart, and sliced down vertically with the scalpel. She slid the pericardium away, as though removing bubble wrap, and exposed Kristen's globular pinkish red heart.

"How are we doing for time, Peter?" she asked.

"Fifteen minutes," he grunted. "Or four hours and ten minutes of cold ischemia."

Desperate to get the donor heart implanted within the five-hour window, Erin knew she needed to speed up. Not too fast, though; rushing surgery only guaranteed mistakes. "Okay, I need the first cannula. Let's prep for CPB," she said, referring to cardiopulmonary bypass.

Someone wheeled the freezer-size heart-lung machine—an external pump and oxygenator that allows the heart to be disconnected from the human circuit by providing artificial blood circulation for the body—closer to the table, while the scrub nurse handed Erin the tools she needed. As her focus became absolute, Erin's anxiety receded from her consciousness. She freed the superior vena cava, the largest vein in the body. Making a small nick in its side, she slid a garden hose–like tube, or cannula, into position, and then tied it into place. Feeling the pressure of time as viscerally as footsteps behind her in a dark lane, Erin rapidly repeated the procedure with each of the three other great vessels. She calmed a little more after each cannula had been secured.

Accepting the clamps offered by the scrub nurse, she fastened off the great vessels, one by one, as near to their insertion into the heart as possible, thus separating the heart from the rest of Kristen's blood vessels. Under the watchful eye of the perfusionist, or bypass technician, the heart-lung machine whirred to life as its transparent tubing turned red with the blood it mechanically pumped in the place of the patient's own heart.

A nurse dabbed at Erin's sweaty brow. She glanced over to the perfusionist, who nodded his approval that the bypass machine was functioning well. "Time to remove the organ," Erin said.

Robards grabbed the syringe full of potassium chloride and injected it into the cannula that Erin had inserted directly into the left ventricle of Kristen's heart. It pumped away for several more beats and then quivered to a halt.

Erin reached inside the chest cavity and wrapped her fingers around the now-still heart. "Scalpel," she called.

She sliced through the vessels beyond the clamps, separating Kristen's heart from her body. Pulling the organ free of the chest, Erin was reminded again of an Aztec priest yanking the heart out of a victim and offering it up as a sacrifice to the gods. With her blood-soaked glove, she deposited the organ into a waiting basin. "Time?" she called out to Peter.

"Four hours, twenty-five minutes," he replied, giving only the cold ischemia time.

*Thirty-five minutes to implant the new heart!* She had never done the procedure in anywhere near that short a window. She wondered if anyone had. The tingling started in her fingers again, but she willed herself calm. *One step at a time, Erin!*

"The donor heart, please," Erin said.

A second nurse opened a metallic chest near the table. She withdrew the heart from the ice bath and carried it in both hands to Erin with the reverence of someone holding a holy relic. Erin grabbed it in her right hand. The heart felt unnaturally cool through her glove. Although taken from an adult male, it was still smaller than the badly damaged swollen organ Erin had just excised from Kristen's chest. On inspection, the donor heart looked to be in excellent condition, but she knew that her eyes could not discern the whole story. Besides, she was way beyond the point of turning back.

Slowly rotating the donor heart 360 degrees, Erin mentally aligned it with Kristen's great vessels that she needed to attach. "Suture and needle driver, please."

Erin gently lowered the donor heart into Kristen's chest. She lined up the edge of the donor and recipient pulmonary artery and stitched in the first suture of Kristen's new heart.

Working rapidly, Erin attached the rest of the great vessels to the new heart. The challenging fastidious work was the perfect antidote to her irrational anxiety. She deliberately avoided asking about the time until she tied off the last suture, securing Kristen's largest vessel, the aorta, to her new heart.

As soon as her assistant cut the last stitch, Erin turned urgently to Proust. "Time?"

"Five hours and sixteen minutes," he muttered.

*Better than I expected, but still too long!* "Let's unclamp now," she snapped.

One at a time, she removed the clamps from the great vessels, allowing Kristen's blood to pass into her new heart for the first time. Each time, Erin stopped and watched intently for any sign of bleeding at the suture lines but was relieved to remove the last clamp without spotting any leaks from the blood vessels.

The new heart lay utterly still inside Kristen's chest.

"Okay. Let's restart it. Paddles, please."

Someone passed Erin the set of internal defibrillator paddles, which resembled a pair of electrified salad spoons. She slid one of the sterile paddles underneath the heart and cupped the other paddle on top, as if squeezing it between tongs. "Okay, charge to ten joules."

A high-pitched buzzing sound cut the room's somber silence. "Charged," a nurse called.

Like everyone else, Erin watched the squiggly horizontal blue line on the cardiac monitor above the OR table. The reading showed ventricular fibrillation—the transplanted heart's erratic, but expected, rhythm. She simultaneously depressed the two little red buttons on the handles. The paddles vibrated almost imperceptibly as they released their shock.

A solitary spike from the shock shot up the monitor like a line across a page, but the squiggly fibrillation pattern held firm.

"Dial up to twenty joules," Erin said, as calmly as possible.

She shocked the heart again but the ventricular fibrillation held fast.

The anesthesiologist shook his head gravely. Fingers crept tighter around Erin's neck. "Recharge!" she barked.

Erin shocked three more times in succession, but she didn't need to look at the monitor to know that the donor heart had not responded. It flopped between her paddles as unresponsively as a thick steak lifted by a pair of tongs.

Erin dropped the paddles on the nearest tray and then turned to the anesthesiologist. "Peter, run an isoproteronol drip," she told him. "I need a milligram of epinephrine and a cardiac needle."

Reaching for the syringe held out by the nurse, Erin noticed her own hand had begun to tremble again. "Come on, Kristen," she muttered under her breath as she poked the long needle through the thick ventricular wall of Kristen's nonfunctioning new heart and squirted the medication directly into its major chamber.

Erin wrapped her other hand around the transplanted heart and gave it several pumps in open cardiac massage to try to coax it into activity. She glanced over to the monitor. It still squiggled away in fibrillation.

The imaginary ligature tightened around Erin's neck. "Another syringe of epinephrine," she croaked. "And have an external ventricular assist device on standby to implant."

Proust glanced at her, his eyes rife with doubt. Erin knew he was right. Kristen Hill was running out of time. The bypass machine was still filling in for the work of her heart, but with or without mechanical assistance, the chances of the donor heart restarting were diminishing by the second.

Erin's own heartbeat crashed like cymbals in her ears. As she pulled her fingers out of Kristen's chest cavity, the rough tremor was visible to all. Her tiny female assistant eyed her with silent concern, but Erin ignored her. She shot her hands out for the defibrillator paddles on the tray. She almost dropped one of them as she fumbled to position it behind the nonresponsive heart.

"Come on, Kristen," Erin muttered under her breath. She glanced at the nurse. "Okay, charge to twenty joules."

Erin shocked the heart again. No response. She repeated two more times, but the wavy line on the monitor refused to budge from its deadly fibrillation pattern. She exchanged the paddles for another syringe of epinephrine. She almost missed the chamber as she jabbed it into the heart and injected again.

"Listen, Erin." Proust's tone was uncharacteristically sympathetic. "We're at well over five hours of cold ischemia. How long will we continue?"

"She deserves longer," Erin said, in a whimpering voice that surprised even her.

Proust shrugged and turned back to the respirator.

"I need syringes of vasopressin and dopamine." Erin cited two other drugs meant to stimulate the heart.

She reached for the paddles again and repositioned them inside the open chest. She applied three consecutive or "stacked" shocks. Barely glancing at the monitor, she dumped the paddles back on the tray and grabbed for the new syringe that the nurse was holding out to her.

"We got something," Proust muttered as he pointed to the monitor.

Erin looked up and saw the change. At regular intervals, a wide blip interrupted the line that had otherwise flattened. She leaned forward and shone her bright headlight onto the donor heart. It took her a second to realize that its walls were now quivering slightly. Holding her breath, she watched as the flicker grew stronger. Soon the heart began to visibly beat.

"Yippee!" Woo whooped, and a wave of relieved laughter spread through the OR.

Erin backpedaled away from the table. She felt as though she might faint. But her sudden light-headedness and cold sweat were a small price to pay for the torrent of relief washing over her.

*2*

The ground-shaking staccato rhythm of the helicopter's blades drowned out the noise from the huge air compressors that cooled the Alfredson Medical Center. Tyler looked up and squinted into the sun as he watched the large red bird swoop down toward the landing pad atop the Henley Building. He had heard rumors of another VIP—a former presidential front-runner—being flown to the Alfredson for specialized neurological care, but as this chopper dropped effortlessly from the sky, Tyler had no idea whom it carried, nor did he care. He focused on the visual grace of the landing, a sight that had awed him since childhood.

The choppers arrived frequently, shuttling patients from all over the Pacific Northwest and beyond. Patients came by car and ambulance, too. Occasionally, they even walked from nearby Oakdale, Washington. The Alfredson counted movie stars, tycoons, and world leaders among its clientele but—because the medical center had never turned away patients without means—the mix also included underprivileged inner-city kids and single-parent families. Rich or poor, they came for the Alfredson's state-of-the-art treatment in fields as diverse as pediatrics, neurosurgery, maternity, joint replacement, and, especially, cardiac care.

Remembering he was already late, Tyler peeled his eyes from the helicopter and hurled himself back into motion. A glance at his wristwatch transformed his jog into a run. With the tail of his lab coat flapping behind him in the warm breeze, he darted past the towering glass-and-steel research facility and followed the path behind the distinguished redbrick building that was once part of the original Alfredson Clinic but now housed an overflow of administrative offices. Tyler still had a cluster of buildings to circumvent before he would even glimpse his destination.

*Hospital? More like a goddamned city,* he thought. *Why did I come back here of all places?*

"Tyler!" a baritone voice called from somewhere to his right.

He stopped and scanned the landscape before he spotted the source of the voice emerging from the arched doorway of the redbrick building. Dr. William McGrath approached with the same purposeful stride that carried him everywhere. At seventy, the Alfredson's president and CEO had a thin, wiry body and ramrod posture that defied age. As always, his graying brown hair was cropped short and he wore no tie under his navy jacket.

"You're a long way from home," William said good-naturedly, though his gray eyes brimmed with inquisitiveness.

"I had to review spinal fluid cytology with a pathologist," Tyler said.

William squeezed his Cary Grant chin between his index finger and thumb. "Our paths hardly cross these days. Are you settling in okay?"

"*Settling in?*" Tyler frowned. "I've been here for over a year."

"A year already? Amazing."

Tyler shifted from foot to foot. "A patient and his family are waiting for me—"

"The spinal fluid?"

William's dehumanizing habit of labeling patients by disease or procedure—remarks like "How did your Wilms' tumor do in surgery?" or "Is your astrocytoma responding to chemo?"—riled Tyler, but he had no time to take issue. "He's only eleven," he said coolly.

William squinted at the younger doctor. "The news is not good, I take it."

"Not what they want to hear." Tyler shook his head. "Not what anyone would."

"Of course," William said without a glimmer of emotion. "Is Jill doing all right?"

The hair on Tyler's neck bristled. "Busy. Fine. The usual." Tyler began to edge away. "Dad, I can't keep them waiting."

"Go." He flicked his hand and wrist in an away-with-you gesture. "Your sister would love it if you and Jill could make it to one of their Sunday family dinners."

*And you?* Tyler wondered without voicing it. "Not this Sunday, I'm on call. The week after, for sure," he called out as he broke back into a run.

Tyler raced across the rest of the complex, wove through the main-floor labyrinth of the Alfredson Children's Hospital, and reached the oncology isolation ward—the sixth-floor unit, or SFU as it was referred to by most of the staff—in seven minutes. Normally, he appreciated the floor's bright modern décor, its walls splashed with cheerful pastel murals and colorful ceramic plaques boasting the names of donors. But as Tyler stood scrubbing his hands at the stainless steel sink outside Nate Stafford's room, the upbeat ambience struck him as cruelly deceptive by offering the illusion of hope to people like the Staffords who had practically none.

Tyler switched off the tap. He dried his hands, slipped his arms into a yellow gown, and donned a surgical mask and gloves. He took one slow breath and then, with hands held up safely away from other contact, backed through the double set of sealed doors that maintained positive pressure respiratory isolation inside the room. The precautions were meant to shut out the ubiquitous airborne viruses and bacteria that, while posing no threat to healthy people, represented potentially lethal infections to critically immunosuppressed patients like Nate Stafford.

Inside the room, Nate's gowned parents flanked his bed. His compact muscular father, Craig, swiveled his square head to stare over his mask at Tyler with a mix of concern and expectation. Nate's mother, Laura, barely took her eyes off her son. She clutched his bare left hand in hers and mopped at his brow with the cloth she held in her other gloved hand. Wired to multiple lines and tubes, the eleven-year-old boy on the stretcher resembled a bald marionette. Skeletal and gray, he strained to lift his head off the bed and look over at Tyler. Nate was the only maskless person in the room. His dry fissured lips broke into a small grin that stirred Tyler's sympathy.

Tyler joined Nate's father by the bedside. "How's my star ball player this morning?"

"I'm not ready to pitch yet, Dr. M," Nate croaked.

"Your headache still bad?" Tyler asked.

Nate swallowed his confirmation.

Tyler rubbed the back of Nate's hand. "Baseball season is still a while off yet."

Craig leaned closer. "What did the spinal fluid show?" he demanded in a low growl.

Laura's eyes widened and darted momentarily from Craig to Tyler. Her son immediately picked up on the furtive warning. "C'mon, Mom, I want to hear it, too," Nate said with a slight whine, sounding more like a kid demanding to see an R-rated movie with some friends than a patient waiting to hear if his cancer had spread to his brain.

Tyler squeezed Nate's hand and felt only bones. "It's not completely gone, Nate."

Laura gasped involuntarily and then tried to cover the noise with a cough. Craig squinted hard at Tyler, his intense eyes ablaze. Nate simply stared at Tyler with a look of brave determination. "So what do we do now, Dr. M?"

"You know me, Nate." Tyler winked. "I always have a backup plan up my sleeve."

Nate nodded dully. "More chemo?" His hoarse voice quavered slightly.

"In a way, yeah."

"What the hell does that mean?" Craig snapped.

Tyler didn't take his eyes off Nate. "Targeted therapy."

"What's that?" Nate asked nervously.

"Remember, Nate, when I explained how leukemia is a disease of your immune system?"

Nate nodded slowly. "You said something goes wrong with the cells that fight off infection and stuff. Some of them go crazy and multiply out of control. Then they take over the bone marrow like a rebel army attacking from the inside."

"I forgot how smart you were for a jock," Tyler said, impressed by the boy's military analogy. "The usual chemotherapy we give attacks all living cells in your body. We hope it poisons the bad cells—the cancer cells—worse than the others. But with targeted therapy, we use specially designed drugs that are immune active."

"What's that mean?" Nate asked.

"These drugs are designed by scientists to seek out and destroy only the defective cancer cells by recognizing what we call 'tumor markers' on the outside of those cells." Tyler struggled for a concrete comparison. "It's kind of like guerrilla warfare."

"More like counterterrorism commandos working in hostile civilian country," Nate said.

Tyler chuckled. "I stand corrected."

Nate shrugged modestly. "I play a lot of video war games."

Tyler patted the boy's arm. "We haven't used targeted therapy much with the kind of leukemia you have, but we have seen some good results with other types."

Nate shifted in his bed. "Will it hurt?" he murmured sheepishly.

Tyler heard Laura's choppy breathing as she fought back sobs. He felt Craig's stare burning into him. But he didn't take his eyes off the boy's stoic face. "No." Tyler shook his head. "You have my word on that, Nate."

The sealed door hissed open. All eyes in the room were drawn to the slim, black-haired nurse who carried a pill cup in one gloved hand and a syringe in the other. Even if her entire face had been covered by her surgical mask, Tyler still would have recognized Nikki Salazar from the effortless way she swept across the floor, moving like the dancer she had once trained to be. He turned back to Nate without making eye contact with Nikki, but her proximity brought a familiar bittersweet rush.

Nikki nodded to the parents—holding Laura's gaze for one empathetic moment—and then turned to Nate. "Time for painkillers and antibiotics," she groaned in an exaggerated way, as if offering cod-liver oil. She waved the pills in the small paper cup at him. "If we get this over with fast, then maybe we can get the controllers out and I can whip your butt in football again."

Nate huffed a laugh. "As if!" The worry drained from his face, and even his color seemed to improve as he forced himself up a little higher in his bed. He slipped his hand out of his mother's. "I got to teach Nikki *another* lesson, Mom," he said almost apologetically as he pulled farther away from Laura.

Tyler decided to capitalize on the distraction. "Come on, Mom and Dad, let's leave it to the pros." He turned for the door. Craig followed right on his heels, but Laura stood by the bedside, reluctant to move.

"It's okay, Mom," Nate said. "Go have one of your boring grown-up conversations outside."

Nikki's presence always affected Nate, filling him with prepubescent bravado, but Tyler knew that the kid was also giving his mother permission to take a break from her relentless vigil.

Laura took a step, wavered a moment, and then followed Tyler and Craig out the door. Without exchanging a word, they walked together down the bright hallway. The parents had been through this enough to know they were heading to the same conference room where all the news—most of it bad—had been broken before. By the time they stepped into the daylight-flooded room, tears were flowing freely down Laura's cheeks. She rushed over to the nearest rolling chair and collapsed onto it.

As soon as Tyler shut the door, Craig turned on him. Though almost six inches shorter than Tyler, he seemed to rise to the same height. Craig's chest swelled and his right fist curled at his waist, looking as if it might strike at any second. "What the fuck was that in there?" he said in a low-pitched tone that came across angrier than a yell.

Tyler did not move. "He had a right to know, Craig."

Craig's lip curled into a sneer. "And we had the right to know before him. To be fucking prepared." He nodded toward his wife. "She almost dissolved in front of the boy."

Tyler shook his head. "I only found out a few minutes ago."

"You know our goddamn cell number!" Craig said, unmoved. "I thought you were better than that amateur shit back there."

Tyler lowered his eyes and nodded. He knew Craig desperately needed somewhere to vent his rage and helplessness at the disease ravaging his only son. And Tyler was more than willing to play the scapegoat. At least, it was *something* he could offer them.

After a long simmering glare, Craig pivoted, stomped over to the table, and sat down beside Laura. He wrapped his thick arm around her. Tyler noticed that the hand gripping his wife's shoulder trembled slightly. He gave them a private moment, walking slowly around the far side of the table before sitting down across from them.

Laura gaped at Tyler. He was accustomed to seeing those eyes bloodshot and teary more often than dry, but now they were clouded with even more defeat than usual. "That last round of chemo . . . ," she said. "I don't know why, but I was sure he was going to respond."

"I know," Tyler said.

"God, he's been through so much. The endless chemo. All that radiation. The bone marrow transplant." Laura sniffed several times. "But I've never seen him look so weak, Dr. McGrath. So gray. He doesn't have any immune system left, does he?"

"Not much of one, no."

"And now the cancer is back again around his brain. . . ." Her words petered out.

Craig pulled his wife closer into his side, as though sheltering her from a blizzard. "What about this targeted therapy thing?" he grunted. "Were you just blowing smoke up our asses?"

Tyler paused to consider his response, aware how fragile the moment was. Craig and Laura were too experienced to be taken in by false promises— which Tyler would never stoop to—but the wrong word or phrase might drain the last of their reserve. And no one had the right to steal a parent's last drop of hope. Tyler was particularly concerned how Craig would digest the news. Despite appearances, inwardly Laura was stronger than her husband.

"Look, this field is evolving all the time. Every year the outcomes improve," Tyler said without overstating the case for optimism. "In certain adult forms of leukemia, targeted immune therapy has replaced chemotherapy altogether. With excellent results. I think it's the long-term direction for all types of blood cancers." He paused. "Granted, we have not yet seen as good results in the leukemia like Nate's. But we have brand-new experimental drugs. One in particular I would like to try on him."

Craig let go of his wife's shoulder. He leaned forward and pushed his hands against the table, rising out of his chair. "Have you used it before?"

Tyler shook his head.

The veins at Craig's temples pounded visibly. "Has anyone?" he choked.

"At St. Jude's, in Tennessee, they have run a few small trials."

"Small," Craig scoffed. "That doesn't sound encouraging."

"I know the principal investigator—the woman running the trials. She's one of the very best in the world. And she believes in this drug."

Craig stared at him, unappeased. "So what's involved?"

"Another intravenous. And like with the chemo, we're going to have to do a lumbar puncture and put the drug directly in Nate's spinal fluid because it won't otherwise cross the blood-brain barrier and get to the cancer cells in the fluid around his brain."

Laura shuddered in her chair, and Tyler hurried to add, "But it's not as toxic as the standard chemotherapy. Less nausea and vomiting. No increased risk of infection. Nate's such a trooper. He'll probably tolerate it even better than previous treatments."

Craig slammed a fist onto the table. "And if he doesn't?"

Laura put a hand up to her husband's chest and gently pushed him back in his seat. "Dr. McGrath, you told us before that if the cancer came back after Nate's bone marrow transplant, the prognosis was poor. . . ."

Tyler silently cursed as he listened to his own words come back to haunt him. It was unavoidable, though. With limitless Internet information and, even worse, *misinformation* available with a few keystrokes, he had to warn his patients and their families about possible adverse outcomes. "Poor is not the same as hopeless," Tyler insisted. "As I said, every day we're making strides—"

"What do the statistics say?" Craig demanded.

"Statistics only apply to groups of patients," Tyler said. "They don't take into consideration each individual case and new experimental treatments."

"You've given us numbers before," Craig said. "Be honest with us now."

Tyler held up a hand. "The success rates—what we call the five-year survival—are all out of date for this disease. Our treatments are totally different than five years ago. Different from six months ago. I can't give you an accurate—"

"Please, Dr. McGrath," Laura snapped uncharacteristically. "Just give us a damn number!"

Tyler cleared his throat. He refused to let himself break off eye contact with either of them. "The textbooks quote a figure of five to ten percent."

Laura caught her breath in mid-inhalation. "Nate has less than a ten percent chance of surviving?" she whispered.

Craig's shoulders heaved, and he brought a hand quickly to cover his face. It was the first time Tyler had ever seen the man cry.

Tyler thumbed toward Nate's room. "Listen to me, both of you." His tone took on an edge. "Did you see your son back there? Nate has *not* given up. So you can't either!" His voice rose. "Do you understand?"

"Yes," Laura said weakly. And Craig nodded.

"Good." Tyler offered each of them the most hopeful smile he could muster. "I'm going to need to get you to sign some consent forms for the new treatment protocol. I want to get started as soon as possible."

After the parents consented to the new therapy, there was nothing left to say. Filing out of the room, with an arm still draped around his wife's shoulder, Craig turned to Tyler. "Look, Dr. McGrath, I said a lot of things today . . ."

Tyler held up a hand to interrupt. "You had every right. You're a good dad, Craig."

Craig's shoulders sagged and his back stooped as he seemed to shrink in front of Tyler's eyes. "I don't know how you do this, Doctor," he mumbled.

Most times, the answer was easy for Tyler. He took enormous satisfaction from doing the best job he could, even under difficult circumstances. But today was an exception. Despite downplaying the statistics, he knew how horribly the odds were stacked against Nate.

Tyler had seen more than his share of cancer-related tragedy. Even when pediatric oncology was practiced perfectly, treatment failures and young deaths were an unavoidable part of the job. He knew that at times like these, the best oncologists detached themselves emotionally from patient and family. What the Staffords needed most—in fact, all they needed—from him was the absolute professional objectivity that would allow Tyler to make the soundest clinical decisions.

But the Stafford case hit him harder than most. Nate reminded him of his twin nephews—the kind of kid he would have wanted for his own. The embodiment of the child Jill and he had worked so hard, and so unsuccessfully, to conceive.

Tyler felt sad, drained, and powerless. Worst of all, he knew that as soon as he gathered himself up, he would have to go see Keisha Berry and essentially repeat the whole ordeal for the family of the eight-year-old with the adorable missing-toothed smile, infectious laugh, and an equally rare and malignant blood cancer.

# 3

An overgrowth of shrubs and weeds cluttered the once meticulously land-scaped grounds, and the house's faded tan exterior begged for a coat or two of new paint. As Lorna Simpson stood at the imposing marble-and-stone entryway, she could see beyond the dilapidation and envision what a grand estate it must have been. She remembered visiting almost forty years earlier when she was only four. She recalled how massive the mansion had seemed and had a vague memory of a strange doll collection inside, but she had no idea whether the place looked even more run-down than on her previous visit.

Lorna had risen at dawn and driven three hours from her town house out-side Portland to the row of heritage mansions in Seattle's Queen Anne dis-trict. She had come to see her great-aunt, Dorothy "Dot" Alfredson. Lorna had expected a servant or caretaker to meet her at the door, so when the huge oak door creaked open she was surprised to find her eighty-nine-year-old great-aunt on the other side.

With arms folded across her chest, the shrunken woman wore leopard-skin leggings and a long black cardigan, accessorized with a bright orange scarf. Dot's white hair was shaved in a buzz cut, and she had generously ap-plied lipstick and eye shadow to a face that looked as if it might have been surgically lifted more than once.

For a silent moment Dot assessed Lorna, who, in old jeans and a simple black V-neck, wore no makeup and had her hair tied in a limp ponytail. "Darling, look at you!" she finally said. "You grew up *exactly* as I imagined you would." She stepped forward and wrapped her bony arms around Lorna, pulling her into a surprisingly tight hug.

"You look well, Dot," Lorna said, self-consciously breaking free of the embrace. "Thanks for seeing me on such short notice."

Dot chuckled. "These days, my social calendar boasts the odd hole, darling. In fact, my next standing engagement is my own funeral." Her eyes twinkled as she pointed to Lorna's beaten-up knapsack. "Leave your *luggage* here, darling. Juanita will take it to the room. Now what can I get you to drink? You *must* need a vodka tonic after that interminable drive."

As appetizing as the offer was, Lorna feigned indifference with a shake of her head. "A glass of water would be great."

"Fortunately, the taps are one of the few things that still run inside the old dump." Then she added in a mutter to herself, "Water, I could have guessed."

Ignoring Lorna's drink request, Dot led her inside the house, through the high-ceilinged marble foyer, and into a wood-paneled living room decorated with dark teak furniture. The younger woman's gaze was immediately drawn to the array of phallic carvings and sexually explicit sculptures (ranging widely in size, age, cultural origin, and depicted act) that covered the living room's ornate mantel and were dispersed throughout the room. Amused and slightly embarrassed, Lorna realized they must have constituted the "doll collection" of her childhood memory. Seemingly indifferent to the provocative artwork, Dot strolled over to a chaise by the fireplace and eased herself onto it. "Tell me, darling, what brings you to the old ruin?"

*You or the house?* Lorna wondered as she sat down in the wingback chair across from Dot. "I was hoping you could shed a little light on the history of the Alfredson for me."

Dot smiled as though responding to an inside joke. "The little hospital Grandfather built."

Lorna nodded, trying to ignore the erotic statuettes and figurines that stood on the mantel directly in her line of sight. She had not seen her great-aunt in well over thirty years; not since the Alfredsons abandoned their yearly family reunions. Even in those days, Dot had seemed strange. Eccentricity aside, the woman had a reputation as a firebrand and agitator, which helped explain how she had chewed through four marriages and why she flaunted her collection of pornographic memorabilia inside the otherwise classically furnished mansion. Lorna had heard that Dot's memory was as ironclad as ever, and she knew that the old gossip was the keeper of most of the family secrets. That alone had drawn Lorna to the largely forgotten mansion.

Dot fluttered a hand in the air like a bird taking flight. "So you have an interest in the history of *our* little hospital, do you, darling?"

"Very much so." Lorna caught sight of a dark wood carving of a naked Polynesian thrusting his disproportionate anatomy toward her. She stifled a laugh as she adjusted her rimless glasses. "I'm teaching a course next term on the Pacific Northwest's twentieth-century history."

"Wonderful," Dot said with a sidelong glance. "At that little community college of yours?"

Lorna bristled at the barb, all too aware of her stalled academic career. But she forced a smile. "Exactly. I am considering including the Alfredson in the syllabus. Seems to me it has played a significant role in local history."

"How so?" Dot said, fighting off a yawn.

"Putting aside its worldwide reputation for medical innovation, think of all the famous people who have been treated at the Alfredson over the years. Elvis, John Wayne, Howard Hughes, the Shah of Iran, Bing Crosby, Rock Hudson, and too many other VIPs to count." Lorna folded her arms across her chest. "Even a sitting president."

"Darling, that's *all* Ike did by the end of his term—sit and wait for the next heart attack."

"Some people consider it the Mayo Clinic of the West Coast."

"I suppose one could make that argument," Dot said with little interest.

"I just finished that book, *The Alfredson: The First Hundred Years*. I was hoping—"

The elderly woman sat up with an agility that startled Lorna. "That so-called biography was utter drivel! *Painfully* inaccurate. That ridiculous man, Gerald *Fenton* Naylor, did not even bother to interview me or anyone else who might have known something about the real history. Instead, that hack toed the party line. I think Fenton transcribed his entire book from old newsletters and whatever other official propaganda he could get his greasy hands on." Dot flung her head back dismissively. "*My Gawd*, if you suffered all the way to the end of it, you would have thought the Alfredsons and McGraths were two of the righteous tribes of Israel!"

Lorna bit back a smile. It was exactly the reaction she had hoped to elicit. "Are you saying we're not?"

The cagey old woman eyed Lorna for a suspicious moment. "I doubt you could have earned a Ph.D. from any institution by being *that* simple. You and I both know how little love lost there is among the Alfredsons." She touched her bright red lips. "And as for the hundred years of loving collaboration between the Alfredsons and the McGraths . . . honestly, have you *ever* heard such *utter* horseshit?"

"But Marshall Alfredson and Evan McGrath must have been close."

Dot spat a laugh. "My grandfather *loathed* Evan McGrath. And the feeling was entirely mutual."

Lorna glanced at the ceramic copulating Japanese couple on the end table. "What about the Alfredson's legendary beginnings?"

" 'Legend' being the pivotal word."

"So Evan McGrath didn't save Olivia's life?"

"Oh, he very much did," she said. "It was just never *enough* to compensate for everything else."

Lorna leaned forward. "What else?"

"A long, sordid tale." Dot heaved an exaggerated sigh. "Surely this sort of trivial ancient history would bore you to tears."

Lorna recognized the spark of glee in Dot's eyes and knew that the old woman was playing coy, angling to be begged. "Hardly! I'm already hooked, Dot. Please . . ."

"I doubt I can still do justice to the story. I am an *absolute* relic. Almost ninety. I can hardly keep breakfast and dinner straight."

"Dot, your memory is fabled." Lorna held her hand out to the older woman. "Besides, you are the only one who knows the whole story. The true story. And I would kill to hear it."

"Kill? *Really?*" Wariness suddenly wiped away Dot's façade of benign befuddlement. "Tell me, darling, why could this possibly matter *that* much to you?"

Lorna shifted in her seat as her mind raced to concoct an excuse.

But Dot's suspicion vanished as quickly as it appeared. Her lips broke into a conspiratorial grin as she glanced in either direction. "You see, even Naylor's hopeless whitewash of a book was right about the very beginning.

Marshall Alfredson and Evan McGrath *did* first meet in August of 1895." She pointed up to the coved ceiling. "In this very house."

---

> Destiny, in the form of a gravely ill loved one, originally brought
> Marshall Alfredson and Evan McGrath together. A good judge
> of character, Marshall trusted Evan from the outset. And he willingly
> placed the fate of the most important person in his world in the
> young doctor's capable hands.
> —*The Alfredson: The First Hundred Years* by Gerald Fenton Naylor

The balding butler led Dr. Evan McGrath into the spacious second-floor office with windows looking out on a manicured English-style garden and rolling lawn below. Still sweating in his black jacket from the sweltering carriage ride, the twenty-nine-year-old physician lowered his heavy doctor's bag, laden with extra instruments and bottles of medicine, as the butler silently backed out of the room.

With a pipe clamped between his teeth, Marshall Alfredson sat behind an oak desk and stared at his guest without expression or comment. The barrel-chested giant had a shock of graying red hair, muttonchop whiskers, and freckled pale skin. Everything, even his huge desk, seemed undersized relative to Marshall, whose blue vest—adorned with a thick gold fob and matching pocket watch—strained to contain his bulk. Marshall's piercing gray eyes scanned the young doctor up and down. Evan felt suddenly self-conscious in his well-worn black suit. Automatically, he touched the patch over the elbow where the wool had frayed most.

Marshall rose from his seat and limped around the desk toward Evan. Though Evan was tall himself, Marshall towered four inches over him. He extended a massive hand to the doctor, and his grip was as crushing as Evan expected. Forgoing introductions or pleasantries, Marshall said, "Dr. Montgomery tells me you're a decent belly man."

"Dr. Montgomery flatters me, Mr. Alfredson," Evan said. "However, I have taken extra training in San Francisco with some of the most reputable surgeons at the Morgan Clinic."

"Reputable perhaps," Marshall snorted. "But I still have my doubts about the whole profession. During the war, when I was only eighteen, I spent time in a Union field hospital. It was my first exposure to the *medical* world. Frankly, I never noticed much of a difference between the work of the surgeons and the pig butchers."

Evan didn't flinch at the insult. Fear of surgery was still pervasive in society and, as in Marshall's case, often justified by traumatic firsthand experience. "Drastic advances have been made in our field since the Civil War."

"Glad to hear it," Marshall muttered, unconvinced. He consulted his pocket watch. "Time is wasting, Dr. McGrath. Perhaps you will examine my daughter now?"

"Of course."

Marshall turned for the door and Evan followed, clutching his bulky bag close to his hip. "Mr. Alfredson, when did your daughter first fall ill?" he asked.

"Five days ago Olivia began to complain of discomfort below her chest. She soon lost all appetite. Then the ague set in. The Sisters have been using cold compresses and ice, but the fevers have persisted."

"Of course," Evan said. "Has there been vomiting?"

"Every day. Sometimes several episodes."

"And her bowels?" Evan asked.

Marshall's pale skin flushed and he looked away in embarrassment. "I was told they have not been at all right."

They stopped outside the closed door at the end of the corridor. Marshall turned to Evan. "Olivia's mother passed a few years ago." A glimmer of vulnerability flitted across his face. "Olivia is all the family I have in this house." His expression hardened. "I hope you understand, Dr. McGrath. It is essential that she be treated with the absolute best of care."

Evan met Marshall's warning stare. "Mr. Alfredson, I believe that every patient deserves that same level of care."

Marshall gripped the knob and pushed the door open. Evan followed him into a room that was noticeably cooler than the rest of the house. A loud, steady buzz immediately drew Evan's attention to its source—a machine perched on a night table near the bed. Evan had read about electric fans, but he had never seen one. He was momentarily transfixed by the blur of motion from the invisible blades and the breeze that flapped the bedsheet covering Olivia Alfredson. On the far side of the four-poster bed, a nurse in a full white nun's habit held a compress to Olivia's cheek.

Olivia possessed the same wild red hair and pale complexion as her father, but now her face was flushed crimson and the pillow around her head was ringed with sweat. Eyes closed, she moaned and her head rolled from side to side. "Mother?" the twenty-one-year-old muttered. "Mother, can you please come? My dress is all wrong."

Evan turned to her father. "When did the delirium set in?"

"Only this morning." Marshall's features creased with concern. "When she began calling for her deceased mother."

Evan dropped his bag to the floor and strode over to the bed. He nodded to the Sister and then turned to Olivia. A bead of sweat ran down from the edge of the girl's hairline, which the nurse immediately dabbed away.

"Miss Alfredson, I am Dr. McGrath," he said. "I have come to see if I can be of service."

Evan waited for a response, but none came. He sniffed a few times and, under the scent of perspiration, picked up a subtle stale aroma that he recognized well. He did not need to touch her brow to know that she was suffering from toxemia, but when the back of his hand brushed her forehead he was alarmed by the height of her fever. He slid his fingers to her neck and felt the rapid weak pulse. His concern deepened. Evan looked over at Marshall, who now hovered at the end of the bed. "Mr. Alfredson, I will need to examine your daughter's abdomen."

Marshall grunted his consent and then turned his head to look away. Evan pulled the sheet down to the level of Olivia's bloomers. Her thin chest rose and fell in rapid shallow respirations, and her plain white chemise was soaked around her neck. She had yet to open her eyes, but her head swiveled more rapidly from side to side.

"Miss Alfredson, I must lay my hand on your belly now," Evan said softly. "Is that all right?"

Olivia's head stopped moving and her eyelids snapped open. She gaped at him with widely dilated green eyes. "Of course, Doctor," she said in a whimper.

Evan slid Olivia's undergarment up to the level of her breasts. He gently rested his right hand on the center of her upper abdomen. The moment he made contact, she caught her breath. He pressed a little harder, and the muscles in her abdomen stiffened in response. He moved his hands over the rest of the belly, repeating the light pressure and meeting the same rigidity each time. When he reached the right lower quadrant, she grimaced and gasped involuntarily.

*How did they let it get this far?* Evan wondered with disgust. He smoothed the chemise over her exposed skin and pulled the sheet back on top of her. "Thank you, Miss Alfredson." He nodded once. "If you will excuse me, I need to have a few words with your father."

Outside in the corridor, Marshall had barely closed the door when he demanded, "Well, Dr. McGrath?"

"Your daughter is afflicted by generalized peritonitis, I am certain. And I strongly suspect that an inflamed appendix has initiated it."

Marshall nodded gravely. Out of habit, he reached for his pocket watch and checked the time. "Dr. Montgomery felt much the same," he grunted.

"Then you will agree to surgery?"

"*Surgery?*" Marshall dropped the watch and it fell to his hip, dangling by its chain. "Certainly not! The girl is far too ill to even consider it."

"An operation is the only reasonable course of action."

"Nonsense!" Marshall snapped. "Look at you. You are still wet behind the ears. How dare you come in here and tell me that the only way to save my Olivia is to slice her open? It is preposterous."

Evan understood the father's visceral reaction, but it didn't stop his own temper from rising. He took a long slow breath and measured his words. "In San Francisco, I performed several appendectomies—the procedure for excising an inflamed appendix. Though it is a relatively new surgery, I have witnessed good results."

"Maybe you have, Dr. McGrath," Marshall said through gritted teeth. "But I will not allow you to risk my daughter's life in order to establish your reputation on the back of our family name."

"I care nothing for your family name!" Evan spat before salvaging his calm. He locked eyes with the man. "Mr. Alfredson, I will put it to you in these simple terms: If Olivia does not have surgery, and very soon, it is my opinion that the toxemia will kill her."

Marshall folded his arms across his chest and glowered for a long moment. Finally, he uncrossed his arms and pointed at Evan with a long finger. "Again, let me put it to you in these simple terms, Dr. McGrath: If my daughter dies because of *your* surgery, you will never ply your trade in the Pacific Northwest again."

Evan summoned the last of his restraint and broke off eye contact. His entire life, he had refused to relent to men like Marshall Alfredson. He wasn't about to back down from Alfredson, but he appreciated that now was not the time for confrontation. "Olivia is too unwell to be carried to the hospital," he said. "We have to perform the operation here."

Marshall swallowed. "I see."

"I will need two pots of boiling water and at least four sets of clean linens," Evan said as he reached for the door handle.

"I intend to watch the whole endeavor," Marshall announced.

Evan turned incredulously to the man. "That is entirely inappropriate, Mr. Alfredson. It is accepted practice that only trained medical personnel and assistants will attend an operation."

"This is my house. And Olivia is my daughter. And by God, I will be present when you do this to her!"

Evan recognized the futility in arguing. "I need those supplies now," he said as he opened the door and reentered the bedroom.

Thirty minutes passed before the servants had gathered the necessary supplies. After Evan had carefully unloaded his bag onto the table he had moved to the right side of the bed, he spent his time sterilizing instruments in the boiling water, laying out the tools in the order he would require them, and threading catgut onto needles of various sizes. After he deemed his equipment ready, he removed his jacket and slipped into the long white apron and cap that he had brought with him.

When Evan insisted that Marshall Alfredson cover his clothes with a clean sheet and a pillowcase tied over his hair, the older man balked. "What kind of quackery is this?" Marshall said. "Are you some kind of druid now?"

Swallowing more anger, Evan scrubbed his hands with soap and washed them in a pot of cold water. "I expect you have not read the work of Dr. Louis Pasteur or Dr. Joseph Lister on germ theory?"

"Sounds like bunkum to me," Marshall said, pushing away the pillow cover that the Sister was trying to apply to his head.

"Germs are everywhere, Mr. Alfredson," Evan said. "We carry them on our clothes and in our hair like leaves on a tree. We cannot see them without a microscope, but if they get into open wounds they can initiate lethal infections. Nowadays, all competent surgeons practice aseptic techniques. And you will not stay in this room without taking similar precautions!"

Olivia lifted her head and spoke up for the first time in ages. "Please, Papa. Listen to the doctor."

Marshall melted at his daughter's voice. He dropped his hand and stooped forward so that the nurse could tie the pillowcase over his scalp.

Evan turned to Olivia. Her pretty plaintive face set his heart racing. Despite his air of self-assurance, he knew that the procedure would be risky for a patient so gravely ill. As he stared into her wide jade eyes, it occurred to him how high the stakes were. He mustered a smile to mask his sudden case of nerves. "Miss Alfredson, I'm going to have to put you to sleep now."

She nodded understandingly. Evan glanced over at Marshall. He reached out and squeezed his daughter's foot through the sheet. "You remember, Liv. We Alfredsons come from the heartiest stock." His voice cracked, and he paused to clear his throat. "You will improve quickly after this, you understand." The words emerged as more command than reassurance.

Evan reached for the bottle of ether and the facecloth on the table. He uncorked the bottle and carefully poured the colorless liquid onto the cloth until it was saturated. The smell of ether drifted to his nostrils, and the pungent aroma relaxed him. He pressed the cloth gently over Olivia's lips. She stared up at Evan, her eyes brimming with trust.

"I'm going to count aloud now, Olivia. All I need is for you to breathe deeply," Evan soothed. "One . . . two . . . three . . . four . . ."

By the time he reached fifteen, Olivia's eyelids fluttered and then shut. He passed the cloth to the nurse and told her to keep it near the patient's lips and reapply at his command. Then he moved over to the side of the bed and pulled the sheets down and Olivia's chemise up, exposing her belly from the bottom of her chest to the tufts of pubic hair poking from above the lowered waist of her bloomers. He washed his hands again, and then soaked a cloth with an iodine solution. Beginning around the belly button, he meticulously cleaned her abdomen in circular motions from the center out, repeating the procedure three times.

Evan glimpsed Marshall again. The man held the same clenched-jaw stare as ever, his face etched with silent threat.

Evan mentally walked himself through each step of the procedure as he reached for the scalpel on the table beside him. *One layer at a time, McGrath,* the words and Scottish lilt of his surgical mentor, Dr. Hugh Dundee, rang in his ears. With his left hand, Evan palpated the area over the appendix known as McBurney's point. And with his right, he brought the scalpel blade down and drew horizontally for six inches as though applying a pen to paper but with slightly more pressure. Evan glanced up at Olivia, relieved to see she maintained her blank-faced anesthetized gaze.

He picked up a pair of steel forceps and used them to bluntly dissect through the scant amount of fat beneath Olivia's skin. Lost in concentration, he lifted the scalpel again and cut through the beefy red abdominal muscle. As soon as the blade penetrated through the peritoneum and into the abdominal cavity, pus welled up through the incision. The putrid smell of infection permeated the room. Evan glanced to Marshall. Though his face had drained of color, Marshall's expression remained steadfast as he kept a tight hold on his daughter's foot.

Evan grabbed for a fresh cloth and sponged urgently at the thick greenish yellow discharge. He jammed the scalpel back into the wound and extended the incision another three or four inches to allow him to visualize the area more clearly. The lacerated edges of muscle leaked fresh blood that mingled with the pus and turned the discharge a disconcerting brown.

Sweat trickled into Evan's eyes. Without prompting the nurse reached over and mopped at his brow with a clean cloth. Then she reached a hand out and felt Olivia's neck. "Dr. McGrath, the pulse is faster and weaker," she said in an even voice, though her implication was clear: Olivia was verging on a state of shock.

Evan grabbed for one of the needles that he had loaded with catgut. Deftly, he threaded the suture around the largest of the bleeding veins and tied them off. The blood flow lessened to a trickle. And after a few more dabs of his now-soaked cloth, the yellow ooze slowed.

Evan dug his bare hand deep inside the wound and grabbed hold of the slippery loops of bowel. He ran his fingers blindly along the rubbery intestine until he felt a thickening that he recognized as the cecum, the beginning of the colon. He pulled the cecum through the open wound. He twisted it over to expose the underside of the bowel, where the attached appendix was so black that it stuck out like an embalmed thumb. He tied off the base of the gangrenous appendix with three coils of his suture, and then cut it free with the scalpel blade and dropped it into the bowl the nurse held out for him. Evan tucked the cecum and attached bowel back into the abdominal cavity. He ran his hand along the inside of her belly to make sure he had not missed any other pockets of infection.

"The pulse has improved, Dr. McGrath," the nurse said in a relieved tone.

Evan squeezed the last of the pus out of the belly and pulled his hand out of the wound. Satisfied, he began to suture the peritoneum closed with a continuous thread. He sewed all the layers that he had cut through back together until he reached the skin, which he chose to leave open to lessen the chance of a wound infection.

Evan put the needle back down on the table and dipped his blood-caked fingers into one of the pots, clouding the water inside. "Sister, will you please bandage the wound?"

"Certainly, Doctor," the nurse said.

Marshall squinted hard at the surgeon. "Will my girl be all right now?"

"Olivia is still very ill, Mr. Alfredson." Evan lifted the steel bowl containing the necrotic appendix. He held it out to show the pale giant, exhibiting it for a shade longer than he knew was necessary. "Now that *this* is no longer festering inside her, I hope she will make a full recovery." He looked down at his fingernails, which were still encrusted with Olivia's blood and pus. He thought of those jade eyes. "But that is out of our hands now," he said quietly.

*4*

Tyler McGrath didn't leave his office at the Alfredson's outpatient clinic until after seven p.m., and only then to rush back to the SFU to treat a patient, Paige Newcomb, who had broken out in a severe allergic reaction to her first dose of chemotherapy. The allergy was easy enough to treat, but the fourteen-year-old—already devastated at the prospect of losing her hair from chemotherapy—was inconsolable at the sight of her swollen lips and neck and the diffuse blotchy rash covering her body.

Tall and gangly with a scattering of pimples over her cheeks and forehead, Paige teetered in the awkward stage between child and adult. But with huge eyes and sculpted cheekbones, she was destined to grow up beautiful. *Only if she survives the cancer,* Tyler thought grimly.

As the antiallergic medication ran into Paige's intravenous line, Tyler sat on the edge of the bed trying to calm her. Desperately self-conscious, the girl recoiled from his initial attempt to squeeze her puffy hand, so he avoided any further contact. But he stayed where he was, hoping his proximity might reassure her.

Paige had pulled a handheld mirror out of her nightstand when the rash had first broken out, and she had clung to it ever since despite Tyler's encouragement to put it away. She consulted the mirror again in disgust. "Dr. McGrath, my friends can't see me like this," she sputtered. "They just can't."

"They won't, Paige." He nodded at her engorged face and discolored arms. "In thirty minutes this will all be a distant memory."

"Promise?" she asked desperately.

"Promise."

She snuck one more horrified glimpse of herself in the mirror and then lowered it to her chest. "Doesn't matter," she groaned. She ran her hand through her lustrous brown hair. "This is all going to fall out soon."

Tyler nodded sympathetically. "You wouldn't believe how quickly it grows back, Paige."

"In a year or something," she muttered.

He forced a smile. "I remember when I got these horrible braces in eighth grade. I don't think I smiled for a year and a half. Now, I can barely remember them."

"At least you could hide your braces." She looked up at him hopelessly, tears welling again. "Everyone is going to see me bald."

They had already had this conversation multiple times, but Tyler didn't mind running through it again. He hoped to see just a glimmer of acceptance in the girl's desperate eyes. "Remember Agnes? The lady who came to see you about the wigs."

Paige nodded.

"Agnes makes them out of real hair. I've seen lots of patients wearing them. And if I hadn't known different I would've been fooled every single time."

"Honest?"

Tyler brought his hand to his chest. "I swear. And if you want to mix it up and go blond and short, or red and curly . . ." He winked. "Hell, if you want a blue Mohawk, Agnes can do that, too."

Paige giggled, but the reassurance was short-lived. Her face crumpled again. "Everyone's still gonna know." She plucked at her eyebrows. "You can't make a wig for these."

Tyler spent another fifteen minutes trying to calm Paige. He didn't begrudge a moment of the time, but he left with the niggling sense that the teenager wasn't much, if any, more at ease than before his arrival.

As he drove away from the hospital, Tyler tried to focus on anything aside from work, but it didn't help. His thoughts kept drifting back to his patients, especially Nate Stafford and the almost insurmountable odds the boy was facing. By the time Tyler pulled into his driveway, he decided that his thirty-fifth birthday had fallen on a particularly lousy day.

Jill and he had lived in the house for over a year but it still didn't feel like home to him. They had bought the recently renovated two-story house soon after relocating to Oakdale. The once-sleepy town, sixty miles outside of Seattle, had grown in step with the Alfredson, which was its primary employer and sole industry. They had not bought the house because of its country charm or elaborate wine cellar—though those were definite plusses—but because of its proximity to the hospital, a five- to ten-minute drive. On drier days, Jill or Tyler could cycle or even run to work, but neither of them ever seemed to find the time.

Though Tyler had grown up in Oakdale, he had not wanted to return to the town or the Alfredson. He doubted he would ever be able to escape the shadow of his family name or establish his own professional reputation there. But Jill had argued that the move was critically important to her career and so, against his better judgment, he relented. While it may have been the right career decision, it had proved the wrong step for their marriage. Their emotional divide had only deepened. At times, it seemed as though they were living independent lives under the same roof. He wanted things to change, but his guilt over recent events made it even harder to reach out to his wife.

Tyler stepped into his house just after nine o'clock. Closing the front door behind him, he called out, "Hello? Jill?"

His only birthday greeting came from their fat old calico cat, Kramer (named after Jill's favorite sitcom character), who rubbed against his leg and meowed for his dinner. Tyler reached down, halfheartedly scratched the cat behind his ears, and then filled a bowl with a mix of wet and dry food, which the cat attacked as soon as it hit the ground. He would have replaced Kramer—or at least augmented him—with a dog or two, but both Jill and he were gone for too much of the day to leave a dog alone at home. Only cats were self-sufficient enough to survive such extended periods of neglect. Tyler wondered how they would cope if Jill ever did become pregnant but, fertility issues aside, that wasn't much of a possibility lately.

Tyler wandered upstairs, undressed, and stepped into the shower. Standing under the hot spray, he tried to scrub away the remnants of his day. He heard the bathroom door whoosh open. "Happy birthday," Jill Laidlaw called out from somewhere behind a cloud of steam.

Tyler switched off the nozzle and pushed open the shower door. His wife's form emerged out of the mist as she leaned forward and pecked him on the cheek. "This bathroom has a fan, you know," Jill said as she swirled a finger through the mist. "But I guess people of your advanced age start to forget those kinds of things."

Tyler held up four fingers and wiggled them. "A few months and you'll be looking at the wrong side of thirty-four, too."

At one time, Jill would have shed her clothes and hopped into the shower with him, but he knew that the passionless kiss on the cheek would be as much affection as he would see. Even if they weren't mired in their rut, she was swamped with a major research grant reapplication and their personal, romantic, and sex life always ground to a halt in its wake. Suppressing a sigh, Tyler reached for a towel, dried off, and wrapped it around his waist before stepping out of the shower.

Jill studied him with those keen blue eyes that had so captivated him. Stylish as ever in funky black low-cut pants and a pale work blouse that still managed to accentuate her slight curves, Jill leaned back against the vanity's countertop. Her blond hair was clipped behind her ears and she wore just a trace of mascara and lipstick to look polished. A distant smile parted those full lips.

Tyler was very familiar with the almost standoffish pose. Though he had picked up on his wife's remoteness—"the wall around your heart," as he had called it during one bitter fight—from their first meeting, it had grown more pronounced recently. Sometimes her inaccessibility left him cold, while other times he admired it as a sign of her inner strength or just found it desperately sexy. At the moment he felt nothing, but he didn't read anything into that. His numbness was a natural response to an overwrought day.

"Ty, I planned on taking you out for a birthday drink," she said.

Recognizing the beginnings of an excuse, he reached beside her for the brush on the countertop. "But?" he said.

"I have to get my grant renewal proposal finished. It's due in a couple days. And it's a monster."

"No problem." He halfheartedly ran the brush a couple of times through his thick brown hair. "Don't feel much like celebrating, anyway."

Jill misread petulance into his comment. "Ty, this is no ordinary grant. My whole lab is riding on this funding. And I still haven't enrolled enough patients in my study to publish the results."

"You will."

"You can't know that!"

"You always have before, Jill."

She shook her head. "Times are bad now. Government funding for medical research has been steadily drying up since the federal deficit ballooned. The competition for grant money is fierce." She grimaced. "One of my old professors just had his grant renewal rejected. The guy is nationally renowned. It should have been a slam dunk. Would have never happened a few years back." She sighed. "I couldn't be reapplying at a worse time."

"It'll work out, hon," Tyler said. "Besides, I don't feel like going out tonight. I've had a crappy day. All I want to do is to open a bottle of wine and wallow in self-pity." He summoned a smile. "I thought that might appeal to you."

"Normally it would be irresistible, but tonight . . ." Jill glanced at her reflection in the mirror and tucked a wayward strand of hair behind her ear. "What was so bad about your day?"

"Remember the boy with acute myeloid leukemia I told you about?"

She ran a finger along the side of her hair. "The baseball star who failed his bone marrow transplant?"

"Yeah. Nate."

Jill turned from the mirror to face him. "Is it hopeless?"

"We're going to try one of the new targeted therapies, but even if it were to work, his immune system is so shot . . ."

Her eyes lit with momentary tenderness. "I'm sorry, Ty."

"He's such a cool kid. And his parents . . ." Tyler shook his head. "I have another posttransplant treatment failure, too. Almost the same story. Keisha's only eight." He had a mental image of the girl that almost made him wince. "She has this wacky smile with the two front teeth missing . . . melts your heart, you know?"

Jill leaned forward and wrapped him in a brief hug. She pulled back and held him by both shoulders. "It's your job. Think of all the ones you do save. These treatment failures . . ." She shrugged. "They're simply unavoidable."

Though he knew she was right, he resented her matter-of-fact tone. "It all evens out in the wash, doesn't it?"

She let go of his shoulders. "You know what I mean."

He nodded contritely. "I'm just venting on you. Venting and wallowing. It's all part of that same irresistible package." He sighed. "Sure you don't want to stick around to join me?"

She studied his face. "Are you going to be okay tonight, Ty?"

He noticed her steal a furtive peek at her watch. "Yeah, yeah. Go," he said.

Jill started for the door. "I'll try to get back at a reasonable time. Save a glass for me. I'd like to toast the old geezer."

"I'll leave my teeth in till you get home." But he knew, as well as she did, that by the time she got back he would be asleep.

After Jill left, Tyler forced their relationship out of his thoughts. He knew better than to judge their marriage in his current headspace.

The ringing phone drew his attention. He would have ignored it, but as soon as he saw his sister's number on the call display he grabbed for it. "Hey, Erin."

"Happy birthday, Pip!" Erin said, using the childhood nickname—shortened from "pip-squeak"—that she coined for him when he was still a preschooler.

He warmed at the sound of her voice. Four years younger than Erin, Tyler always looked up to his older sister; though he didn't see as much of her as he would have liked, even now that they worked at the same hospital. When they were together, few people recognized them as siblings. Tyler had inherited their mother's blue-gray eyes and lighter angular features, whereas Erin had acquired their father's darker coloring and narrower bonier face. Temperament-wise, the pattern was reversed. Tyler shared William's intensity, while Erin had inherited their mother's easygoing unflappable nature. Erin had always seemed to sail through life, succeeding at anything she bothered to try and rising to the top of her field in cardiac surgery without ever showing much ambition.

"You haven't called me Pip in a while," Tyler pointed out.

"Didn't want to chance one of those famous temper tantrums."

He chuckled. "I could really throw them in my day, couldn't I?"

"I can still picture you lying facedown on the floor in Harris's grocery store, fists and feet flailing, while poor old Mr. Harris tried to negotiate with you like he was talking down someone with a bomb strapped to his chest."

"What can I say? I really wanted those chocolate Pop-Tarts Mom wouldn't buy."

She uttered a small laugh. "My baby brother is thirty-five. You have no idea how old that makes me feel."

"Join the club," he said. "Erin, thanks for the book. I love it."

She had left the gift—a coffee-table pictorial book on the history of flight—for him with his receptionist at the outpatient clinic.

"Maybe you'll get back to those flying lessons one day, huh?"

"Yeah, maybe next spring," he said, though he knew the likelihood was slim.

"I would have preferred to drop it off in person. Give you a birthday hug and all. But I couldn't find you at the hospital, and I knew I wouldn't have time to drive out to your place tonight." They hardly ever bumped into each other on the sprawling medical complex's grounds. And Erin and her husband lived on a farm, twenty minutes outside of Oakdale in the opposite direction, with their twin sons, three dogs, and four cats along with horses, sheep, and too many other animals for Tyler to keep track of or count.

"Long day?" he asked.

"Too long."

"Did you do a transplant?"

"Yeah. I did."

Tyler picked up on his sister's hesitance. "It didn't go well?" he asked.

"The weather delayed the transport chopper." She sighed. "The new heart had over five hours of cold ischemia before we got it re-implanted. A small miracle that it started beating at all."

"How's the patient doing?"

"Not great. I'm not sure she's going to make it. She still has a balloon pump in her aorta supporting her circulation." She exhaled and the receiver whistled in his ear. "She's only in her twenties. A single mom. Two kids. They're twins, just like Simon and Martin."

"Don't some donor hearts take a while to rebound after transplant?"

"Sometimes." She paused. "I don't know what will happen to those kids if Kristen doesn't bounce back. The father is a deadbeat. And she has little other family support. Just one aunt who's not in great shape herself."

"Aren't you getting a little ahead of yourself, Erin?"

Tyler was unaccustomed to reassuring his older sister. He seldom had to. Little seemed to faze Erin. Not the stress of her job, in which she literally held lives in her hands, nor the happy chaos of her home with its own zoo, tireless eleven-year-old boys, and an equally inquisitive and scattered husband, Steve, a chemical engineer who had given up his career to raise their sons and run the farm. But ever since Erin returned earlier in the year from her stint as a volunteer surgeon at an African hospital, Tyler had noticed a change in his once-carefree sister. Less relaxed, she had begun to fuss over details that had never bothered her before.

"How are the menaces?" Tyler said, deliberately changing subjects.

"Busy. Exhausting. You know? Same as ever." She chuckled. "They miss their uncle, though."

"Yeah, it's been too long," Tyler said. "How about this weekend? Maybe they could sleep over Friday night?"

"I'm sure they would *love* to." She paused a moment. "Will Jill be okay with that?"

"You know how much she loves Martin and Simon," he sighed.

"And they, her," Erin said. "I just don't want to impose on either of you."

"It's no imposition. Your kids are fun. Both as crazy as their dad. Besides, Jill is tied up with her research grant renewal. I'm sure it will end up just a boys' night out for us."

"No R-rated movies this time, huh?"

"They hoodwinked me last time."

"Uh-huh," she said skeptically. "So you thought that slasher flick was rated G?"

"They told me PG-13," he muttered. "But I'm onto them now."

"Fair enough." Erin cleared her throat. "Tyler, how are things at . . . your home?"

A few months earlier, Erin and Tyler had gone out to dinner to catch up. After a few beers and half a bottle of wine, Tyler had alluded to his strained relationship with Jill. Erin had not pried, but she had obviously not forgotten, either.

"Yeah, things are all good," he said evasively.

"Great." She laughed. "Anyway, I called to wish you a happy birthday, not to meddle."

"Big sisters are supposed to meddle, aren't they?"

"Especially now that Mom isn't around to do it."

Erin's reference to their mother brought a momentary quiet. Eight years had passed, but the wound had yet to heal. Her death had left a void in the family that no one else could ever fill.

"Hey, Tyler," she said with forced cheerfulness. "Why don't Jill and you come over Sunday for a belated birthday dinner? I'll invite Dad and Lies-beth," she said, referring to their maternal grandmother.

"I'm on call Sunday."

"Weekend after?"

"Done."

After he hung up the phone, Tyler couldn't shake the sense that some-thing, beyond the difficult transplant surgery, was troubling his sister. For a moment, he wondered if Steve and she were going through a rough patch, too. But he wrote the idea off as far-fetched. They had been married almost twenty years. Tyler had never met a closer, more affectionate couple. It had to be something else. *Africa?* he wondered again.

Tyler slipped into his bathrobe. He wandered downstairs and into the basement wine cellar that the previous owner had installed. Spacious with handcrafted cabinets, a tasting table, and sophisticated temperature and humidity controls, the elaborate cellar was wasted on Tyler and Jill. They kept only fifty or so bottles in a room meant to hold several hundred, and their collection consisted of mainly domestic wines that he imagined would have dismayed serious connoisseurs.

Tyler studied a row of bottles with little interest. He was considering cutting his losses and climbing into bed but, out of a halfhearted desire to mark the age milestone, reached for a bottle of pinot noir. He had just tucked it under his arm when the doorbell rang. Tyler glanced at the wall-mounted digital clock that read 10:12 P.M. before he headed up the stairs.

He opened the door to find his father standing on the other side, still wearing the same blue suit as earlier. William McGrath extended a hand to his son. In his other arm, he clutched a wrapped rectangular box with a small red bow and an envelope attached.

"Dad?" Tyler squinted, unable to mask his surprise.

In the past year, his father had visited the house only a handful of times. Tyler never put much weight into Jill's theory that it was her presence that kept William at bay. Tyler had few memories, even as a child, of time spent with his father. An inveterate workaholic, William had dedicated his life to the Alfredson, first as a kidney specialist and now as the senior medical ad-ministrator. The hospital was William's home and, for all intents and purposes, his first family. For much of his childhood, Tyler had relied on—without even realizing it—his maternal grandfather, Maarten Vanderhof, to fill in for his absent father. Maarten, not William, had inspired Tyler to choose medicine. Tyler had even followed his grandfather's huge footsteps into the specialty of pediatric oncology, a field that Maarten had pioneered in the fifties and sixties.

"Happy birthday," William said stiffly as he broke off the handshake and handed his son the present.

"Thanks." Tyler was surprised at how pleased he was to see his father had not forgotten his birthday. Too embarrassed to show it, he looked down at his watch. "Dad, it's after ten."

"I meant to come sooner, but the day got away from me." William cleared his throat. "I hope I didn't wake you."

Tyler held up the bottle of pinot noir to show him. "I haven't reached the point of taking one of these to bed yet."

"Maybe when you're thirty-six," William said in his usual dry delivery. He followed Tyler into the house. Despite his son's objections, he insisted on stopping to slip out of his shoes before joining Tyler in the living room. "Where is Jill?" he asked, sitting down on a sofa.

"Writing a research grant."

"Of course. The MS stem cell research?" William raised his eyebrow slightly. "Good. The controversy always spices up our Research Ethics Committee meetings."

Tyler had heard, though not from his father, that William had to repeatedly defend Jill's right to conduct studies within the ethical minefield that was stem cell research. "Don't you have enough controversy without dragging Jill into the mix?" he asked.

William's shoulders slumped. "Plenty."

Again, Tyler noticed how tired his father looked. He could not believe how much the man had aged in the past year. "What's the latest, Dad?"

"A few patients and staff members are unwell with a mysterious GI bug. Infection Control has suggested we may need to shut down a few outpatient clinics." William waved away the concern and sat up straighter. And then he added, as if an afterthought, "Oh, and the Alfredson board is holding an extraordinary meeting in two weeks. I have to prepare for it."

"Prepare for *what*?"

"The usual dog and pony show. No doubt it's just another glorified photo op. You know that family. They like to appear involved in their namesake hospital."

"But you said it was an 'extraordinary' meeting."

"Gets them more publicity that way. I've been down this road before." William pointed to the gift still in Tyler's arm. "Open it. Please."

Tyler separated the envelope, tore it open, and pulled out a generic birthday card. When he opened it a photo fell out and fluttered to the floor. He reached down to pick up the faded color snapshot. It showed a three-year-old boy wearing a red cowboy hat and mounted gleefully on a brown horse. It took Tyler a split second to realize that he was the boy in the picture, because he had no recollection of the occasion or the photograph. He turned it over and saw that his father had scrawled on the back:

*Happy thirty-fifth birthday, Cowboy.*

*Dad*

Showing a hint of a smile, William shrugged. "Your mother would have wanted you to have it."

In the last few years of her life, Jeannette had taken to the habit of including old photographs in the kids' birthday and Christmas cards. That tradition had ended suddenly on a bitterly cold November morning, eight years before—the day his mother dropped dead of a burst aneurysm in her brain. She was only fifty-three.

"Open the present," William said.

Tyler lifted up the box and tore off the wrapping paper. Underneath, he found a long wooden box. He unlatched the clasp and opened it. Inside was a bottle of red Beaucastel from Châteauneuf-du-Pape, 1970 vintage. Tyler suspected it had cost a fortune. He smiled gratefully at his father. "Older than me, huh?"

"You know the expression about wine?"

"That it gets better with age."

William rose to his feet. "But it's only true to a point. Sooner or later, all wines will spoil." He nodded to the bottle. "In this case, with proper care, you still have a little way to go."

"Will be interesting to see which one of us spoils first," Tyler said. "Will you join me for a toast?"

"I can't. I have an early meeting."

"Well, thanks for dropping by, Dad. And for the bottle. It will be a huge upgrade to our cellar. I imagine it will embarrass the hell out of the other bottles around it."

William showed a slight grin as he strode for the door. He stopped to slip his shoes back on. "Listen, Tyler, I know the Alfredson doesn't hold the same relevance for you as it does me."

*Here we go!* Tyler thought, suspicious he was about to hear the real purpose of his father's visit.

"The McGraths have been an integral part of the Alfredson for a hundred years," William went on. "I think it's fair to say that it's in our blood."

"This is not exactly news, Dad."

"I suppose not. Nonetheless, I'm glad you and Jill have come back to work here."

"And?"

William held up a palm. "Maybe not now, but at some point, you should consider a nonclinical role—"

"You mean medical administration? Me?" Tyler croaked. "You've got to be kidding."

"In the next two years, there will be a new division head of pediatric oncology. In fact, the department head for pediatrics—"

"Don't waste your breath." Tyler raised a hand. "Why don't you talk to Erin?"

William shook his head. "That would be pointless."

Tyler couldn't argue. Erin was as far removed from all things bureaucratic or organizational as possible. "Well, I'm certainly not interested, Dad."

"At your age, I wasn't interested either," William said. "I thought administrators were all stuffed shirts and parasites. I didn't care about budgets and expenditures. I cared about my patients. I wanted to make a difference for them. One day, though, I listened to my uncle's advice. As a doctor, you make a difference one patient at a time. As a health-care planner, you can make a difference to the whole system."

"Goddamn it, Dad! This is exactly why I didn't want to come back here in the first place," Tyler said, suddenly unleashing a day's worth of pent-up frustration. "I work at the Alfredson because it's well staffed, well run, and doesn't choose its patients based on the size of their parents' wallets. But I couldn't give a flying fuck about the McGrath family's hundred-year medical dynasty or our destiny in the Alfredson's future. For me it's just a bunch of buildings with a lot of fancy bells and whistles, nothing more. You understand?"

"I think I do," William said quietly. They stared at each other for a tense moment. "Tell me, Tyler. Are you sure the Alfredson would be such a world-class hospital with its open-arms policy of caring if our family had not been involved since its inception?"

"I don't know," Tyler mumbled sheepishly, aware that he had overreacted.

William nodded knowingly. "I realize you don't have much interest in the place," he said with a trace of hurt. "But it might be worth your while to have a brief look at its history. After all, history has an uncanny knack of repeating itself."

# 5

*I'll give the old crackpot this much: She can spin a yarn,* Lorna Simpson thought as she leaned forward in the wingback chair, absorbed in Dot Alfredson's telling of the initial encounter between Evan McGrath and Marshall Alfredson and the improvised appendectomy the young surgeon had performed over a century before, one floor above where the two women now sat. Lorna had never received the water she requested, but she had already dropped her pretense of teetotalling. Now, like Dot, she gratefully cradled a tall drink that was far more vodka than tonic.

After Dot finished her tale, Lorna held out her free palm to the other woman. "I don't understand. Evan saved the life of Marshall's only daughter. What possible reason could Marshall have had to hate the doctor?"

Dot's bright red lips broke into another self-amused smile. "Hatred doesn't always have a rhyme or reason to it, darling. Take the present-day version of our Alfredson clan. Frankly, putting money squabbles aside, I suspect many of us would still *loathe* each other."

"I'm not so sure," Lorna said, though she silently agreed with her great-aunt. "When I was a kid, we used to have those family reunions."

"Ah, the annual screaming matches. They hardly lasted, though, did they?" Dot eyed her with a glimmer of mischief. "Of course, the whole *merry* tribe will be reuniting for the Alfredson board meeting in a few weeks. Will you be attending, darling?"

Lorna buried her nose in her drink. "I haven't decided yet," she lied. "How about you?"

Dot's eyes lit. "I wouldn't miss it for the world!"

Eager to change the subject, Lorna put her glass down on the coffee table. She fixed her great-aunt with a penetrating stare. "Dot, there has to be more to it. What went so wrong between your grandfather and Evan McGrath?"

Dot sipped her own drink unhurriedly. Her gaze drifted to the mantel bearing graphic figurines. "The thing that usually comes between two men."

Lorna nodded. "A woman."

"Dr. McGrath was right, of course," Dot said vaguely. "Within hours of being stitched up, Olivia began to improve. The fever broke. And soon she began to eat again." Dot ran a hand over her shorn white hair. "Yet every day, for weeks on end, he would still come back here to this house, riding Seattle's new electric trolleys as far as they would carry him and then walking the last mile."

"Was he falling in love with Olivia?"

Dot shrugged. "Evan insisted that it was merely a matter of conscientious postoperative care. Of course, as Olivia improved, the young doctor and patient had a chance to branch out beyond dressing changes and dietary restrictions."

Lorna raised an eyebrow. "Branch out?"

"Mind out of the gutter, darling." Dot winked. "Theirs was still an innocent relationship. But they had a shared passion. After reading fantastic accounts of Florence Nightingale's exploits, Olivia was *fascinated* by all things related to health care. Evan, of course, was passionate on the subject. He dreamed of opening a new clinic in the Pacific Northwest. Olivia would hang on every longing word of his description. *Naturally*, the friendship blossomed."

"I take it Marshall did not approve."

Dot laughed. "About as much as Romeo's or Juliet's father might have."

"Was Marshall that much of a snob?"

"Oh, probably," Dot said. "But this had nothing to do with social status or even patient-doctor etiquette."

"What then?"

"Evan was already married."

Lorna fought off a smile, realizing that her long drive was proving worthwhile. "Ouch. Awkward."

"Awkward, *indeed*, darling." Dot raised a bony finger. "Now if you've ever seen erotica of the period, you would realize that behind closed doors those randy old Victorians—in all likelihood my grandfather among them—were up to sexual exploits that would make an X-rated-film star blush. But in public, prudishness and naïveté reigned supreme. Marshall didn't appreciate the *appearance* of a deepening relationship between his daughter and her married surgeon."

"No." Lorna sputtered a laugh. "I suppose he wouldn't."

"Marshall was *so* outraged that he found Olivia a new doctor and banned Evan from his house."

"I'm guessing that didn't keep them apart, though."

"Olivia secretly went to work for Evan."

"*Secretly?*" Lorna frowned. "How do you secretly work at a doctor's office?"

"I imagine you don't, darling. Olivia came to work for Evan at his own home. To help his wife, Virginia."

Lorna shook her head and sighed. "Okay, now you've lost me."

"At that time, Virginia McGrath was a shut-in. *Utterly* disabled. Out of gratitude to Evan, Olivia came to his house to help out. A companion. The kind of horrid care aide thing my nieces and nephews want to impose on me now." Dot rolled her eyes and scoffed. "Could you imagine?"

*The poor care aide*, Lorna thought, but she shook her head sympathetically and smiled. "What was wrong with Virginia?"

Dot swept a hand from her knees to her hips. "The 'creeping paralysis' is what they used to call it."

---

The partnership between Alfredson and McGrath sprang almost spontaneously from their first meeting. In Evan, Marshall recognized a visionary. And in Marshall, Evan found a champion.
—*The Alfredson: The First Hundred Years* by Gerald Fenton Naylor

Evan and Virginia McGrath lived in a four-bedroom home of the newly popular four-square style. Identical houses had begun to pop up all over Seattle in subdivisions that sprouted around the new cable car lines like barnacles on a dock. Having little interest in architecture or social appearances, Evan had chosen the house because of its proximity to the city's only hospital (a modest two-story structure on Fifth Avenue, run by the Sisters of Providence) and its setting on a flat, easily accessible street that would allow wheelchair entry.

Outside of his work, Evan's sole focus for the last few years had been the care of his ailing wife. But in the past three months a new distraction had crept into his life.

Sitting in the dining room across the oak table from Evan, Olivia Al-fredson wore a blue high-waist jacket and matching skirt with her long red hair piled and pinned above her head. Her pink cheeks were scattered with light freckles, and Evan noticed how agreeably they had filled out in the weeks since her surgery. She had shed some of her shyness and, despite her well-mannered deportment, a spark of mischief danced in those jade eyes.

The McGraths' regular housekeeper, Mrs. Shirley, was at home tending to her ailing son. Her cousin, Miss Adele, was coming twice a day to perform light housekeeping and prepare meals, neither of which she did nearly as well as her cousin. But Evan considered Olivia a godsend. Without her, he would have had to leave Virginia alone during stretches in the daytime.

Olivia reached for the pot of tea she had steeped and poured it into two waiting cups. Leaving the third one empty, she put the pot down and covered it with a colorfully embroidered cozy. "Will Mrs. McGrath nap for long?" she asked.

Evan rubbed his eyes wearily. "Perhaps. As you know, these days, Virginia is so fatigued."

"Is that because of her multiple scler . . ." Olivia struggled to finish the term.

"Multiple sclerosis," Evan said.

"I had not heard of this disease before," she said sheepishly.

"Most people have not," Evan said. "Many still know it as 'creeping paralysis.' Dr. Jean-Martin Charcot only discovered it twenty-five years ago on cadaver dissections. Prior to his astounding work, even doctors used to consider the disease a type of hysteria or acquired imbecility."

Olivia passed Evan the sugar. "It is a disease of the nervous system?"

He nodded. "Dr. Charcot showed that multiple sclerosis affects the entire nervous system from the spinal cord to the deepest areas of the brain."

Her eyes burned with curiosity. "Are people born with this illness?"

Her interest fueled his enthusiasm. "No. The symptoms do not usually set in until adulthood. That is when the brain damage begins. Virginia did not suffer her first attack until she was twenty-one."

"So there was a time when Mrs. McGrath could walk?"

"*Walk*? It was not that long ago that she used to run on the tennis court, Miss Alfredson!"

Olivia reddened. "I'm sorry, I did not know."

He held open his hands. "How could you? All you have ever seen of her . . ."

Olivia tilted her head and her lips formed a tentative smile. "What was Mrs. McGrath like . . . before? Please, I would like very much to know."

"Virginia is such a spirited woman. She used to love the outdoors—to go for long strolls and to swim. And whenever we could find someone with a tennis court, she was a lioness on the grass." He smiled at the memory. "And she used to sing in the church choir. She was a contralto with a low voice that was as lovely as she was—as she is."

Olivia looked down at her teacup. "Of course."

"The illness struck five years ago. At first, it was just numbness in her hands. We thought it was a matter of overexertion. Then she developed the tremors. Of course, when her vision began to tunnel—"

"*Tunnel*?" Olivia shook her head. "What does that mean, Dr. McGrath?"

"The field of vision closes in from the sides, like looking through a tele-scope." Evan pantomimed peering through his touching forefinger and thumb. "Once she developed the tunnel vision, I realized the diagnosis. The answer had been staring me in the face all that time. I should have recognized it much sooner."

Olivia clasped her hands together. "Perhaps you did not want to, Dr. McGrath?"

"No question, clinical judgment becomes clouded with loved ones." Evan stared into her sympathetic eyes. "Three years ago, the disease attacked her sense of balance. That was a cruel blow. Virginia has not been able to walk in over two years. And, as you know, her speech has become difficult to un-derstand at times."

Olivia nodded. "Do you know what causes this affliction?"

Evan shook his head. "Some doctors believe it is a problem with the sweat glands—a lack of proper secretion—but I think that is nonsense."

"What do you believe?"

Evan stared into the bottom of his cup. "There are diseases, like sugar di-abetes or kidney failure, where organs that had once worked perfectly well simply fail. I have seen the autopsies. It's not merely a matter of these organs wearing out, as with old age, but more as if they were specifically targeted for attack. As if their own bodies had turned against them. I believe the same has happened with Virginia's nervous system."

Olivia nodded. "Is there medicine that will help?"

"No." Evan felt the bile rise in his throat again. "Of course, there are no shortage of charlatans promising cures. That is what brought us to Seattle in the first place."

"You came here seeking treatment for your wife?" Her face creased, bewildered. "But . . . but you are a doctor."

"My area of specialty is limited to surgery. No surgical procedure can help Ginny. Even in the reputable hospital where I worked in San Francisco, none of my colleagues could offer her anything. Then someone told me of a man in Seattle who specialized in chronic debilitating diseases. A Dr. Garth Sibley." His lip curled on speaking the name. "I corresponded with Sibley for a while. He had an understanding of multiple sclerosis, but I did not trust his hypotheses, and I was very leery of his grand promises." He shook his head angrily. "I should have never read his letters to Virginia, but they made her so happy. In her mind, Sibley became her savior. I could not refuse to bring her to see him."

"It did not go well?"

"No, it did not." The memory of it stoked Evan's ire. "For a small fortune, the quack treated her with one of his patented panaceas, Sibley's Elixir. His snake oil almost killed her. I had to threaten to beat the life out of him before he confessed that his 'curative' was nothing more than red wine with a small portion of sulfuric acid added."

Olivia wrinkled her nose in shock. "*Sulfuric acid?*"

"Sibley and his ilk," he growled. "They are the problem with my profession. Anyone can present himself as a doctor or a healer. These people offer nothing but lies and pseudoscience. Worse still, they break the first law of medicine."

"Which is?"

"Hippocrates said, 'Above all, do no harm'!" He gazed at her intently, his chest thumping with a blend of indignation and affection. "I have seen this maxim contradicted far too often, Miss Alfredson. Patented 'cure-alls' thrown together with whatever chemicals are lying about. Outdated and dangerous treatments like bleeding or even the drilling of holes into people's skulls.

People want so badly to find something to help that they will trust anyone. However, these unproven procedures and spurious medications kill patients. I have signed far too many death certificates as a result."

Olivia shook her head in distaste.

"In San Francisco, at the Morgan Clinic, we practiced medicine supported by scientific principles and evidence," Evan went on. "There is nothing comparable here or anywhere in the whole state."

Olivia leaned forward, her eyes suddenly wide with excitement. "You could establish such a facility, Dr. McGrath. Right here in Seattle!"

"Could you imagine it, Miss Alfredson?" He reached forward and almost grabbed her hand in his exhilaration, but stopped himself. "A clinic where the best practitioners and researchers in medicine come together to care for patients, share their knowledge, and search for new and better remedies."

Evan looked away in embarrassment. He had never discussed the idea with anyone, but he longed to see such a clinic built, and not only for professional reasons. He was also thinking of his wife, imagining her in an environment that offered a glimmer of hope for the future.

Cheeks flushed, Olivia stared at Evan in awe. "How wonderful!" she gasped.

Evan experienced another surge of the elation, which was happening more often in her presence. He had not had an opportunity to teach students since he had left San Francisco. To have such a hungry pupil, who was so quick to understand, was a pleasure for him.

Their eyes locked warmly. "Dr. McGrath, this clinic could really be something important."

"Yes."

A high-pitched moan from Virginia's room broke the moment. Evan began to rise from his chair. "No!" Olivia jumped to her feet. "Allow me to help Mrs. McGrath up. Please. You look so very tired."

Evan nodded gratefully. He was exhausted, having stayed at the hospital until four A.M. with a gravely ill man who required amputation of his gangrenous leg. "Miss Alfredson, you have been such a help to Virginia and me," he began awkwardly. "I do not know how to thank you."

Olivia showed him a big smile. "Dr. McGrath, I believe that a little help around the house is minor compensation in return for saving a person's life."

Evan watched her disappear into his wife's room. He heard voices. Though he could not make out the conversation, he picked up snippets of his wife's anxious jumbled words and Olivia's reassuring answers. Impatient for their return, Evan tried to convince himself that he was just eager to see his wife again.

Ten minutes passed before the floorboards creaked and Olivia pushed Virginia's wooden wheelchair through the doorway and into the dining room. Evan rose and walked over to meet them. Virginia was wearing a shawl over her shoulders and a long nightgown. She sat slumped in the wheelchair, a blanket over her lap. The sight reminded Evan how much his wife had aged. At twenty-seven, Virginia's drawn face already looked middle-aged.

She offered her husband a very shaky hand. He clutched it in his as he ran his other hand tenderly over her forehead. "Good sleep, Ginny?"

Virginia appraised him blankly. "At least I can still swim in my dreams," she slurred, showing a glimpse of her former self. Then it was gone. A confused suspicion clouded her uneven expression. "Evan, who is this lovely young woman?"

Though Olivia had been visiting daily for weeks, Virginia's memory for recent events had worsened of late. "Remember, Ginny? Miss Alfredson helps us out in the afternoons."

Virginia turned to Olivia. "You're very young." She added warily, "And so well dressed for a housekeeper."

Evan picked up on the paranoid tone in his wife's voice. As her memory slipped and her grasp on reality weakened, Virginia was prone to fits of unjustified accusation, often questioning her husband's faithfulness. Olivia had yet to witness any of these episodes, but Evan realized his wife was verging on one now. "Miss Alfredson is not a housekeeper, Ginny." He held his wife's shoulders reassuringly. "She volunteers to help us. Out of the goodness of her heart."

"The goodness of her heart?" Virginia said. "That is most selfless of her."

"I performed surgery on Miss Alfredson," he soothed. "She is eager to help out in return. And you know that while I am at work, you can use the company."

"Where is Mrs. Shirley?" Virginia asked.

His wife had forgotten that their regular housekeeper was at home with her own very ill nine-year-old. Evan had been caring for the boy—who had suffered from asthma and chest colds his entire short life—but this time his pneumonia had not responded to the daily injections of silver. "Tommy has another chest infection," he said, downplaying the gravity of the illness.

"That poor, poor little boy," Virginia cooed.

A heavy pounding at the door interrupted them. Evan hurried over to open it.

In an overcoat and derby, the bearlike figure of Marshall Alfredson filled the doorway. "McGrath, I know she is in here!" the older man boomed, close enough for Evan to smell the remnants of his most recently smoked cigar.

Evan eyed him steadily. "This is my home, Mr. Alfredson. I do not appreciate your tone."

Marshall pointed over his shoulder to where Olivia stood. "And how do you think I appreciate discovering this *situation* involving my own daughter?!" He cocked his massive fist and shook it menacingly at Evan.

"Papa, this is not—," Olivia began.

Without taking his eyes off Marshall, Evan raised a hand to interrupt her. "Perhaps we should continue this discussion inside?"

Marshall grunted his agreement. As soon as Evan stepped out of the way, Marshall stormed toward his daughter. He had made it several strides before he stopped abruptly, noticing Virginia for the first time. He pulled off his hat, brought it to his chest, and bowed toward her. "Pardon me, madam, I am . . . er . . . ," he stammered to Virginia. "I am Olivia's father. Marshall Alfredson."

"Mr. Alfredson, allow me to introduce my wife, Mrs. McGrath," Evan said pointedly.

Always self-conscious of her tremor and slurred speech in the company of strangers, especially men, Virginia merely said, "A pleasure, sir."

Evan joined the others collected around Virginia's wheelchair. He viewed Marshall's mortified face with a satisfaction he found hard to suppress. "You see, Mr. Alfredson, the *situation* is that our regular housekeeper has not been able to come due to family illness. Miss Alfredson has been kind enough to keep Mrs. McGrath company while I attend to my patients."

"I see." Marshall nodded, regaining some of his composure. He glanced over to his daughter, his expression a contrast of approval and annoyance. He turned back to Evan. "Olivia has not been so forthright. I was not aware of her contributions here."

"You are now, Papa," Olivia said evenly.

"Would you care to join us for tea, Mr. Alfredson?" Evan asked.

"No, thank you," he said stiffly. "I really must be on my way."

"Papa, I would like you to listen to Dr. McGrath," Olivia said. "He has a wonderful idea. I think you could help him realize it."

Marshall shook his head. "I don't see what possible help I could offer Dr. McGrath."

Olivia reached out and grasped her father gently by the elbow. "Listen to him, Papa, please. This is something truly good and visionary. With your sense for business and your backing—"

Evan flushed. "Miss Alfredson, this is neither the time nor the place," he said.

Ignoring Evan, Olivia stared at her father. "Please, Papa."

His defiance withered under her stare. "Of course." He cleared his throat. "Dr. McGrath, I would be most interested in hearing this idea."

"Excuse me, Mr. Alfredson," Virginia said. "I am fatigued and need to retire to . . . my bedroom."

With a pang of melancholy, Evan realized that Virginia wanted to hide her appearance from the distinguished-looking gentleman.

Olivia moved quickly to Virginia's wheelchair and began to push her toward the bedroom. "I am happy to help Mrs. McGrath," she said. "Perhaps, Dr. McGrath, you might take the opportunity to explain your concept to my father."

Evan led Marshall over to the dining room. The businessman folded his arms across his chest. With the women gone, his demeanor assumed a semblance of its previous edge. "Your grand vision, Dr. McGrath?"

"It's not that grand or original, really," Evan began uneasily. "In fact, it is similar to what I saw in San Francisco." He went on to explain his disillusionment with the state of health care in the Pacific Northwest and then, though in a more restrained tone, shared his idea for the clinic he had earlier described to Olivia.

Marshall unfolded his arms and rested his hands against the edge of the table. The ruddy skin around his large features wrinkled in concentration, and Evan could see that he was running mental calculations. "Where would you house such a facility?" he asked.

"I do not know," Evan admitted.

"And how would you attract all these great minds to come work in the Pacific Northwest?"

"I would hope that if one furnished the space and opportunity, the talent would follow."

"You hope?" Marshall huffed. "As I understand your description, this hospital would not charge patients for the care."

"Only those who could afford to pay."

"Another charity hospital. Just like the Catholics." Marshall sighed. "And how do you assess whether a patient could afford to pay or not?"

His self-consciousness growing, Evan simply shook his head.

"And the total cost of building and maintaining this hospital?"

"Mr. Alfredson, I am a doctor, not a businessman. I would have to rely entirely on someone else to manage the finances."

"I think what you mean, Dr. McGrath, is that you would need to rely on someone else to build and finance this hospital for you."

Evan said nothing. The two men stared at one another for a long moment. "I am a lumber trader," Marshall said. "I know nothing about endowing hospitals. And frankly, I do not even see the necessity for this utopian medical clinic you dream of."

"Perhaps you might have seen it better when your daughter was still ill," Evan snapped.

"Perhaps," Marshall said grimly. "However, I am not Andrew Carnegie. I cannot afford to throw money at some half-baked idea, regardless of the good intentions behind it. I have a family to provide for. Olivia will find a husband soon," he said. "And grandchildren will soon follow. I have their futures to consider first."

Angered and humiliated by Marshall's brush-off, and the perception that he had ever intended to solicit from the businessman, Evan broke off the eye contact. He rose to his feet. "Mr. Alfredson, I believe you told me earlier that you needed to be off."

Marshall rose to his full height, too. "Yes, I did. And I will escort my daughter with me. I have no doubt you can find a temporary chambermaid somewhere outside of my family."

*6*

William McGrath's back throbbed as he stepped out of the climate-controlled environment of the administrative building into the unseasonably hot fall sunshine. Each of the ten steps down to the cement pathway below intensified the exquisite pain in his low back, but he was conscious to keep his posture straight and his gait steady, so as not to let on to any passing personnel that he was suffering. As the hospital's CEO, he believed he shouldn't show any sign of frailty or weakness, especially now that he had reached seventy.

William stopped a moment to give his back a break, pretending to study the redbrick building that was the original site of the Alfredson in 1896. Though engulfed by newer and larger surrounding structures, the three-story building, with its simple elegance and stalks of ivy snaking up its walls, was still his favorite—a slice of living history on the sprawling grounds of the Alfredson complex. William was fiercely proud of his family's role in establishing the hospital and nurturing it into a world-renowned medical center. One that possessed the heart and soul to never turn away patients who needed its specialized care; not even those who lacked the means or insurance to pay for it.

*But all that will go by the wayside if the Alfredsons vote to sell,* William thought with a heavy heart.

Resisting the temptation to massage his back, he turned and began down the pathway. He walked past the green space of the enclosed courtyard—once part of the front lawn of the original clinic—where some staff lounged their breaks away. He heard the beating blades of the helicopter and knew, without looking up, that it was about to alight on the pad atop the Henley Building. He walked on past the waffle-shaped façade of the Adler Diagnostics Building. Though he found the building an eyesore, he knew it housed one of the most high-tech and innovative radiology and diagnostic imaging facilities in the country.

William rounded the corner and saw the children's hospital looming ahead of him. His thoughts drifted back to his conversation—*More like confrontation*, he thought—the evening before with Tyler. Though both of his children now worked at the Alfredson, neither showed a glimmer of interest or investment in the family's ongoing administrative presence. Since its inception, a McGrath had always overseen the Alfredson, from William's great-grandfather, Evan, through his grandfather, and three uncles since. And now that legacy was at risk of succumbing to indifference. The idea saddened him.

William shook off the thought and strode on toward his destination, the ten-year-old northeastern Grovenor Medical Tower, known by most people as simply "the Tower." A twenty-six-story cement-and-glass behemoth, the Tower was the tallest structure in a forty-mile radius and occupied the equivalent of a city block. Dwarfing most of the other buildings on the complex, it accommodated thirty-four inpatient wards, forty-five operating rooms, and twenty outpatient clinics. It also housed the world-renowned kidney transplant program and renal dialysis unit. And the Alfredson's main kitchen, which could have easily filled a couple of football fields, was situated in the Tower's labyrinthine basement. The underground food preparation factory ran round the clock and was connected by a subwaylike system of tunnels and electric trolleys to all of the other twenty-seven buildings on site. The kitchen staff prepared over three thousand inpatient food trays for each meal. And they catered to every conceivable diet including—but not limited to—vegan, gluten free, kosher, diabetic, low sodium, hypoallergenic, renal dialysis, low protein, and cardiac.

Approaching the Tower's entrance, William spotted Dr. Norman Chow pacing in front of the glass doors. Chow turned to him and waved his arm as though trying to flag a passing plane. "You're still alive, Bill, thank God!" Chow called out happily.

The tall, stooped Taiwanese microbiologist and head of infection control—who, at fifty-five, still insisted on everyone calling him Normie—was one of the only people since grade school to address William as Bill. And though he would never admit it, William did not mind Chow's use of the nickname.

"Guess I can call off the search party now," Chow went on with a high-pitched laugh. "I wasn't sure who was going to get here first, Bill, you or the Second Coming."

Less than ten minutes late, William still chuckled at his friend's hyperbole. Between Chow's bulletproof cheerfulness and his informal Western idiom delivered in a Chinese inflection, William found it impossible to be offended by the man.

"Good to see you, too, Normie."

Chow pointed to the building behind him and then tapped his own chest with two thumbs. "Sadly, Bill, you're staring at the prettiest thing you're going to see once we get inside this joint."

William's mood clouded. "The infection has spread, I take it."

"You take it right, amigo. We had to close two medical short-stay units this morning because of three new infections. This *C. diff* is becoming one major pain in the butt. . . ." He patted his backside. "Specifically, for this cute Asian derriere."

William had already heard about the closures. "Is there something else, Normie? You made it sound urgent in your message."

Chow nodded, suddenly grave. "The superbug has hit the dialysis unit."

William's stomach knotted. In the past week, the antibiotic-resistant bacteria, or superbug, *Clostridium difficile*—known more commonly as *C. diff*—had spread rapidly through the Tower. William had always thought of *C. diff*, and its characteristic severe diarrhea and flulike symptoms, as a relatively benign infection. Up until recent years, simple outpatient antibiotics fought off all *C. diff* infections. But the Alfredson's new superbug strain had developed multiresistance to antibiotics, and doctors were running out of treatment options. From his years working as a nephrologist, William realized that the consequences of the superbug reaching the kidney-failure patients— all of whom were already immunocompromised to one degree or another— would be grave.

"How many patients?" William asked.

"Only three so far."

The small number brought little relief. Once the microorganism established a toehold at a site, it inevitably spread. Though William had not practiced clinically in over twenty years, as a kidney specialist the dialysis unit was near to his heart. He hated the idea of it being overrun by rogue bacteria.

Moreover, he worried over the health of one specific patient—a reclusive VIP who almost no one even knew had been admitted to the hospital.

"I want to see the renal floor," William announced.

"Yeah, I figured as much." Chow sighed exaggeratedly and turned for the door.

They rode the elevator to the Tower's third floor. The doors opened to a sight that chilled William. It looked like a scene from some postapocalyptic sci-fi movie. The staff all wore full head-to-toe body precautions, including gowns, gloves, face masks, hoods, and booties. A large sign posted above the closed double doors to the renal dialysis unit stated that no visitors were allowed on the floor.

A gowned and masked security guard hurried over to them. He glanced at their hospital identification badges and then said, "I'm afraid, Doctors, everyone has to wear protective gear on this floor."

Chow flashed the guard a thumbs-up and then turned to William. "My orders, Bill. Normie's done being Mr. Nice Guy. We're not screwing around with this superbug no more."

Chow led William into the makeshift changing room that was formerly a patient lounge. A bank of portable lockers had been installed along one side of the room. Piles of clean gowns overflowed from a large hamper while boxes of booties, gloves, and masks rested along the windowsills.

They changed into the full protective garb and then headed out to the ward. A tall African-American woman waited for them outside the door. William recognized the reedy woman behind the mask and cap as Dr. Roselle Garland, a world authority on kidney disease and head of the Alfredson's renal program. Her usually calm gray eyes shone with uncharacteristic alarm.

"What's going on, Roselle?" William asked.

"You've heard about our three cases of *C. diff*?" Garland said.

He nodded. "What's their status?"

"Two of them are very ill. One is verging on critical." Garland paused. "William . . . it's Annelise Nygaard."

William's heart leapt into his throat. "Oh, no."

Chow viewed Garland with a grimace. "Who the heck is Annelise Nygaard?"

She turned to William and searched his eyes for permission.

"That's not her real name," William said.

"Figures." Chow shrugged. "Sounds more like one of the characters from those romance novels that the wife is addicted to."

William glanced around to ensure no one was within earshot, and then said in a low voice, "Normie, Annelise is the alias Princess Catherina goes by."

"Princess Catherina?" Chow did a double take. "Holy crap! That Swedish royal who used to party naked with the rappers and rock stars?"

"She's Danish." William viewed Chow sternly. "Normie, only a handful of people know the princess is here. And she is desperate to keep it that way."

William remembered the news coverage. In the early 1990s, when still in her late teens, the young Danish princess had gone through a rebellious phase when she partied with famous musicians and movie stars and was rumored to be sexually involved with several of them. Because of her striking good looks and royal title, she quickly became the target of gossip columnists and the paparazzi. Thirty-five now, Catherina had since dropped out of the limelight. But a notorious photograph from the time—picturing her dancing topless on the deck of a yacht outside Nice with a rapper (who was gunned down in a drive-by shooting two weeks later)—had immortalized her reputation as the Party Princess.

Catherina had since tried to maintain a low profile. After her childhood-onset diabetes destroyed her kidneys and almost claimed her eyesight, she had become a recluse. That only fueled the paparazzi's interest. And the more they hounded her, the more obsessed the princess had become with her privacy. She had not been seen in public in nearly ten years but the rumors still swirled, placing her anywhere from dead and buried in an unmarked grave in Wales to living in the commune of a South American cult.

Catherina had first come to the Alfredson for treatment of her damaged eyes. Several years later, after her immune system rejected her first kidney transplant, she had chosen to return to the Alfredson for a combined kidney and pancreas (islet cell) transplant. But, like many celebrities before her, the princess had registered under an alias. Only William and a few of Catherina's doctors, like Roselle Garland, knew the woman's true identity.

"I want to see her," William said.

Garland nodded and headed toward another set of closed double doors that normally would have been kept shut only during fire alarms. William and Normie followed Garland onto the renal ward, stopping at the last private room at the far end of the main hallway. She rapped on the door with a gloved hand.

The door opened a crack. A petite middle-aged woman slid out through the small opening and then quickly shut the door behind her. Despite the woman's mask, William recognized Jutta Lind as the princess's executive assistant. On their previous encounters, the unsmiling Lind had always struck William as being as officious as she was blindly loyal to her princess.

"Ms. Lind, may I introduce Dr. Chow, our hospital's chief of infection control," he said.

She nodded, but eyed him with suspicion. "Dr. Chow," she said coolly.

"Dr. Chow is aware of the . . . situation," William said, which only deepened the woman's frown lines. "We would like to speak to the patient."

"She is exhausted, Dr. McGrath," Lind said without budging from the door.

"It's important, Ms. Lind."

Lind viewed them for another long moment before she slid her hand behind her back and opened the door. She stepped inside and held the door partly open for them. The three doctors filed into the room. William had barely passed through when he heard the whoosh of the door closing behind him.

The blackout curtains were drawn tight and the room was illuminated by only one fluorescent light above the bed where Princess Catherina lay propped up with a blanket drawn up to just below her neck. Despite the room's dimness, she wore chunky opaque sunglasses that covered a third of her face but did not hide her drawn cheeks or bony jaw. Even in the weak light, her complexion was ghostly pale and starkly contrasted with her short jet-black hair. William saw little likeness between the prematurely aged and emaciated woman in front of him and the lovely vibrant princess he remembered from the magazine and TV images.

Catherina's head moved slightly in his direction. Through her dark lenses, William could not tell if she was looking at him, or even if her eyes were open. As he neared the bed, he heard her heavy breathing and saw that her translucent lips were cracked and fissured. Up close, her skin was tinged with a worrisome greenish hue.

William bowed his head slightly. "How are you feeling, Your Highness?"

Catherina's head bobbed slightly. "I have been better, thank you, Dr. McGrath." Her raspy voice was much weaker than last time they had spoken.

William introduced the princess to Chow. In an exaggerated attempt at etiquette, Normie bowed forward at the waist. "Your Majesty."

" 'Your Highness,' " Lind corrected with a note of sharpness.

"I prefer simply Annelise," Catherina croaked. She covered her mouth with a slender hand and her shoulders bucked in a gagging gesture. After a moment, she pulled her hand from her lips. Breathing even heavier, she gasped, "Jutta, my basin, please!"

Her assistant rushed to offer the princess a bean-shaped bowl. Catherina rested it on her chest as though she had trouble holding the weight of the empty plastic container.

Garland stepped closer to the princess. "Annelise, because of your . . ." The nephrologist searched for the right term. "Gastrointestinal symptoms, your blood sugars are very volatile and your electrolytes are even more brittle. We need to perform more frequent dialysis. Daily."

The princess's shoulders heaved again as she brought the basin closer to her lips. After the spell passed, she reached up and pulled off her sunglasses. Her eyes were deeply sunken in their sockets, and the skin tented and crinkled around them. But her large pale blue irises were as captivating as ever. William now saw the resemblance to the Party Princess.

Catherina looked from Garland to William. "Am I too . . . unwell to proceed with the transplant operation?"

Garland nodded. "Until you've recovered from the infection. Yes."

For a moment, the princess viewed them with unconcealed anguish, but then she hurriedly fumbled to put her sunglasses back on. "I see," she breathed.

"Your Highness—Annelise," William said. "On behalf of the entire staff of the Alfredson, I wanted to tell you how very sorry we are—"

Catherina raised a shaky hand to interrupt. "Pardon me, Dr. McGrath, but I just need a few moments alone," she rasped as she clutched the basin nearer to her chin.

"Of course." William recognized that Catherina was embarrassed by her display of nausea.

"Thank you." The princess tried a smile but her lips pursed and she gulped back a gag, before jerking her head away from them.

The others headed to the door, but Lind stopped them from leaving. "Doctors," she said in a conspiratorial whisper. "I know you are aware of the importance of the princess's privacy to her. It is absolutely paramount. *We* hope that we can rely on you to protect her identity from any prying eyes or ears. No one can know the . . . condition Princess Catherina is in."

*You have no idea how important it is for the Alfredson, as well,* William thought, but before he could reply a low mournful groan came from the direction of the princess. It was followed by a series of sickening retching noises and then the splashing sound of vomit hitting the floor.

A moment of silence was broken by the crash of the bowl hitting the floor and then Catherina's plaintive cry. "*Jutta!*"

## 7

Driving through the breaking dawn light, edgy and brittle with exhaustion, Jill Laidlaw fought off a twinge of guilt for having left Tyler alone and demoralized on his birthday. It soon turned to irritation. Her husband was bringing work home too often recently. It was sad about the kid, but Tyler didn't have a monopoly on heartbreak. As a specialist in neurodegenerative disorders, Jill faced her own share of tragic cases. But she trusted that, rather than pity, what patients needed from their doctors was the best medical care possible. She had learned early in her career that too much emotional attachment only clouded a physician's clinical judgment, which never benefited the patient.

Jill realized that their careers were now driving a wedge between them, whereas before their professional ambitions had once deepened their bond—each of them the cheerleader for the other. If work kept them apart for stretches, they used to compensate with romantic weekend getaways, often spent almost entirely in bed. Lately, the passion and the laughter had petered out. The move back to the Alfredson, which Tyler had resisted at every step, had strained their relationship. And their repeated and futile attempts at pregnancy had worn them down. No matter how hard Jill tried to bury her mixed feelings about motherhood, she suspected Tyler must have known. Though he was too decent to ever raise the subject, she wondered if he blamed her ambivalence, at least in part, for their failure to conceive.

At times, she ached for their previous intimacy. Some nights, she would wake with a start and pat the bed beside her to ensure Tyler was still there. Lately Jill could not escape the sense that she would rise one morning to find him gone. The irrational insecurity was so unlike her that it embarrassed her. But she sensed he was slipping away, and hated the thought of losing him. Despite their current troubles, she still loved him more fully than she would have once thought possible.

Jill's thoughts drifted back to her looming career crisis. Her current research grants supported her lab with its staff of more than twenty, including several postdoctoral students who were full of promise. But like all academic physicians, Jill had to apply to renew those grants every three to five years. She had never felt more vulnerable. The federal government, her major sponsor, provided the lifeblood for her potentially groundbreaking multiple sclerosis study. But with the federal deficit soaring, funding was being cut at every level. The competition for grants was fiercer than ever, and the chance of rejection higher. Jill knew there were no guarantees, especially since she did not have enough data to publish yet.

Jill was weary from the politics of academia. These days, science was only a fraction of a scientist's job. Medical research had become a business— awards and published papers its commodities. Jill knew how to play the game. She considered herself equal parts manager, writer, advocate, and publicist. And she was willing to fulfill any role needed. She had sacrificed far too much to see her work fall apart now.

With another pang of guilt, Jill thought of her mother, Angela, and how she had to put her law career on hold to care for her ailing husband. Alzheimer's disease had made Jill's father so unpredictable that it was impossible to leave him alone. Consequently, Angela had been forced to turn down the chance to become a district court judge—her lifelong career ambition. Instead she continued to practice law part time from her own home. Though dedicated to her husband, Angela exuded her resentment like steam seeping from a vent. Especially to her daughter.

Jill phoned often and returned to San Diego every few months to look after her father for weekend stints. She felt ashamed for not committing more time to her parents, but her work would not wait for anyone. Her study was too important. She had used that same rationalization to move her lab to Oakdale and drag her husband to the one hospital where he vowed to never work, because the Alfredson was the acknowledged leader in multiple sclerosis research and the destination of last hope for some of its victims.

People like Senator Calvin Wilder.

Jill could still picture the robust and charismatic forty-six-year-old senator from the news clips and advertisements two years earlier when he was the front-runner for his party's presidential nomination. Billed by some as the Republican JFK, the Washington State senator had been a shoo-in for one side or the other of the party's presidential ticket when he pulled out unexpectedly in mid-campaign, citing "family issues." Despite rumors about his health, Wilder's handlers had done a good job at keeping the media at bay.

Stepping into the senator's room, Jill was jarred by the sight of the former presidential front-runner sitting slightly stooped in his electric wheelchair. Wilder could walk short distances—though unsteadily and not without the aid of a cane—but he was forced to use the wheelchair much of the time. He had lost weight since the campaign, and the strong jawline that once made his face both handsome and authoritative now looked disproportionately oversized. Most noticeable was the change in his speech. His once deep silky timbre, the epitome of a leader's voice, now often emerged as halting. Occasionally, he even stammered or slurred his words. But the man had lost none of his indescribable presence. Standing beside him, Jill felt as though she were in the shadow of authority.

Wilder flashed one of his winning smiles and extended a slightly shaky hand to Jill. "Hope you didn't come so early on my ac-account, Dr. Laidlaw," Wilder said.

Jill shook his hand and smiled back. "I try not to keep senators waiting."

"You ought to." He chuckled. "No one has more time on their hands than former politicians. . . ." He winked. "Except maybe the *current* vice president."

With a polite laugh, she pulled up a wire chair and sat down across from Wilder.

He studied her face. "You worried at all about the Alfredson?"

She frowned. "Why would I be worried about the hospital?"

"A very interesting gov-governance structure," he stuttered. "The board of directors are all descendants of Marshall Alfredson. The same folks own the land and buildings. The whole shootin' match. You understand?"

Jill had no idea where the senator was going with this. She even wondered if the digression might be a medication side effect. "So basically the Alfredson family still owns the hospital, right?" she said, trying to humor him.

Wilder nodded. "It's a fairly unique setup among m-major academic hospitals."

"And has been like that forever, probably," Jill said lightly, hoping to be able to steer the conversation back to his condition.

"True. But aside from Catholic hospitals, which are all owned by that guy in Rome," he chuckled, "most teaching hospitals are endowed by benefactors or charities. They are auto-auto . . ." He took a slow breath and tried again. "They are autonomous. They don't have to answer to any one person or family."

"Senator, I know practically nothing about hospital politics," she said. "I am far more interested in MS and innovative treatment options."

"I still have a few friends in high places," Wilder went on, undeterred. "I hear an extraordinary meeting of the board has been called for the end of the month. Very hush-hush. Apparently, Alf-Alfredsons from all over the country will fly in for it."

Jill forced a laugh. "You think they plan to raze the hospital and put up condos?"

Wilder stared back without smiling. "Don't you think some HMOs or other health-care corporations might . . . might be interested in trading on the Alfredson name?"

*Of course!* she thought, reddening at her obtuseness. The Alfredson effectively functioned as a public hospital, providing care regardless of the patients' capacity to pay. But it was far better known worldwide from media coverage of the rich and famous who came for treatment of their exotic and deadly diseases. Jill suddenly saw Wilder's point—a corporation could trade on the Alfredson name and reputation and charge its VIP clientele a small fortune. But no private-interest group would offer anything more than the legislated obligatory emergency care to uninsured patients or, even more alarming from Jill's point of view, support the current research programs that cost the Alfredson millions every year.

"You don't really think the Alfredson family would sell the hospital?" she asked quietly.

"I don't know." For a moment Wilder's two eyes drifted apart but then they snapped back into alignment. "Isn't your father-in-law the CEO?"

"Yes." *But he would never discuss confidential hospital business with me.* "He's pretty tight-lipped about administrative issues."

"Still . . . ," Wilder encouraged.

"I'll try anyway," Jill said, as much to herself as the senator.

Wilder's face relaxed into an asymmetrical smile. "I never used to gossip so much before. Wonder if I can bl-blame the MS for that, too? Hell, why not? I blame it for everything else." He held open his quivering hands. "Dr. Laidlaw, I was hoping to find out a little about that study of yours that you mentioned the last time."

"Of course, Senator."

"I hate to waste your time, but do you mind walking me through the process again?"

"*Mind*?" she said. "I would never enroll you in a study unless you were fully aware of all the potential risks and benefits."

His lopsided grin grew. "With that kind of thor-thoroughness, you will never become my aide, but I appreciate your approach, Dr. Laidlaw."

Despite his physical disabilities, Wilder's legendary charm continued to shine through. Jill saw why he had earned a reputation as a heartthrob among female voters. "If it's all right with you, Senator, I'm going to start with the basics?"

He nodded. "Please."

"All neurons, or nerve cells, in the body have a coating—like the rubber insulation around an electric wire—made out of a phospholipid called myelin," Jill explained. "As you know, multiple sclerosis is an autoimmune disease. In other words, for reasons unknown the patient's own immune system begins to misinterpret the myelin lining of their own nerve cells as foreign, like they were an invading germ. As a result, the white blood cells— the body's natural defenders—are programmed to attack their own body's myelin."

"Like rats gnawing through a power cable," Wilder offered.

"Not the prettiest analogy, but basically . . . yes." Jill frowned. "As you know, people with milder disease have only one episode or a single nerve affected. Others have intermittent flare-ups, what we call the relapsing-and-remitting form of MS." She held her palm out to him. "Unfortunately, Senator, you suffer from a type of MS that is progressive. The most severe form."

"I never do th-things half-measure." His engaging smile resurfaced.

"Traditionally, we've had limited treatment options," Jill said. "At first, all we could do was treat symptoms. In the past ten or fifteen years, we have been using interferons to try to modulate—in other words, switch off—the immune system's self-attack."

A fleeting look of bitterness crossed his face. "Interferons have never helped me."

"I know." Jill sat up straighter in her seat. "But my lab has taken a different approach. Rather than try to modulate the immune system—which is like slowing the leak without touching the flood—we've been looking for ways to stimulate repair of damaged neurons. To regenerate myelin and even replace the damaged cells." She looked hard into his eyes. "In other words, we're not trying to just slow the progression. We hope to reverse the course of the disease."

"To turn back time." Wilder lifted his hand and it banged into the handles of the wheelchair. "How does it work?"

"We grow stem cell cultures in the lab. These stem cells are very immature, what we call multipotent cells. That means they can differentiate—or turn into almost any type of cell: bone, muscle, skin, even brain tissue." Jill nodded. "We've genetically engineered two enzymes that we introduce into these multipotent cells. Those enzymes steer the cells into growing brain cells like oligodendrocytes."

"The k-kind of cells that produce myelin, right?"

"Exactly!" Jill leaned closer, her voice warmed by her passion. "Now we harvest these newly grown nerve cells and inject them directly into your spinal tissue and brain stem. And we hope that the new cells will repair or replace the damaged ones."

He raised an eyebrow. "You *hope?*"

"It's worked well in the animal models," she said. "And in our early human studies, we are seeing promising results."

"What about the risks?"

"There are always those." Jill nodded. "We have to give you immuno-suppressing drugs. So you'll be at risk of infection, even cancer. And of course there are all the usual drug side effects."

Wilder nodded, unperturbed. "These stem cells. Are they embryonic stem cells?"

*Oh, not this!* Jill squeezed her leg in frustration. She knew where Wilder was heading. Many people, particularly on the religious right, but from across the political spectrum, fundamentally opposed embryonic stem cell research because it involved the use of aborted fetuses and had a theoretical potential to lead to human cloning. That anti–stem cell lobby had hounded her from the outset, and she was fed up with having to defend her research to them.

"No," she said. "We would harvest your stem cells from the lining of your nose. The olfactory neurosensory cells—the nerve cells responsible for smell."

His features clouded. "But you do use embryonic stem cells in your research?"

She sighed. "I have. Yes."

Wilder's right hand trembled more noticeably. "I have always been opposed to embryonic stem cell research."

"You're not in the Senate anymore." She pointed up and down, indicating his scooter. "Stem cells are the future of treatment for MS and all other degenerative neurological diseases. I don't mean to sound fatalistic, but I don't know of anything else that might offer you hope of reclaiming what you have already lost."

"Lost? *Lost?*" He gaped at her. "This disease has *stolen* so much from me! I want my life back. I want to have another chance to make a diff-difference for people. To advocate for their hopes and interests. Maybe even a return to the Senate or . . ." He stopped short of mentioning another run at the presidency, but Jill inferred it from his tone. "But what would I have left, if I let this rotten disease steal my principles, too?"

*8*

The Alfredson Medical Center's parking garage stood ten stories high and could have serviced a megamall somewhere in the suburbs. Tyler Mc-Grath's stomach flip-flopped as he wound his car around floor after floor. The evening before, he had stayed up late trying to fulfill his promise to share a birthday toast with his wife. Tyler ended up downing most of the bottle of wine and still nodded off before she returned. He woke fully dressed on the living room couch, draped by a blanket that Jill must have placed over him. Yet despite the hangover, he had shaken off his birthday blues. He even managed to drag himself out for an early morning jog, though the first few queasy blocks were touch-and-go. He arrived at the hospital revitalized and eager to start Keisha Berry and Nate Stafford on their new treatment protocols.

The mammoth lot, even the doctors' parking area, was often completely full by eight A.M., so Tyler was lucky to find a spot on the eighth floor. The engine whined as he backed his new car into the lone spot. Though the six-month-old Japanese hybrid helped ease Tyler's green conscience, the car had not won him over yet. It wasn't nearly as versatile or peppy as his old SUV.

On his way to the stairwell, Tyler stopped for a moment to peer out of the opening between the concrete walls. Under the cloudless blue skies, the sprawling Alfredson Medical Center shone before him, a tasteful blend of sleek modern buildings and towers on the north side of the complex and, on the south, the older brick structures that possessed more character. There was living history in those buildings, and Tyler experienced an uncharacteristic wave of pride.

*Maybe Dad's right. Maybe it is more than just bricks and mortar.*

While his father's words might have resonated more than he wanted to admit, he still had no interest in personally weaving the McGrath name any deeper into the fabric of the Alfredson's history. What he wanted to do was help Nate, Keisha, and the other unlucky kids on the sixth-floor unit. The thought reminded him of another historical familial connection, though this one from his mother's side. His maternal grandfather, Maarten Vanderhof, had almost single-handedly established the childhood cancer wards in the late fifties. Maarten was still a legend in pediatric oncology circles. So much so that Tyler was relieved not to share his surname. One medical dynasty was more than enough to shoulder.

Enjoying the day's warmth, Tyler opted against the more direct underground tunnel route that connected the parking garage to the children's hospital. Instead, he strolled the path between buildings beside the central courtyard garden, past the rainbow of uniforms worn by various workers lounging in the early morning sunshine. He returned the friendly wave from a small group of staffers from the SFU who were enjoying a smoke break. He bit his tongue, amazed that the same people who worked with cancer victims believed they could light up with health impunity.

He reached the children's hospital. Energized by the gorgeous day, he bounded up the stairwell, forgetting that there was an extra maintenance level between each of the numbered floors. By the time he had climbed all twelve flights, he was panting as he strode into the nursing station. Rounding a corner he spotted Nikki Salazar before she saw him. In mauve scrubs, she leaned gracefully against the countertop, charting. She stood with one leg crossed behind the other, the toes of her back foot barely touching the ground, as if en pointe.

Nikki looked up and their eyes locked briefly. "Hi." She nodded and then dropped her gaze back to the chart. A slim smile creased her lips. "Guess it's true that age eventually catches up to everyone."

"I wish I could blame my lack of fitness on my age. Be less embarrassing." He managed to slow his breathing and thumbed toward the patient rooms. "The kids do all right overnight?"

"All stable," Nikki said, meaning that none of them had died or developed sepsis during the night, always a small victory in and of itself. "Nate had a tough time sleeping. Jan finally had to sedate him around two A.M."

He nodded. With all the poor kid must have had on his mind after the news of his cancer's recurrence, Tyler couldn't imagine sleep would come easily, if at all.

"Did you have a happy birthday?" Nikki asked, without making eye contact.

"Happy enough," he said. "Very quiet. Just a glass or two of wine at home."

The forced words were almost as many as they had exchanged, outside of patient care–related issues, since the night they closed O'Doole's Pub together. Three weeks had passed, but the memory was still vivid enough that it clouded their subsequent encounters with newfound awkwardness.

Nikki shut the chart. Tyler expected her to walk away, but she didn't. She touched the scar that ran from the bridge of her nose to her cheek. That one flaw made her even more attractive in his eyes. "You ever see the movie *Logan's Run*?" she asked.

"No. Why?"

"It's a cheesy seventies sci-fi flick." She shrugged. "It's set in a futuristic society where—if I remember right—they kill anyone as soon as they hit thirty-five."

Tyler chuckled. "And Logan doesn't like this policy?"

"Not when he turns thirty-five, he doesn't."

"Then I guess my birthday went better than it could have."

"Better than Logan's, anyway." With that, Nikki turned and headed out toward the patients' rooms.

Tyler was still grinning when he plopped down in front of a keyboard at the back of the nursing station. He began to call up his patients' latest lab reports and imaging studies online, but his thoughts kept drifting back to that night at O'Doole's.

Three Fridays before, a group of them from the SFU had headed out to the pub. Despite their closeness at the hospital, the staff hardly ever socialized outside of work. Tyler always assumed they needed the time apart to distance themselves from the intensity and tragedies of the work they shared. But this particular Friday, they had gone out to celebrate the news that Michael Houston—an irascible two-and-a-half-year-old African-American who had won over the entire staff during his four-month stay—had finally been discharged home.

Miracle Mikey—as he had been dubbed—was originally admitted with the most common, and treatable, type of childhood leukemia: acute lymphoblastic leukemia (ALL). But nothing went smoothly for the boy from day one. The trouble started as soon as Mikey was given his initial, or "induction," phase of intense chemotherapy. He developed multiple serious side effects. And once those drugs knocked out Mikey's immune system (as they were supposed to) he was clobbered by one overwhelming infection after another. Few of the staff expected Mikey to survive even his induction phase.

But Mikey was a fighter. Each time he emerged from a coma or was weaned off the life-support system, he would do so with a smile on his face and, if he had the strength for it, mischief on his mind. After he had weathered a particularly aggressive case of sepsis, or blood poisoning, one of the nurses nicknamed him Miracle Mikey. The moniker proved prophetic. With normal blood counts and no cancer cells detectable in his bone marrow, Mikey was sent home to begin the maintenance phase of his treatment as an outpatient. His prognosis was excellent.

While the majority of the children treated by the sixth-floor team did survive their cancer, even the veteran nurses acknowledged Miracle Mikey as a special case. He represented a triumph of will and personality over disease and complication. And so, the evening after his discharge, the staff had taken the opportunity to head to one of the few bars in Oakdale and celebrate the occasion over what turned out to be several pitchers of beer.

Tyler and Nikki sat at the far end of the long table in the corner. They were close enough to have a good view of the surprisingly talented piano player—who sounded, and even looked, a lot like a younger Billy Joel—but far enough away to hold a private conversation over the music and ambient noise.

Tyler lowered his empty pint glass to the table and nodded at Nikki's full glass. While the pitchers had been steadily draining around her, she had barely touched her beer all evening. "Can ye nae down a single glass o' stout in honor of the wee lad's triumphant discharge?" he said, struggling to feign a Scottish accent.

Nikki shook her head and pointed to the neon shamrock behind the bar. "You do realize O'Doole's is an *Irish* pub?"

"I can't do an Irish lilt."

"You canna do a Scottish one either, laddie," Nikki said with a much more authentic-sounding accent. She pointed to her glass. "Anyway, this stuff is liquid calories. I might as well stuff the pitchers directly down the back of my pants instead of drinking it."

"*You*? Right. The ballerina." Nikki had told him once of her childhood ballet studies, but even if she hadn't, Tyler would have assumed from her gracefulness and arched posture that she had trained as a dancer.

"In a previous life. I haven't danced seriously since I was sixteen."

Tyler drank in her chocolate brown eyes, delicate bone structure, and smooth complexion, save for the scars under her eye and above her lip. "I am not buying your calorie-counting excuse for a second."

She shrugged. "All right, I'm the designated driver."

"Except no one drove here," he said. "You planning to hijack the cab on the way home?"

Her smile faded. She glanced around to ensure that none of the others were listening. "Truth is, I'm a recovering addict."

Tyler realized she wasn't joking. "Oh . . . I'm sorry, I didn't mean . . . um . . . to—"

Nikki laid a hand on his arm. The amused smile lit her eyes again. "I'm the one who ought to apologize. I had no right to lay that on you!" She laughed self-consciously. "That's as bad as being trapped on a flight beside a stranger who's hell-bent on saving your soul before the plane touches down."

"Not that bad." He returned her grin. "Well, not as bad as say . . . if my seatmate were a Scientologist, and it was a transatlantic flight."

"I guess not." She sipped her beer. "Besides, I've never had an issue with booze. I don't really like it much. But they tell me it's a good idea to avoid all drugs, including alcohol."

Nikki struck Tyler as too self-possessed and devoid of nervous energy to be an addict. He wondered if cocaine or narcotics were her previous crutch, but, sensing silence was his best response, he merely nodded.

She reached for the nearest pitcher and filled his glass without asking. "Five years ago, I was involved in a bad car accident," she said. "My fiancé was driving on a highway outside Phoenix. A van drifted over the median. The driver had fallen asleep at the wheel. He hit us head-on."

"Oh, my God!"

"I got off easy. Aside from a few lacerations"—she flicked a finger near the scar under her eye—"worst injury I sustained was a couple crushed vertebrae in my lower back." She swallowed. "Glen died."

"Oh, Jesus, Nikki . . ."

"The back pain was so intense," she went on. "The hydromorphone was the only thing that seemed to numb it. In retrospect, I guess I wanted to numb more than just the physical pain. Anyway, long after the bones healed, I kept popping those beautiful little pills. The problem was, my doctor recognized that I didn't need them anymore. And he decided to wean me off my supply."

Tyler could guess where she was heading but didn't interrupt.

"By this point, I was back working again, in Tucson." Nikki looked down at the table. "As you know, there's no shortage of painkillers on an oncology ward. I didn't think anyone would notice if I borrowed a few pills here and there."

"But someone did."

Nikki nodded. "Suffice it to say I lost my nursing license in Arizona, followed by doing a stint in rehab. I was lucky to get my papers in Washington."

"Does anyone else here know?"

"Janice Halverson did. Right from our first interview," she said, referring to the headstrong SFU nurse manager who fluctuated in her staff's eyes between hero and slave driver, depending on the person and time of day. "She has been unbelievable. She took a chance on me when she absolutely didn't have to."

"Janice is no fool," Tyler said. "She recognizes a superstar when she sees one."

"Thanks," Nikki mumbled, as she began to redden. "God, you'd probably trade me for that Scientologist on the transatlantic flight about now."

He leaned closer and gently elbowed her in the ribs. "Are we talking New York–London or L.A.–Moscow? Because that could make it a much different choice."

She looked up at him affectionately. "Dr. McGrath, you're a pretty good listener for an MD." She bit her lip. "And you? You have any dirty laundry that I could wash for you?"

"Don't think your machine would have room for it all."

"Try me."

"Well, for starters, the Alfredson was the last place I wanted to come to work."

She frowned. "But your family's name is synonymous with the hospital. Like the royal family, or something."

"Except we're not exactly the Romanovs or Windsors." He shook his head. "It's only a hospital."

"Well, if that's how you feel, then why do you care one way or the other? It's still a very good place to practice."

"True, but this job is hard enough to get right *without* feeling like you have history watching over your shoulder."

"I guess so."

"Besides, moving back here has not been good for the home front, you know?"

She said nothing. He doubted he was letting her in on much of a secret—the hospital gossip mill being legendarily efficient—but something in her placid expression invited more. Finishing a third pint of beer, Tyler explained how much Jill and he had drifted apart since they arrived in Oakdale. He never mentioned their infertility issues, but he sensed that Nikki appreciated something other than their respective hectic careers had strained their marriage.

The alcohol combined with the opportunity to open up—in a way that Jill and he had not done in ages—heightened the sense of closeness. Then the Billy Joel impersonator at the piano launched into a series of sing-along standards, from "Sweet Caroline" to "American Pie." Soon, Tyler and Nikki found themselves linked arm in arm with each other and the two people on either side, as they belted out the tunes and swayed to and fro.

By midnight, the crowd from the hospital had thinned, and canned music replaced the pianist. The remaining staff all gathered on the makeshift dance floor. Though Tyler had danced with several of the other women from the SFU, by the time the last song—Elton John's "Your Song"—played, Nikki was in his arms. Even drunk, he was acutely aware of the pitfalls of holding her warm supple body against his, but her gentle curves, fluid dancing, and vanilla fragrance were irresistible. The sexuality of the contact was less mesmerizing than its intimacy. He couldn't remember the last time Jill and he had held each other the same way.

Tyler lowered his head and spoke into her ear. "You working tomorrow?"

"Day off."

"Me too. Maybe we could grab a coffee somewhere?" Drunk as he was, he recognized the inappropriateness of the offer but was too caught up in the moment to stop himself.

"Oakdale is no Seattle, Tyler. Unless you like gas station coffee, we don't stand a chance of finding a cup at this time of night."

"Yeah, I suppose—"

She pulled back and studied him, eyes aglow. "My place is less than a mile away. Even my sponsor tells me I'm still allowed to drink coffee . . . provided it's decaf."

"Yours as good as the gas station?"

Nikki leaned forward and stood on her toes to whisper in his ear. "Don't pressure me, Dr. McGrath." She giggled.

He pressed his cheek against hers while Elton John sang, "How wonderful life is now you're in the world."

The lights came up. Tyler and Nikki lagged behind the rest of the group filing for the door. Near the doorway, he stopped her by the arm. "Let's grab a cab of our own."

She viewed him with an unusually indecisive expression before slowly nodding. "We could walk. It's not that far."

He leaned nearer and snuck in a kiss on her cheek. "Don't feel like walking," he whispered in her ear.

They stepped outside. Despite the suburbia enveloping them, the unusually warm breeze reminded Tyler of the tropics. He spotted a waiting cab. They hurried over and climbed in the back. Nikki gave the driver her address. As soon as the car pulled away from the bar, Tyler reached out and cupped Nikki's chin in his fingers and turned her face toward him. She nuzzled her face against his hand. In the car's dim interior he could not see the scar under her eye, but he leaned forward and kissed her on the same cheek.

She pulled away from the contact.

Tyler straightened. "Nikki, I . . . um . . . didn't mean to—"

Before he sputtered another word out, she grabbed the back of his neck and pulled his face to hers. Their lips met, and the moist contact catapulted his desire. Pressing his mouth harder against hers, he slipped his hand under her shirt and caressed the skin of her back.

Nikki's tongue gently probed his lips. Tyler pulled her even closer, lifting her off the backseat. Lithely, she balanced on one knee and leaned into him without breaking off their kiss. Her hand massaged his scalp and neck as their tongues meshed frantically.

Tyler slid his hand around to her abdomen and let it skitter over the smooth firm skin. His fingers ran up until they reached the silky fabric of her bra, and he squeezed one of her small, firm breasts. She uttered a soft sigh into his mouth that only tightened the hardness inside his jeans.

The car slowed. "We're here," the driver said in a singsong, knowing voice as he brought the cab to a stop in front of a modern-looking condominium complex.

Nikki slipped out of Tyler's grip and furtively straightened her shirt. They shared a glance. She bit back a laugh and hopped out of the car. He groped in his back pocket and pulled out his wallet. He rushed to pay the happy driver, leaving a tip larger than the fare.

As soon as Tyler reached the sidewalk, Nikki grabbed his hand in hers. She squeezed it once and then pulled him toward the front door. Resisting his attempts to kiss her there, she fumbled in her purse for the keys. She unlocked the door and led him inside. Hand in hand, they rode the elevator in silence to the fourth floor.

Nikki led him halfway down the hallway to her apartment. She opened the door and Tyler followed inside. He barely had a chance to take in the interior, because the moment the door closed behind them she vaulted into his arms, pinning him against the door. Her legs straddled his hips. Her mouth hungrily explored his as her hands squeezed his shoulders and upper back.

"Bedroom?" Tyler panted between kisses.

Nikki thumbed over her shoulder. With her legs still wrapped around him, he carried her light frame through the open doorway. With a tap of her elbow against the wall switch, two floor lamps lit the room. Tyler carried her over and deposited her on the textured blue comforter on top of her bed.

Hitting the mattress, Nikki pulled Tyler down by his shirtfront on top of her. He kissed her hard on the lips and then eased out of her grip. "I just need the bathroom for a moment."

"First door on your left." She winked. "Hurry."

Tyler rushed to the bathroom and stepped over to the sink. He cupped his hands in front of the faucet and splashed the cold water generously in his face. Looking up, he caught his reflection. He studied his slightly hooked nose, square jaw, and blue eyes, but saw none of the attractiveness that women sometimes remarked on. Instead, a sudden wave of disgust overcame him. He was staring at the face of a con artist.

Tyler had a mental vision of adorable Miracle Mikey, and all the years of needles and drugs the boy still faced before he would be anywhere close to being cured. He thought of Nikki, and how she had watched her fiancé die and then had to overcome a career-threatening battle with addiction. His thoughts turned to Jill. For all their differences and recent strife, they had been there for each other for ten years. And Tyler was poised to take steps that he would not be able to undo.

A wave of shame chilled him more than the cold water dripping off his face. He ran a hand through his hair, turned off the tap, and dried his hands on the towel. The line between fantasy and reality had grown starkly clear under the bright bathroom lights.

Tyler trod back to the bedroom. Nikki lay under a comforter, her skin bare from where the edge of the comforter ended just above her breasts.

She viewed him with an open-mouthed smile. "It's toasty under here."

For a split second, Tyler almost forgot the guilt and hopped into bed with her. Instead, he dropped his gaze to the floor and muttered, "Nikki, I have to go."

## 9

Erin McGrath surveyed the family room. Her sons' stuff—sweaters, jerseys, baseball mitts, tennis rackets, books, and DVD cases—was scattered everywhere. Couches were buried under their junk, while the pillows and throw blanket were strewn haphazardly across the floor. A bomb might have left less fallout.

The anger surged inside her. "Martin! Simon!" she shouted. "You get your sorry asses down here. And I mean *now*!"

There was no reply, except from their Australian shepherd, Tobi, who had been sleeping on a couch half buried under a pile of jackets. The dog sprang up, jumped to the ground, and, assuming she was in trouble, scurried out of the room with ears back and tail tucked between her legs.

"*Boys! Don't you push me today!*" Erin hollered.

Still no response. Erin looked down and noticed her hands were shaking.

*What's gotten into me?* she wondered. The state of the family room wasn't much different from usual. Clutter was as much a part of their family life as the many animals they kept.

*Must be the fatigue*, Erin rationalized away her uncharacteristic tantrum.

She had been up, operating, through most of the night. As the on-call cardiac surgeon, she had to rush in to the Alfredson at midnight to replace a heart valve that had ruptured in a sixty-year-old accountant after he suffered a massive heart attack. He survived the surgery only to succumb to his mangled heart minutes later in the recovery room. The futility of the procedure combined with his wife's quiet devastation had compounded Erin's weariness.

*I'm exhausted, that's all*, Erin reassured herself. But the tremor didn't subside. Instead, the imaginary fingers crept around her neck. *Not again, damn it!*

Anxiety mounting, she felt herself falling into her second panic attack in as many days.

*Slow your breathing!* she commanded herself. But her lungs wouldn't co-operate, and the pins and needles spread up from her toes and fingers. Help-less to stop it, she felt her respirations deepen to the point of hyperventilation. And then, as she expected, her throat closed over. No matter how hard she breathed, she couldn't get enough air.

*It's not real!* she repeated again and again. But the mantra failed miser-ably to reassure her. Light-headedness overcame her. She shot out a shaky hand to grab the wall beside her and support her weight on legs that had turned to spaghetti.

"*Rin?*"

Erin jerked her head over to see her husband standing at the doorway in a T-shirt and jeans, plumbing snake in his hand. Steve Aylsford gaped at his wife. "What is it, hon?"

"I . . . am okay," she choked out.

Steve dropped the tool on the floor and raced over to her side. Grabbing Erin tightly by her upper arm, he guided her away from the wall and led—practically dragged—her to the nearest couch. He pushed a stack of books and magazines out of the way, and then lowered her into the spot he had just cleared.

Steve's presence—his forceful grip on her upper arm and the faint familiar smell of his deodorant—helped calm her slightly. The weight on her chest diminished and her breathing eased. But she could not stop trembling.

Steve released her arm and dropped onto the couch beside her. Draping his arm over her shoulders, he pulled her closer. "Talk to me, Rin."

"I'll be okay in minute," she gasped.

Steve ran his hand along her brow, mopping away rivulets of sweat. "What the hell's going on? You look like you just saw a ghost . . . or ten."

Erin forced herself to take slower, shallower breaths and to pause between them. She clasped her hands in her lap to lessen the shake. "Lately, I've been having these . . . episodes."

"Episodes?"

"More like attacks." She sighed. "Panic attacks, I think."

"Panic? *You?*" he cried. "Rin, in twenty years, I've never seen you spooked. Not even a little scared. I'm the only chicken on this farm."

She laughed nervously. "Yeah? Well, make room in the coop. There's two of us now."

He squeezed her shoulder. "Panic attacks, Rin. Come on."

Still struggling to speak in sentences, Erin merely nodded and snuggled tighter against him. The bristles of at least three days' worth of stubble tickled her cheek. Ever since he had forsaken his engineering career to stay at home with his sons and run their farm, Steve shaved less often. And his cheeks, his whole face, had filled out over the past years. He used to be as wiry as a distance runner, but he had put on weight while his reddish-blond hair steadily thinned. At forty-three, he resembled his father more than she would once have ever dreamed possible. Erin didn't care, though. She loved him as much as ever. An incredibly involved father, he had boundless patience for their sons, and he shared their insatiable curiosity. Simon and Martin had inherited his irrepressible enthusiasm.

Steve loosened his grip and studied her face. From the amused glint that had returned to his eyes, Erin figured she must look a bit better. She felt it, too. Either this attack had been minor or her husband's presence had helped to abort it.

"Rin, how many of these 'episodes' have you had?"

"Six or seven."

"How long have they been going on?"

She shrugged. "Couple months."

"*Months?*" He grimaced. "Erin, when were you going to tell me?"

Steve only called her by her proper name on the rare occasions when he was upset with her. "I thought things were getting better after I started the medicine," she said.

The skin around his eyes furrowed. "You're on drugs? Who prescribed them?"

"I did."

Steve shook his head, disapproving. "What's that old saying about the physician who treats herself?"

"That she has a fool for a patient." Erin pulled away from him. With her panic gone, irritation began to rise in its place. "I know that, Steve."

But he didn't let up. "You're a cardiac surgeon. I don't imagine panic attacks exactly fall into your realm of expertise."

"I did go to medical school."

He rolled his eyes.

"Don't you get it, Steve?" Her words caught in her throat. "Heart surgeons aren't supposed to have panic attacks."

His expression softened. "I suppose not."

"Would you put your heart in the hands of someone who might panic at any moment?"

"Rin, you have to talk to someone."

She reached out and touched his furry cheek. "I'm talking to you."

He chuckled. "Lot of good that'll do you. A chemical engineer might even be less useful than a chest cutter on this one." He tilted his head. "Isn't there someone at the Alfredson? A therapist?"

She nodded. "There's a psychiatrist who sees some of my open-heart patients. She's very good."

"Will you talk to her?"

"Yeah, I should," she muttered halfheartedly.

He shook a finger at her. "Yeah, you'd better."

She leaned forward and kissed him on the lips. "You were my knight in shining armor just now."

Steve grinned self-consciously. "With a toilet snake instead of a lance."

"The right tool for the right job is what I say." She got to her feet, pleased to find that the strength had returned to her legs. "Where are the boys?"

"Down at the school, shooting hoops."

Erin glanced at her watch. "I better head back to the Alf. I have to do ward rounds."

She began to walk away, but Steve caught her gently by the wrist. "Ever since you came back from that African mission—"

"It wasn't a mission," she snapped. "I didn't go there to convert tribesmen to Christianity."

"Okay. Okay." Steve released her wrist and raised his hands. "Poor choice of words. Rin, you know how much I believed in that trip."

She stroked his shoulder. "I know."

"It's just that ever since you came back, you seem . . ."

She folded her arms across her chest. "I seem what?"

Steve met her stare. "Reserved. A little more irritable. Not quite your easygoing self."

She shrugged.

"Rin, it's like you left a little of your spark in Kenya."

"Shit, Steve. That's a bit much."

"I'm not the only one who noticed," he said gently. "Your brother did, too."

"Tyler? He never said anything."

"You hardly talk about Kenya, Rin."

"Medical stuff bores you to tears."

"You know what I mean." He frowned. "Could your episodes have something to do with that incident in the operating room? With those militia fighters?"

*That incident*, Erin thought grimly. She turned from her husband with an evasive shrug. In the more than half of her lifetime that they had been together, Erin had shared everything with him, except the real story of what had happened that day in Nakuru. She didn't fully understand why she had glossed over the details except that it had happened on the other side of the world—the Third World—and the best way to keep it compartmentalized, she rationalized, was to not talk about it, not even with Steve.

Erin tried to hold the memory at bay now, but it didn't work. Her mind flashed back to that crowded operating room in Nakuru. She could feel the room's oppressive heat. She pictured the skeletal, ebony-skinned patient—a tribal elder—still awake on the table. She fought off a shudder as she remembered the sudden cadence of footsteps marching nearer. And she would never forget how, at the noise, her patient sprang up from the table. "*The Kikuyu!*" he had whispered, his eyes huge with fear.

*Those damn footsteps.*

"What, Rin?" Steve asked.

Afraid the memory might trigger another panic attack, she shook her head. "I'm really late." She leaned forward, brushed her lips over his cheek, and then headed for the door. "I should be home by mid-afternoon."

Erin raced out the door, faster than she needed to, and drove to the hospital in an adrenaline-depleted fog.

As she performed rounds on her postoperative patients, Erin had trouble concentrating on her work. When she reached the surgical ICU, she was surprised but pleased to discover that the ICU team had gotten her transplant patient, Kristen Hill, off the ventilator. It was a positive sign to see her breathing on her own, even though Kristen still depended on the assistance of the balloon pump inside her aorta and was wired to more lines and tubes than a home furnace.

A fragile smile crossed Kristen's lips as Erin reached the bedside. "You got it started," the young mother said in a croak not much louder than a whisper. "I heard it was touch-and-go for a while."

Erin nodded. "Sometimes transplanted hearts are like cold, stubborn car batteries. They just take a few cranks."

Kristen lifted her hand from under the covers and touched the sleeve of Erin's lab coat. "Thank you, Dr. McGrath."

Her gratitude delighted Erin, and she grinned widely. "Can I have a look at the incision?"

Kristen nodded.

Erin reached forward and pulled back the sheet, uncovering the woman's chest. In the center, a broad white bandage covered the area between Kristen's breasts. The surgeon gently peeled the top of the bandage away from the skin to have a peek at the surgical wound. Erin was satisfied with the wound's bruised but healthy appearance. She carefully laid the bandage back into position. "Are you having much pain?" she asked.

Kristen shrugged her shoulders slightly. She nodded to the narrow white tubing by her hand that ended in a hub with a red button. "The morphine pump helps a lot."

Erin nodded. "Hopefully you won't need that much longer."

"Dr. McGrath, do things . . . look . . . okay now for me?" Kristen's voice was tentative rather than weak.

Erin studied her patient. Kristen had survived her transplant and made it off the ventilator, but even with the assistance of a pump inside her major artery and the best drugs medicine had to offer, her blood pressure was still critically low. Any reassurances she offered would be hollow and potentially misleading. "Kristen, it's still too soon to know for sure."

"I see." Her face fell. "I'm not out of the woods, am I?"

Erin would never lie to a patient, but she chose her words carefully to avoid traumatizing Kristen. She patted the back of her patient's hand. "You've done as well as we could have hoped up to this point. Your new heart was 'on ice' for longer than we would have liked. It's sort of stunned right now. We call that 'posttransplant cardiomyopathy.' But it's beating and you're off the life-support system." She mustered a light smile. "All good signs."

Kristen's eyes reddened and tears crested over her lower eyelids. "Not good enough for my kids. I have to be there for them." She swallowed. "There's no one else."

Erin felt another pang of empathy for the young mother. "Kristen, things are looking better than they did a week ago. A *lot* better than they did in the operating room. We just have to take it day by day now. But you're a fighter. And you have something very special to fight for. That is going to be a huge help."

Kristen nodded. She sniffed and wiped away tears with the back of her hand as her expression stiffened with resolve. "And feeling sorry for myself isn't going to do much for Katie and Alex."

Erin winked. "I think you've earned the right to a little self-pity."

Kristen laughed weakly. "Doesn't help to play the victim. Believe me, I tried when my husband walked out on us. Now I'm going to focus on positive things, like getting better."

"That's the spirit, girl."

Kristen reached up and caught Erin's hand again. "Whatever happens, Dr. McGrath, I want to thank you from the bottom of my . . . new . . . heart. You've given me another chance. That's all I could ask for."

## 10

The ornate millwork, high slanted ceilings, and crystal chandelier did not compensate for the pervasive musty smell in the uncomfortably warm guest bedroom. The small east-facing windows provided little in the way of breeze, and by six thirty A.M. the sun was already beating through the worn blinds. The brightness yanked Lorna Simpson from her first hour of decent sleep.

Fed up and restless, Lorna would have dug up some excuse to flee the house the previous evening—especially when Dot Alfredson drunkenly boasted that, fifty years before, she had held a small orgy with three of the better known Beat poets in the very same guest room—but her wily great-aunt had trapped her in the mansion with the promise of an "explosive family secret."

However, neither the secret nor any further details regarding Evan Mc-Grath and Marshall Alfredson had ever emerged. Citing a hoarse voice and exhaustion, Dot had napped away the afternoon. Then supper came, served by a middle-aged Hispanic maid, Juanita, who seemed to materialize out of nowhere. Eating ravenously, Dot evaded any attempts to steer the conversation back to the nineteenth century. By dinner's end, the old woman had polished off most of the decanter of red wine that accompanied the rack of lamb, and she was in no position to share anything other than scattered rumors about her once-famous-now-forgotten social contemporaries and lewd details of seventy years of sexual disinhibition. Finally, Juanita helped the babbling Dot off to bed.

Fuming at the memory of the wasted day, Lorna showered under a weak stream of water, barely able to wash the shampoo out of her hair. She decided that her great-aunt had already provided enough background and there were still other sources to tap into to fill in the rest of the story.

*I still have a few more weeks*, she reassured herself.

When Lorna walked into the breakfast nook, she was surprised to see that Dot was already dressed—this time in a set of tiger-print leggings with a long white cardigan—and reading the newspaper as she sipped her coffee. "Darling, I do hope you slept as well as I did," she chirped.

"Fine, thanks," Lorna grumbled.

"Coffee?" Dot said. "Juanita has brewed a drinkable pot this morning. Then we'll have her porridge. Juanita is an *absolute* marvel at porridge!"

"No thanks, Dot." Lorna didn't budge. "I'll have a quick cup of coffee, but then I have to head off."

"But darling, you haven't heard anywhere *near* the best part of the story!"

Lorna rested her hands on her hips. "Will I ever?"

"So you do have a streak of the Alfredson drama in you, after all!" Dot laughed. "I'm *aching* to share the story with you. I simply ran out of steam yesterday. At my age, one never knows when the fatigue will incapacitate. But I awoke fresher than the morning dew. And I'm ready to sing like a songbird." She punctuated the point with a comical tweeting sound as she patted the seat beside her.

*What an irritating old crow.* Reluctantly, Lorna pulled back one of the chairs and sat down across from Dot. Juanita appeared with a pot of coffee, two steaming bowls of porridge, and a fresh fruit salad. The complementary morning aromas made Lorna's stomach churn with hunger.

Dot continued to avoid the subject of the birth of the Alfredson all the way through breakfast and instead offered a surprisingly current running commentary on local and national politics. As Juanita cleared the plates, Dot loudly outlined her draconian ideas for solving the illegal alien problem, either oblivious to the Hispanic maid's presence or—more likely, Lorna decided—to antagonize the poor woman. Finishing the last bite on her plate, Dot lowered her fork and said, "Now where were we with McGrath and my grandfather?"

Lorna relaxed in her seat. "Marshall was just dragging his daughter out of Evan's home."

"So he was." Dot smiled and shook her head. "My grandfather was one stubborn son of a bitch. You would have thought he would have shown a little more gratitude to Dr. McGrath for saving Olivia's life."

Lorna considered the chronology, realizing that the fall of 1895 was not that long before the Alfredson opened. "Still, I assume he soon changed his mind about funding the Alfredson?"

"*Gawd* no!" Dot threw up her small hands and a bulky charm bracelet slid noisily down her wrist. "What he did was to forbid Olivia from going anywhere near Evan or his wife ever again."

"I take it Olivia didn't comply?"

"Darling." Dot's face lit in that odd familiar lascivious smile. "The quickest way to get a randy young woman to do absolutely *anything* is to forbid her to do it. Adam and Eve taught us that, way back, didn't they?"

Lorna stifled a sigh; her great-aunt's sexual innuendos were wearing thin. "What did Olivia do?"

"What any resourceful person would do. She had her friends cover for her," Dot said. "Olivia arranged a series of alibis for nonexistent card games, recitals, walks, and who knows what else!" She stopped to consider it a moment. "But my grandfather was no longer Olivia's only problem."

"No?"

"Olivia was being relentlessly courted by the son of a family friend." Dot sighed. "Another heir to a lumber fortune. Arthur Grovenor. The poor boy was hopelessly in love with her."

"Was Arthur jealous of Evan?"

"I suppose," Dot said. "Arthur was a bit of a spineless sap. He couldn't quite figure out how he had lost Olivia's affection—not that he ever really *had* it—or how to win her back. He would have stood *no* chance at all, had Fate not intervened."

"How?" Lorna demanded.

Dot smiled to herself. "I might be giving Fate more credit than *she* is due. Many people lent Arthur a big hand. Some deliberately, and others, like Virginia McGrath, inadvertently."

"Evan's wife?" Lorna asked, confused.

Dot nodded. "In Virginia's weakened mental state, she had grown increasingly suspicious of the lovely young redhead who had spent so much time at her home over the past months." She stopped to dab at a flake of lipstick at the corner of her mouth. "Of course, sometimes the paranoid are the first ones to recognize what is *really* happening, aren't they?"

––––––––––––––––––––

Evan held the local Seattle medical community in the highest regard.
He wanted to pool that existing talent in one innovative
center—his new clinic.
—*The Alfredson: The First Hundred Years* by Gerald Fenton Naylor

As they had done for numerous afternoons over the past months, Evan and Olivia sat at the undecorated dining room table, again sharing a pot of tea.

Olivia had told her father that she was attending an afternoon piano recital, so she wore an elegant green dress with a high neckline, which she knew accentuated her eyes. But Evan appeared too agitated to notice the dress or her eyes.

Though still awed by the handsome doctor, Olivia had shed most of her original shyness in his presence. As their intimacy continued to deepen, she allowed more glimpses of her feisty nature to show through. In the past week, they had even spontaneously dropped the convention of referring to one another by surnames.

"Evan, please tell me what happened at the hospital this morning," she said, surprising herself with the firmness of her request.

"Two people died."

"Oh, I am sorry." Olivia nodded somberly. "But I thought such things were not unexpected in a hospital."

"Of course people die in the hospital," Evan snapped, but his tone quickly softened. "Death is the natural extreme of all disease, Olivia. But these two people were healthy. A twenty-year-old mother and her baby. There was no reason for either to die."

"Childbirth?"

Evan nodded.

"What went wrong?"

"It did not go wrong. It was steered to disaster by sheer and unforgivable negligence."

"How was it steered, Evan?"

"I do not think the details are at all appropriate to share with you. The event was most . . . unpleasant."

She fixed him with a defiant stare. "After what I've been through these past months, I believe my delicate constitution will cope."

"I suppose you might." He showed a glimpse of a smile that was replaced by a scowl as he began to recount the event. "As soon as I arrived at the hospital, one of the Sisters rushed me to the birthing room where the women who do not have access to midwifery at home often come for childbirth." He shook his head. "Inside, it was a most terrible scene. Dr. Andrews—the *fool*—was trying to deliver the baby. It was obvious from across the room that there was a shoulder distocia."

She frowned. "What does 'distocia' mean, Evan?"

"After a baby's head has passed the birth canal, sometimes the shoulder becomes lodged under the mother's pelvis. The blood supply to the child is interrupted at a time when he still cannot breathe, so it is of the greatest urgency to deliver the baby's body as quickly as possible. And there are well-documented maneuvers to help accomplish this."

She nodded vigorously. "I see."

"The poor child's head was navy blue! God only knows how long he had been without oxygen."

"What was Dr. Andrews doing?"

Evan shook his head, and his lip curled in disgust. "He was killing them, is what that quack was doing!"

Her jaw fell open. "How could he possibly do that?"

Evan held out his hands as if cupping a baby's head. "The key to shoulder distocia is to raise the mother's hips as high as possible to maximize the opening of the birth canal and then press down on the pubic bones of the pelvis." He pushed his hands down against an imaginary pelvis. "To squeeze the shoulders through. Sometimes you even have to break the child's arm. But it is a highly effective maneuver."

"Dr. Andrews was not doing so?"

Evan's hands fell to the table. "The poor woman was positioned no differently from a normal birth. And *Dr.*"—he snorted the term—"Andrews was cutting and slashing away at her like he was practicing his fencing skills. Granted, a well-placed incision will assist with the delivery, but this was butchery. And it served no purpose except to cause the mother even more undue agony. Oh, and the bleeding!"

Olivia gasped involuntarily. Evan reached out to her, but she shook it off. "No, Evan, please. I want to hear what happened."

"I pushed the imbecile out of the way. With the simple technique I described, in less than a minute I delivered the little girl. But of course, she was already dead." He swallowed. "And that poor mother. Olivia, if you could have seen the heartbreak in her eyes. And her complexion . . . how gray it had turned." His face crumpled with distress. "The woman was hemorrhaging out from all of Andrews's unnecessary slashes. I had no time . . . no equipment at the ready. . . ."

"Of course, Evan, how could you possibly be prepared?" she murmured.

"I had the Sister apply pressure," he went on, as if reliving the experience in his head. "And I readied my tools and loaded the needles as quickly as I could. There was no time to even anesthetize the woman. She was so very brave. Not a word of complaint. I had barely started to suture those horrible wounds that Andrews had inflicted on her, when she suddenly stilled . . ." His words petered out.

Olivia rose to her feet and rushed around to his side of the table. She knelt in front of him and took both his hands in hers. She was astounded at her own forwardness but unwilling to release her grip. "Evan, what else could you have possibly done?"

"If she had been attended by an experienced midwife at home, everything would have turned out so much better." Evan shook his head. "I am so very ashamed of my medical fraternity today."

Olivia stared up into his tormented gray eyes. She desperately wanted to comfort him, but could not find the right words so she just clasped his hands and said nothing, aware of the electricity in the contact between them.

"We came here to find better care for Virginia," Evan went on. "The quality of medicine I have seen here is worse than what we left behind. Almost barbaric, at times. And Virginia grows weaker by the day." He cleared his throat. "Olivia, I think it might be best if I take Ginny back to San Francisco. To her home."

"No. You cannot!" Olivia flushed crimson at the exuberance of her outburst and the heat of their contact. "You cannot give up so easily, Evan. What about the clinic you dreamed of in Seattle? That is what would be best for your wife! And others like her. If only that poor woman who passed today had such a clinic to attend . . ."

Evan shook his head helplessly. "Your father is right, Olivia. I have no business sense. I have no means. I have no land. It *is* all just a half-baked dream."

Olivia let go of his hands and jumped to her feet. "Do not say that! It is a marvelous vision. And you are the best person to see it built. The *only* one. You have the knowledge, the determination, and the compassion to see the job through." She brought a hand to her chest. "I will speak to Papa again."

Evan smiled tenderly, but his expression filled with resignation. "It will do no good, Olivia. We both know that."

Olivia felt tears welling, but she fought them off. "Do not be so sure. And if not Papa, then I will speak to my friends. Some of them have fathers even wealthier than mine." Reckless with affection, she reached out and touched the light stubble on Evan's cheek. "We can find a way to make it happen."

He rose to his feet, put his hands behind her back, and drew her closer to him. "Olivia, you are such a wonderful hopeless dreamer."

His warm breath tickled her cheek. A fresh wave of heat overcame her. It felt like the summer before when she had kissed Arthur Grovenor after the church picnic, only so much more intense.

"Oh, Olivia," Evan murmured.

She leaned forward and touched her lips to his. The past months of confusion, denial, and guilt melted away. All she wanted was to stoke the fire that now ran from her toes to her scalp.

*11*

Reading glasses riding near the tip of his nose, William McGrath struggled to find a position that would take the edge off his searing backache. Even his beloved high-back rolling leather chair, which had served him his entire forty-one-year career, offered no relief. The pain was getting worse by the day.

"The data is up to date as of eight A.M.—" Normie Chow lowered the pages he was holding and nodded to William. "You doing okay there, Bill?" he asked, upbeat as ever, despite the bleak news he had brought with him.

"Fine, Normie, I tweaked my back on the weekend."

"Golf, right?" Chow asked. "You WASPs love to chase that little white ball through the grass, water, and sand. You old fellas are especially obsessed."

William chuckled despite the double insult. "I haven't golfed in ages."

Chow ran a hand across the hair that he combed over his noticeably bald pate. "It's not a Viagra-related injury, is it?" he asked.

William rolled his eyes. "Just a long-standing bad back."

"You need to stretch more, Bill," Chow advised. "That's the ticket. The Chinese have known that for years. Ever see those ancient Asians doing tai chi in the parks? That slow-motion kung fu meditation stuff really works. My grandma's pushing a hundred—which is thirty more than what she weighs—but she could still probably lift a piano."

"I'll be in the park tomorrow with a Steinway." William reached for the report on his desk. "Now about these numbers . . ." Trying to push the burning throb from his mind, William grappled with the details on the busy spreadsheet in his hand. Though he had trouble digesting all of the various numbers on the page, he understood the gist of it—the outbreak at the Alfredson was far worse than originally presumed. The *C. diff* had spread like wildfire through the Tower. The superbug had already shut down several outpatient units, but the huge building housed too many ill people to find appropriate space elsewhere, so they had to keep most of the Tower's inpatient wards open, though under the most stringent isolation conditions. Three patients had died. Others were facing the same fate, especially if the *C. diff* ever reached the critical care units or the oncology wards with their already immunosuppressed patients.

*And, of course, poor Princess Catherina*, William thought, though she would never appear in any official tally. Earlier in the morning, the princess had left via helicopter for the airport and the private jet that would carry her home, for the last time, to Denmark. William had seen her off. The memory of her swathed in layers of blankets tugged at his heartstrings.

Overwhelmed by the superbug, Catherina had deteriorated rapidly, and her doctors all agreed that she needed to be transferred to the ICU and put on a life-support system. But she had flatly refused. Minutes before her transport chopper arrived, William had gone to see Catherina, accompanied by Dr. Roselle Garland, who wanted one last stab at convincing the princess to reconsider. Catherina's nurse had stepped out to gather the medications needed for the journey, so only Catherina and her faithful assistant, Jutta Lind—who was more agitated than ever—were in the room.

Catherina's deterioration shocked William. Her cheeks had sunken to deep hollows and her skin was so sallow it verged on gray. An oxygen mask covered the lower half of her face, but the muscles in her neck still retracted with each hungry breath. Despite her grave condition, the princess was as dignified as ever. She even managed a small smile for her visitors and thanked them for coming.

Catherina panted while listening to Garland's attempts to convince her to stay in the Alfredson's ICU. The princess brushed away the doctor's advice with a single weak wave. "I've already lived through too much unwanted attention and controversy." She gasped. "I do not want it to follow me in death."

William knew she was right. If Catherina died of the superbug, the media would jump all over it.

"Your Highness, you are still young," Garland persisted. "With aggressive treatment, you could still beat this."

Catherina's pale blue eyes clouded with resignation. She stared at her doctor for a long moment. "No, Dr. Garland, I won't."

Garland clasped her hands together in frustration. "How can you know?"

"I am so tired, Roselle." Catherina's lips cracked in a grateful smile. "You have done all you can. I have been fighting for a long time. Too long. Now, I just want to go home. To be left in peace."

Garland opened her mouth as though to argue but appeared to change her mind. Frown still fixed to her features, she merely nodded.

William realized that the princess's insistence on decamping the Alfredson without leaving a trace of her presence—or the deadly infection she had acquired there—would spare the hospital negative publicity at a pivotal time. But rather than feeling relieved, he felt sad, ashamed, and partly responsible for her poor outcome at his hospital.

Normie snapped William out of the memory with a waving hand. "Bill, what's going on here?" he asked. "You having one of them seniors' moments?"

"Probably." William sighed as he pushed away the memory of Catherina's departure. "Normie, what's the status of the kitchen?"

"I wouldn't eat off the floors yet." Chow laughed. After two food preparers had acquired *C. diff* infections, the food services team had had no choice but to shut down the central kitchen. "We're doing another terminal clean of the whole works but then we still have to retest the surfaces for any trace of *C. diff.*"

Stifling his frustration, William merely nodded. The Alfredson was now outsourcing most of its food preparation. No hotel or catering company in Oakdale had a kitchen large enough to support such a massive meal order that was complicated by so many special dietary requirements. The food services managers were forced to truck food trays in from a Seattle-based airline caterer. It was proving to be a logistical nightmare.

"How much longer would you estimate?" William asked.

Chow shrugged merrily. "Three days. Minimum."

"Not good." With the fire heating at the base of his spine, William focused on the paper in front of him. "Am I reading this right? Did we have twelve more *C. diff* cases overnight?"

"Probably more, Bill."

"What does that mean?"

"Those are just the inpatients," Chow said. "We haven't got all the sick calls from staff yet. If yesterday is anything to go by, we'll dig up five or six more cases by noon."

William exhaled heavily. He could not fault Chow's infection control team for how they had managed the crisis so far. They had reacted swiftly to the outbreak with what some considered severe and excessive measures: full-body precautions, banning visitors, confining inpatients to their rooms, and closing all break rooms. The aggressive steps were an absolute necessity. If the *C. diff* spread to other buildings, they might have to shut the doors of the entire complex. In over a hundred years since the Alfredson opened, it had never once closed, not even when the Spanish flu decimated the complex in the fall of 1918. William was determined not to let it happen under his watch.

"Normie, can you give me an idea of what to expect over the next week?"

"Hard to know." Chow squinted. "If we can keep the *C. diff* out of any other buildings and the staff is rigorous about washing their hands and thumbs—people always forget their frigging thumbs!—then we should see the number of new cases plateau in the next couple days."

"Plateau" was not the word William had hoped to hear, but it was at least better than some of the alternatives.

"Then again, you know me, Bill," Chow went on. "I'm a glass-is-half-full kind of guy. Don't count out the frogs and swarms of locusts just yet."

"So noted," William sighed.

Chow glanced at his watch and rose to his feet. "I got a debriefing with my team."

"Normie, please remind them of how confidential all this information is."

"Got it." Chow turned for the door. "Just name, rank, and serial number. Right?"

"Exactly," William said as he watched Chow hurry out of the room. *If the media gets wind of this now . . .*

He picked up the spreadsheet to study it closer. Another sizzling dagger dug into his spine. He felt so tired that the figures swirled in front of his eyes. He refused to use exhaustion as an excuse, but the fatigue did remind him he was overdue for a blood transfusion. The lack of circulating red blood cells was affecting his concentration, but he did not know when he would find the time to go in for another bag or two of blood.

Six months earlier, he had been diagnosed with multiple myeloma, a cancer of the bone marrow that shuts down the body's blood cell production. He had declined aggressive treatments, such as intravenous chemotherapy or a bone marrow transplant. Every time William saw his hematologist, the specialist insisted that William would have at least a 50 percent chance of long-term survival if he would agree to maximal treatment. But William steadfastly refused, because he knew the chemotherapy would make him far too ill to work. Believing the Alfredson could not afford to have its CEO sidelined at such a critical juncture, he opted, instead, for oral medication and blood transfusions, realizing that both steps were merely stopgaps, buying him a few years at best.

Aside from his hematologist, no one, not even his family, knew of his illness. He did not want to have to face his children's reaction. He imagined Tyler would badger him to accept the ultra-aggressive treatment. As a surgeon, Erin might be more accepting of her father's decision, but she would insist on including Tyler in discussions William didn't want to hold yet. He knew the time would come in the not-too-distant future when he could no longer hide his illness, but in the meantime he saw no value in letting his family fret and fuss over the inevitable. If Jeannette were still alive, she would have understood. Of the many things he missed about his wife, her level-headed wisdom was high on the list.

William had so much he needed to accomplish before the cancer caught up to him. Under calm blue September skies, a hurricane was building around his beloved hospital. This *C. diff* outbreak was only the tip of the iceberg. However, its timing could not have been worse in light of the Alfredson's extraordinary board meeting that loomed less than two weeks away.

As much as William had downplayed the importance of the meeting to Tyler, Erin, and others, he was deeply concerned. Only direct descendants of Marshall Alfredson had voting authority with the board. Though several responsible family members—including the current chairperson, Eileen Hutchins—had built upon their inheritance, many of the offspring had frittered away the sizable fortune left to them when Marshall died in 1929. The

Californian branch of the family had been particularly wasteful. William had heard that almost all of them planned to attend the board meeting. Few, if any, had ever come to a previous meeting, and it was hard to escape the obvious conclusion—*they're coming to cash in.*

William knew he had a strong ally in Eileen Hutchins. She was as committed to the medical center as he was. He had known her for over thirty years, since her husband had first become his patient for treatment of his failing kidneys. The disease eventually killed Richard Hutchins after years of dialysis and two rejected kidney transplants. In the fifteen years since Richard died, Eileen had never remarried. And, in William's eyes, she had only grown more elegant without losing an iota of her attractiveness. But despite her unwavering support, William recognized that her influence only ran so deep with the more distant Alfredson cousins. Those board members felt no affiliation to Eileen or the hospital, and yet they were the ones who might end up deciding its fate.

William tried to turn his attention back to Chow's spreadsheet, but he couldn't stop ruminating over the possible disastrous fallout if the board voted to sell.

"Hello, William," a familiar voice called. "Is now a bad time?"

He looked up, surprised to see his daughter-in-law standing at the doorway. "Never for you, Jill." He rose as fluidly as he could manage through his backache.

Jill Laidlaw swept into the room, stopping a few feet from him. Her subtle French perfume reached his nose, but she did not come any closer. In earlier days, William and his daughter-in-law might have hugged their greetings, but they had long since given up the ritual. It had little to do with their lingering tension; neither was the hugging type.

William waved her into a chair, then circled behind his desk and eased back into his own seat. Despite their sometimes-adversarial relationship, he still had a soft spot for Jill. He admired her intelligence, strength, poise, and ambition. And he wasn't too old or too ill to appreciate her captivating blue eyes, chiseled facial features, or her flair for smart sexy ensembles like the black blouse, skirt, and black pumps that she currently wore. On paper, his son had landed the perfect catch. And vice versa. But whenever William saw them together lately, he could not help but suspect that significant problems boiled under the placid front they presented to the family.

"To what do I owe this rare pleasure?" he asked.

Jill smiled. "I missed you the other night. And I wanted to say thank you."

"For?"

"The birthday present you dropped off for Tyler. He was touched."

*Was he?* William wondered, recalling their angry argument on his way out of the house. "I hope the two of you find a special occasion to crack that bottle."

"We will." Jill eyed him with fleeting distrust but her smile soon resurfaced. "William, you look pale. Are you feeling okay?"

"Just a hazard of my job." He shrugged, embarrassed. "I never see the sun, and I don't get as much time under the tanning lamps as I would like."

"Somehow, I can't picture that," she said with a laugh, but the skepticism clung to her features. "You sure it's nothing else?"

"Quite." William leaned back in his chair, and was rewarded with another jolt of pain. "It's a long trek from the neurosciences building to my office," he said, attempting to steer Jill away from a discussion regarding his health.

"I assume you heard that Senator Wilder has been admitted?" she asked.

"Multiple sclerosis."

Jill nodded. "An aggressive form."

"Do you have new treatment options for him?"

"Nothing mainstream," Jill said matter-of-factly. "Other neurologists have tried all the known disease-modifying agents. They've done little to slow his deterioration."

"Are you planning to enroll him in your study?"

"We've discussed that." She shifted slightly in her seat. "Senator Wilder is a very insightful man. He's considering his options carefully."

"I see." William felt a mix of excitement and apprehension at the prospect, recognizing the potential upside and pitfalls of having such a high-profile research subject at the Alfredson.

Jill looked down at her hands. "The senator mentioned something to me that I'm sure you must already know about."

Still weighing the implications of having a former presidential frontrunner as a research guinea pig, William said distractedly, "Oh, what's that?"

"It's related to the upcoming Alfredson board meeting."

William snapped back to the moment, on guard again, though he tried not to let on to his daughter-in-law. "What about it, Jill?"

"Senator Wilder implied that the Alfredson family is considering selling the hospital."

"It's not entirely theirs to sell."

"Really?"

"While it's true that Marshall Alfredson paid for the initial construction and the family still owns the land on which the hospital is built, the hospital's finances are complex. For example, there is an Alfredson Foundation—funded by years of donations—that has covered much of the capital costs in terms of the newer buildings and equipment."

"But couldn't the family just sell the land out from under it?"

"Not without a drawn-out legal battle." Though his assessment was technically true, he was not nearly as confident as he sounded. "Why did the senator raise the subject?"

"To warn me, I think." Jill studied her fingernails, appearing to lose interest. "Actually, I think he was using *me* to warn *you* that the Alfredsons might decide to sell the hospital to some HMO or other private-interest group."

"Very good of him," William said with a lightness he didn't feel. Clearly, Wilder and others had reached the same conclusion he already had. "Did he happen to mention where he heard this rumor?"

"No. I just thought I should pass it along."

"Consider it passed. Thanks."

Jill rose from her seat. "I'm up against a major grant reapplication. I better get moving."

He stood painfully to his feet. "How is that going?"

Doubt flittered across her face. "You know how these things are. It gets more and more competitive every year. Still, I think we're in okay shape."

"I wouldn't have headhunted you and your team for the Alfredson if I didn't believe that your lab was in better-than-okay shape."

"I thought hiring me was your way of getting Tyler back to the family homestead."

"I can't deny it's good to have family close." He frowned. "Speaking of Tyler, did he mention our conversation at all?"

"Only the gift. But we've hardly had any chance to chat since."

William hesitated a moment. "I suggested that he consider taking a more active role in shaping the future of the Alfredson."

"You mean medical administration?" She shook her head. "I don't imagine that would have gone over too well."

"No. Not well at all." William measured his next few words before speaking. "Listen, Jill, you're both young. You've got bigger hopes and aspirations. I understand that. But one day, Tyler might see the upside in having a nine-to-five job. You, too. It's rewarding and less stressful—for the most part—than the high-level clinical or research work you both do. And in many ways, it's more conducive to a family lifestyle."

She pursed her lips. "Which family?"

William held up his palm. "I don't presume to know what your long-term plans are, but one day you might consider children."

"*Consider*?" Jill snapped. "William, you know that Tyler and I have more than just 'considered' children, but none of our efforts have panned out so far."

"That must be disheartening." He shook his head. "But it seems to me that Tyler and you are burning the candles at both ends. I don't imagine that helps."

Her cheeks flushed. "It's simple biology, William. And, since there's apparently nothing wrong with your son's sperm count, it has to be some issue with my eggs or uterus or whatever." She looked away in embarrassment. "Please don't insult me by trying to pin our infertility on my overambitious career."

He folded his arms across his chest. "I think you're misinterpreting my meaning, Jill."

"Am I? I thought you were just lecturing me on what's best for my family. Did your career choices give you the freedom to enjoy a family-conducive lifestyle with your wife and children?"

He took a long slow breath. "I was consumed by my practice and then my administrative work for most of Erin and Tyler's childhoods. I am not necessarily proud of my choices. Time slips away so very quickly." He sighed. "And before you know it, sometimes it's too late."

"Too late for what?" Her voice cracked. "Too late to have children?"

"Too late to see what really matters in life," he said quietly.

"That's it, isn't it?" she said with quiet anger. "You're concerned I won't produce the precious McGrath heir to the Alfredson."

Without waiting for a reply, she spun and raced out of the office.

*Maybe she's right,* William thought as he watched her go. *Maybe I am obsessing over what will amount to nothing more than a historical footnote.*

Still, he had only one son. And the McGraths had not multiplied as prodigiously as the Alfredsons. There were only three other males from Tyler's generation with the McGrath surname; none of them had shown any interest in medicine or the Alfredson.

William hobbled back over to his chair and sank into it. With all the brewing catastrophes, the chance of the Alfredson lasting in its current form—with or without McGrath representation—was rapidly dwindling. Besides, he wasn't sure he had enough energy, or red blood cells, left to keep fighting for its survival.

## 12

Rather than the head-to-toe sterile garb he had to put on to visit Nate Stafford in his isolation room, Tyler wore only his civvies, black jeans and a navy polo shirt, to see Keisha Berry and her parents in her private room. In the past four months, Keisha's immune system had fully rebounded from her bone marrow transplant; she no longer required isolation or any special precautions. Wearing a pink gown and with her hair tied in a ponytail, Keisha sat on top of her bed drawing in a sketchbook with thick colored markers, which she switched often and rapidly. Cheeks full and flushed, the eight-year-old African-American looked the picture of health.

The sight reminded Tyler how cruelly deceptive appearances could be.

Despite her bone marrow's recovery, Keisha was facing a battle almost as lopsided as Nate's. Her most recent screening blood tests had revealed what they all feared most: Keisha's leukemia had recurred despite chemotherapy and bone marrow transplant. Because her remission had lasted for only a few months, her prognosis was statistically even worse.

Had Tyler not personally delivered the demoralizing news to Keisha's parents the day before, he would have assumed that they hadn't heard. They were smiling when he entered the room, and little he had told them so far had dented their positive outlook. He knew their profound faith helped explain their unwavering hopefulness. Keisha's father, Jonah, was a Baptist minister. Her mother, Maya, was a high school teacher who also taught Sunday school. The family had moved to Tacoma only a year before, from Mobile, Alabama, after Jonah had been recruited to lead a large church in the Pacific Northwest.

Tyler had treated children of devoutly religious families before. Even when compared to those families, the Berrys' acceptance of Keisha's condition bordered on extreme. Neither Maya nor Jonah had shown Tyler more than an occasional glimpse of the desperation that Nate's parents never stopped exuding. Even Keisha was remarkably philosophical about her illness. "I don't think God would take me now and leave Mommy and Daddy alone in the world," she had told Tyler matter-of-factly the day before.

Tyler was convinced that the Berrys' religiousness amounted to an alternate form of denial, though he realized his own atheism, which ran deep in his family, might be influencing his opinion. He had grown up without any exposure to organized religion. The random cruelty and senselessness of the childhood cancers he dealt with—especially in children like Keisha, who sometimes suffered the worst of chemotherapy without seeing any benefit—had only pushed him further away from a belief in any possible divine rhyme or reason to existence.

While Tyler respected the Berrys' beliefs and admired their unshakable faith, their ever-present gratitude embarrassed him to the point of annoyance. Standing beside Keisha and clasping her husband's hand in hers, Maya viewed the doctor as though he had just pulled her from a sinking ship. "I don't know where we would be without you, Dr. McGrath," she said in her strong Southern accent. "You've been a godsend."

*What good have I done?* Tyler wanted to scream. *Keisha's cancer is back, likely for good.*

But as he stared into the woman's kind brown eyes, he simply accepted the compliment with a shrug. "Did you have any questions about the pamphlets I gave you yesterday?"

Maya turned deferentially to her husband. No taller than his wife, Jonah was as skinny as she was full-figured. He had a long, thin face and a receding hairline that made him look older than he was. Tyler imagined that Jonah's penetrating ocher eyes and deep resonant voice would have commanded serious attention from a pulpit. "Dr. McGrath, I have read all the pages," he said. "However, I'm still not entirely clear on how this . . . Vintazomab"—he pronounced the name tentatively but correctly—"works."

"It's a monoclonal antibody that targets the tumor marker CD thirty-three." Tyler turned to his patient with a smile and a wink. "How's that for a mouthful of gobbledygook, Keisha?"

Absorbed in her coloring, she replied without even looking up. "You sure talk boring sometimes, Dr. M."

"Keisha!" Maya looked embarrassed.

"You can't argue with her, Mom." Tyler chuckled, turning back to her parents. "You see, leukemia cells don't look the same as normal white blood cells. On their surface, they have an abundance of molecular cell markers, which are kind of like the unique spots on a leopard. Except the cancer cells tend to overexpress—or make too many copies of—those markers."

"Like a leopard with too many spots?" Keisha suggested in mid–marker stroke.

"Exactly! Hey, I didn't think you were even paying attention, smarty!" Tyler said, drawing a wide grin from Keisha that showed the gaping space where her two front adult teeth had yet to grow in.

"About those cell markers, Dr. McGrath," Jonah encouraged.

Tyler nodded. "One marker in particular that is overexpressed on the surface of leukemic cells is a receptor called CD thirty-three."

Maya held up her hand, as if wanting to ask a question in class. "Is that why they call it 'targeted therapy'? Because the drugs attack those tumor markers?"

Tyler nodded. "Up until recently, we didn't have drugs that could distinguish between the 'good' and the 'bad' cells. Most chemotherapy drugs attack them all, and we just hope the cancer cells are selectively destroyed because they multiply so quickly and that's when cells are most vulnerable." He smiled at Maya. "But a few years ago scientists infected mice with human leukemia cells. They were able to grow and isolate antibodies that specifically attack certain tumor markers. Thus creating drugs like Vintazomab." He made a fist with one hand and clamped his other over it like a Venus flytrap closing over its prey. "Vintazomab binds to the CD thirty-three receptors on the cells which have the most markers—in other words, the leukemic cells— and selectively destroys them."

Both parents nodded their understanding. Jonah held out his hand. "So this Vintazomab won't harm Keisha's good blood cells?"

"Well . . . some normal blood cells also have the CD thirty-three markers on their surface, but not nearly as many as the leukemia cells," Tyler hedged. He remembered the case reports of the three children, out of the roughly three hundred already treated with Vintazomab, who had died during early treatment. As with other chemotherapy-related deaths, no one knew for certain if the drugs or the cancer was to blame. However, one death per hundred patients treated made the drug less toxic than many other chemotherapy agents. "In early clinical trials, there have been a few serious side effects, but most patients have tolerated the drug well."

Still holding each other's hands tightly, Maya and Jonah shared a quick glance in which Tyler recognized a trace of the raw vulnerability that such decisions always elicited. But it didn't last. Jonah reached over and squeezed his daughter's shoulder affectionately. "When can Keisha begin the Vintazomab treatment, Dr. McGrath?"

"In the next two or three days, I hope."

Keisha wriggled free of her father's hand. "Daddy, I can't draw with you harnessing me!" she squealed.

"You mean *harassing*, hon," her mother, the teacher, corrected.

Keisha shrugged. "I'm drawing you a pony, Dr. M," she said without looking up.

Tyler studied the page. Earlier, he had mistaken the brown creature for a cow, but he realized that it could pass for a horse, too. "It will be perfect for the wall behind my desk," he said.

"I think I'll draw you riding him," Keisha said. "You ever ridden a pony?"

"Not for a long time." Tyler had a flashback to his father's birthday card with the loose photo inside of him mounted on a horse—a three-year-old cowboy. "How about you, Keisha?"

"I like to ride ponies," Keisha said. "Not horses, though. They are too high. And I don't want to fall, because Mommy and Daddy say I bruise too easy now. "

Keisha drew on happily for several moments. When she finished, she held the sketch up coyly for his assessment. It still looked more like a cow, now with a broom straddling it, but he was touched by the effort. He reached up and pantomimed tipping an imaginary hat. "Perfect. I'm mighty obliged, ma'am."

Keisha giggled. Then she lowered the sketch to her lap. The smile left her lips. "Dr. M, are you going to have to put another needle in my back when you give me this Vintazo stuff?"

Tyler swallowed, realizing Keisha had been paying attention to every word of the drug's description. He nodded. "Remember last time, Keisha? We're going to put that magical numbing medicine on your back again. Did you feel it then?"

She shook her head minimally.

"You won't this time, either." He pulled off the imaginary hat and pretended to hold it over his heart. "I'll cowboy swear on that!"

The door opened and Nikki Salazar poked her head through. Her face was uncharacteristically pale. "Dr. McGrath, I'm sorry to bother you, but may I have a word?"

Reading the urgency in her features, Tyler excused himself and hurried out to join Nikki in the hallway.

Nikki stared hard into his eyes. "It's Nate," she said quietly. "They've moved him to the ICU."

Tyler's heart sank, but he wasn't entirely surprised. An hour earlier, Nate Stafford had spiked a fever. With the immunocompromised patients, infections often struck with the speed of a cobra. Tyler knew Nate must have had pneumonia because the boy had started to cough as soon as his temperature rose. "Is he intubated?"

Nikki nodded. "They had to put him on the ventilator. He could hardly breathe."

Tyler turned and rushed toward the staircase at the end of the hallway. Nikki stuck by his side. "If we're going to try him on Vintazomab then we shouldn't wait for his pneumonia to be treated," he said.

"So let's start treating him in the ICU."

"Yeah, we better."

"I'll get the supplies and meet you up there," she said as they reached the door to the stairwell.

"Okay." Tyler opened the door, stepped into the stairwell, and raced up the stairs.

Outside Nate's ICU room, Tyler slipped into the full sterile gear. Though he was expecting the sight, his heart still ached when he stepped inside and saw the boy with a breathing tube sticking between his lips and multiple lines hanging over him like a nightmarish cobweb. An ICU nurse attended to the infusion pumps on the near side of Nate's bed, while his parents hovered over their son from the other side.

Craig Stafford's masked head snapped up in Tyler's direction, but Laura could not tear her eyes away from her boy. Nate's face was even grayer than the tubing that ran from his mouth and led to the life-support system. His glassy, half-shut eyes drifted over to view the new visitor.

"What do we do now?" Craig demanded before Tyler even reached the bedside.

Tyler didn't say a word until he made it to the bed. "Hi, Nate," he said in his most reassuring tone as he laid a hand on the boy's shoulder. "Everyone misses you downstairs, so let's make this a short stay here, okay?" He forced a smile. "Trust me, Nate, you've sailed through tougher binds than this one."

The child's mouth moved around the tube but no sound emerged except the whooshing noise of the ventilator that now breathed for him.

"Don't try to talk, Nate. You've got to rest." Tyler turned to his parents. "Craig, the plan has always been to start the new treatment today. And that's exactly what we're going to do."

"But his pneumonia!" Laura croaked.

"The ICU team is treating it," Tyler said. "We need to jump-start Nate's immune system. The only way I know how to do that is to start him on targeted therapy."

Laura stared at him a long moment but then she nodded. "Okay."

Craig looked far more hesitant, but he, too, nodded his consent.

Tyler turned back to his patient. "Nate, I know you can't speak, but I want you to understand that we have to get this new medicine going."

Nate's eyelids widened momentarily. Tyler recognized the fear despite the boy's sedation. He squeezed his shoulder a little harder. "Remember, Nate? I promised we wouldn't hurt you. In fact, we're going to make you sleep through the whole thing."

Nate blinked once, and his mouth appeared to relax around the tube.

Tyler took a deep breath. Nate was so sick and his cancer so advanced that he knew the chance of any intervention helping was unlikely. They were verging on "a wing and a prayer" territory, but he forced those thoughts out of his head and focused on the immediate steps.

Tyler walked Nate and his parents through the intravenous infusions of Vintazomab that they would need to run and the lumbar puncture—known by some as simply "LP" or "spinal tap"—he had to perform to ensure the medicine reached the leukemic cells near Nate's brain.

Craig snapped his fingers in frustration. "How is the medicine going to reach Nate's brain if you only stick it in his back?"

"We thread a hollow needle between the backbones, or vertebrae," Tyler explained patiently. "The medicine flows directly into a layer—what we call the subdural space—that goes all the way up the spine. It runs into the space at the base of the skull—the intrathecal sac—and then into the fluid surrounding the brain."

"Like a drainpipe," Craig grunted.

"Exactly." Tyler went on to explain the potential complications and side effects associated with the drugs. However, he opted not to tell them that the only fatalities in the Vintazomab treatment group had occurred in the smaller subset of patients who, like Nate, needed to have the medicine injected directly into their spinal fluid. This drug was the patient's last hope, and Tyler saw no point in adding to Craig and Laura's overwhelming burden.

Almost half an hour passed before the pharmacy sent up all the necessary bottles and vials of medication. Tyler used the time to prepare his LP tray while Nikki assembled the lines and extra tubing required to run in the drugs. Against the wall behind them, she lined up a series of IV poles holding the tinted glass bottles of Vintazomab they planned to infuse into Nate's bloodstream and spinal fluid.

Tyler had offered Nate's parents the opportunity to stay in the room but, understanding that their son would be under a general anesthetic, neither of them wanted to watch him endure the invasive procedure.

A chunky young anesthesiologist, Dr. Jane Lomas, soon joined them in the room. Sitting at the head of Nate's bed, she plugged a syringe loaded with a foamy, white general anesthetic agent into one of the tubes. She glanced over to Tyler, who nodded his consent for her to begin.

"We're going to start now. All right, Nathan?" Lomas pushed down on the syringe's plunger. "Count down from twenty in your head."

"You won't even make it to ten," Tyler said from the far side of the bed. "Have a good sleep, buddy. Dream of all those ball games you've stolen for your team."

Within fifteen seconds Nate's eyes fluttered and then closed. Nikki came around to the near side of the bed, uncovered his emaciated body, and rolled him with ease onto his side, his back facing Tyler. She repositioned the boy's legs so that his bony knees and hips were bent and he was curled into the fetal position.

Tyler sat down at the stool facing Nate's back. As a pediatric oncologist, he had performed countless LPs. The procedure was second nature to him, but as he reached for the alcohol-soaked sponges and began to sterilize the central back where he intended to insert the needle, his heart thumped harder. He couldn't shake the sudden sense of foreboding.

With other patients, he would have needed to feel along the spine for the bony prominences to find the right spot (between the third and fourth lumbar vertebrae) to puncture with the spinal needle. But Nate was so skeletal that Tyler could spot his entrance point from across the room. He reached for the local anesthetic syringe and stuck the needle through the skin, raising a weal of tissue at the site of insertion. Nate didn't flinch, which indicated he was sufficiently anesthetized. Tyler inserted the needle farther and froze what little deep tissue Nate had between his skin and spine, so that the boy would not feel any procedural pain when he awoke.

The smell of the alcohol-based skin cleanser drifted to Tyler. He had grown to despise the bitter scent, which he associated with all the painful taps and biopsies he had to inflict on so many young patients. Still feeling inexplicably uneasy, he grabbed the long, skinny spinal needle off the surgical tray. Tyler applied the tip of the spinal needle against the skin. Satisfied that his alignment was perfectly straight and in line with the rest of the spine, he applied steady pressure, piercing the skin and slowly advancing the needle.

He felt the familiar pop as the needle penetrated into the subdural space of the spinal canal and was sucked inside by a vacuum force. Leaving the larger hollow needle in place, Tyler withdrew the sharp stylet introducer from its center. As soon as the stylet came free, spinal fluid—looking as clear and harmless as tap water—dripped from the near end of the needle like a faucet with a very slow leak.

Sweating now, Tyler reached for the dangling end of the tubing that Nikki passed him and then hooked it up to the free end of the spinal needle. He waited for a moment as Nikki adjusted the flow into the tube. She nodded once. The connection was good.

Tyler reached for the IV poles behind him. With a quick scan of the bottles' labels, he pulled the third one toward him. He read the wording on the bottle twice. As per protocol—because of past medicolegal tragedies that had occurred in other hospitals when the wrong medicine was infused into the spinal space—he waited for Nikki to read it as well before proceeding.

"Vintazomab," she confirmed aloud.

Satisfied, he plugged the free end of the medicine, "piggyback" style, into the tubing that led to the spinal needle in Nate's back. With a thumb, Tyler released its roll dial and tapped a button on the electronic flow meter. The fluid began to run. He watched as the medicine coursed freely along the tube and into Nate's back through the spinal needle.

With nothing left to do but watch now, Tyler leaned back in his seat. His own worries—like his marital strife and conflicted relationship with his father, and even Nikki—all seemed so trivial and petty in relation to the near-hopeless battle Nate was waging.

"Tyler," Nikki said with an urgency that snapped him out of his introspection.

His eyes darted over to her. The skin exposed above her mask had gone pale as a sheet. "What is it?" he asked.

Nikki pointed at Nate. "His hands," she said.

Tyler jumped to his feet and leaned over the bed to see what Nikki was pointing at. Both Nate's hands lay palm-down on the bedsheet in front of his belly. They were trembling like leaves in a heavy wind.

Tyler's breath caught in his throat. He shot a hand out and grabbed the nearby IV pole that held the Vintazomab running into Nate's spine. He frantically rolled the dial to shut off the infusion. "Get four milligrams of IV lorazepam into him stat!" Tyler called out for the standard, first-line antiseizure medication.

He raced around to the other side of the bed just in time to see Nate's eyelids go into a rhythmic spasm and his head begin to bob.

"Damn it," Tyler muttered. "He's going to seize on us."

Within seconds, Nate's mouth clamped down on his endotracheal tube. Then his arms and legs joined his eyes in uncontrolled convulsions. Unconscious, Nate thrashed wildly on the bed.

Tyler dove across the seizing child. It took all his strength just to prevent Nate from bucking right off the bed.

*13*

After breakfast, Dot Alfredson and Lorna Simpson returned to the wood-paneled living room with its substantial hearth, somber furniture, and unabashed clutter of erotic artwork. It was barely nine in the morning, but the dark, cavernous room, lit by a floor lamp and a dim chandelier, gave the feel of perpetual evening. Dot had yet to suggest drinks, but Lorna suspected that the vodka tonics would not be long in arriving.

Lorna was engrossed by her great-aunt's story and was hungry for more details. "So after Olivia Alfredson and Evan McGrath shared that first kiss, what happened? Did they—"

"Like rabbits in heat, you might say." Dot nodded in the direction of the ceramic copulating Japanese couple.

Lorna frowned as she considered the implications. Dot mistook her expression for disapproval. "How can you *possibly* blame them?" the old woman asked. "Remember that Evan's wife had been disabled for years, and Olivia was a twenty-one-year-old virgin. *Imagine* how much lost time and opportunity both of them had to catch up on!"

Lorna smiled to herself at the absurdity of her great-aunt's sexual fixation, considering that the woman was pushing ninety. "No one else knew?" she asked.

Dot's bony hand took off like a bird leaving its perch. "The Victorians excelled at discretion," she said vaguely.

"True, but in 1895, Seattle wasn't a big town."

"Not much more than a one-horse town, really." She rolled her eyes. "And you know how well secrets are kept in small towns."

"So their affair was exposed?"

Dot looked down at the tiger stripes on her leggings, lost in her own thoughts. "Nothing lasts forever, darling."

---

Family meant the world to both men; Evan's priority was his ailing wife, while Marshall's focus was his motherless daughter. Mutual dedication to their loved ones only strengthened the bond between the two pioneers.

—*The Alfredson: The First Hundred Years* by Gerald Fenton Naylor

An unusually cold and early winter had besieged the Pacific Northwest. By late November, Seattle had already seen more snow than the whole season sometimes brought. Despite the coal burning in the corner fireplace, there was a chill in the room. But Evan was warm under the thick comforter, especially with Olivia pressed up tight against him in nothing but her petticoat. He was astounded, and hopelessly aroused, by how much heat her flushed skin gave off.

Until they began their tryst, Evan had never stayed at a hotel before. But over the past month, he had rented a room once a week, or more, at the Sherman Hotel, on Yesler Street behind Pioneer Square. The bearded old clerk with a blind, opaque left eye and dull stare always gave them the same second-floor corner suite with the coal fire already burning. Evan had heard of men using aliases for similar purposes, but he never falsified his name. However, he never dissuaded the clerk from referring to Olivia as Mrs. McGrath, though he doubted that the one-eyed man was fooled.

Evan reached out and stroked Olivia's silky cheek. She nuzzled her face against his hand and kissed it. They had just made love, but he longed to possess her again. Though Olivia had begun the affair as a virgin, she was a fast learner and remarkably open-minded. Over the past weeks, they had quickly found new ways to touch, caress, and kiss to draw out the moment and heighten the ecstasy of each encounter.

Evan's pervasive self-disgust at his own disloyalty did not dampen his desire for Olivia. It was all-consuming; as intense as his sexual awakening during his honeymoon. At the thought of his wife, another stab of guilt tore through him and he gently pulled his hand from Olivia's face. Virginia had fallen ill during their second year of marriage, and they had not been physically intimate in almost four years. Evan never once considered the forced abstinence as justification for his actions. On the contrary, he had sworn a commitment to her—"for better or for worse"—and in his eyes, Virginia's condition made his affair with Olivia even more inexcusable. He had never before broken his word; nor would he have ever forgiven someone else in the same predicament.

With a sense of shame, he remembered how he had treated his mentor, Dr. Hugh Dundee. The gregarious Scotsman was a surgical genius, an unparalleled teacher, and a generous man. He had taken Evan under his wing professionally. Dundee had also shared his home in San Francisco with the young doctor, inviting Evan and Virginia to countless family meals with his charming wife and three children. The surgeon had helped entrench in Evan the principle of providing humane care to all patients, regardless of sex, social status, or race. Dundee's adherence to the belief had caused a stir that rippled through the San Francisco medical community when the surgeon admitted a Chinese woman to the Morgan Clinic for removal of her infected gallbladder. Old Dr. Morgan, long retired, had intervened, intending to throw the woman out of the hospital, but eventually relented when Dundee threatened to quit.

However, the two men's relationship had soured after Dundee admitted a prostitute to the clinic for a hysterectomy to manage her cervical cancer. The Scotsman readily admitted that he had met the woman at her brothel, which he frequented. Evan was outraged at Dundee's conduct and told him so. The surgeon accepted his protégé's consternation good-naturedly. He argued that not only what his wife did not know would not harm her, but that his weekly visits to the brothel made him an otherwise better husband and father. Evan tried to accept the explanation with worldly understanding but found it impossible to sit eating and laughing at the family table as though Dundee's duplicitous behavior had no bearing on his family or the rest of his life. The two men soon drifted apart socially and then professionally, which influenced Evan's decision to relocate to the Pacific Northwest.

Olivia grabbed Evan's hand in hers. The sensual squeeze drew him back to the moment. "What are you thinking, my darling?" she asked.

He forced a smile. "I am reminiscing."

She slipped her hand out of his and pulled back slightly. "Oh, about better times?" she asked with a spark of hurt.

"No, no, my love." He reached for her shoulder and drew her closer again. "I have never lived a better moment than this one. I was just thinking about San Francisco and my work at the Morgan Clinic."

Olivia assumed Evan was referring to his desire to see a similar clinic built in the Pacific Northwest. "You will have something comparable here in Seattle. Soon, Evan! I know it."

Evan nodded, drinking in her shining green eyes and full lips. He would have been content to stare at that lovely round face forever.

"My fath—," she started, but faltered. "I am certain it will work out for you. I feel it in my bones."

"Oh, Olivia, I love your youthful optimism." He leaned forward and ran kisses along her cheek. "I love you so very much."

"And I you," she said, kissing him on the mouth.

The pressure of her lips on his launched a fresh wave of arousal through Evan. He reached for the silky cloth of the simple slip she wore and ran a hand over it until his fingers touched her bosom. He squeezed through the fabric.

Olivia uttered a quiet noise that differed from the soft moan he had come to crave. He released his grip and pulled back to study her. She was sobbing.

He reached out and wiped a tear away with his finger. "Olivia?" he said softly.

She dabbed at her eyes. "Oh, it's nothing really. I am just lost in a perfect moment." She smiled again, though Evan could see that her lightheartedness was forced.

"I love you," he said again, self-conscious but unable to help himself.

She nodded. "I love—," she began to say but her voice quavered and more tears flowed down her cheeks.

His chest ached. "What is it, Olivia? Tell me. Please."

She did not bother wiping the tears from her eyes. "I have never dreamed that I could be so happy, Evan."

"Then what is wrong?"

She pointed from Evan to her own chest. "How can *this* possibly last?" Her voice dropped to a near whisper. "My father . . . your wife . . . Oh, Evan, how much longer can we continue to go on like this?"

Evan took both her hands in his. "As long as we have to, Olivia. Until we can find a better . . . more suitable . . . way to be together." He squeezed her hands tightly and stared deep into her eyes. "I want us to be together forever."

"There is no such thing as forever," she said in a steady voice.

"There is for us, Olivia," he insisted, but his chest was burning as he spoke the words. He suddenly felt on the verge of tears himself, because he knew she was right.

They parted later in the afternoon, committing to another rendezvous soon. Heavyhearted, he checked out of the hotel. Rather than ride the cable car up the hill to his house on Capitol Hill, he chose to walk through the biting wind and crisp layer of snow. He had forgotten his gloves at home and the pockets in his wool coat offered minimal warmth. His fingers were tingling from the cold when he finally reached the door to his house.

Mrs. Shirley, whose son had miraculously rebounded from his latest bout of pneumonia, was in the kitchen preparing dinner. The smell of roasted chicken wafted out to Evan accompanied by the high-pitched, and at times off-key, strains of her singing. The tune today, "It Is Well with My Soul," was one of her favorite hymns.

In the drawing room, Virginia sat alone in her wheelchair, covered, as usual, by the blanket and shawl. Her face had grown even more drawn. She looked frailer every day. But her mind had cleared over the past weeks. Her memory was keener, and she had not voiced a single irrational or delusional thought in weeks.

Virginia's lips broke into a lopsided smile as Evan neared.

As always, her proximity heightened his guilt. He felt two inches high as he leaned down to kiss her forehead softly and squeeze her bony arm. "How is today, Ginny?"

"I am afraid I am not yet ready for a tennis match," she said in her halting speech pattern.

Virginia had maintained her sense of humor throughout her ordeal, but her sarcasm often left Evan at a loss for words. "Did you sleep this afternoon?" he asked.

"For an hour or so," she said. "Mrs. Shirley read to me. It was *The Jungle Book* today. The poor woman struggles with some of Kipling's more challenging verses." She looked away. "I wish we had toured India together,

Evan. It sounds so very exotic. I think it would have made for a wonderful adventure."

Evan smiled sadly. "Providing, of course, we did not come face-to-face with any tigers."

"There are worse fates to confront." She lifted a shaky hand to him. "How was the hospital this morning?"

He cleared his throat. "Quite manageable. Of course, I will have to return for evening rounds after dinner."

"You work too hard, Evan," Virginia said.

He shrugged. "No harder than most doctors."

"Most doctors have wives who tend their homes and offer them a place of rest and sanctuary at the end of a long day's work. Whereas I merely add to your burden."

Evan squeezed her arm lovingly. "Come now, Ginny."

She stared at him, her left eye twitching. "There is so much you deserve. So much which I cannot provide you."

"Oh, Ginny, please," Evan said, his voice cracking. "Do not talk like this. You are the one who has suffered. I wish with all my heart that there was more I could do for you."

"You are a good husband." She struggled to show him another smile.

Feeling like an utter fraud, he hollowly returned her smile.

"Evan?"

"Yes, Ginny?"

"There is a small favor I would like to ask."

"Anything."

"Miss Alfredson . . . Olivia."

Evan went cold. He dropped his gaze to the blanket covering his wife's lap. "What of her?"

"Mrs. Shirley has returned," Virginia said. "I believe I am well cared for now. I would like you to please thank Olivia for her generosity of time and spirit. However, I was hoping you might inform her that I no longer require her visits or her companionship."

Evan shifted his weight from foot to foot. He buried his still-burning fingers in his pockets. "Are you absolutely decided? I believe Miss Alfredson enjoys your company."

Virginia nodded. "She is an enchanting young woman. I like her dearly."

She stared at him without speaking. There was no mistaking the sudden look of betrayal in her watery eyes. "It is her scent, Evan. I smell it everywhere. Each time I inhale it, it breaks my heart anew."

*She knows!* The breath caught in his throat. The shame swallowed him whole. "Ginny . . . ," he started to say, but he faltered to find the words.

Virginia's hand swung out and barely caught his elbow, squeezing it clumsily. "Mrs. Shirley is making our favorite chicken," she said, her voice much lighter. "I do hope it's ready soon. I am famished."

At dinner, Virginia seemed as energized and upbeat as Evan could remember. Her mood bordered on euphoric. She reminisced about the trips they had taken along the northern California coast. She discussed her favorite musicians and poets, and which of their works meant the most to her. And she even questioned Evan about the clinic he was still hoping to establish and whether he had found any potential backers.

Barely touching his plate of chicken and potatoes, Evan fought off his nausea and tried unsuccessfully to hold up his end of the conversation. He found it excruciating to maintain eye contact with his wife. Evan was relieved when Mrs. Shirley finally collected their dinner plates. He excused himself and hurriedly dressed for the hospital, this time remembering his scarf and gloves. After bundling himself up, he said a quick good-bye to Virginia and headed out.

The freezing night air came as a relief from the stifling guilt and forced joviality inside. The gas streetlights lit the snow-covered sidewalk in front of him. A few fresh tracks cut through the snow on the road, but Evan did not see a carriage or another person for the first half of the eight-block walk from his home to Seattle's only hospital, on Fifth Avenue. As he was crossing at a street corner, he heard the jangle of bells and the beat of hooves behind him. He looked over his shoulder and saw a carriage rapidly approaching.

The driver eased the horse to a stop beside Evan. The carriage door opened and two young men, both dressed in natty navy suits and bowler hats, climbed out of the carriage and hurried toward Evan. "Evening, Dr. McGrath," the shorter stocky one said in a menacing tone. "Mr. Alfredson would like a word."

"I am needed at the hospital now," Evan said. "Perhaps I can call on Mr. Alfredson tomorrow afternoon."

The taller one took a step forward and clamped his hand around Evan's upper arm.

"Mr. Alfredson would like to speak to you *tonight*," the shorter one said.

The grip tightened like a steel trap until Evan's arm ached. Realizing the pointlessness of resistance, he took a step toward the carriage.

Inside, the taller man sat on the leather seat beside him while the other sat down across from him. No one spoke during the twenty-minute cold bumpy ride.

Evan recognized the Alfredson mansion by the torch-lit driveway. As the carriage slowed to a stop, his heart skipped a beat at the memory of the visits he had paid to Olivia while she convalesced from her surgery. Whether or not she was at home, Evan realized that Marshall would not let him anywhere near his daughter.

The shorter man climbed out of the carriage and then the taller one shoved Evan out behind. The two men each grabbed one of Evan's shoulders and dragged him away from the main entrance and toward the coach house.

They pushed Evan through the doorway. Inside the front room, a fire crackled loudly in the hearth against the far wall. The pleasant smell of fresh-cut pine from a pile of wood beside the fireplace filled the room but did little to stem his growing apprehension.

Marshall Alfredson waited by the fire. He was jacketless but wore a vest over his shirt with the sleeves rolled up. His ever-present watch fob hung from his front pocket. He stood with legs apart and big hands dangling at his sides. His normally ruddy face was scarlet, and his jaw clenched. He said nothing as he hobbled nearer. Marshall stopped less than two feet away, and Evan was hit by a blast of breath as strong as cigar smoke.

"In my dealings, Dr. McGrath, I have found that most people have come to regret taking me for a fool," Marshall said quietly.

Evan stared back. Equal parts shame and fear already bubbled inside him, and now indignation joined the mix.

"The lumber trade can be a slippery business," Marshall continued in a more conversational tone. "I find it important to keep a close watch on my competitors. To that end, I employ Mr. Wellsby." He nodded at the shorter man, who returned the gesture. "Mr. Wellsby is an investigator. And he is very discreet and most reliable."

Evan's stomach tightened, but he maintained steady eye contact with the redheaded giant.

"Are you familiar with the Sherman Hotel, Dr. McGrath?" Marshall asked.

Evan did not reply.

Marshall's fist shot out and slammed into Evan's midsection. He doubled over from the surprise and pain, but the two thugs on either side of him hauled him straight up by his armpits.

"The Sherman Hotel?" Marshall asked, almost pleasantly, though fury leapt in his eyes.

"Yes, I am familiar with it," Evan gasped as he fought to catch his wind.

Marshall hit him again in the same spot. As Evan reached out to clutch his belly, Marshall punched him in the face twice, with either hand. The second blow broke a tooth and sent blood spraying from his lip.

"How dare you?" Marshall cried out.

Evan panted, fighting for air. He felt the blood dripping down from his nose and his lip. Even through his anger and distress, Evan realized the beating was justified. "Olivia and I are in love," he said, mostly to himself, realizing the remark was ill-advised but beyond caring.

The big man moved like a trained fighter. Evan tried to raise his hands to protect his face from the flurry of fists, but the two other men held his arms back and left him helpless to the assault.

Light-headed with pain and breathlessness, Evan swayed on his feet. The vision in his left eye was rapidly receding as his eyelid swelled shut. "I love her," he moaned again.

"You are a married man." Marshall punctuated it with another punch. "You have no right."

"We didn't plan it, Fate brought us together," Evan said with a spray of blood.

The remark drew another blow to his gut that doubled him over again. "*I* brought you together, you scurrilous dog!" Marshall growled, breathing heavily now from the effort of the beating. "I wish I had never admitted you to my house." He cocked his fist again but did not strike. "You are ruining Olivia's life. And you have disgraced our good name. Do not dare assume I owe you anything other than this!"

Only the grip of Marshall's henchmen kept Evan from collapsing.

Nausea filled him. He could barely breathe. His left eye had closed completely. He thought of Olivia and realized he might never see her again. "Were you never in love, Mr. Alfredson?" he croaked.

Without answering, Marshall pivoted and stormed toward the fireplace. He bent down and lifted and dropped a few of the logs until he decided on one, weighing it in his right hand.

Instinctively, Evan struggled against the two men holding him as he realized Marshall's intent. He tried to backpedal away as the giant approached but the two men easily held him in place.

"Yes, I have been in love, Dr. McGrath," he said through gritted teeth. "With Olivia's mother, God rest her soul. But there was nothing lascivious, shameful, or scandalous about the love Mrs. Alfredson and I shared."

Evan watched in horror as Marshall raised the log over his head. There was a jolt of pain and his teeth slammed together. Then everything went dark.

The next moment, Evan was lying on a sofa. His head throbbed as if a vise had tightened over his skull. At first, he had no idea where he was but the smell of pine grounded him. He opened his right eye and saw Marshall and the two men hovering over him.

"Can you hear me, Dr. McGrath?" Marshall asked.

Evan nodded, and his head felt as though it might explode from the minimal gesture. But he no longer feared for his life. His outrage drained away, replaced by only self-disgust.

"I want to be extremely clear, Dr. McGrath," Marshall said in a suddenly businesslike tone. "If not for the state of your poor wife, you would already be dead. Do you understand me?"

"Yes," Evan whispered.

"If you go near my daughter again, I will kill you with my own hands." He raised his bruised knuckles to emphasize the point. "That, of course, will be of little advantage to your wife in *her* condition."

Evan swallowed painfully. The man was right. Virginia's fate would be doomed if he were to die. "I understand," he slurred.

"Swear it!" Marshall demanded.

"I swear I will stay away from Olivia," Evan said, his heart breaking as he spoke the words.

## 14

Jill Laidlaw stayed at the hospital and worked through dinner, which consisted of the other half of her smoked turkey sandwich left over from lunch. She reworked and massaged her grant renewal proposal, desperate to inject more appeal into it for the academic jurors who would decide her lab's fate.

Jill didn't reach home until after nine o'clock but still arrived to an empty house. In the kitchen, Kramer meowed loudly as he swatted his empty bowl with a paw, demanding food. Admiring her old cat's directness, Jill knelt down and scratched him behind the ears and then reached for his bowl. As she peeled back the lid on the can of cat food, she experienced an unexpected rush of nausea at the meaty broth's pungent odor. *Was the turkey in my sandwich okay?* she wondered.

The doorbell rang, pushing the thought from her head. Had she still lived in a bigger city like San Diego, Jill might have ignored it, but in the sleepy town of Oakdale she felt very safe in answering the door after dark.

Her sister-in-law stood on the other side. Erin wore a T-shirt and sweats and, as Jill could have predicted, no makeup. Still young-looking at thirty-nine, Erin had exotic, striking features, sharing her father's dark eyes and slightly curved nose. She had been thin as long as Jill had known her, but Erin never made any effort to highlight or complement her natural looks, seeming content with a permanently dressed-down appearance that verged on sloppy.

Erin leaned forward and wrapped Jill in a quick hug. "How are you?"

"Good." Jill slipped out of the embrace, uncomfortable as ever with Erin's tactile approach. "And you?"

"Fine. No complaints."

Despite the words, Erin appeared more uneasy than Jill ever remembered seeing her. "You sure?"

"Yeah, all good," Erin said distractedly. "Is Tyler home?"

"No. He's not back yet."

"Oh."

Jill allowed a longer than necessary pause before she said, "He could be home any time, though. Do you want to come in?"

"Um . . . sure."

Jill led Erin into the kitchen. "Tea?" she offered.

"Okay." Erin nodded, glancing to either side. She appeared preoccupied and nervous, totally unlike her usually relaxed self.

"Erin, is something wrong?" Jill asked.

"I've . . . um . . . been . . ." She shook her head and then waved away Jill's question. "I just wanted to catch up with Tyler. I never saw him on his birthday."

Jill boiled the kettle and steeped a pot of chai tea, assuming that would be the beverage of choice for her earthy sister-in-law. "How are Steve and the boys?" she asked.

"Haven't you noticed? Steve *is* one of the boys." Erin's taut face relaxed slightly. "They're doing well, thanks. It's good Simon and Martin are back in school, though. Too much destructive energy on the loose during those long summer days. Something—or someone—was liable to get blown up."

Jill smiled. Though her feelings for Erin were mixed at times, she had a soft spot for her twin nephews. Despite their innate mischievousness, the eleven-year-olds worshiped Tyler and her. And, if Jill were to believe the legends about terrorized babysitters, they always behaved better for their aunt and uncle than the others who looked after them.

"Sixth grade, huh?" Jill shook her head. "I still remember pushing them around in that double stroller."

Erin grinned, seeming to have overcome whatever had been troubling her earlier. "I can't even remember them at ten. I guess it's different for parents."

Jill doubted Erin meant anything in the comment, but she still felt her irritation rising. "Oil and water" was how Tyler once described the two sisters-in-law's relationship. And he wasn't far off. Jill was insightful enough to recognize that her innate competitiveness only compounded the antagonism. Everything came so easily to Erin: marriage, motherhood, and especially her career. She had already cemented her reputation as one of the best heart surgeons on the West Coast, while Jill was still struggling to establish herself as a leading neurology researcher.

"Tyler said you were busy on your grant reapplication," Erin said. "How's that coming along?"

"It's going," Jill muttered.

"Must be a beast at crunch time, huh? You have to roll out the dog and pony show all over again for the jurors on the funding committees. That's got to be a lot of pressure."

Jill bit her tongue, aware she might regret any knee-jerk response. Instead, she poured the tea into two cups.

"I don't know how you do it, Jill," Erin went on. "Practicing clinical neurology while running a major research lab like you do."

"No, you wouldn't, would you?" Jill said, unable to mask her sarcasm. *You just stick new hearts in people, raise kids, and run a farm while still enjoying the perfect marriage*, she almost added.

Erin looked as if she might reply but instead reached for her cup and sipped her tea.

"How are things in the world of cardiac surgery?" Jill asked, forcing conversation.

Erin shifted in her seat. "Same as ever. Although people are getting a little nervous about that *C. diff* outbreak in the other buildings at the Alf. It would be bad if that reached our floor. Very bad."

Jill nodded. "I hear it's causing your father no end of grief."

"Yeah, I don't think he's slept in days. You know Dad. Any threat to the Alfredson—"

"Is like a threat to his own child."

"No, it's *far* more serious than that," Erin said, and they both laughed.

"William dropped by on Tyler's birthday. He tried to talk him into getting involved in medical administration."

Erin's eyes lit with amusement. "My little bro in med admin? Can't see it."

"Has William ever approached you about it?"

"He doesn't waste his breath anymore." The amusement slid from Erin's expression. "Jill, how do you think Dad looks lately?"

"Pale," she said without hesitation.

Erin nodded. "I saw him a few days ago. He looked like crap."

"Maybe the stress of being CEO is finally catching up to him."

"Maybe," Erin said distantly.

Jill shrugged, still stung by her father-in-law's insinuation that her career might be adversely affecting her fertility. "I get the feeling William would like to see me gestate a male heir to the McGrath throne."

"No doubt. My boys don't share the McGrath name. Besides, I can't see a medical future for either of them." Erin put down the cup of tea and viewed Jill earnestly. "How's that going, anyway? You guys still trying?"

Jill looked away. "Not actively."

"Friends of mine adopted a little girl from China. They're so happy that they're now planning to adopt a little boy from Korea."

Jill's frustration surged, and she slammed her cup down on the countertop. "We're not idiots, Erin," she snapped. "We're aware of the other options out there."

"I am sure you are, Jill. I just thought—"

"Thought what? Because you had no trouble having kids, you could offer me advice on the best way to?"

Erin shook her head. "I wasn't trying to advise you, Jill," she said in a quiet but firm tone. "And I didn't mean to offend. I thought you might be interested in my friends' experience. But I guess not."

"I know people who have adopted kids from Asia as well," Jill said in a more conciliatory tone. "Sorry, Erin. As you can probably tell, this whole child issue is a bit of a sore point for me these days."

"Fair enough. I could have been a little more sensitive." Erin checked her watch and then rose to her feet. "I think I'll have to catch up with Tyler at the hospital."

*Oil and water*, Jill thought again as she walked Erin to the door, where they shared a cursory good-bye.

By eleven P.M. Jill had still not heard from Tyler. That was unusual. Most times, he would have at least called to explain his lateness. Stewing with frustration and worry over the future of her lab, the run-ins with her in-laws, and Tyler's whereabouts, Jill drew a bath and uncorked a bottle of wine.

Lying in the tub, she performed the breast self-exam that she performed monthly (whenever she remembered) since her favorite aunt had been diagnosed with breast cancer the year before; the second of her mother's sisters to develop cancer. Jill found no lumps, but her breasts were tender to touch. She remembered she was due to start her period any moment, so that would explain their sensitivity. Out of reflex, she considered taking another home pregnancy test but decided there was no point. She had not conceived during their regimented sexual schedule while on fertility-enhancing drugs and—as Tyler and she had made love only once in the past month or so—she was unlikely to get pregnant now.

Besides, she thought her breasts, which were never particularly large but always shapely enough to draw attention, had shrunken over the past year. She had lost weight, as she was prone to, due to her recent career stress. She knew those lost nine pounds included her chest, still she couldn't help but see her reduction in cup size as symbolic of further-dwindling fertility.

*You're not even thirty-five yet! Get a grip, Jill.* She had little time for anyone's self-pity, least of all her own.

She had just climbed into bed and reached for her book when Tyler walked in. His face was haggard, his eyes bloodshot. For a moment, she had a fleeting premonition that he was about to announce he was leaving her. *What the hell is wrong with me?*

Jill dropped her book on the nightstand. "What's the matter, Ty?"

Arms dangling at his sides, Tyler stood on the other side of the bed looking like an automaton. "Nate Stafford died."

Jill couldn't place the name at first, but then she remembered. "Oh, the baseball player?" She felt a pang of relief that the news wasn't of a more personal nature.

"The former ball player."

"Sorry." Jill held out a hand to him. "But you made it seem that this was inevitable," she said as gently as possible, aware of how sensitive he had been lately to her tone when it came to his patients.

"True." He looked away. "I just never guessed that I would end up killing him."

"*Killing him?*" She sat up in the bed. "What are you talking about?"

Tyler dropped onto the bed. He sat hunched over the end of it with his head in his hands, rocking in place. "Nate was in the ICU with pneumonia." He went on to describe the boy's septic condition and his decision to rush Nate onto the experimental Vintazomab treatment protocol. "Right after I ran the dose through the spinal needle, he began to seize. We gave him every drug we could think of, but nothing would stop those goddamn convulsions. Finally, we chemically paralyzed him with neuromuscular blockers." He held up a hand and then dropped it to his side. "By that point, it was too late. The damage was done." The emotion drained from his voice entirely. "Nate died two hours later."

Jill's shock receded as she absorbed his explanation. She shuffled down the bed until she sat beside him. She laid a hand on his thigh and squeezed gently. "Ty, you did exactly what was needed. What any good doctor would do. You tried a medicine of last resort when all else had failed." She sighed. "It didn't work. That's not your fault."

"I was cavalier, Jill," he said flatly. "I rushed the treatment."

"Sounds to me like he needed urgent treatment."

"I should have done a CAT scan of his head to make sure there was no sign of elevated pressure from the cancer load before I gave him the spinal Vintazomab. I think that dose pushed his cerebral pressure over the edge."

"You don't know that!" Jill snapped, frustrated by her husband's determination to hold himself accountable for something so obviously beyond his control. She willed her voice calmer, and squeezed his leg supportively. "Listen to me, Ty. I'm a neurologist. I know a thing or two about seizures and raised intracerebral pressure. The boy was awake and alert when you saw him. There was no reason to get a CAT scan before starting the drug. We both know it would not have affected his outcome."

"Do we?"

"He was dying, Tyler," she said more firmly. "No matter what you did or did not do. At least he was unaware at the end."

"So were his parents, Jill," he said, his voice catching. "They never even had a chance to say good-bye."

Jill had run out of ways to defend Tyler to himself, so she left her hand where it was and said nothing. Her thoughts drifted back to ideas for enhancing the grant renewal application, which hung over her like a guillotine. With the current state of her data—and still months away from potential publication in a high-impact journal—she was less and less certain of re-approval.

"You know, Nate was the first patient I saw at the Alfredson," Tyler murmured, still staring straight ahead. "I had such a good feeling about his prognosis last year. I basically told him he was going to beat his cancer."

"You gave him every chance to," Jill said absentmindedly.

"Hmmm," Tyler grunted.

Jill turned and studied her husband. She had never seen him so shaken. Part of her wanted to cradle him until the pain eased, while the other wanted to slap him back to his senses. She squeezed his leg harder. "Listen to me, Tyler. You can beat yourself up forever. But when you step away from your personal attachment, you know that this poor boy was destined to die." She numbered the points with the fingers on her other hand. "He was riddled with cancer. He had failed all therapy. His immune system was shot. And he had acquired an overwhelming infection." She reached out with the same hand and cupped his chin between her thumb and index finger and gently rotated his head toward her. "The truth is, no doctor or medicine was going to save Nate."

He nodded slightly.

"Ty, do you think you'll be able to let this go?" she asked.

"With time," he said, and mustered a small smile. "Thank you."

She shrugged. "Hey, that's our deal, right? We cover each other's backs."

Tyler studied her tenderly for a long moment. Then he leaned closer and kissed her on the mouth. She met his kiss with little interest, but that did not discourage him. He seemed to need her physical consolation.

It had been weeks since they had made love, and normally the pressure of his lips and the minty taste of his breath would have stoked her interest, but the stress of her looming grant showdown had doused her libido.

Despite her minimal responsiveness, Tyler did not stop as he might have at other times. He moved his mouth across her cheek to her ear and began to lick and nibble at her earlobe. He slipped a hand under her pajama top and massaged her lower back in slow deep circles.

Feeling his warm breath on her ear and the steady pressure of his fingers against her spine, Jill's body began to respond in spite of herself. Her husband's desperate need for sexual solace was arousing, too. Soon the checklist of next steps on her grant dissolved from her mind, and she focused on the pleasing rhythm of his fingers and lips. When he slipped off her pajama top, she felt the warmth between her legs. She was surprised by how excited she had become at the sudden anticipation of their nakedness, and the touching, licking, and pleasure that was to follow.

After they had made love, twice and with more intensity than they had in months, Jill drifted into an easy contented sleep, her worries sweated away.

But she awoke shortly after four A.M. with a sense of looming dread even more acute than the previous evening. Tyler tossed restlessly beside her, but when she looked over his eyes were shut and he appeared to be dreaming. She wondered if he was experiencing a nightmare related to his patient's death, but she did not wake him up. She had no energy to console him again this morning.

Jill crawled out of bed and tiptoed to the bathroom. The scale showed she had lost another two pounds since her last weigh-in. She showered, changed, and headed downstairs. She hesitated a moment outside the kitchen. Based on the scales, she knew better than to skip another meal, but feeling the pressure of time, she promised herself she would grab a bite of breakfast at the hospital.

Jill arrived at the Alfredson's neurosciences center at 5:05 A.M. It was still dark, but several of the floors were lit inside the sixties-style, white-and-blue tile building that Jill always considered hideously ugly. Regardless, it was one of the larger buildings on site, indicative of the prominence of the neurology program within the Alfredson. Someone had once told her that the hospital's focus on multiple sclerosis and the neurosciences in general dated back to the original chief of staff, Tyler's great-great-grandfather, whose first wife had died of the disease.

Aside from a nurse who was having a smoke break outside, and the night-shift security guard inside the lobby, Jill saw no one else until she reached her ninth-floor lab. She unlocked the door and let herself in to find that the lights were already burning. She wondered for a moment if she had left them on the evening before but dismissed the idea. Even if she had, the cleaners would have turned them off.

"Jill!"

The loud voice startled her. It had come from down the hallway housing the inner offices. "Andrew? Is that you?" she asked, recognizing the voice of one of her research assistants.

Andrew Pinter stuck his head out of Jill's office, the last one down the corridor. The twenty-eight-year-old Ph.D. in biostatistics often used her office computer to analyze data for their study, claiming it was faster than the others, though Jill suspected Pinter preferred the size and privacy of her office. With a mop top, scraggly beard, and studded earrings in both ears, Pinter could have passed for the front man of a grunge band. Despite his trademark torn jeans and chronic scruffiness, or maybe in part because of them, he exuded an effortless animal magnetism. Jill understood why a steady stream of gorgeous young women dropped by the lab to bring him food or pick him up after work. Pinter was a charmer when he chose to be, and Jill usually enjoyed his playful flirtatiousness.

"You got to check this out," he said, waving her into the office.

"What is it?" she asked, stifling a yawn as she walked toward him.

"You'll see." He winked and his head disappeared into the room.

Jill stepped inside. Pinter had plunked down behind her desk and was typing away at the computer. A coffee cup sat on one side of the keyboard, and on the other side lay an open wrapper with muffin crumbs that sprawled beyond its edges and onto her desk. The sight raised her hackles; Jill was meticulous about keeping her workspace clean.

Pinter didn't seem to notice her exasperation. He waved her around to his side of the desk and pointed proudly at the screen. Jill studied the simple graph it showed. Two colored lines started from the same point near the bottom of the vertical axis on the left-hand side of the screen. As the lines progressed over the time axis, the one labeled TREATMENT diverged dramatically upward from the line labeled CONTROL.

Jill eyed him skeptically, though excitement had begun to bubble inside her. "Where is this data from?"

"I plugged in what data we had on the six-month follow-ups on the stem cell implantation subjects," Pinter said.

"We're still enrolling patients. Besides, we haven't even finished collecting that six-month follow-up data yet." Jill tried to sound dismissive, but her chest had begun to pound and she warmed with excitement.

Pinter's smile grew wider but he said nothing. Jill focused back on the screen. She could not ignore the promise depicted in those diverging lines on the graph. The data had come from the same stem cell study in which Senator

Wilder was considering enrolling. Their first step on the road to publication was to analyze the subjects' functional disability scores—their ability to perform simple tasks such as using a keyboard, grasping utensils, or pronouncing specific words—to compare before stem cell transplantation and every six months following.

Jill had heard anecdotes of patient improvement, some dramatic, within months of re-implantation. However, she knew better than to read much into those case reports. Placebo benefits and observer bias, where both the enrollees and researchers subjectively note improvement because they so desperately want to see positive results, were the rule in nonblinded studies. Most times, such outcomes could not be statistically validated or reproduced, which was the kiss of death for a major medical study.

The graphs facing Jill on the screen were objective measurements collected by "blinded" research assistants who were unaware of which patients had received stem cells. They meant so much more than the anecdotes. Aglow, Jill still tried to mask her exhilaration from Pinter. "It's so early," she said. "Why bother even running the data at this point?"

" 'Cause of this." He laughed.

Pinter clicked the mouse a few times and the data suddenly appeared in table format on the screen. Jill was so familiar with this type of table that she could mine it at a glance. Two numbers immediately popped out at her and sent her heart slamming. The first was the variance, the difference (in this case, improvement) in the scores between the groups. She saw that the treatment group had averaged a 38 percent improvement over the untreated group in neurological testing. *In only six months!* The number was staggering—higher than she had dared hope for. The second value, the P value, ratcheted her mood to near delirium. It was well under 0.05, the magic mark for the P value in any study. A low P value like that meant that the chance of improvement in the treatment group occurring randomly was almost nonexistent.

Unable to contain herself, Jill smiled from ear to ear. She laid a hand on Pinter's shoulder. "Is this really right?" she asked, barely above a whisper.

Pinter shrugged. "I'm just the dumb monkey who plugs in the numbers." His beaming face contradicted the modest words. "But I did plug 'em in right, if that's what you're asking."

"Do you know what this means?" Jill said, as much to herself as Pinter.

"Yeah, I'll still get paid next month."

"You and me both. And everyone else in the lab." She laughed. "Andrew, I could just kiss you right now."

He tilted his head and touched a finger to his stubbly lip. "Oh, yeah? So what's stopping you?"

She leaned her head in closer as if to kiss him, but pulled back at the last moment and punched him playfully on the shoulder. "Alimony payments."

Andrew's eyes lit with menace. "You only have to worry about those if you get caught."

She giggled again, giddy with relief and thrilled by the implications of the early findings. Her grant renewal would be a slam dunk now. Suddenly, the likelihood of publication in one of the most prestigious journals, such as *Nature* or *Science*, loomed large in her mind. She sensed that big scientific accolades might greet such a landmark stem cell study, including major awards or prizes. Maybe even *the* prize.

*Don't get too far ahead of yourself, Jill!*

But her silent reprimand did little good.

## 15

As her narration wore on, Dot visibly lost steam. Her usual animation—flying hands and exaggerated facial expressions—diminished until she sat slumped back in the chaise with her hands folded across her abdomen. A few times she lost her train of thought or used the wrong name.

Lorna worried that her great-aunt might soon pack it in as she had the day before. She dreaded another evening spent in the warm musty guest room with its unsavory history. Out of desperation, Lorna fell back to flattery. "Dot, it's unbelievable the way you breathe life into Evan, Marshall, and these other historical characters. I feel as though I know them personally."

Dot sat up straighter and ran her hand through her cropped white hair. "They were colorful people, *our* ancestors."

"Technicolor, for 1895, I would say." Lorna found it curious that Dot lumped Evan in with their ancestors but she kept the thought to herself. "I still don't see how a vicious beating and a death threat led to an endowment for a hospital."

"Come, now, darling." Dot smiled humorously. "It's a *positively* Alfredson family trait to say one thing and do another."

"Maybe, but I don't see how that applies—"

"Take the upcoming board meeting, for example," Dot said. "We speak in glowing terms about the little family hospital, but many of our *dear* relatives are perfectly prepared to sell off the Alfredson as though it were an old trailer that we could auction off on that eBay program."

Lorna shrugged, careful not to show interest in present-day events. "I'm an academic. I don't get too involved in the business side of the family."

Dot stared at her for a long moment, and Lorna again spotted a disconcerting flicker of insight in the old woman's eyes. "There is *no* Alfredson family business," Dot said. "The lumber business was sold off eons ago. Granted, a few of Marshall's offspring have been prudent with their inheritance, but most have squandered it. All we have left of his legacy is our position at the Alfredson. And if not for the many strings Grandfather attached to the original endowment, we would have no say whatsoever in that, either."

"Point well taken," Lorna said, hoping to gently steer Dot back onto course. "Why did he attach those strings? Few hospitals are privately owned by families."

Dot sighed heavily. "Sometimes I wonder if you're hearing any of what I am trying to tell you, darling," she said with more than a hint of annoyance. "Marshall Alfredson never had *any* interest in building or financing a hospital."

Lorna held up her hands. "Then why, Dot? Why in God's name did he go from trying to kill Evan McGrath to helping him realize his lifelong dream?"

Dot shook her head. "Marshall was a businessman, through and through. For him, everything in life had a price tag. The hospital was simply one more bargaining chip."

"Bargaining for what? Surely he didn't need to buy off Evan McGrath with a hospital? Sounds like Marshall was powerful enough to have just driven the man out of town, or worse, had he wanted."

"That's the problem with you academics." Dot flashed Lorna another knowing smile. "You never want to accept the simple answers, do you?"

"Hold on!" Lorna's frustration with her great-aunt's riddles suddenly vanished. "It had nothing to do with Evan, did it?" In her excitement, she rose from her seat. "Marshall was bargaining with his own daughter, wasn't he?"

Dot smiled approvingly. "Yes, he was."

"But back then, what kind of influence would a twenty-one-year-old girl have had on an overbearing father like Marshall?" Lorna asked. "Especially in light of her tryst with Evan."

"Olivia was no shrinking violet," Dot said. "She was a forward-thinking woman. A nineteenth-century feminist, of sorts."

Lorna shook her head. "But even before Evan and Olivia were found out, Olivia couldn't talk her father into the idea."

"*Talk him into it?*" Dot threw up her hands. "*Gawd, no!* She would have had better luck talking him into wearing a ball gown to his men's club! What Olivia did was trade on the one thing that mattered most to Marshall Alfredson."

"The family name?" Lorna guessed.

"You really are catching on, darling." Dot touched the side of her nose. "Back in those days there was something *even* more scandalous than a high-society lady having an affair with a married man."

---

For Marshall, the new clinic was always an Alfredson family endeavor.
He included Olivia in the planning from the outset.
And her input proved invaluable.
—*The Alfredson: The First Hundred Years* by Gerald Fenton Naylor

Olivia hurled herself off her bed and scrambled on all fours until she found the pail near the bed. Just as the brim reached her mouth, she vomited violently into it.

Theodora Douglas watched Olivia with calm concern. "You sure you're all right, child?" she asked.

Embarrassed, Olivia wiped the drool away from the corner of her lip. "It must have been something I ate at dinner."

"And the four dinners before that one, too," Theodora grunted as she walked over to pick up the bucket. "I best get you a clean one. Or maybe three or four of 'em."

Theodora had been with the Alfredsons since Olivia was born. The skinny black maid with the pox scars, broad nose, and expressive brown eyes never seemed to age. No one knew exactly how old she was. As she had no family of her own, she lived in the servant quarters at the back of the coach house. A tireless worker, Theodora was afraid of no one, not even Marshall.

Theodora liked to pretend her commitment to the family was solely professional. Much as she maintained that Olivia was a continuous burden to her, she provided companionship and grudging guidance to the young woman. Olivia would trust her life in Theodora's weathered hands. In Olivia's mind, she already had, the moment she made Theodora the go-between in her clandestine correspondence with Evan McGrath. Every day, the maid would stop by the Catholic hospital on Fifth Avenue to drop off or receive letters from Evan via the hospital's black handyman, Moses Brown, who acted as Theodora's counterpart in the letter exchange.

Ten days earlier, Theodora had brought home an unexpected and devastating letter. While Evan had reiterated his enduring love for Olivia, he insisted that they had to end their affair for their sake and those of their loved ones. "Being a surgeon," he had written, "the only way I can possibly accomplish this is with one swift, deep, and complete cut. I could not bear it any other way."

Olivia had cried for the better part of three days, reading the letter over and over. Then the vomiting set in. At first, she assumed it was merely part of her grief. But when her breasts swelled more and she passed through her seventh week without her monthly bleed, she realized that she was pregnant. Distraught, Olivia had written Evan three times begging him to reconsider his decision. In her most recent note, she pleaded for a meeting, although she could not bring herself to break the news of her pregnancy in a letter.

As Theodora reached to collect the bucket of vomit beside her, Olivia, still on her knees, grabbed for her arm. "Dora, are you certain there are no envelopes for me?" she gasped.

Theodora looked down at her and exhaled impatiently. "I may not be able to read, ma'am, but I am pretty sure even old Theodora remembers how to pick herself up an envelope." She affected a Southern freedman accent, although she was born free in Massachusetts and had read every book in Olivia's library.

"Stop it, Dora!" Olivia snapped, fighting back another wave of nausea. "I have to speak to Evan. It is imperative."

"Child, you read his letter how many times? The doctor ain't going to change his mind now. You just punishing yourself by drawing it out."

"But he does not—" Olivia stopped herself.

Theodora's face scrunched into a series of deep lines that hid the darker pigmentation of her pox scars. "Are you telling me your doctor friend doesn't know about his own baby?" she said.

Olivia froze in mid-breath. "You know?" she whispered.

"'Course I know!" Theodora flicked a finger in the direction of the bucket. "What kind of imbecile you take me for?"

"I . . . I never thought . . . ," Olivia stammered, still stunned by the revelation.

"Doesn't matter a rooster's feather what old Theodora knows, but are you saying that your friend does not know about your condition?"

Olivia nodded, now warding off tears along with her nausea.

With surprising strength, Theodora pulled Olivia up to her feet. She guided her toward the desk in the room. "You get over there and you write him a letter and tell him," she instructed. "I'll take it to Moses straight away."

Olivia frantically waved a hand in front of her. "Not like that, Dora! Not by sneaking him a letter. I will not tell him that way!"

Theodora's stern expression relaxed into a sympathetic smile. She reached forward and brushed a few loose strands of Olivia's hair away from her eyes. "Child, you do get yourself into some situations, don't you?"

"Oh, Dora . . ." Olivia could no longer hold back the tears. She threw her arms around Theodora and buried her head in her shoulder, sobbing heavily.

Theodora rubbed Olivia's back without saying a word.

After a minute or two, Olivia released Theodora and straightened up. She dried her eyes with her sleeves. She fixed the maid with a determined stare. "Tears will not solve anything," she said, her voice gaining strength.

Theodora grimaced. "What are you planning, child?"

"I must speak to him."

Theodora considered it a moment and then nodded her approval. "Sounds about right."

Olivia brushed her teeth twice, but she could not shed the acidic taste at the back of her throat. She slipped into her favorite blue dress, noticing that its waist felt tighter than before. Staring at herself in the mirror, she was overcome by self-doubt. She undressed and changed into the green dress that she had worn the day Evan and she had shared their first kiss.

Olivia left the house, walked the mile and a half to the nearest cable car stop, and rode it up to Capitol Hill. She had never been inside Evan's ground-level office, but she had often walked by, concocting excuses to visit the area. Even during those secret visits, she had never been so nervous. Her heart was in her throat as she neared the door to the office.

Inside, the older receptionist accepted Olivia's story that she had come to see the doctor regarding intestinal colic. She led Olivia into the examining room.

Evan sat at the desk in the far corner with his head down, writing furiously on the pages in front of him. "Dr. McGrath, may I introduce Miss Alfredson," the receptionist said.

Dropping his pen, Evan snapped his head up. "Of course." He banged his knee loudly on the desk as he sprang to his feet. "Thank you, Mrs. Mickleson. That will be all."

The woman turned and left the room without another word, shutting the door behind her.

Mouth parched and hands damp, Olivia gaped at Evan from across the room. Despite her nerves, she was so elated to see him again that for a moment his facial wounds did not register. Then she suddenly recognized the extent of his injuries.

"Evan!" She rushed toward him. Up close, the distortion of his handsome face appeared far worse. Black and yellow bruising encircled his eyes like a raccoon's mask. He had a cut across the bridge of his nose and his upper lip was split and scabbed. "What happened?"

His swollen lip parted into a sad smile, revealing a markedly chipped upper incisor. "I slipped on the ice and landed headfirst on the ground. I could not have been more clumsy."

The explanation rang false to Olivia. She reached out to touch his face, but he drew away slightly, and she dropped her hand to her side in embarrassment.

Evan looked down at his feet. "Olivia?"

"Yes?"

"Listen, Olivia, I am a man of science, not words," he said stiffly, without looking at her. "So I cannot begin to describe the depth of my feelings for you. My words would be inadequate and hollow."

Despite his flattery, dread welled in her chest at the undercurrent of finality that accompanied his tone. She tried to swallow away the lump filling her throat.

Evan looked up at her, his eyes full of the same longing and adulation she had seen before at the Sherman Hotel. But unlike previous times, he did not reach for her with those gentle hands. "Olivia, I wish with all my heart that our circumstances were different . . ."

"They are different now, Evan," Olivia croaked.

His bruised face crumpled with pain. "No." He sighed. "I mean I wish I had the freedom to pursue a life with you."

"Evan, you have to know—"

Evan stopped her with a raised hand and a shake of his head. "Anything you say will only deepen the hurt." He dropped his hand back to his side. "My wife has suffered so much in her short life. I simply cannot add *this* to her misery, Olivia. I will not." His voice cracked. "It would kill Ginny. Do you understand?"

An unwanted image of his helpless wife sitting crumpled in her wheelchair flashed to Olivia's mind. As always, a wave of shame—as though she had taken something precious from a little child—overcame her. She lowered her head. "Yes, I do."

"I was so wrong to have misled you." He touched his chest. "Olivia, you must know that if it were up to me alone, I would give up everything to be with you."

She nodded slightly.

"I have come to realize that it is not my decision to make." He paused and added quietly, "No matter how painful, sometimes the needs of others have to come first."

Olivia said nothing. A statue could not have been more still.

"When spring arrives, I intend to move Virginia back to San Francisco."

A sense of loneliness consumed Olivia, even worse than the moment she heard that her mother had died. But with the emotional void came sudden clarity. Evan was right about the needs of others. Suddenly, Olivia saw a way to realize so many of those needs all at once.

Olivia reached out and brushed her fingers over the large bruise near Evan's left eye. He winced slightly but did not pull away. She smiled lovingly. "You need to take care of yourself, too, Evan," she said. "That is just as important for Virginia's sake."

He raised his hand to his cheek and caught hers, squeezing it.

She pulled his fingers to her mouth and kissed them, lingering for a moment at the feel of the soft hairs against her lip, and then released his hand. "Good-bye, Evan."

"Olivia . . ."

She pivoted and rushed for the door without looking back.

Out on the street, Olivia shed no more tears. She had much to do, and little time to accomplish it. She silently vowed to never let Evan know about his child. However, she had no intention of "going to visit relatives in the country" (the popular euphemism used for unmarried women sent away to have their bastard children out of sight), nor would she dream of slinking off to some backstreet butcher who might illegally terminate the pregnancy.

Her plan was as simple as the man central to its success: Arthur Grovenor. Poor sweet Arthur still doted on her like an abandoned puppy might. Though he did not challenge her intellectually or emotionally, Arthur had a good heart. He was even charming in his own way. His greatest shortcoming was that he was not Evan. But he was now the only future Olivia could envision. And she was prepared to accept his open-ended marriage proposal, on one condition that had nothing to do with Arthur.

As heartsick as she felt, Olivia took comfort and even pride in realizing how well her scheme might unfold for everyone other than herself, even her unborn child.

As soon as she reached home, Olivia went off in search of her father. She found him in his upstairs office, chomping his cigar more than smoking it as he scanned through the large black ledger on the desk in front of him. When Olivia walked into the room, he lowered the book. "Hello, Olivia," he said coolly. As gruff and temperamental as her father could be with others, Marshall usually softened in her presence, but in the past few weeks he had treated her with a cool reserve she was unaccustomed to.

"Hello, Papa."

"You look very flushed," Marshall grunted. "You do not have another fever, do you?"

"I am fine," she said.

They stared at each other for a few moments. "Well?" Marshall finally asked. "What is it?"

"Papa, I would like you to reconsider Dr. McGrath's clinic."

Marshall's eyes locked on hers. With his still-bandaged hand, he crushed the remainder of his cigar in the waiting ashtray. "Did you see *that* man after I forbade you?" he asked hoarsely.

For the first time in her life, Olivia felt afraid of her father. She hesitated and then steeled her nerves. "Yes, I did," she said. "I continued to see him up until last week."

He sat very still in his chair, but his expression darkened. "Do you honestly expect your complete disregard for my authority—and your own decency—will convince me to throw money at him and his rattlebrained schemes?" His voice grew louder with each word.

"No."

He slammed a hand against the desk so hard that Olivia almost jumped. "*Hell and damnation!*" he bellowed. "What are you thinking, child?"

Olivia had never heard her father swear. Trembling slightly now, she stood her ground. "I am thinking about the future of the Alfredson family."

"I believe that is one factor that you have not considered at all!"

She held his gaze. "On the contrary, Papa. All I'm thinking about right now is our family." She paused and then rested a hand on her belly. "And the future generation of Alfredsons."

Marshall glared at her, angry and confused, but then his eyes lit with sudden and catastrophic understanding. His face fell and he slumped back in his seat. "Oh, Olivia, no. Not that! Do not dare tell me . . ."

Her wordless stare was confirmation enough. He closed his eyes. "Thank God your mother is not alive to hear this," he whispered.

"Papa, everything will be all right."

"How is that possible?" he asked miserably.

"I am prepared to accept Arthur Grovenor's marriage proposal."

Marshall's eyes popped open and he sat up straighter again. "Of course you will!" he said, suddenly recognizing an escape from social calamity. "We will have the reception here at the house. We will make it a New Year's Eve event! It is only a few weeks away. Yes, of course. That will explain the short notice. It might work. Yes, it just might!"

The words struck Olivia as being as damning as a prison sentence.

"Of course, we will need invitations printed immediately," he went on. "And I will need to meet tomorrow with James Grovenor to finalize a guest list. There will be many people not to forget . . ." Marshall was almost smiling as he ran through the permutations in his head. He seemed to have forgotten his anger, or even Olivia's continued presence.

"Papa?"

"Hmmm?"

She took a long, slow breath. "I will not go through with this unless . . ." She faltered.

His eyes darted over to her. "Unless what?" he snapped.

"Unless . . . you agree to invest in Dr. McGrath's clinic."

Marshall jumped up from his seat and stormed toward her, stopping only a few inches away. He raised an open hand over his head, like a broken branch that was about to fall on her.

"After all you have put me through, you would force me into this devil's compromise?" he growled. "How dare you!"

She looked up at the towering figure over her. He had never before laid a hand on her in anger, but she had no doubt that he would not hesitate now. "If you agree to this, I will marry Arthur." She swallowed. "And I will never see Dr. McGrath again."

"And if I do not?"

She steeled her nerves with two more deep breaths. "I suspect there are many places far from Seattle—towns where a qualified doctor and his new wife and child would be welcomed, without questions being raised about either of their pasts."

Daggers shot from Marshall's eyes. Olivia instinctively flinched, expecting to feel the blow from her father's open hand at any moment.

## 16

As Tyler's car wound and whined its way around the seventh floor of the Alfredson's parking garage, he continued to try to convince himself that Nate Stafford's outcome was inevitable and that such cases were unavoidable in his job. He mentally cataloged other heart-crushing tragedies he had already seen in his career: parents who had struggled for years to adopt a daughter from China only to lose her to cancer within months of her arrival, an eleven-month-old who died of leukemia the day before his first birthday, and a mother losing her battle with breast cancer who still lived long enough to see her teenage daughter die first, of a brain tumor.

He reminded himself that the only way to cope was to keep the emotional attachment at arm's length and to focus on the success stories that mercifully outnumbered the losses by a significant margin. But Nate Stafford's death seriously rattled him. Tyler could not distance himself from the loss because, for the first time in his career, he felt responsible.

He had hoped his return to the hospital would distract him from the guilt by keeping him focused on other patients who needed his attention. It hadn't worked so far. In his head, he kept sifting through the events of the boy's last hours, trying to discern what had set off his internal alarm that something was very wrong even before he slid the needle into Nate's back.

Tyler knew Jill was right: Nate was going to die, regardless of the chosen treatment. Though her logic was impeccable, it brought him no solace. Without Vintazomab, Nate might have survived weeks or even months. A long time in the life of a child, and too many irreplaceable memories for a parent.

Tyler spotted the only open parking spot on the seventh level and tucked his car into the tight space between a van and a cement pillar. The sun had risen over Oakdale again and brought temperatures in the mid-seventies.

A light summerlike breeze carried the scent of fresh-cut grass. But Tyler had little interest in taking the scenic route through the grounds of the Alfredson on this perfect fall morning. Instead, he strode down to the basement floor and followed the underground tunnel along the most direct route to the children's hospital.

Most days, he walked onto the sixth-floor unit with a sense of purpose verging on ownership. But today he slunk onto the SFU almost as if returning to a crime scene. His hands were sweating, and his heart galloping. He half expected to run into one of Nate's parents, like he had so many previous mornings. Tyler had a flashback of that terrible moment when he broke the news to them in the ICU's family conference room. He could still see Laura rocking, catatonic-like, on the couch while Craig, tears rolling down his cheeks, stormed up and down the room, stopping only to punch two holes through the drywall.

This morning, nothing on the SFU struck Tyler as out of the ordinary. He received the usual friendly greetings from other staff members. No one else appeared to be hand-wringing over the boy's sudden death. The staff had accepted the naturalness of his passing, and Nate would soon be put out of mind like other children who had died before him. People who staffed the oncology wards were remarkably adept at looking ahead, and not dwelling on losses.

However, when Tyler reached the back desk of the nursing station, he spotted the first sign that he wasn't entirely alone in his grief. In dark green scrubs, Nikki Salazar stood charting at the nearby countertop. Puffy black bags darkened the skin under her bloodshot eyes. She looked as though she had been crying recently. As he neared, she broke into a sympathetic smile. "Hi," she said softly.

"Nikki, you okay?"

She instinctively touched the bags under her eyes with a finger and thumb. "I missed my Botox refresher. When that happens, I'm like Cinderella at ten past midnight. It ain't pretty."

"Botox, *right*." Tyler chuckled. "Did you get any sleep last night?"

She shook her head. "You?"

"I slept. Almost wished I hadn't."

"Nightmares?"

"Yeah," he said. "Well, not exactly. I dreamed Nate was still alive. I told him I wanted to try him on a new treatment, but he refused. Said he was sick of the hospital, and he was going to leave to go pitch a Little League game."

"If only," she said with a slight shake of her head.

Tyler smiled. "You were always his favorite, Nikki."

Her neck bobbed as she swallowed hard. "Tyler, do you think . . ." She stopped.

"That the Vintazomab caused his death?"

She nodded.

"Yes, I do."

"Me, too." Her face fell. "I don't understand. I double-checked all the bags from the pharmacy. I didn't confuse any of the infusion rates on the pump. I don't—"

He grabbed her by the shoulders. "Christ, Nikki, it was nothing you did!"

She frowned, not looking the least consoled. "It's supposed to be a harmless drug. So if we didn't do anything wrong, then how—"

Tyler squeezed her shoulders once before releasing his grip. "There were three deaths in the early drug trials involving Vintazomab. They all came in the group that had spinal infusions." He felt his face heating. "I chose not to tell his parents that 'small' detail, because I thought it might spook them."

"And it would have! You know Laura and Craig. It would have paralyzed them with indecision. And Nate needed desperate measures to stand *any* chance."

"Maybe too desperate," Tyler said. "I didn't even do a CAT scan before I started the drug. Nate could have had dangerously elevated intracranial pressure when I ran that extra fluid in around his brain. That might well have been what pushed him over the edge."

Nikki's fingers wrapped around his elbow. Her kind smile exuded encouragement. "Tyler, I've worked with you long enough to know that your judgment is impeccable," she said. "But imagine for a moment that Laura and Craig had known about the added risk and chosen to proceed anyway, which we both know they would have in the end. The sense of responsibility would have destroyed them. Believe me, it's almost better it happened this way."

For that brief moment, Tyler did.

His phone rang. He would have ignored it, but Nikki let go of his arm and said, "Go ahead, take it. I've got a dose of chemo to administer." She turned and hurried from the nursing station.

Tyler dug his phone out of his pocket.

"It's me, Ty!" Jill's voice bubbled. "Catch you at a bad time?"

"No. Not at all." But he felt oddly sheepish hearing her voice with Nikki so nearby. "What's up?"

"The data, Tyler! From my stem cell study!" Her words tumbled out in a rush as she told him about the early data demonstrating a marked improvement in the functional ability of the MS patients who received stem cell implants.

"Congratulations, hon," he said with heartfelt pride. "The timing isn't so shabby, either, huh?"

"Ah, yeah." She laughed. "This is going to save my lab!"

"Might mean a lot more than that."

"You think?" she asked giddily.

"Aside from bone marrow transplants, has any other stem cell treatment ever been proven to show clinical benefits so far?"

"Not that I know of. No."

Tyler knew Jill must have gone over the implications multiple times but still probably wanted to hear his validation. He was more than willing to indulge her. "Exactly!" he said. "This is going to be earthshaking stuff when you publish. For you and the Alfredson."

"Let's hope," Jill said with another giggle. "You think your father will be pleased?"

"I think Dad will be over the moon," he said. "Sounds like the Alfredson is under siege, politically, these days. This news could be a huge help. The timing couldn't be better."

"Would be nice if one of my studies actually helped William out, instead of causing him more headaches."

"It might even save you some Christmas shopping this year."

"No more unappreciated scarves," Jill joked, referring to her last Christmas present that William had neither worn nor acknowledged. "I think I'm done with my grant reapplication. Maybe tonight we could go out to celebrate? After all, we didn't ever get that birthday drink the other night."

"Yeah, I'd like that," Tyler said as he hung up. But despite how pleased he was for her, celebrating was the last thing on his mind.

Jill had not asked him about Nate, but Tyler didn't blame her. She had worked so hard for this breakthrough. With blood, sweat, and tears, she had climbed the academic ladder, one painful rung at a time. Now she was poised to hit the scientific equivalent of a grand slam. Tyler would not expect her to dwell on his problems at that moment.

Walking down the hallway, lost in his thoughts, he almost ran into Maya Berry where she stood in front of the long mural. Her husband was nowhere to be seen. Before she spoke a word, Tyler noticed a difference in the generously proportioned woman—the serene calm she had miraculously maintained throughout her daughter's ordeal had vanished, replaced by an expression bordering on panic. "Dr. McGrath, thank God you're here!"

"What is it, Maya?"

"Keisha's not right." She shook her head gravely. "She's complaining of a headache. She won't touch her breakfast. The child is not even interested in her coloring book."

Keisha and her sketchbook had been inseparable in Tyler's memory. But he was not surprised to hear that her condition had deteriorated. He had seen her blood work and the MRI of her brain. It was inevitable that she started to show symptoms sooner than later. "I am coming to see Keisha right now."

"Oh, that's good. I'm relieved." Maya turned for her daughter's room.

Tyler stood where he was. "Maya, the cancer in Keisha's spinal fluid must be causing the headache and lethargy."

Maya stopped and turned back to him. "So she needs that targeted therapy we discussed, right?" she exclaimed. "The Vintazomab. You're going to start it right away, aren't you?"

Tyler's chest began to flutter. "Well, it's an experimental drug," he hedged. "We still need approval from the team."

"*Approval?*" Maya grimaced. "You never mentioned anything about that before."

Tyler had not raised the issue because it was generally a rubber-stamp process. According to hospital policy, all experimental treatment protocols had to be discussed with the entire oncology medical staff at the twice-a-week rounds where the complicated cases were reviewed by Tyler and his peers. Normally, no doctor would impede his colleague from starting a treatment deemed potentially life-saving. However, as a result of Nate's sudden death, the department head, Dr. Alice Wright, would likely suspend the use of Vintazomab until a full mortality review was conducted. Tyler knew in his heart that such a formality would never have stopped him before, but he was suffering his first professional instance of cold feet. And he could not bring himself to tell Maya about Nate.

"I am sorry, Maya," he said. "I still need to get the go-ahead from my colleagues."

"When will that happen?" she asked, her hands flapping in agitation.

"We have rounds the morning after next. I should have the green light by the end of that meeting."

Maya's expression crumpled. "What do we do in the meantime, Dr. McGrath?" she croaked.

"I'm going to start Keisha on steroids, now," Tyler said. "That should help with the headaches."

"But steroids won't get rid of my child's cancer!"

Tyler shook his head. "They will buy us time to start the treatment that might," he said, realizing how hollow his reassurance must have sounded.

"I pray to God you can start Keisha on that Vintazomab soon, Dr. McGrath."

For the first time since he had met her, Tyler saw recognition in Maya's eyes that faith alone would not be enough to guarantee her daughter's survival.

Wordlessly, they walked together into Keisha's room. Inside, Tyler realized Maya had not exaggerated. In little over a day, the girl had withered. Her cheeks had lost color. The lovable missing-toothed smile was nowhere to be seen. Even her sketchbook lay neglected on the nightstand beside her. Eyes half open, she stared at the TV above her bed without much interest. Holding her neck bone-straight and her head in neutral, Keisha was clearly uncomfortable. But she still managed a slight grin for Tyler.

"How bad is the headache, Keisha?" he asked.

Keisha started to nod but the pain stopped her. "It hurts, Dr. M. Even my neck. Like when Jimmy Adams squeezed me in that headlock for too long."

Tyler bared his teeth and punched his fist against his palm. "I'd love to have a talk with that Jimmy."

Keisha laughed weakly. "Have to be long-distance. He still lives in Alabama."

"Good thing for Jimmy." Tyler winked. "Keisha, we're going to give you some medicine to take away that headache."

Her eyelids lowered to half shut. "That Vintazo stuff you told us about?"

"Not yet, Keisha." He explained to her about the steroids, stressing they were pills and could be crushed into juice or applesauce. Though subdued, Keisha accepted all of it in her usual stride.

Tyler left Keisha and her mother to go write the orders for steroids and painkillers. Uncharacteristically, he double-checked his calculation on the steroid dosage based on her weight. The unnecessary step bothered him. He wasn't used to second-guessing himself like that.

Tyler slogged through the rest of his hospital rounds on autopilot. Fortunately, his inpatient load was light; he had only eight other children admitted under his care. Though they all appeared to be relatively stable, they were cancer patients and deserved his absolute focus. But he could not stop his thoughts from wandering back to what went wrong with Nate Stafford and what might happen to Keisha if he were to start her on the same treatment. *What other option does the girl have?*

Tyler arrived at the children's outpatient clinic at noon. The three-year-old sleek glass building was as large as the neighboring children's hospital and connected to it via a second-floor glass walkway. Parents from all over the country and around the world brought their children to the center for second and even third opinions. Not only cancer victims. The Alfredson's world-class areas of pediatric care ranged from muscular dystrophy to cystic fibrosis. The only common denominator was the life-threatening nature of the illnesses.

As soon as Tyler walked into the front office of the oncology clinic, the young redheaded receptionist, Lela, with a row of studs along her left earlobe, rushed up to him anxiously. "Dr. McGrath, I'm so sorry," she sputtered. "He wouldn't take no for an answer."

"Who wouldn't?"

"Craig Stafford," Lela said. "He insisted on seeing you now. He was real pushy about it."

Tyler's veins ran cold. "Where is Mr. Stafford?" he asked.

She thumbed behind her. "Waiting in the first exam room for you." She clicked her studded tongue and frowned. "I'm sorry, Dr. McGrath."

"Don't worry, Lela, you did the right thing." He headed toward the exam room, dread rising with each step. At the door, he gathered himself before turning the handle and stepping inside.

In jeans and a black T-shirt, with his back to Tyler, Craig Stafford stood absolutely still as Tyler approached. "Craig?" Tyler stopped, close enough to pick up on the stale smell of body odor.

Craig turned slowly to face him. He was unshaven, and his wavy black hair was matted on one side and stuck out in untamed spears on the other. Eyes sunken and cheeks hollow, Craig looked just as lousy as Tyler had expected.

Struggling for the right remark, all Tyler came up with was, "How is today?"

Craig's eyes narrowed. "Today isn't so great," he said throatily. "Laura hasn't said ten words since Nate . . ." He rubbed his eyes. "She can't get out of bed. I had to take Brittany over to my parents in Redmond. Brit can't stop crying. Says she doesn't believe her big brother's really gone."

Sensing Craig did not want his sympathy, Tyler simply nodded.

"You don't have any kids, do you, Dr. McGrath?"

"No."

"I didn't even think I wanted to be a dad," Craig said, his tone remote and his gaze far away. "I was only twenty when Laura got pregnant. It all seemed like way too much responsibility to me. Then this colicky baby comes along who cries all the time for the first four months. I'm holding two jobs and not sleeping in between, thanks to little Nate." He grunted. "Something weird happened in that first year. Never even really saw it coming. But one day, I suddenly can't imagine life without the little guy around."

They lapsed into a long silence that Craig finally broke. "I wanted to ask you something, Dr. McGrath."

"All right."

Craig dug in his pocket and pulled out a crumpled sheet of paper. He held it, still folded in his hand, without even glancing at it. "This Vintazomab drug. You told us serious side effects were rare, didn't you?"

Tyler held steady eye contact. He knew now for certain where Craig was heading, and he wasn't surprised. Even before the man showed up at the clinic, Tyler had expected he would have to hold this conversation with

Craig at some point. The loss of a child often elicited unpredictable reactions in parents, but not in Craig's case. At every setback, Nate's father had lashed out with anger. The more helpless he felt, the greater his fury. And Tyler knew he was facing a volcano moments from eruption. "Craig, I said that serious side effects were uncommon, not rare."

"There's a difference?"

Tyler nodded. "To doctors, 'uncommon' usually means less than one in a hundred, whereas 'rare' would be more like one in a thousand or less."

"Maybe I was too emotional to understand you right." Craig slowly unfolded the paper in his hand. "Your memory is obviously better than mine. Did you happen to tell us, too, that deaths from this Vintazomab only happened in kids who got the drug through spinal needles?"

"No," Tyler said. "I didn't."

Craig's eyes widened with the first flickers of fury. He waved the page, which looked like an Internet printout, at Tyler. "You mind if I ask, Dr. McGrath, why *the fuck* you didn't share that *little* detail before we signed the consent?" he growled.

"Nate had cancer cells in the fluid around the brain," Tyler said evenly. "Drugs like Vintazomab don't cross the so-called blood-brain barrier. The only way to reach the cancer is by infusing the medicine through a lumbar puncture."

With his free hand curled into a fist at his side, Craig took a sudden step closer. A waft of body odor hit Tyler and registered like a visceral warning, but he resisted the urge to back away.

"That's not what I asked," Craig said through gritted teeth. "Why didn't you warn us of the *real* risks before we went ahead with it?"

"Nate's leukemia was so advanced." Tyler sighed. "I had run out of treatment options. Vintazomab was my very last shot. My Hail Mary."

"*Your Hail Mary?*" Craig's lip curled into a full sneer. "You arrogant prick. You can chuck those all day long from your fucking ivory tower, can't you? Using kids like Nate as your guinea pigs. And you'll get all the glory when one of them connects!"

"It wasn't like that." Tyler crossed his arms and shook his head fervently. "I would never expose a patient to an experimental drug unless I thought the benefit outweighed the risk. Especially Nate. I cared about him. A lot."

Craig lunged another step nearer. His face was inches from Tyler's. "You hardly knew him!" he shouted, exhaling flecks of spit along with a sour blast of stale coffee and cigarettes.

Tyler stood his ground. "Well enough to know how special he was."

Tyler braced himself for the punch or blow he expected to fall at any moment, but Craig left his slabs of fists at his sides. He squinted hard. "Nate was going to do big things, one day. Might have even been a pro ball player."

"No question, Craig."

Stafford stepped back and shook his head in disgust. "We'll never know now, huh?"

"I'm sorry."

"Maybe Nate didn't stand much of a chance by the end," Craig croaked. "Maybe there wasn't much left to do. But I know this: You and that shitty drug took his last few days from Nate. From Laura, Brit, and me, too." His eyes glowed with indignation and his voice faltered. "We didn't even get to say good-bye."

Ashamed, Tyler dropped his gaze to the floor. Craig was right. Maybe he had stolen the only chance for Nate's family to ever find closure in his death. He looked back up at Craig and extended his hand. "I am so sorry for your loss," he said.

Craig just stared at him for a long moment. Then slowly he raised his right arm, but instead of a handshake his fingers curled until only the fore-finger was extended. He shook it at Tyler like a gun. "Sorry doesn't cut it!" he snapped. "I might be just some dumb cement layer, but I been doing some reading about informed consent. And best as I can tell, you didn't get it from us."

Tyler knew better than to argue. He just dropped his hand to his side.

"We're going to sue you and your precious fucking hospital for every dime we can!" Craig barked. "And I'm going to the press, too. To warn others. I don't want you screwing over any other families. Making decisions that aren't yours to make!"

## 17

For the second evening in a row, Jill Laidlaw had the house to herself. In the sexy new black dress that she had saved for months, waiting for the right occasion, she sat at her desk in the home office with a lipstick-kissed glass of red wine in her hand and her cat, Kramer, balled around her ankle, purring.

She finished the last sip of wine and glanced at her watch again: 9:44. Their celebratory dinner was beyond salvaging; the male couple who ran the best restaurant in Oakdale, Le Bistro, would never seat them after ten. Besides, when Tyler called two hours earlier promising to hurry home, he had sounded even more shaken than the previous evening.

Still, Jill felt too upbeat to slip out of her dress. She poured herself a second glass of wine and turned her attention back to the computer screen. For the umpteenth time, she pored over the spreadsheet that Andrew Pinter had constructed from her data. She scanned the list, row by row, studying the patients' functional scores in the areas of speech, mobility, and coordination. She carefully compared the scores of each of her MS patients before and six months after implantation with reengineered stem cells. Her smile broadened as she saw the consistently positive trend—improvement in some, a lack of disease progression in others—among the treated patients.

Then Jill turned her attention to the spreadsheet showing the results from the control (or untreated) group, none of whom had received stem cells. Most of the control patients had worsened and were less functional over the same period that the treated patients had improved.

Despite herself, Jill was still astounded by the dramatic improvement in the treated group. Even before Pinter had shown her the spreadsheets, she had seen patients who, for the first time in months or years, could dress themselves, speak more clearly, or use a keyboard. Two patients had even escaped the confinement of their wheelchairs and were walking with the aid of only a cane. Over the past months, a few patients had tearfully hailed Jill as their savior, claiming the stem cells had given them a new lease on life. But she knew how strong the placebo effect was, and so she had not fully trusted the patients' accounts or even her own eyes. Now that she saw those beautifully diverging lines on the graph, and their accompanying low P value, Jill suddenly appreciated the significance of her new treatment approach.

Another tingle ran through her. It felt better than all the spelling bee championships, scholarships, and other academic distinctions combined. After all the frustrations and setbacks, her experimental treatment appeared to offer fresh hope for patients with advanced multiple sclerosis. And, she realized with another quiver, it promised to cement her reputation internationally.

"There are worse things than surprising yourself, huh, Kramer?" She reached down and swept her fat cat off the floor and onto her lap, indifferent to the fur that stuck to her new dress and the animal's squirms of protest.

"It's almost too good to be true," she said to the cat as she stroked his neck. She fought off a sudden glimmer of a worry that she could be overlooking something. *Don't ruin this moment by overanalyzing it!* she reprimanded herself. *That's something Mom would do.*

Growing up, Jill had often thought of her emotionally remote mother as a killjoy. But that same temperament made Angela Laidlaw an excellent lawyer. She would have become an even better judge, had her husband not been stricken with Alzheimer's. The memory rekindled Jill's guilt.

The cat began to whine and claw at Jill's wrist. "Trust me, Kramer, Dad is still with it enough to be proud of me for this," she said, before lowering the cat to the floor. "Besides, if my treatment works for MS then the same approach might help in Alzheimer's, too," she rationalized, though she wasn't convincing herself much more than the cat.

Jill realized she hadn't spoken to her parents in almost a week. It was too late to phone, but she knew her mother often logged on to the Internet to catch up on e-mails after her husband had gone to bed. Jill clicked on the videoconference icon on her screen. As the tinny ring shook the speaker, an image of herself from the perspective of the computer's camera popped up on the monitor. In her fitted black dress, with blue eyes highlighted by eye shadow and tawny hair worn down past her shoulders, Jill recognized her own attractiveness but only in a cold-eyed sense, as though staring at a stranger. Or, at least, an out-of-date image—one captured from her life before she became so caught up in her academic ambition that she thought of almost nothing else.

After ten unanswered rings, Jill gave up. Gently shaking Kramer free of her ankle, she rose from the desk and carried the glass and bottle back to the kitchen.

As Jill stood at the sink washing the glass, her thoughts turned to Tyler again. He was taking his patient's death so hard. She wondered again if her husband had chosen the wrong specialty, having to deal with critically ill and dying children. He had more trouble than she did keeping emotions at bay.

Tyler had once brought the same passion to their relationship. She recalled the romantic surprises he used to spring on her—the unexpected dinners, the wrapped jewelry boxes hidden in coat pockets, the unscheduled getaways, and the flowers . . . so many flowers. But it had been months since a bouquet had arrived for her. Jill knew she shouldered some of the responsibility. At times, his romantic excess crawled under her skin. Just because she loved him—was even still *in* love with him—didn't mean that she needed big romantic gestures. They were outside her comfort zone.

After finishing the dishes, Jill turned off the lights and headed up to bed. With the research funding worries alleviated, she expected to sleep better than she had in months. But her giddy excitement kept her awake. She had already sworn Andrew Pinter to secrecy. She planned not to tell anyone else until the results were verified and her paper was ready for publication; the risk of intellectual theft—or worse, the humiliation of being publicly refuted—was too high. However, experience dictated that the early results would leak out sooner than later. When it came to high-profile studies, academics were as discreet as gossip columnists.

She warmed with anticipation again as she considered the awe, respect, and even jealousy her study might engender among her colleagues—the lifelong validation she had sought.

Eventually, she drifted off into a dreamless sleep.

She woke up just before six A.M. to find Tyler lying quietly on his back beside her. Feeling more aroused than she had in recent memory, Jill ran her fingers along his bare shoulder and rubbed his arm gently. Without waking,

Tyler stirred and then rolled away from her. Giving up, she climbed out of bed.

In the kitchen, Jill ate a breakfast of toast, fruit, and eggs; as much as she had eaten for the last week of breakfasts combined. She even combed through the entire newspaper—stopping to complete the crossword puzzle, like she used to—before she headed in to work.

She was still riding a natural high when she arrived at the Virginia Mc-Grath Neurosciences Building. Inside, she barely took note of the bright yellow signs warning staff to take special contact precautions. As the *C. diff* outbreak had not touched her work environment, it was easy to push the alerts out of mind.

On the way into the hospital, Jill had received a text message that Senator Wilder wanted to see her. As soon as she reached his floor, she went directly to Wilder's private room. As usual, she had to stop outside his door to flash her credentials for the Secret Service agent on duty, a bald burly man who would have looked more natural in military fatigues than a navy blue suit.

Inside, Wilder lay in pajamas, propped up by the raised head of his bed and covered by a blanket. Jill thought his color had drained, but she kept the impression to herself.

"Thank you for coming again, Dr. Laidlaw." Wilder's face broke into another beguiling, slightly lopsided smile. "I'm sure I'm becoming one of your most bothersome patients."

"Never, Senator." Jill pulled up a metal chair to the bedside. "How are you today?"

"I can't complain." He chuckled. "Well, I can—and believe me, I do—but it d-doesn't help much."

Jill smiled politely. "I spoke to my father-in-law, Senator."

Wilder nodded shakily. "Dr. McGrath dropped by yest-yesterday."

"Did he reassure you about the sanctity of the Alfredson?"

His shoulders twitched in what passed for a shrug. "He tried."

Jill tilted her head inquisitively. "You're not convinced?"

"Bit of a job hazard." Wilder waved his hand clumsily. "After all those years on Capitol Hill, I just assume people always mean the opp-opposite of what they tell me."

Jill chuckled. "You mentioned you had other sources. Have you heard any different?"

"Putting aside the brand-name value of the Alfredson," he said, without answering her question, "have you any idea how much the land beneath it is worth?"

She blew out her cheeks. "A fortune."

"At least double that."

"William told me that most of the hospital's funding and capital costs come from the foundation, not the family," she pointed out. "He said it would be a legal nightmare for the Alfredsons to try to sell off the hospital."

"One person's legal nightmare is another's opportunity."

She eyed him intently. "Senator, do you know something my father-in-law doesn't?"

Wilder considered the question for a moment, before offering a slight shrug. "All just rumors."

"Well, I've just learned some promising news about my study. If the data holds up, it should bring some good publicity to the Alfredson. Might even make the hospital harder to sell."

"Or easier." He smiled widely and waved again. "Forgive me, Dr. Laidlaw. I am a born con-conspiracy theorist." Wilder burped loudly. "Excuse me."

"Are you okay, Senator?"

Wilder's cheeks puffed and he swallowed rapidly a few times, as though gagging. "Guess I can't talk about Washington without getting a little queasy." He smiled again and held out his trembling hand. "Now tell me about your great s-success."

She hesitated. "Most of the people inside my lab haven't even heard yet."

"Dr. Laidlaw, I'm famous for my discretion. To this day, my campaign manager still thinks I'm stumping in New Hampshire." He winked. "Please, I want to hear about your breakthrough."

Enthused by his interest, and inexplicably eager to please him, Jill summarized her early findings and their hopeful implication for MS victims.

"Congratulations, Dr. Laidlaw." He smiled widely and wiped a few beads of sweat from his brow. "On behalf of all MS patients, thank you."

Jill felt her face flushing. "It's still early."

"I understand," Wilder said. "I have been thinking about your study a l . . . lot lately."

Jill's pulse quickened. The senator's enrollment would be the icing on the cake. "Have you reconsidered?"

He began to speak, but his face darkened and he looked as if he might choke.

"Senator?" Jill raised a hand out to him, but he waved it away.

"I'm okay." He breathed heavily. "I just want to be clear about the stem cells you are using."

"What about them?" she said warily.

"If I were to . . . to . . . be enrolled," he said, raising his head off the bed with obvious effort, "I would have to be sure that no cells from human embryos would be involved in my treatment."

"This study only uses autologous cells, Senator. In other words, your own cells. If you consent, we will only use scrapings from the lining of your nose to harvest your stem cells. Then we'll transplant them back into your spinal fluid and brain stem."

Satisfied, Wilder sank back into his bed. "Okay."

Jill's chest welled with exhilaration again. "So you'll agree to enroll?"

"If it's all right with you, I would like to do more than just enroll."

"What do you mean?"

"Since I dropped out of the cam . . . campaign," Wilder said with a note of sadness, "I have avoided all public appearances. With good reason." He made another gagging noise.

"Senator?"

"I'm okay." His head steadied. "Dr. Laidlaw, if you are agreeable, I would like to go public with my support of your research."

Jill could barely contain her excitement. "I am not asking—"

"I know you're not." He smiled. "I want to. Listen, I know how difficult it is to fund research nowadays. I want people to see what I've become. What multiple sc . . . sclerosis can do to a person—to a life. Maybe together, we can raise awareness. And if I res . . . respond to the treatment, the added publicity might help your cause. Lord knows it would help mine." His chuckle turned into another burp, but it didn't deter him. "I want another shot at public service. There's so much more to accomplish." He sighed. "I want my life back, Dr. Laidlaw."

*And what if you don't respond, Senator?* Jill considered the stakes and immediately saw that the huge upside of having a former presidential front-runner as her study's spokesman outweighed its risks. "Thank you, Senator. You have no idea—"

Suddenly, Wilder's face turned dusky and he began to gag uncontrollably. He lurched forward in the bed and his head almost slammed into the blanket covering his legs. He uttered a horrific retching sound.

Just as Jill leapt to her feet and grabbed him by the shoulders, vomit erupted from his mouth.

*18*

Erin scanned the inpatient chart in her hands. "Damn that storm," she muttered to herself as she considered how negatively the weather-delayed transport chopper might have impacted Kristen Hill's future. The young woman had improved minimally since her surgery. Her transplanted heart was still badly stunned from its protracted time spent on ice. With each passing day, the possibility of it never recovering grew more likely.

Erin thought of Kristen's twins, Katie and Alex. She had run into them the day before as they were being led away from the Henley Building by a stooped and pale woman, Kristen's aunt, the only other relative involved in the children's lives. They had dressed up—Katie wore a blue sundress and Alex had on a matching short-sleeved shirt and bow tie—for their first visit to see their mother after her surgery. Erin had to resist the urge to sweep them both in a big hug, but neither of them seemed to even notice her. The kids shared the same wide-eyed, overwhelmed look that she had seen so often in people of all ages after a first visit to an intensive care unit.

Brushing off the memory, Erin stepped into Kristen's room to find her patient crying. She hurried over to the bed. "Kristen, are you in pain?"

Kristen shook her head.

"What is it?"

"The kids." Kristen sobbed through her oxygen mask. "They're not allowed to come visit me anymore."

"I know. I'm so sorry." Earlier in the morning, Erin had received a dire e-mail from her father, copied to the entire surgical staff, warning that a patient in the surgical ICU had contracted *C. diff* infection. Everyone in the unit was now at risk. As a consequence, the whole unit had been placed on the most stringent infection-control measures to prevent further spread.

Only essential staff members would be permitted inside, meaning no visitors, not even family, would be allowed.

Erin reached for Kristen's free hand and squeezed it in hers. "I know it sucks, Kristen, but the hospital has to take these precautions. You understand?"

Kristen shrugged.

"They're meant to protect you. Katie and Alex, too."

Kristen's tears stopped flowing, but she clung tightly to Erin's hand. "Dr. McGrath, if I were to pick up this infection—"

"That's what these measures are supposed to prevent."

"Yeah, but with my recent luck . . ." Kristen laughed bitterly. "I'm so weak. And I know my new heart is not working as well as it should."

Erin knew Kristen was right. Her frail body could not cope with the added insult of a major infection.

Kristen swallowed. Her voice cracked again, but her eyes remained dry. "I'm not going to see Katie or Alex again. Am I?"

A lump formed in Erin's throat. "You can't think—"

"I am only trying to be realistic."

"Kristen, maybe you haven't bounced back as quickly as we'd like. But you're not worse. That's the important thing."

Kristen's lips formed a brave smile. "Dr. McGrath, I know I don't have any right to ask you . . ." Her words petered out.

"Go ahead, Kristen. Ask."

"You have twins. You know what it's like." She paused and her voice lowered. "If something happens to me . . . if I don't make it, will you keep an eye on Katie and Alex for me?" Her face creased with concern. "Not all the time or anything like that. Just, you know, from time to time. To make sure they're doing okay?"

Erin squeezed Kristen's hand even tighter. "What Katie and Alex need is for you to come home."

"I know, but if . . ."

Erin closed her eyes and nodded. "Of course, Kristen," she said. "*If* . . . I would make sure that they're doing okay. I promise you."

"Thank you," Kristen said with obvious relief.

After Erin finished her rounds, she headed toward her office in the newly erected cardiac sciences building. Her brain was knotted with unpleasant thoughts and worries. The promise she had made to Kristen weighed heavily on her. She knew she had already become too enmeshed in her patient's life.

As she neared the office building, the imaginary fingers encircled her neck again. The sense of suffocation was as acute as in earlier episodes. Dread seized her again. Her hands went numb from the wrists down. Gasping for air, she staggered over and collapsed onto an empty wooden bench in front of the building. She clasped her head in her wooden hands and rocked back and forth, desperate for the attack to abate.

She felt someone touch her arm. "Dr. McGrath? Erin?" a voice asked.

Erin pulled her hands from her face to see a nurse in navy scrubs kneeling in front of her and checking her pulse. There was something familiar about the woman's kind face, and especially the scar running underneath her eye, but Erin was too distressed to place it.

"I'm Nikki Salazar," the nurse said, pulling her fingers from Erin's wrist. "I work with your brother, Tyler. We met once in the cafeteria."

"Oh, of course," Erin sputtered.

"Erin, what's the matter?"

She shrugged.

"Can I get you anything? Maybe a glass of water—"

"No. No." Erin fought to slow her breathing. "Just a migraine. Like a terrible ice-cream headache. Thankfully, they never last too long."

Nikki eyed her doubtfully. "Your color is a little off."

"I get light-headed from the pain sometimes. I'm okay now."

Nikki straightened up but continued to view her with concern. "I saw Tyler on the ward earlier. I could page him for you—"

"No! Nikki, please. I'm better now." The words tumbled out more frantically than Erin intended. She forced herself to her feet to prove her soundness. The world spun around her, but she managed to hold her footing. "Honestly, I'm feeling better. Thank you."

"Good," Nikki said, though her tone was still dubious. "I'm on break for another half hour. You want some company where you're going?"

Feeling calmer, Erin forced a smile. "Thanks, Nikki, but I'm good to go now. I do appreciate your concern."

"Okay. I better get back to minding my own business now." Nikki turned and, with a quick wave over her head, was gone.

As soon as the ground stilled under her feet, Erin trudged toward the

building and up to her office. By the time she reached her door, a slight resid-
ual dizziness was all that remained of the most recent panic attack.

Erin wasn't scheduled to see patients and was looking forward to the soli-
tude. But no sooner had she slipped her key in the deadbolt than she heard
her father's somber voice coming from behind her.

"Erin, do you have a moment?" William asked.

"Hi, Dad." She hesitated. "Sure. Come on in."

Erin watched as William strode toward her. Were it anyone else, she
wouldn't have noticed anything unusual in his approach, but her father's normal military rigidity was off-kilter. He listed slightly to his right, as though
favoring his hip or back. And he looked even paler than the last time she saw
him. "Dad, you okay?"

"Slight flare-up of my sciatica. Nothing really." The corners of his lips
hinted at a smile. "I think I'll have to cut back on my triathlon training."

"I didn't know you had sciatica," Erin persisted.

"For years," he said as he followed her inside. "Besides, I came by to discuss your injury, not mine."

"Injury?" It took Erin a moment to make the connection. "Oh, the
carpal tunnel," she said, looking away.

The evening before, Erin had informed her department head, Dr. José
Chavez, that she intended to take a leave of absence for health reasons.
She told him she had a flare-up of carpal tunnel syndrome, a common
nerve compression in the wrists that caused needles-and-pins discomfort
and weakness of the fingers. She claimed the numbness was interfering with
her ability to safely perform certain precision surgeries in the OR. Chavez—
a good surgeon, whose people skills were at times wanting—was not particularly sympathetic but, for medicolegal reasons alone, had no choice but to
grant her a leave.

Erin wasn't surprised the news had already reached William's ears. It
seemed nothing went on at the Alfredson without her father knowing.
"How long have you suffered from carpal tunnel?" he asked.

"Ever since I was pregnant." Erin turned away as she spoke the half-truth.
While she had suffered from carpal tunnel syndrome in the later stages of
her pregnancy, she had not experienced a single symptom since she shed the
extra thirty pounds soon after the boys' births. She felt sheepish about lying
to her department head, and even worse for misleading her father. But the

alternative—admitting that she had become too terrified to step back into the OR for fear of being immobilized by another panic attack—was unthinkable.

"How long will you be sidelined?" William asked.

"Not sure," she evaded. "I'll give it a week or two and then see how they're feeling."

"Are you planning to have it fixed? Joe Gallant is a terrific plastic surgeon. He performs the surgery through an endoscope. The recovery time is minimal—"

"Dad, I just want to rest my hands for a little while and see if that helps before I stick them under the knife." She frowned. "If that's okay with you."

"I see." William's hand drifted behind his back, and he began to rub. "Erin, you're acknowledged as the best transplant surgeon we have here."

"That's not true. Mitch Halverson and Abdul Qatar are just as good or better—"

"I am not telling you because you're my daughter—in fact, I never told you before precisely because of that. Erin, it's the truth. And the heart program needs you operating again. As does the Alfredson."

She shrugged off her father's rare compliment. "I need a few weeks. That's all. Meantime, we have enough surgeons here to cope with my load."

William eyed her without comment.

"Dad, why does it matter to you or the hospital if I take a short leave?"

It was his turn to be evasive. "There's a lot going on right now."

"Thanks, Dad. Now everything makes sense." For a moment, she felt like a petulant teenager again.

William viewed her for a long moment. Then, without another word, he limped over and lowered himself gingerly into the chair across from her desk. Erin walked around and dropped in the chair across from him.

"I haven't told anyone else, but I suppose you will all find out soon enough anyway," William said in a defeated tone. "The hospital—at least as we know it—is in trouble."

He might as well have told her that the oil or beer industry was on the brink of collapse. "The Alfredson in trouble? Come on."

"The Alfredson family is meeting at the end of the month to decide the hospital's future."

Erin shook her head. "Why would its future be any different from its last hundred years?"

"Some members of the family want to sell the hospital."

"*Sell* the Alfredson?" She rose from her seat without even realizing it. "To whom?"

"An HMO or some other private health-care corporation. I suspect those behind the motion already have a buyer in mind, but I have no idea whom."

"If the Alfredson is sold to a company in the private sector . . . ," she said to herself, already calculating the consequence to Kristen Hill and patients like her who would never have the insurance coverage or means to pay for the care they needed.

Reading her thoughts, William sighed. "Exactly, Erin. It would become another private hospital."

"Can they really do it, Dad? Sell the entire medical complex?"

"Probably. The family still owns the hospital and the land. However, it's legally complex with the foundation involved." He exhaled again and, with obvious discomfort, repositioned himself in the chair. In the space of a single breath, he suddenly looked old to Erin. "Regardless, if the family tries to sell the Alfredson it would cause irreversible upheaval."

Erin was still struggling to wrap her mind around the far-fetched idea. "Do you think they really will try?"

"All they need is a simple majority vote. There are several family members who would never support the motion, and almost as many who certainly will. The fate of the Alfredson will rest with the unknowns and the undecided." He sighed again. "That is why it's so important that all stays quiet in the days leading up to the vote. This damn *C. diff* outbreak is not helping. Nor will the fact that our top heart surgeon is taking an indefinite leave."

She reached across the desk and squeezed William's arm through his jacket, surprised by the boniness of it. "Dad, I just can't see how it will matter to anyone if I take a couple of weeks off."

"You're probably right, of course," he said, sinking deeper in his chair. "I just don't want to give the other side any more fodder."

She mustered a reassuring smile. "Surely the Alfredson has survived bigger threats than this one."

"Of course it has, but . . ." He grimaced. "When I still practiced medicine,

I had this patient, Harry Olsen. Harry was an overweight smoker with high blood pressure, out-of-control cholesterol, diabetes, and kidney failure. He survived three heart attacks, two bypass surgeries, and a lung cancer scare. After all that, Harry still refused to give up smoking or stop eating donuts. You know what finally killed him?"

She shook her head.

"A bee sting. Harry didn't even realize he was allergic until a bee stung him on the lip." He stared hard at his daughter. "Erin, sometimes it's the most unexpected, seemingly harmless threats that inflict the most damage."

She released his arm. "Dad, is there any other way I can help?"

William rose awkwardly from his chair. He smiled stiffly. "No. Just get your talented hands operating again as soon as possible."

Self-conscious, she folded her arms across her chest, tucking her hands underneath them. "I'll give it a week and see."

"I hope you're feeling better soon, Erin."

"You, too, Dad. Are you planning to see a physical therapist about your back?"

"I think I will follow your same strategy. I'll give it a week and see."

She smiled. "Hard to argue with that."

He shuffled toward the door, stopping with his hand on the doorknob. "Erin, there's nothing else, is there?"

"What do you mean?"

"Aside from your carpal tunnel syndrome, everything else is okay? With Steve? The boys?"

"Fine." She cleared her throat. "Why do you ask?"

"Lately, you've seemed subdued."

She felt her face flushing. "I don't know what you mean."

"You're not quite the same outspoken tireless girl I remember." He chuckled. "That thirteen-year-old who insisted on continuing to play the part of Maria in her junior high's production of *The Sound of Music* despite the crutches, cast, and broken leg."

"Maybe I've matured a touch since ninth grade."

"I suppose that can happen." He opened the door. "I just haven't seen a lot of the old Erin since you came back from Kenya. To be honest, I miss her a little."

After William left, Erin slumped back in her chair. She could not continue to hide or bury her anxiety attacks for much longer. She was not accustomed to lying, and she was obviously doing a lousy job of it. Not only had the panic attacks incapacitated her at work, but they were taking a toll on her family life. Her poor sleep, preoccupation, and irritability were driving a wedge between her and Steve and the boys.

Involuntarily, her thoughts drifted back to Africa and that hospital in Nakuru. By the time she returned stateside, Erin had almost buried the memories of that harrowing standoff in the muggy operating room. Somehow they had crawled back into her consciousness. At first only in her nightmares, but now they were terrorizing her waking hours. Earlier that morning, she had practically jumped out of her skin at the pounding footsteps of the Code Blue team as they raced past her in the hallway.

In her mind's eye, she could still see the old man's pupils dilate until his brown irises disappeared altogether. And she could practically hear his forlorn cry as the first swing of the machete fell.

Despite her promise to Steve, Erin had not yet made an appointment to see a therapist. But she could no longer deny to herself that she needed to talk to someone.

Palms sweating, she reached for the phone and punched in the number for her brother's pager.

# 19

Dot Alfredson had found her second wind. Or perhaps, Lorna Simpson thought to herself with a smile, the old girl's cocktail (a triple vodka tonic) accounted for her renewed vigor. Not that Lorna was in any position to judge. The bitter smell of tonic hit her nose like an invitation. Though still enjoying her first drink, she was already anticipating the second.

While Dot seemed to rely on her maid, Juanita, for most necessities, she insisted on attending to her own bartending. She now stood in the corner of the room, with only her head and shoulders clearing the leather-sided mahogany bar, as she lovingly dispensed Grey Goose vodka into two fresh glasses.

For Lorna, the lull in Dot's storytelling was like a spell breaking. Her thoughts turned to the other purpose of her visit. "Dot." She stopped to have a sip of her drink as if only making small talk. "That Alfredson board meeting in a couple of weeks."

In mid-pour, Dot glanced up from the bottle without spilling a drop. Her gaze drifted back to her task, but her voice carried that same note of suspicion Lorna had heard before. "What about it, *darling*?"

"How many voting Alfredsons are there?" Lorna asked.

Dot lowered the bottle and stirred the drink with a long narrow spoon. "As you know, I've fallen off the Christmas card lists of most of our dear relatives," she said lightly. "According to the charter, only direct descendants of Marshall Alfredson twenty-one years and older are entitled to vote. Everyone else from my generation has had the good decency to die. Last time I checked that would leave sixty or so voting Alfredsons."

The number was consistent with Lorna's estimate. "Nearly all of whom are coming to the extraordinary board meeting," she said, as much to herself as her great-aunt.

Dot fixed her with another probing gaze. "Darling, I thought you had no interest in things that happen in *this* century."

"Only a passing interest." Lorna laughed as she tossed back the last of her drink.

"Of course, we will be making history at this meeting, won't we?"

"Oh?" Lorna said with her nose still buried in her glass. "How so?"

" 'Money first.' That was Grandfather's credo," Dot said. "And most of our dear clan still lives by the same belief. Certainly many of the Alfredsons, *especially* the Californian collection, could use the windfall that would come from selling off the only family asset left."

Lorna stood up and carried her empty glass over to the bar and exchanged it for the fresh drink waiting for her. She took a sip, pleased to taste even more vodka than in the previous glass. "You think the family will vote to sell?" she asked, trying to sound as casual as possible.

"I imagine so, yes."

"Do you intend to vote?"

Dot's bright red lips parted in one of her lascivious smiles. "For me, this is like hunting big game on safari. I'm *merely* going for the sport of it." She ran her hand over her short white hair. "And you, darling? How will you vote?" She paused and then added with a trace of sarcasm, "Assuming you even bother to attend, of course."

Lorna considered her answer carefully. Her great-aunt was no fool. She needed to reinforce her credibility or risk losing the old woman altogether. "To be honest, Dot, that is one of the reasons for my visit. I'm still trying to decide."

Dot's smile withered. "Really? All this ancient family history will *actually* influence your decision one way or another?"

"In a way." Lorna mentally composed her words before continuing. "The Alfredson has never meant much to me aside from its status as a minor landmark and the family name, which I don't even share. But now, listening to you describe its history and how it touched people—my ancestors—has given me a far greater sense of . . . ownership. You understand?"

Blank-faced, Dot nodded. She reached for her own drink, sniffed it, and then took a long sip.

"Dot, there's something confusing me about the chronology of your story."

"Oh? What's that?"

"Olivia was your aunt. So your father must have been her brother, but you have yet to mention him once."

She shrugged her narrow shoulders. "He was considerably younger than Olivia."

Lorna frowned at her great-aunt. "But Marshall's wife died when Olivia was in her early teens. Correct? Did your father and Olivia share the same mother?"

"No."

"So they were only half siblings," Lorna said. "When did Marshall remarry?"

"He never did."

Lorna threw her hands in the air. "Okay, now I'm totally lost."

But Dot simply shook her head and laughed. "Darling, why ruin a perfectly good story by cutting to the end?" She picked up her glass but didn't drink from it. "Now where were we?"

"Olivia was just about to blackmail her father into funding Evan's hospital."

"Ah." Dot smiled. "So she was."

---

Reserved and unassuming, Marshall initially balked at the suggestion of naming the clinic after himself, but Evan insisted. The young doctor convinced Marshall that it was only right, since there would be no clinic without the Alfredsons.

—*The Alfredson: The First Hundred Years* by Gerald Fenton Naylor

By the early 1890s, Seattle's only hospital was no longer large enough to accommodate the city's booming population. Every day Evan McGrath spent at the hospital, he grew more convinced he could design and run a superior clinic that, despite the Sisters' tireless efforts, offered better and more humane care. But like a fire deprived of oxygen, his hope of realizing the dream had withered and died in the wake of losing Olivia's loving support and encouragement.

This morning, Evan walked onto the women's ward to find it even more crowded than usual. The bare walls were lined by narrow beds with cloth partitions separating some, but not all, of the beds. The nuns had laid extra mattresses on the floor to house the overflow of patients. They were laid so tightly together that Evan had to tread carefully to avoid stepping on patients. As usual, they ranged from young to old with diagnoses that ran from heart ailments to wound infections and almost everything between. As always, there was a disproportionate representation among the "seamstresses" (as the Sisters euphemistically referred to the city's prostitutes). Despite the modest nightgowns in which the nuns dressed them, these women were easily recognizable by their skeletal faces and blank stares. Advanced syphilis and cervical cancer were the common culprits. As a surgeon, Evan rarely had any treatment to offer the cervical cancer victims, whose tumors were invariably too advanced to remove.

But the prostitutes accounted for a smaller than usual fraction of the admitted women on this cold December morning. An outbreak of influenza had hit Seattle hard in the late fall, and most patients were sick with the virus. Many others admitted with alternate diagnoses had since acquired the flu from their sick and contagious neighbors. And the virus had spread among the staff, too. Several of the Sisters were now too sick to leave their own beds.

A devout follower of the germ theory teachings of Lister and Pasteur, Evan had always been conscientious about hand-washing, but he had become obsessive during this influenza outbreak. He could not afford to become sick. While the flu was usually no more than a nuisance to healthy adults, he feared he might bring the virus home to Virginia and put her, in her weakened state, at mortal risk.

Recently, Evan's concern for his wife's health had soared, as he helplessly watched the multiple sclerosis continue to ravage her. However, despite her steady physical deterioration, her mental status had actually improved. Her paranoia and forgetfulness had dissipated. She was acting more like the old Ginny, which, compounded by the lingering guilt over his adultery, only deepened his attachment to her.

Shaking off the worry, Evan focused on his rounds. He stepped from bed to bed and mattress to mattress. Unlike many doctors, Evan believed firmly in his patients' right to privacy during examination. He often addressed people in a whisper to avoid being overheard by neighboring patients. And whenever possible, he pulled partitions around patients before uncovering a body part to examine. But this morning any hope of modesty was lost.

Evan assessed the belly of a woman whose gallbladder he had removed three days before. Her wound was closing nicely, but she had developed a high fever that he believed was more attributable to the flu than her surgery. Still, he intended to instruct the Sister to change her dressings three times a day until her fever broke.

He was on his way to find the nun when he bumped into Moses Brown in the hallway. The hulking black man had a broad nose, crooked front teeth, and intelligent brown eyes. He wore, as always, the same fraying navy blue suit that was too short in the pants and sleeves, and in all likelihood had belonged to a patient that had died in the hospital (the nuns were very practical about recycling clothes to the needy). Six months earlier, Evan had reset Moses's badly broken forearm that was shattered in a fall from the hospital roof. Moses's radius and ulna had healed straight, and the successful treatment won his devotion.

"Excuse me, Dr. McGrath, sir," Moses rumbled in his low baritone.

"Yes, Moses," Evan said, trying to portray his usual sense of calm. But the sight of Moses always sent his heart pounding with the anticipation of word from Olivia. Even though Evan had not responded to her last three letters, he had read them countless times, lingering over each phrase and word. Sometimes he would just stare at her looping penmanship or the monogram in the corner of her personal stationery. The familiar scent of the paper alone was enough to conjure the vivid memories of those ethereal hours spent together at the Sherman Hotel.

Evan had not seen Olivia since the day she had shown up unexpectedly at his office. Despite his worry and affection for Virginia, he missed Olivia more than he ever imagined possible.

"How can I help you, Moses?' Evan asked, reining in his expectation.

"I have a letter," Moses said in a low voice.

"All right then."

Discreet as ever, Moses glanced to either side before slipping his hand inside his jacket pocket and withdrawing the envelope.

Even before it reached Evan's hand, his hopes fell. The tan-colored envelope looked nothing like the pastel ones from Olivia. He turned it over. On the back was written DR. MCGRATH, without an accompanying address. Then Evan spotted the MA monogram in the left-hand corner. Instinctively, he reached up and touched the rough scab above his lip that covered the laceration from the beating Marshall had laid on him.

"Did Theodora give you this?" Evan asked.

"No sir, Dr. McGrath." Moses shook his head. "I have not seen Dora for the best part of a week."

The disappointment in the man's tone matched Evan's crestfallen mood. "Who did, then?"

"A gentleman I'd never seen before, sir. He called himself Mr. Wellsby."

Evan touched his lip again, remembering the unsavory little man who had spied on Evan and Olivia and later dragged him to face Marshall's wrath. "Oh," he mumbled.

Moses's forehead furrowed. "Dr. McGrath?"

"Thanks for bringing this to me," Evan muttered as he tucked the envelope in the inner pocket of his jacket. He saw no urgency in opening it. "Is there something else, Moses?"

"Dr. McGrath, do you . . . er . . . expect to receive more . . . um . . . letters?" he stammered, and then hurried to add, "I mean, ones that Dora might bring for you."

Evan shook his head. He felt a sudden pang of empathy for the man, who was clearly smitten with Olivia's courier. "No, Moses. I do not expect Theodora to bring any more letters."

"Oh, well, I best be going," Moses said, embarrassed at his show of emotions. "I have to fix the second-floor window before the patients get a chill, or worse."

Evan ran a hand over his jacket pocket and felt the letter again, irrationally wondering if Olivia had borrowed her father's stationery to write him. *And send Wellsby to deliver it? Don't be such a lovesick fool!*

Once he was alone in his office, Evan reached into his pocket and extracted the envelope. The monogram on the outside stoked his unease. He grabbed the letter opener on his desk, and sliced open the envelope feeling as though he were cutting into an angry abscess. Unfolding the single slip of paper, he noticed that the neat script was composed of short harsh strokes, the antithesis of Olivia's wavy fluid penmanship. The note was as short as Olivia's were long.

> *Dr. McGrath, I wish to meet to discuss a business proposition. I anticipate your presence at my home tomorrow at four o'clock in the afternoon to discuss the matter further.*
>
> *Marshall Alfredson*

Evan stared at the page. The impolite invitation had left no recourse for rescheduling or refusal. Frustrated, he balled up the paper and threw it into the wastebasket beside his desk, vowing to simply ignore it.

By noon the following day, his resolve had weakened. He had little appetite to hear Marshall's proposition, assuming it might be another ultimatum, but the prospect of again being inside the house where he had first met Olivia excited him. He realized Olivia would be nowhere in sight, but the draw was almost irresistible. Ashamed of his lack of restraint, he closed his office early and rode the cable car to the stop nearest the Alfredson home.

As Evan walked the mile from the trolley stop, conflicting thoughts swirled in his head. The still-sizable welt on the back of his scalp ached as he neared the house. His mouth was dry and his palms damp as he reached the door and rapped with the large knocker.

Stanley, the English butler who used to welcome Evan with a polite smile, greeted him with only a stiff nod. "Good afternoon, Dr. McGrath. Please follow me to the drawing room."

Evan spotted Theodora hurrying down the hallway and his heart skipped a beat. He waved discreetly to her when she looked up. Without slowing, she showed him a trace of a smile.

In all the many times he had visited the Alfredson mansion while Olivia was recuperating from her appendectomy, he had never before been invited into Marshall's library where Stanley led him now. Poorly lit with high ceilings and the furniture and moldings all constructed of dark heavy wood, the room struck Evan as foreboding.

The imposing mantel clock read five minutes after four, but Evan was kept waiting another fifteen tense minutes before Marshall entered. In a black suit, with the gold chain of his watch dangling from his pocket, the redheaded goliath limped toward Evan, who rose to his feet. Neither man extended his hand to the other.

"Won't you please sit down, Dr. McGrath?"

Evan lowered himself into his seat as Marshall lumbered over and sat behind his desk directly across from him. He reached for the cigar box on the desk and offered the open box to the doctor. The rich tobacco aroma didn't tempt Evan, who declined with a shake of his head. Marshall shrugged and then chose a cigar and lit it with a long match. He took three slow puffs before he pointed the cigar at Evan. "Dr. McGrath, I have been thinking about our previous discussion."

Evan tensed. The throb in his scalp intensified as he braced for another threat.

"Perhaps your idea is not as far-fetched as I had originally thought."

Confused, Evan held up a hand. "My idea?"

"I own land sixty miles from here, near the Cascade mountains. I am told there is good building soil there."

Evan gaped at the man.

"That clinic of yours." Marshall waved his cigar impatiently. "I am prepared to build it for you."

Evan was dumbfounded.

Marshall squinted at him. "Do you understand me, Dr. McGrath? That utopian clinic you describe with such fervor. I have decided to finance it. To build it for you."

"Why would you do that?" Evan blurted.

"That is no concern of yours." Marshall took another few puffs of his cigar. Then his features softened. "I suppose I have come to realize that you were more helpful in curing my daughter's ailment than I have credited you for."

Though he was still dubious of Marshall's motives, an inkling of excitement sparked in Evan.

"On a more pertinent note, I see tremendous growth in the future of the Pacific Northwest," Marshall went on. "I think we might need better medical facilities than what the city currently provides."

Evan sat up straighter. "You say the proposed site is sixty miles away?"

Marshall nodded.

"I find it hard to imagine the roads are well developed between here and there."

"Good enough for a horse and carriage," Marshall snorted. "There is a rail line, too."

"It will keep me a long way from Seattle."

Bitterness flitted across Marshall's features. "Forgive me, Dr. McGrath, but I do not view that as a particular disadvantage."

*Of course not.* "I'm thinking of Virginia, my wife," Evan said, but his exhilaration mounted. If he could establish the clinic he had always envisioned and attract some gifted physicians and experts in their field, then, perhaps, he could find new hope for his wife.

"I see." Marshall shifted in his seat. "The town of Oakdale is near the site. Perhaps you could find a comfortable home for Mrs. McGrath there?"

"Perhaps," Evan said, his thoughts already focused on the logistics of building a new hospital. "What size clinic do you have in mind, Mr. Alfredson?"

Alfredson shrugged again. "I own hundreds of acres in the area, so the land is not an issue. I am a lumberman with my own construction crews, and therefore can control the costs as I see fit. Largely, I would defer to your needs and the plans of our chosen architect." Then he added, "*Within reason,* of course."

Evan was stunned by the unexpected opportunity. He suspected there had to be more to Marshall's proposal, but he was too elated to care. He struggled not to show his excitement. He folded his arms across his chest and eyed Marshall earnestly. "If I accept your offer, will you invest me with the authority to direct the medical care of this clinic? To hire the people I see fit and to choose the manner in which care is offered?"

"Yes, yes," Marshall snapped. "I am offering you the chance to run this clinic."

Evan couldn't keep the smile off his lips.

Marshall yanked the cigar out of his mouth and ground it out aggressively in the ashtray on his desk. "But make no mistake, Dr. McGrath, this will *not* be your clinic. It will always be owned by the Alfredson family." He glared at the doctor. "Do you understand me?"

"Yes."

Marshall rose to his feet. "Good. Then I think our business here is done."

Evan stood up, too, his head swimming with the recent developments. He extended his hand to Marshall, who shook it perfunctorily.

"Good day, Mr. Alfredson," Evan said as he turned to leave.

"Dr. McGrath?"

Evan turned back to the man. "Yes?"

"I suppose I should inform you that Olivia is to be wed."

The words hit Evan harder than the blow from the fire log. His breath caught in his throat. The anticipation of seeing his clinic built was washed away by a fresh wave of heartache. "When?" he sputtered.

"New Year's Eve." An icy smile crossed Marshall's features. "Oh, and Dr. McGrath, please do not expect an invitation."

*20*

Blood. What a difference an extra couple of pints made to William Mc-Grath. Since he had slipped into the outpatient department the evening before and received a blood transfusion, he no longer felt light-headed or breathless after a single flight of stairs. But the infusion of energy provided no escape from the crisis swirling like a cyclone around his beloved hospital.

His mood had been even lower since reading the third-page newspaper article on the death of Princess Catherina. According to Reuters, she had died peacefully at her home from complications of kidney failure. Neither the Alfredson nor the superbug was implicated, or even mentioned, just as Catherina would have wanted. However, William was annoyed to see that the brief obituary dredged up a reference to her infamous topless photograph.

And now, as William sat at his desk drumming his fingers on the desktop and listening to Normie Chow describe the Alfredson's worsening *C. diff* outbreak, his mood steadily blackened. Chow reviewed the situation with the aid of an electronic presentation that included tables, charts, and pie graphs, but not a sliver of good news, as best William could tell. His back throbbed—a harbinger of worse news to come—and his frustration mounted with each new slide.

Chow's unflinching smile seemed to contradict his bleak news. Not even William's steady glare dented his grin. "Listen, Bill," Normie said happily. "This isn't just a run-of-the-mill case of poopie-pants picked up at the salad bar of some two-star Caribbean all-inclusive. We're talking about an aggressive pathogen here. If you look at the numbers—"

Showing a rare glimpse of temper, William interrupted Chow with a heavy groan. "Normie, I get it! Six more deaths, forty-five new cases, and we've seen further spread of *C. diff* to other wards and buildings despite our infection-control measures." He slapped his palm on the desk. The crack was louder than he'd intended. "What the hell is going on?"

Chow scratched his balding head. "This little bugger isn't playing by our rules."

"That's your best answer?" William glowered.

"As good as it's going to get, methinks," Chow said.

William took a deep breath, struggling to regain calm. "Humor me, Normie. Explain why we're having so much trouble controlling the outbreak."

"*Clostridium difficile* is a hardy bug." Chow flexed his arm Popeye-style, as if showing off his biceps. "A nasty piece of work, too. It's from the same family as the anaerobic bacteria that causes gangrene and botulism. Trouble is *C. diff* can live inactive as a spore. These spores can exist on almost any surface."

William nodded. "And survive all our repeated cleans?"

"The spores are only a few microns in size. They can hide anywhere within this small country you call a hospital. Even the best cleaners in the world can't get bleach into every nook and cranny." Chow chuckled. "They're already doing a helluva lot more than I would for the meager wages you pay 'em!"

The housekeepers were working for overtime now, but William didn't feel the need to justify that to Normie.

"Besides," Chow went on, "even if we got the bathrooms clean enough for Martha Stewart to cook in, there are still the asymptomatic hosts to worry about."

"People like us?"

"Yeah. Or any staff member. Healthy people are the biggest threat of all, because we might be transporting the little devil all over hell's acre without even knowing it."

William suppressed another groan. The cancerous ache in his back reminded him that he wouldn't qualify as healthy. For a moment, he considered letting Chow in on his secret—it would be a relief to share with someone, and Normie was one of the few people he would trust with the news—but he dismissed the idea, deciding now was not the time to discuss his own health problems. "So anyone can carry *C. diff* spores without showing symptoms or even realizing they are contagious," he summarized.

"Bummer, huh?" Chow nodded. "Can't even test for the spores, if someone doesn't have diarrhea. That was the problem in Quebec. And we're facing the same strain here."

William tilted his head. "Quebec?"

"In 2003, a big hospital in Montreal had an outbreak of *C. diff* on their wards. Same aggressive subtype as we're seeing now. It's multiresistant and less responsive to antibiotics. A superbug." Chow chuckled again. "'Superbug' always makes me think of a little bacterium wearing a mask, cape, and tight pants."

"Did they manage to eradicate it in Montreal?"

"They have it under control." Chow sighed. "Not sure they can ever eradicate it."

"How long did it take them?"

"About a year."

"*A year?*" William's heart sank. "We don't have a year," he said, more to himself than Chow, wondering if he would live to see the Alfredson's outbreak controlled. "How many cases did they have total in Montreal?"

"About fourteen hundred," Chow said matter-of-factly. "Around a hundred deaths."

*A hundred dead!* William envisioned the potential *New York Times* headline. The Alfredson could not afford that kind of publicity, especially with the hospital's future hanging on the next board meeting. "That will not happen at the Alfredson!" he said definitively.

"If you say so." Chow scratched his head again. "Meantime, you might have bigger fish to fry."

"How so?"

"Didn't you hear about the senator?"

Confused, William shook his head. "Wilder?"

Chow nodded. "He's our latest *C. diff* victim."

William shot to his feet. The pain fired up his spine as though he had been speared. "*Victim?* Is he dead?"

"Not too far off, from what I hear," Chow said. "They moved him to the ICU this morning."

Ignoring the searing ache in his back, William headed for the door, Normie right behind him. Unlike Princess Catherina, if Senator Calvin Wilder died from a superbug acquired at the Alfredson, it would not be kept secret; the headlines would be plastered on the front page of every major newspaper.

Marching almost half a mile from his office to the Henley Building, William had to stop twice to catch his breath. The second time, Chow remarked, "Tai chi, Bill. That's the ticket. My grandma could run this route with a sack of rice strapped to her back."

William was too concerned about Wilder, and too winded, to respond. He kept his head down and trudged on for the Henley Building.

Inside, William and Normie had to clear a Secret Service checkpoint set up in the ICU. After donning sterile gowns, gloves, and masks, they stepped into the isolation room where Wilder was confined. Dr. David Leavenworth, an internationally renowned intensive care specialist, was already at the bedside. Pale and soft-spoken, the middle-aged doctor had two hoop earrings and a ponytail that in William's opinion clashed with every other aspect of his meek appearance and temperament.

Senator Wilder lay unconscious on the bed with a respirator tube jutting between his lips. His waxy skin was almost translucent. A number of intravenous lines converged at the central line inserted into his neck, delivering crucial fluids. Several wires connected him to a flat-screen monitor above his bed. William saw at a glance that all the electronic readings boded poorly—the senator's heart rate was dangerously rapid and his blood pressure critically low.

Leavenworth nodded at the monitor. "We've got him on antibiotics and multiple meds to try to support his circulation, but . . ."

"It's still not good," William said.

"Not good at all." Leavenworth clasped his gloved hands together and laid them over his prominent belly. "On top of his *Clostridium difficile* colitis, he has developed a significant urinary tract infection. The dehydration from his *C. diff* and the sepsis from his urinary infection have tipped him into severe shock. His heart is struggling. And now his kidneys have shut down, so we need to start him on dialysis."

Sweating behind his mask, William turned away from Wilder to look Leavenworth in the eyes. "What is the prognosis, David?"

"Guarded, at best." Leavenworth's gaze drifted off somewhere beyond William's shoulder. "If we can control his fluid loss, rehydrate him, eliminate his urinary infection, deal with the *C. diff*, and support his cardiac and kidney function throughout . . . then he *might* have a chance."

Chow shook his head and exhaled as though he were blowing out candles.

"Holy crap, Dave, I don't think I've ever heard so many 'ifs' squeezed into a single sentence."

William squinted at the intensivist. "David, what are the odds of his pulling through?"

"The man is relatively young but he has organ failure on top of two infections," Leavenworth continued emotionlessly. "If I had to put a number on it, I would say Senator Wilder has less than a fifty percent chance of surviving."

"Less than fifty percent," William muttered to himself, estimating that the Alfredson's odds were no better. He had visited Wilder three times since the senator's admission. He liked the man and felt genuine admiration for the dignity with which he faced his disease, but now William focused solely on damage control. If the senator were to die, William wondered how he could stall the public revelation of the *C. diff* infection and the Alfredson's culpability until after the pivotal board meeting.

William was still mentally wrestling with the potential public relations fallout as he stepped back into his office. Eileen Hutchins, the chairperson of the Alfredson's board of directors, was already waiting in his office. She pushed away her coffee cup and rose from her chair when she saw William enter the room. The attractive sixty-year-old widow had the same fair complexion as her great-grandfather, Marshall Alfredson. An impeccable dresser, Eileen wore a stylish teal suit with an open-neck white blouse complemented by a simple, tasteful gold-and-silver chain necklace.

Eileen smiled warmly as William neared. She met his hand with both of hers and clasped it for an extra second or two. "Ah, William, always a pleasure. The telephone never does you justice," she said in her slight Bostonian inflection.

Eight years after Jeannette's death, William missed his wife—and the little romantic moments they had shared throughout their more than thirty years of marriage—as much as or more than ever. He still experienced bouts of stark loneliness whenever the hectic pace of his administrative work slowed. He had not dated another woman since; none had even caught his eye. Except Eileen Hutchins. He sensed interest on her part, too. But despite how eagerly he anticipated their meetings, William thought that in light of his illness, it would be futile, potentially cruel, to act upon his attraction.

He inhaled her lilac-scented perfume. "Thank you for coming in, Eileen," he said, conscious of the stiffness in his tone.

"Any excuse, William." She smiled. "I want to show you something." She sat back down in her chair, reached down for a file, and opened it on his desk.

Ignoring the throb in his back, he hurried around the other side of the desk and sat down across from her. She pulled a page out of the file and pushed it toward him. He noticed her short, impeccable nails and the understated diamond solitaire ring she wore on her right hand. Eileen looked up and caught him viewing her. She smiled again.

Flushing, William quickly diverted his eyes to the page. He recognized the long list of Alfredson family members. "Are all of the Alfredsons coming to this extraordinary board meeting?" he asked.

"We have confirmed that sixty of the possible sixty-three voting family members will attend."

"Sixty?" William said with alarm. "That many?"

"It will be the largest meeting in the board's history, but I think that works in our favor."

He looked back up at her. "I don't understand, Eileen. How does such a large turnout help us?"

"For the motion to pass, it will require the vote of a simple majority of those present. In other words, fifty percent plus one."

"Or thirty-one votes in favor."

"Exactly." She tapped the list with her index finger.

William had met almost half of the people listed and recognized the names of several more. He saw that beside each name someone had penciled in a plus sign, a minus sign, or a question mark.

"Are those your marks?" he asked.

She smiled bashfully. "Some of them are just guesses, of course."

"What is your count, Eileen?"

"Right now, it stands at twenty-six in favor of selling, twenty-nine against, and five unknowns."

William nodded. "So all of the unknowns would have to vote in favor for this motion to pass?" he asked.

Eileen shrugged. "Providing I'm correct about the other family members' intentions."

William glanced over the list again. Of the ones he knew well enough to quantify, he agreed with Eileen's categorization. "How confident are you, Eileen?"

Eileen pursed her lips, deep in thought. "I cannot deny that some of my extended family—arguably an entire branch—see this motion as a huge financial opportunity." She shook her head. "Did you ever hear of my uncle, Tommy Alfredson?"

"From California?"

"Yes." Eileen sighed. "The second of Marshall's five grandchildren. The black sheep of the family. Tommy took his share of his inheritance to Hollywood in the forties. Dreamed of becoming a movie producer. Instead, he whittled away the money in no time." She scoffed. "Still, Tommy tore through three loveless marriages, thoughtfully leaving the board with a total of sixteen voting members, so far, and several more on the way as soon as they reach the age of twenty-one."

"I take it those will be sixteen votes in favor?"

"Two won't be coming, but of the other fourteen, twelve yesses and two unknowns." Eileen's smile faded. "One of Tommy's grandchildren is promoting the ludicrous notion that we can sell the Alfredson and still capitalize on its name."

"How so?"

"I've heard from a few board members that my second cousin, Jason Alfredson, has been looking for partners in a venture to set up a string of private Alfredson clinics. He wants to take advantage of our surname's association with excellence in health care."

"He seriously thinks that the family can gut the real Alfredson and still bastardize its name for profit?" William grumbled.

"I wouldn't worry too much," she reassured. "Jason has never been particularly successful or reliable in his previous schemes. I doubt anyone in my family will trust him with a dime of their money."

But William did feel worried. He leaned forward to relieve the pressure in his back. "Eileen, do you honestly believe we have enough votes to block this motion?"

"It will be close. *Very* close." Eileen reached for the page and turned it back to face her. She ran a finger down the list and then, satisfied, nodded. "I think we'll come out okay."

The pressure eased in his back and William smiled at Eileen. She reciprocated, and he noticed again how lovely her dark green eyes were.

"Of course, it will help if all stays calm and quiet until the meeting," she said. "Speaking of, is that infectious outbreak under control?"

He broke off eye contact. "No." He cleared his throat. "In fact, we have a bit of a situation."

"Situation, William?"

"It's . . . Senator Wilder."

"What about the senator?"

"He's become infected."

Her eyes widened and her mouth fell open. "Not with the superbug?"

William nodded. He updated Eileen as to Wilder's brittle condition.

"This is not good, William. Not good at all." She shook her head gravely. "He has to recover," she said, as if William somehow controlled the man's outcome.

"But if he doesn't?"

"Can you imagine the news stories? It would be a huge embarrassment to the Alfredson." She tapped the list on the desk. "Maybe enough to sway the undecided. I'm not sure my predictions will still be valid if the senator were to die."

A moment of gloomy silence fell between them. Finally, William said, "You know, we have lost a real opportunity here. Senator Wilder was on the verge of enrolling in one of my daughter-in-law's MS studies that is show-ing real promise."

"Yes, I meant to discuss that with you," Eileen said in a cooler tone.

William frowned. "Senator Wilder's enrollment?"

"No. Dr. Laidlaw's stem cell research."

"What about it?" His tone was more defensive than he intended.

"A number of my cousins—all of whom support our side in the vote—are quite religious. Stem cell research does not sit well with them."

William folded his arms across his chest. "Being on the board does not give them the power to dictate the research direction of this center."

"William, I know that," she said with a trace of irritability. "But maybe it would be best not to mention your daughter-in-law's research right now. We have enough to deal with, as is."

William sighed. "More than enough."

Eileen rose from her chair. She extended her hand and shook his. Unlike before, the gesture was purely businesslike. "Please keep me up to date about the senator and this outbreak."

As Eileen strode out of the room, William felt a twinge of regret. He reached a hand behind his searing back and began to rub, but it did no good. He fished in his desk drawer for the bottle of painkillers, realizing they would provide only minimal relief and possibly make him groggy.

A voice drifted in from the doorway. "Dad."

William dropped the pill bottle back into the drawer and slammed it shut. "Hello, Tyler."

"Bad time?" his son asked.

"No worse than others." William cocked his head. "I thought you broke out in a rash the moment you stepped foot inside an administrative building."

"I took an antihistamine before I came." Tyler walked toward him and sat in the chair that Eileen had just vacated. "Dad, you've got a little more color than last time I saw you."

William counted on the fact that, with his gradually dropping blood count, people closest to him were often the last to pick up on his draining color. His children tended to only notice after he had received another blood transfusion. "I got stuck in my car yesterday with the sunroof open. Maybe I got some sun."

"And you lived to tell?"

Despite his son's attempt at levity, William picked up on his troubled eyes. Tyler had inherited those blue eyes, like so many of his other features, from his mother. At times, the resemblance was so strong, William found it painful to look at him. "What's wrong?" he asked.

Tyler stared down at the desktop. "You remember that boy I told you about who had a leukemia recurrence?" he murmured.

"The spinal fluid?"

"Not 'the spinal fluid,' Dad. Nate Stafford."

"Did Nate die?"

Tyler nodded.

"I'm sorry."

All oncologists lost patients. It was inevitable. But William suspected something was different about this boy's death. He sensed it would be best to let Tyler explain on his own terms, so he simply waited.

"Dad, he . . . um . . . died while I was treating him."

"I assumed so."

"No. I mean literally. In the middle of a procedure I was performing."

"Oh."

Tyler went on to summarize Nate's doomed Vintazomab infusion. Nothing in his son's description sounded beyond the realm of an unforeseen procedural complication, yet William felt extremely uneasy. "This treatment is largely unproven," William said, trying to sound supportive. "You offered the family a last-ditch attempt to save their son's life."

Slouched even lower in his chair, Tyler merely shrugged.

"And you mentioned there were three deaths in the early trials of the drug." William lowered his voice. "You did warn the family of the potential side effects?"

Tyler nodded slightly.

"Then what is it, Tyler?"

"Nate's father is upset. Very upset."

"Any father would be."

"He blames me," Tyler said.

"It's not your fault."

"He claims that I didn't warn him of the real risks."

"But you just told me—"

"Dad, I didn't tell them that all three deaths in the previous trial occurred *only* in the subgroup who received Vintazomab directly into the spinal fluid."

Ice ran through William's veins. "You didn't?"

"The parents were so anxious." Tyler shrugged. "Every decision incapacitated them. Vintazomab was Nate's very last hope. And the cancer was in the spinal fluid. I had to get the medicine to it. The boy had no time to wait for his parents to agonize over a decision."

William wanted to accept his son's explanation. He willed himself to say something reassuring, but he was already envisioning the potential legal consequences. "So you didn't really get informed consent, did you?"

Tyler stiffened in his seat. "No. I guess not."

"What are the parents planning to do?"

"Aside from suing me?" Tyler said. "The father is threatening to go to the press."

"Damn it!" William slapped the desktop again. "Do you have any idea how lousy your timing is?"

"I'm sorry," Tyler grunted. "I didn't mean to inconvenience you. Next time, I'll try to schedule my medical legal disasters better."

Despite the back pain, William pushed himself up from his chair. "*Inconvenience me?*" He raised his voice to a near shout. "This hospital is teetering on the brink. And now you show up to give it a push at the moment it needs one least."

Tyler jumped to his feet. "That's all that worries you about what happened to Nate? How his death reflects on your precious fucking hospital?"

William shook his head angrily. "The hospital might mean nothing to you, but I have invested my life into it. And so did many others in our family."

"Romanticize it all you want!" Tyler snapped. "It's just bricks and stones. But Nate was a sweet kid with a whole life ahead of him."

In William's mind, all the crises suddenly melded into an insurmountable wall that was about to topple onto the Alfredson and erase a lifetime of work. In his heart, he knew he should try to console his son, but he felt so infuriated and helpless that he could not control himself. "Are you so pigheaded that you can't see it, Tyler? The Alfredson represents hope to thousands of Nates."

Tyler just glared back, unwavering.

"We provide them a level of care that almost no one else can. And we do so free of charge for families who couldn't possibly afford it elsewhere." William jabbed angrily at the window. "But if the board votes to sell the Alfredson to some private interest, it will become just another for-profit hospital. This country is teeming with those. What will happen to the other children like Nate then? Tell me that, Tyler!"

Without answering, his son slowly turned and walked for the door. Reaching the doorway, he looked over his shoulder at William. The bitterness had left Tyler's features. His eyes were clouded with naked hurt. He opened his mouth as if to speak, but nothing came out. He stared helplessly at his father for a moment longer and then turned away.

## 21

Nikki Salazar imagined she could feel the sunlight activating the vitamin D under her glistening skin. The hard rollerblading in the summerlike heat and brightness was what she needed after having spent so much time indoors, working overtime shifts. She didn't need the extra income, but she had relied on the added work to distract her from her personal turmoil. Her fitful sleep and those extra shifts, with all that time spent on her feet, had only aggravated the throb of her collapsed vertebrae that had dogged her since the car accident. The anti-inflammatories weren't touching the pain.

Two days before, after weeks of resisting, Nikki had dug out the last bottle of hydromorphone tablets from the back of her bathroom cupboard. She had hung on to the bottle "in case of emergency," despite her Narcotics Anonymous sponsor's repeated warnings of the foolishness of doing so.

After almost three sober years, Nikki was surprised by how easy it was to pop that first pink tablet. She swallowed it without regret or remorse, rationalizing that nothing else would touch her pain. And it did help. She attributed the dull sweet euphoria that followed to nothing more than a natural response to finally receiving some decent pain relief. Keen not to wait for the throb in her back to recur, Nikki popped two more pills within four hours of the first. By the time she headed out for her rollerblade, she was pain-free and had already consumed fourteen of those fifty pills.

Since the car accident, her vertebrae couldn't bear the impact of jogging, which used to be her favorite exercise. Nikki had bought a mountain bike but, tired of the mud and the spills, soon gave up on trail riding. She stumbled onto rollerblading two years earlier only after being goaded into it by a blind date (her one and only) who wanted to establish how adventurous and fun he was. Though the date was a complete bust, Nikki was hooked from the first strides. Rollerblading had since become her primary means of exercise and her best stress reliever.

She saw another advantage in skating, too; it was one of the few sports her former fiancé, Glen, had never pursued. Nikki didn't need another activity that reminded her of his absence. The memories waxed and waned, but lately she had thought of Glen often. Especially after Nate Stafford's death.

She found it strange that a little boy could remind her of a grown man, but the more she considered the association, the less odd it seemed. They were both baseball fanatics. They had both died far too young. And even at thirty-two, Glen had been just a little boy at heart. He could be so annoyingly immature—unreliable, overly spontaneous, and unself-conscious to the point of embarrassing—yet he had such a big heart. He could read her moods like no one else; without prompting, he knew when she needed an encouraging word or to be taken out dancing or to be just left alone. Nikki doubted she would ever again find anyone who loved her like Glen did.

*And certainly not a man who is already married*, Nikki thought, still embarrassed at the memory of how she had thrown herself at Tyler McGrath that night at O'Doole's Pub.

Before Tyler, Nikki had never felt the slightest spark for any of the young—or sometimes middle-aged or even older—doctors who had shown interest in her. In the first year of working with Tyler, she had resisted the effect of his blue eyes and disarming smile. Unlike several other SFU nurses, who gushed over and flirted with him as though they were still in the ninth grade, she had steadfastly maintained a professional distance. Nikki couldn't help but admire his bedside manner, though. His patients and their parents routinely bonded with Tyler in a way she rarely saw with the other physicians. And while he was more serious in temperament than her happy-go-lucky former fiancé, sometimes even brooding, Tyler showed a few glimpses of Glen's irreverent antiestablishment streak.

That night at O'Doole's, the celebratory mood, nostalgic music, and warmth of their dance floor contact had all conspired to cloud her judgment. With their bodies pressed together and his sinewy arms wrapped around her, she had lost herself in a moment. It had gone way too far and ended too abruptly. At the time, she felt humiliated, confused, and hurt by his sudden departure. As those feelings abated, she realized he had made the right choice for both of them. An affair would have only led to more emotional upheaval at work. And she had lived through enough of that during her days of painkiller addiction and pill theft.

Every time Nikki had seen Tyler since O'Doole's, the awkwardness pooled anew and she hid behind a frosty aloof front, behaving as though she resented him for his actions. She wanted to let him know otherwise—to tell him how much she missed their friendship at work—but she hadn't found the right moment or mustered the nerve yet.

On the way home from rollerblading, she felt a new twinge in her back and the growing desire for another hydromorphone tablet. Suspecting she would need more than her remaining pills, Nikki considered how best to extract a prescription from her doctor, who was well aware of her addiction history. She considered trying the local walk-in clinic instead.

Once home, Nikki polished off an entire carton of orange juice, drinking it straight from the container—her one habit that used to infuriate Glen. She permitted herself one more tablet of hydromorphone before work. She registered a hint of alarm at how frantically she grabbed for the bottle and dug out a pill.

She ran a hot bath and soaked in the tub until she felt the narcotic kick in and her worries drain away. She toweled off and slipped into a set of mauve scrubs that complemented her improved mood.

Nikki arrived on the sixth-floor unit twenty minutes early for her afternoon shift. She had hoped to catch up on her charting, but before reaching the nursing station, she bumped into Keisha Berry's parents standing hand in hand in the hallway outside their daughter's room.

"Keisha's gone for a chest X-ray," Jonah explained.

"That's routine, isn't it?" Maya asked anxiously.

"Very." Nikki laid a hand on Maya's shoulder and squeezed reassuringly. "You know us, Maya, we always think the roof will cave in if we stop running tests on our patients for even one second."

Maya nodded, though the worry clung to her features.

"How's Keisha today?" Nikki asked.

"She's doing better," Jonah said. "The headache is almost gone with those steroid medicines. And she's getting her appetite back."

"She's even drawing again," Maya added.

"That's a good sign. And good news for me. She's promised to draw me a tiger and a puppy." Nikki winked. "I hope she puts a fence between 'em."

Maya's face creased deeper. "But the steroids are only making her feel better. They're not really fighting off her cancer, are they?"

"They're shrinking the swelling," Nikki said, while evading the question. "That's important."

Nikki had noticed a marked change in Maya over the past days. The helpless anxiety that was so common among the parents of children on the SFU now flamed in her eyes, too. At first, Nikki had assumed Keisha's clinical deterioration had ignited her anxiety, but the day before Maya had made it clear that Nate Stafford's death was responsible. "That poor boy had the same type of cancer as our Keisha, didn't he?" she had said.

Nikki tried to release Maya's shoulder, but the woman reached out and grabbed her hand so that all three of them were physically linked. "Nikki?"

"Yes, Maya?"

"I don't understand this . . . um . . . delay."

Nikki frowned. "What delay?"

"Well, we signed all those consent forms days ago for the experimental treatment protocol. Dr. McGrath seemed to be in such a hurry to get Keisha going on this Vintazomab. And now . . . well, it's like he's changed his mind or something."

Still holding his wife's hand, Jonah shot her a cautioning look. "Now, Maya, Dr. McGrath knows what he's up to. He already explained why he had to wait to start treatment. He needs to get all the right approval first."

"It's just that he was so eager before," Maya said.

Nikki understood exactly what explained Tyler's reticence, but she kept it to herself. "I know the wait is so frustrating," she soothed. "Dr. McGrath has to follow the hospital protocol."

"That's right, baby," Jonah said.

"I just hope he gets it soon," Maya muttered.

Nikki freed her hand and, with a promise to visit Keisha within the hour, continued on to the nursing station. Inside the enclosure, she spotted Tyler sitting at the back desk reviewing lab work on a computer screen. She sat down in the chair beside his.

At the sound, he spun in his seat to face her. "Hey." He showed her a tired grin.

"Hey, yourself." She felt a sudden pang of sympathy for Tyler and decided against adding to his worries by telling him about his sister's apparent migraine and evasive attitude in the courtyard. "How's it going?"

"Busy." He shrugged. "I'm on call, and we have three new admissions to the ward today."

She nodded. "I just ran into Keisha's parents."

"Oh?"

"Maya was asking me about the Vintazomab protocol."

"She's anxious to get Keisha going on it, huh?" he sighed.

"As in yesterday."

Tyler rubbed his eyes. "Nikki, I'm supposed to run all experimental protocols past my colleagues at our clinical rounds to get their approval before proceeding."

"That meeting was this morning, wasn't it?"

Tyler looked down and spoke to the countertop. "I didn't put Keisha's case forward today," he said quietly.

"You didn't?"

"For one thing, the department head, Alice Wright, suspended the Vintazomab trial at our site pending a mortality review of Nate's death. And it was the right thing to do, too."

Nikki nodded, but she didn't buy his explanation. She knew from first-hand experience that the oncologists had considerable leeway in deciding the best treatment for their patients. She suspected Tyler was using the technicality as an excuse. "What else?" she asked gently.

He looked up at her, defeat clouding his features. "Craig Stafford came to see me."

Nikki tensed. "He was angry, I take it?"

"I sensed that, yeah." Tyler grunted a humorless laugh. "Nikki, he's been doing all kinds of Internet searches on the Vintazomab study. He knows that the deaths were exclusively linked with the kids who got intrathecal doses of the med."

"In other words, the very sickest patients! The ones whose leukemia had already spread to their brains." She shook her head in frustration. "That only makes sense, Tyler."

"Not to Craig, it doesn't. He is going to sue me." He cleared his throat. "And that's not the worst of it."

"No?"

"He plans to go to the press."

Nikki threw her hands up. "For what? You were just trying to do the best for his son."

"But it didn't work out that way." His chin dropped lower. "I withheld information from them. He's within his rights."

Eager to ease his pain somehow, she reached out and gripped his forearm. "Listen to me, Tyler. We both know this is how Craig responds to loss. He's been furious with the world ever since Nate was diagnosed. He's lashed out at every step of the way, always desperate for somewhere to place all that blame. That's what this is about. It has nothing to do with informed consent."

Tyler cracked a grateful smile. "Maybe."

"Definitely," she said. "You can't let Craig's overdeveloped sense of vengeance affect the care of other patients."

"I have to learn from my mistakes," he said in a subdued tone.

She met his gaze without releasing her grip on his arm. "So you'll be more careful with the consent next time around. But you didn't make any mistakes with the treatment."

His expression softened slightly, but he didn't reply.

"Tyler, aside from Vintazomab, are there any other possible protocols to start Keisha on?"

"Nikki, you know as well as I do." He sighed. "She's failed her bone marrow transplant and multiple rounds of chemo."

"So you have no option but to start her on Vintazomab."

"No. I suppose not."

"Tyler?" a woman's voice called from behind them.

Nikki immediately released his arm and glanced over her shoulder. Though she had never met Jill Laidlaw, she recognized her from sightings in the cafeteria and parking lot. But Nikki had never been in such close proximity to her. Jill had high cheekbones and striking blue eyes. The blond neurologist wore a sleeveless silky blue shirt and black hip-huggers so chic that Nikki felt self-conscious in her hospital-issue scrubs. Not only was she beautiful, but up close she appeared younger.

Jill's eyes lingered on Nikki's hand for a moment, long enough to convey that she didn't appreciate the way the nurse was touching her husband's arm, before she broke into a smile and extended her hand. "I'm Tyler's wife, Jill."

"Nikki," she said, meeting Jill's cool palm.

Tyler rose from his seat. He smiled awkwardly at his wife. "Hey, Jill, what brings you by?"

"I work here at the Alfredson," she said with a hint of sarcasm. "Matter of fact, just a couple of buildings over."

Tyler eyed his wife with an expression Nikki couldn't discern. "And it's only taken you fifteen months to circumvent those buildings," he said.

"Touché." Jill smiled. Her voice dropped lower. "Tyler, did you hear about the senator?"

Nikki knew she was referring to Calvin Wilder. The hospital rumor mill had been working overtime with the news of how the VIP had fallen ill from the scourge sweeping through the complex.

"I heard," Tyler said.

"He was just about to consent to my study," Jill said.

Tyler shook his head.

"He's a very decent man, Ty."

Tyler reached out and touched the back of his wife's hand. "I'm sorry, hon."

Nikki felt an irrational pang of jealousy. She had a sudden longing for another hydromorphone pill. Fighting off a blush, she backed away from the couple. "I've got meds to dispense," she said.

## 22

Lorna stared down at the cubes of ice rattling around the bottom of her empty glass. The third drink had hit her hard. The oak-paneled room swam a little, and her words had begun to slur. She resolved to resist another refill, despite Dot's coaxing. She could not afford to have her judgment impaired further, especially since her great-aunt seemed to be feeding off the alcohol, growing more animated and articulate with each fresh glass.

Lorna cradled her glass close to her chest, trying to hide its emptiness. "So it's that simple, is it? Marshall Alfredson built the hospital to appease his daughter and push Evan McGrath out of the city? End of story."

Dot laughed. "My *Gawd*, when is life ever *that* simple?"

"So what happened?"

Dot's eyes twinkled with amusement. "If poor Evan McGrath thought 1895 was an eventful year, nothing could have prepared him for the year that followed."

"What do you mean?"

Dot rolled her hand and watched her chunky gold bracelet slide down her arm. "Olivia married Arthur Grovenor on New Year's Eve in front of two hundred guests as planned. I doubt that started Evan's year off on the right foot."

"Olivia was the love of his life, wasn't she?"

"Whatever the hell *that* means." Dot sighed. "She was undoubtedly the love of the moment."

Remembering Dot had plowed through four failed marriages, Lorna understood her great-aunt's skepticism.

"On a more promising note," Dot went on, "my grandfather was not a man to dillydally. The plans for the Alfredson Clinic were drawn up quickly by the *noted* Seattle architect, Samuel Firestone. By early May, Marshall's laborers had cleared enough trees off the land to break ground."

"Did Evan and Marshall agree on the design?"

Dot absentmindedly laid her hand on the back of the fornicating ceramic samurai on the end table beside her. "Those two agreed on very little, but I don't believe Evan was given, or even asked for, much input into the clinic's design."

"Really?" Lorna frowned. "On his dream project?"

Dot shook her head. "Virginia had not fared well that winter. By spring, she was bed-bound. Evan hardly left her side. I imagine he had little time for anything else."

"Was she dying?"

Ignoring the question, Dot nodded toward Lorna's glass. "The rate these glasses leak is *frankly* abominable. Let me patch yours for you."

Tempted as she was, Lorna covered the top of her glass. "I think I've finally stemmed my leak."

"Suit yourself, darling." Dot sprang to her feet and marched off toward the bar.

Lorna marveled at the spryness of her tiger-stripe-clad ancient relative. It occurred to her that longevity ran in the Alfredson family. And yet she remembered that Olivia had not lived very long. She watched Dot pour a generous helping of vodka with a steady hand. She added a small splash of tonic and a couple of ice cubes to the glass, but manners aside, the old girl might as well have drunk directly from the bottle for what little dilution she achieved.

"Dot, how did Olivia die?"

Her great-aunt took a sip and nodded her satisfaction. "Spring of 1896 was an overwrought time for poor old Evan," she said, again evading Lorna's question.

"How so?"

"Because, darling, the events that would shape the rest of his life all happened that spring."

---

After losing Virginia, Evan assumed he would never remarry. He relocated to Oakdale for the sole purpose of helping to oversee the construction of the clinic, and instead met the love of his life there.
—*The Alfredson: The First Hundred Years* by Gerald Fenton Naylor

Sleep deprived and emotionally numb, Evan McGrath stood and watched the men, horses, and steam-powered machines burrow deeper through the rocky soil where the clinic's foundation would soon be laid.

Four days earlier, Evan had stood by a different hole and watched another crew, but those men were filling, not digging, and the plot was much smaller—big enough only for Virginia's casket. From a medical point of view, the only unexpected feature of his wife's terminal pneumonia was how long she had lasted. However, when Evan saw that final breath catch in her throat and the light extinguish from her eyes, he felt as shocked as if Ginny had died in a fall from a horse.

The attendees had filled the small church for her subdued funeral service, but only a handful, including Mrs. Shirley and Moses Brown, braved the torrential rain and watched the grave diggers race to backfill the plot before the loose soil turned into a mud bath. Evan's sudden tears had surprised and embarrassed him. He cried for more than just Virginia's loss. He mourned the time and opportunity her illness had stolen from them both, and the children they could never have. He also wept for Ginny's final years of suffering and the indignity that Fate had cruelly saddled on her. And he spent a little of his sorrow on himself and the happiness of which he had also been cheated.

Now, as Evan stood and watched the laborers excavate, he wondered what was to become of his life. He had invested so much energy into caring for Virginia, especially in the last few months when she had grown so helpless. As a doctor, he had long known that she had no hope of recovery, but as a husband, he had never given up. And while Virginia's death might have been a mercy for her, he had difficulty imagining life without her.

Respecting Evan's moment of introspection, Moses Brown stood a couple yards away and watched the crew at work. Wearing the same undersized suit as always, Moses had accompanied Evan on the indirect four-and-a-half-hour train ride—punctuated by multiple stops—from Seattle to Oakdale.

Evan had marveled at Moses's handiwork in patching, and improving, the rickety hospital on Fifth Avenue; the man was a brilliant carpenter who innately understood all aspects of building. Though Evan had little interest in and even less aptitude for construction, he did not trust Marshall enough to leave the project entirely in the hands of his men. He envisioned a building that would survive a hundred years or more, and he had brought Moses to the site to help ensure that it was built to last.

Evan turned to his friend. "Moses, how deep do they need to go to lay the foundation?"

Moses stroked his chin with an index finger as he considered the question. "For a three-story brick building of this size, I expect they'll have to dig out a few more feet still."

Evan had originally envisioned a five-story structure. Though he had never ridden an elevator in his life, he had read that they were all the rage in new buildings in New York. He had hoped to see one installed at the clinic, to transport the bed- and wheelchair-bound patients between floors. Samuel Firestone had argued that it was wildly impractical and too expensive for such a remote site. Marshall agreed with his architect and arbitrarily set the height of the clinic at three stories with only stairways between the floors.

Marshall had assumed more of a hands-on approach to the project than Evan anticipated. The businessman pored over the plans with Firestone, arguing over even the finer architectural details such as the window sizes and finishing. Most of Marshall's decisions were unilateral. Evan had put up little opposition because Virginia had grown so ill during the days when the plans were being finalized, and he was too consumed with her health to focus on anything else. Evan now regretted allowing Marshall to take absolute control of the clinic's design. He intended to make up for the oversight by remaining nearby as it was built.

"I am surprised Mr. Alfredson has not shown up here to tell everyone what to do and how to do it," Evan muttered, as much to himself as Moses.

Moses glanced at Evan out of the corner of his eye. "Dr. McGrath, I expect Mr. Alfredson doesn't think he can leave his daughter right now."

"No?" Evan kept his tone casual though his heart began to thud at the mention of Olivia. "Why is that?"

Moses looked in both directions and then dropped his voice to a hush. "Well, Theodora told me that Mrs. Grovenor is having early labor pains. And she's supposed to stay in bed."

Bile welled in his throat, as Evan fought to keep the surprise from his voice and the pain off his expression. "Olivia is pregnant?" he said. "I had not heard."

Moses shuffled on the spot. "I'm sorry . . . um . . . Dr. McGrath, I thought you already knew that Mrs. Grovenor is with child."

Not trusting his voice to cooperate, Evan simply shook his head.

"The baby is due to arrive in the early fall," Moses said. "But now with the pains, Theodora is worried the child will come too early. Dangerously so."

"I see." Evan swallowed hard. He did not understand why he was so shocked. Women were supposed to become pregnant once married. But the idea of Olivia carrying another man's child ripped open a wound that had never really healed. There was something heartbreakingly final about her pregnancy. It made Evan feel utterly alone in the world.

"We don't need no audience here." A gruff voice from nearby pulled Evan from his despair.

Ire rising even before he located the source, Evan swiveled his head to see the squat, beady-eyed foreman, Patrick Flynn, marching nearer and shaking a finger at them. The man wore dirty overalls with numerous tools dangling from his belt, and the wooden shaft of his hammer swung back and forth across his hip with each bounding step closer.

"What did you just say?" Evan snapped.

"You heard me," Flynn croaked. "Me and the boys know how to put up a brick shithouse like this one. We could do it in our sleep. We don't need no soft-handed doctor watching over us with his own nigger in tow."

Moses didn't show a trace of reaction, but Evan straightened upright. His lip curled into a sneer, but he was too angry to speak.

"We don't need you here," Flynn went on. "And we don't want you watching over us no more. So why don't you take that nigger pet of yours—"

Evan's recent losses all melded into a fury he had never known. He swung his arm wildly and hit the foreman full force in the mouth with a cocked fist.

Flynn shrieked in surprise and pain. Before he could even raise his hands up to his defense, Evan dove forward and knocked the man to the ground. He struck and punched wildly, but the foreman had quick reflexes. Most of Evan's blows smashed futilely into the dirt. The agile little bulldog soon squirmed free of Evan's grip and managed to land a few punches to the side of the doctor's head. Then Flynn flipped him over onto his back, pinning his surprisingly heavy frame into Evan's chest.

"You lily-livered pansy," Flynn hissed. Bloody spittle flew as the foreman's sour breath filled the air between them. "I'm going to teach you a lesson you didn't get in school," he said as he elbowed Evan in the jaw.

The pain only fueled Evan's rage. He heaved up with all his might and managed to roll Flynn over. The momentum sent them going side-over-side for three or four turns, stopping only when they reached the edge of the pit.

Evan heard the shouts of the workers, who were dropping their tools and hurrying over to watch the fight, but he ignored them. Capitalizing on his size advantage, he was able to pin Flynn's arms back by the wrists and squeeze hard.

His anger subsided as he held the squirming little man in place. "Apologize to Mr. Brown, and I will free you."

"All right, all right," Flynn panted. "Just ease up on my wrists before you snap them. I need 'em for building."

Evan relaxed his grip slightly. Flynn looked over to Moses as if to speak. Suddenly he spun his head back and spat a moist bloody gob straight into Evan's eye. As Evan recoiled in surprise and disgust, Flynn launched his bent knee into Evan's crotch.

The agony winded the doctor. Before he could catch a breath, Flynn had slipped out of the hold and scrambled to his knees. With a flurry of punches and kicks, the foreman wound up kneeling over Evan. Flynn drew his hammer from his tool belt as though he were a gunfighter. He held it cocked above his head, ready to swing. His small eyes were ablaze with hatred. "You have this coming, McGrath."

Evan's arms flew up to protect his head. Shielding his eyes, he endured a moment of blind anticipation. Nothing happened. He lowered a hand and saw that the hammer was suspended over the foreman's head. It took Evan a moment to realize that Moses was holding back the head of the hammer with one hand while his other arm wrapped tightly around Flynn's neck.

"I don't think you want to do that, Mr. Flynn," Moses said calmly, as he wrenched the hammer free from Flynn's hand.

Eyes bulging with fear, Flynn choked, "No."

"I think all your differences have been settled now," Moses said in a tone that was almost soothing. "Wouldn't you agree, Mr. Flynn?"

Flynn nodded as best he could while trapped in the headlock.

"Dr. McGrath and I will be on our way now," Moses said, as he released Flynn from the headlock.

Flynn sputtered and gasped. He hopped to his feet and quickly backpedaled away from Moses and the pit. Evan was in too much pain to move. Moses reached down and with one hand pulled him to his feet.

The shouts and catcalls from the other laborers had grown louder as many of them collected around the two interlopers. The men now formed a semicircle bordered by the edge of the pit. Several glared menacingly. Evan realized that if they were to turn on them, Moses and he might wind up as a permanent part of the clinic's foundation.

Moses acted as though he were oblivious to the angry mob encircling them. He carefully dusted off his jacket sleeves and pant legs. He tossed Flynn's hammer at the feet of the still-coughing foreman. Then, grabbing hold of Evan's elbow, he leisurely led the doctor away from the pit. They still had to pass through the line of laborers who now stood shoulder-to-shoulder. But Brown's unflappable poise had an almost hypnotic effect, and the men parted for them. Even Flynn said nothing as they trudged away from the site.

The next day, Moses Brown returned to Seattle to resume his job at the Catholic hospital, while Evan remained in Oakdale. He soon received a terse letter from Marshall Alfredson, requesting that he "refrain from launching unprovoked assaults on the builders, as it might lead to unnecessary construction delays." Though Evan continued to return to the building site daily, he had no further run-ins with the workers; not even Flynn. They largely ignored him, treating Evan as though he were an immovable landscape feature that they had to work around.

Evan recognized he served no real purpose in Oakdale, but he could not bring himself to return to Seattle. The memory of Virginia's death was still too vivid. And he was unwilling to risk the emotional trauma from a chance encounter with the pregnant Olivia, hoping that maintaining a safe distance from her might ease his heartache. But it didn't.

Evan even found work for himself in Oakdale. The only other doctor in town, an ancient Southerner named Dr. Miles Green, was effectively crippled by severe angina and welcomed the younger doctor's help.

One day, as they stood in their dusty office in the late afternoon, Green offered Evan a sip of whisky from his hip flask. Evan felt obliged to have a drink, but the firewater went down like razor blades and he had to fight back a gag.

"Country doctoring isn't quite the same as the big city. Would you not agree, Dr. McGrath?" Green mused in his Southern twang.

"I would," Evan croaked.

"No nurses. No hospital. Hell, we are our own apothecary." Green assembled an imaginary ball with his weathered hands. "Patch 'em up as best we can. That's all we can offer these folks. And that's all they expect of us, too."

Evan liked the old doctor, but he could not hold his tongue. "With respect, Dr. Green, I think your attitude is outdated. I believe all doctors are obliged to offer a high level of care based on current knowledge and the most sound practice."

Green took another sip from his flask. When he pulled it from his lips, his watery eyes had lit with amusement. "Young doctors!" He laughed. "I remember what it was like to be one, myself. All that solemn passion and blind faith. How I wish it lasted."

Green held out the whisky, but Evan waved it away. The old man toasted him with the flask. "I do hope I live to behold this revolutionary clinic of yours, Dr. McGrath. I surely do."

Nine days after their conversation Green dropped dead of a heart attack. Evan assumed medical care of all residents of Oakdale. He enjoyed his role of small-town doctor, and it still allowed him time to concentrate on shaping the direction of the Alfredson Clinic.

Evan wrote letters to every distinguished physician, surgeon, and medical researcher of whom he knew, inviting them to Oakdale to participate in the new venture. Predictably, he received reams of polite refusals, but he was not dissuaded or discouraged. Within a month of his campaign, he was elated to receive his first letter of acceptance from a noted intestinal specialist practicing in Portland, Oregon, who was seeking a "new challenge." As the word leaked out, other positive responses began to trickle in from doctors as far away as Chicago. By the end of the summer, Evan had commitments from fourteen doctors—though he had yet to work out with Marshall how they would be paid—with specialty interests as diverse as ophthalmology, urology, pulmonology, and pathology.

Evan had been unable to sell his home in Seattle, whose real estate market still stagnated in the wake of the depression that followed the global financial panic of 1893. He could only afford to rent a room in a quaint Queen Anne–style house on the outskirts of Oakdale. It was owned by a pleasant, though nosy, spinster in her early fifties named Stella Hathaway.

An excellent cook, Stella prepared all his meals. Within a few weeks of moving in, Evan noticed that his clothes no longer hung off him as though he were a drying rack.

One day in early July, the short rotund woman excitedly announced that her niece, Grace, would be joining them for dinner. "She is a working woman," Stella whispered with a deference that verged on awe. "A school-teacher."

Returning to the house that evening, Evan was surprised by how much effort his landlady had put into her niece's visit. She had lit decorative red candles in all the rooms. A white tablecloth covered the worn pine table, while crystal and silver flatware replaced the usual plain cups and cutlery.

Stella was atwitter with excitement and nerves as she led her niece into the living room to introduce her to Evan. Grace Hathaway wore a simple blue dress with a bow tied behind her waist. Plump, but not fat, the twenty-two-year-old had a round face grooved with faint acne scars. Her pleasant gray eyes complemented her kind smile, but the feature that struck Evan most was her flaming red hair.

Though reserved at first, Grace soon relaxed in his presence. She had an endearing tendency of hanging on every word spoken. And Evan found her easy soft laugh infectious.

After a feast of fried chicken, garden vegetables, homemade bread, and mashed potatoes, Stella plated generous portions of freshly baked apple pie. Between mouthfuls, Evan asked, "Miss Hathaway, where do you teach?"

She smiled. "In a small schoolhouse near Everett."

Evan knew of the town sixty miles north of Seattle, but he had never visited. "What sort of school is it?"

"Not much of one, I am afraid, Dr. McGrath." Grace uttered one of her infectious laughs. "A simple one-room school, two miles outside of town. The children all live on nearby farms. I teach first through seventh grade."

Evan swallowed a mouthful of pie. "That must be a challenge," he said.

"Indeed. The older children can be real rascals." Grace chuckled again.

"I fear turning to face the chalkboard. I never know what sort of projectiles will be launched at my back."

Evan laughed heartily. "I am afraid I was exactly that sort of a trouble-maker during my school days. And I have the permanently scarred knuck-les to prove it."

"I find that hard to believe, Dr. McGrath." She glanced at his hands as though checking for herself.

Evan lowered his fork. "May I ask what drew you to teaching, Miss Hathaway?"

Grace blushed. "I love children," she said with a slight shrug. "And I love to see them learn. To grow. It is the most rewarding experience to watch a child become a reader, Dr. McGrath."

Evan nodded. "Yes, I imagine it would be."

"And medicine, Dr. McGrath?" she said expectantly.

"I am no good at anything else," he said flatly.

Stella, who had silently beamed in her seat as she drank in the playful-ness between the other two, spoke up. "Dr. McGrath is building a special new hospital outside of Oakdale."

"How wonderful," Grace said. "What will it be like?"

"It will not be that special." Evan shrugged modestly, but he went on to describe it to her in excited detail.

"It sounds more than special, Dr. McGrath. I have such admiration for medical practitioners." Her fair skin flushed deeper. "I have read every book by and about Miss Florence Nightingale. She is so brave and wonderful. I would never have the nerve to do anything like that." She giggled.

Evan stared at Grace, transfixed by her red hair. "What you do is noble, too, Olivia—excuse me—I mean . . ." He stuttered and reddened. "Miss Hathaway."

By the time the plates were cleared, Evan realized that he would marry Grace Hathaway.

*23*

Tyler gazed out the east-facing window at Le Bistro and drank in the panoramic mountain view. The Cascades broke through the low-lying clouds and seemed to hover over the town of Oakdale, as though suspended in the sky like Mount Olympus. Across the table, his grandmother, Liesbeth Vanderhof, was too preoccupied with her meal to notice the scenery. The frail woman struggled to cut another bite of her salmon.

Two years earlier, Liesbeth had been forced to move into an assisted-living elder care home because her rheumatoid arthritis had gnarled her hands and fingers so badly that she could no longer cook, clean, or launder for herself. The widow seemed perfectly happy with her new home, where the meals and cleaning were provided for her. However, despite her busy social life there, Liesbeth refused to entertain anyone from "the outside" at the residence. "It's too pitiful," she once told Tyler in her laughing voice. "I would never drag my family to some nursing home to see me. I don't want them to remember me like that."

Her modern building could have easily been mistaken for an ordinary apartment complex, but Liesbeth was nothing if not proud. Despite her arthritic knees she insisted on walking the three blocks, regardless of the weather, to catch a bus to meet Tyler for lunch. One of the few luxuries she did allow herself was fine food. Le Bistro was her favorite. Over the past year, Tyler and she had fallen into a standing monthly lunch date. Initially she had tried to pay for every meal but, when he threatened to walk, she compromised on alternating turns at picking up the tab.

Tyler looked forward to lunches with his grandmother. His deep affection for her aside, Liesbeth provided a direct link to the memory of his grandfather and, especially, his mother. They had died within three years of each other. Though they were arguably the two most influential people in his life, Tyler had trouble imagining how much Liesbeth must have missed her husband and only daughter. Despite the loss, and her debilitating arthritis, Liesbeth still managed to maintain a sunny disposition and upbeat outlook. Tyler wished he had inherited more of her resilience.

Wearing a pale sweater and black pants, Liesbeth had pinned her medium-length gray hair back with two hairclips. She possessed sharp Dutch facial features with high cheekbones and an upturned nose. Her kindly face was weathered with the same laugh lines Tyler remembered from childhood, but she never seemed to age further. And her laugh was as quick and vibrant as ever. Only her hands bore the brunt of her eighty-six years. They were knobby, swollen, and angled grotesquely at the knuckles and finger joints. Tyler was surprised they could still hold a fork and knife at all.

Noticing his gaze on her hands, Liesbeth put down the cutlery and clasped her hands together self-consciously. "It's a blessing, really." She spoke with a remnant of a Dutch accent. "They might not be pleasant to look at, but they do not hurt like they used to. The disease, my doctor tells me, is now 'burned out.'" She laughed. "Much like the victim herself."

Tyler grinned. "Hardly, Liesbeth." He had been calling her by her first name for as long as he could remember. She never wanted to be called Grandma, or Oma, claiming the title made her feel too old. "You're an inspiration."

"You have always been such a little charmer. Even when you were five years old. Remember? You told me I was as beautiful as a queen." She shook a crooked finger playfully at him. "Of course, you always wanted more licorice back then."

Tyler laughed. "Got any on you now?"

Liesbeth ignored the joke. Her brow furrowed and she gazed at him for a long moment. "Tyler, what is bothering you today?"

Surprised, his hand stopped halfway to the coffee cup. He thought he had donned a convincingly brave face for their lunch. Of course, his grandmother had always been eerily insightful. "It's been a tough week at work," he said.

"Ah. I still remember how Maarten would bring his work home with him."

Tyler leaned forward in his seat. "That's something I always wondered about. When Opa began in the 1950s, pediatric oncology wasn't a real specialty. Chemotherapy and radiation therapy were just in their infancy. It was all wild guesswork. And the most common childhood cancer, acute lymphoblastic leukemia, was almost—"

"They all died, didn't they?" Liesbeth interrupted with a knowing nod.

"Ninety-five percent of them, anyway. Now, it's fewer than ten percent." Tyler shook his head. "I can't imagine how discouraging it must have been for Opa."

Liesbeth viewed him quizzically. "Maarten never expected to save those children."

"He didn't?"

"He would have loved to have saved them all, of course," she said with a small sigh. "But your grandfather was a realist. He committed his life to easing their pain, not prolonging their lives. He couldn't bear to see a child suffer. And in those days, some children used to suffer horribly in their final days with cancer."

"But Opa became a pioneer of leukemia treatment. Under his guidance, the Alfredson boasted the highest survival rate in the country."

"Yes, of course. When Maarten saw that he could offer hope to these children . . . it changed everything. That was later, after he had already established his practice."

Tyler smiled. "He's still so revered, you know?"

Liesbeth's eyes lit with a hint of pride, but she laughed it away. "Maarten always hated that."

"Hated what?"

"The accolades. The attention. It embarrassed him. He never considered himself more special than anyone else at the hospital." She shrugged. "Perhaps less so."

"I can relate."

Liesbeth pursed her lips. "This is so very unlike you, Tyler. You have always thrived on attention."

He sipped the bitter, rich coffee. "There's good attention, and then there's the other kind."

Liesbeth viewed her grandson silently.

"Something went very wrong at the hospital."

Liesbeth waited.

"A boy that I treated for leukemia . . . ," he began.

Tyler had never discussed his work with his grandmother. He certainly had no intention of sharing the specifics of the Nate Stafford case, but once he started he could not stop himself. As he spoke, he realized how good it felt to unload to her. Liesbeth said nothing, but her forgiving eyes brought Tyler unexpected solace.

"I doubt Opa would have fumbled it as badly as I did," he concluded.

She shook her head. "Tyler, you have no idea how much it all haunted him."

"Liesbeth, his judgment was legendary. People still speak of him with awe."

"*People* never know the whole truth, do they?"

"What was the truth?"

"Your Opa hardly slept. He took all kinds of sleeping pills. It didn't help much. If ever Maarten did fall asleep, most nights he woke in a cold sweat." She shook her head again. "The nightmares . . ."

Tyler shook his head. "I always just thought of him as a grandfather— the best one a boy could have—but I had no idea just how important a doctor he was until I started medical school."

Liesbeth shifted in her seat. A vaguely uncomfortable look flitted across her face but then was gone. "Listen, Tyler, do you know how Maarten came to America?"

"You came together from The Hague right after the war, didn't you?"

She shook her head. "Maarten was eight years older. We did not know each other in Holland. I came to Seattle in 1946, to live with my aunt and uncle. I met Maarten here, not in Europe." She paused. "He came before me. As a war refugee."

"A refugee?"

"Maarten was Jewish."

"You're kidding!" Evan sputtered. " 'Vanderhof' doesn't sound Jewish."

"It isn't. He changed it from Hertzog. He didn't want people to know."

"Why not?"

"A young Jew from occupied Holland . . ."

Tyler stiffened in his seat. "Wait a minute. Was Opa in the camps?"

Liesbeth nodded.

"Which one?"

She hesitated a moment. "Auschwitz."

"*Auschwitz*," he echoed, mouth agape.

She lowered her voice and glanced over her shoulder as if to ensure no one was listening. "His parents and his brother and sister were all slaughtered there. Maarten spent eighteen months in that hell. Can you imagine?"

His mouth went dry. "I can't even begin to."

"After what he lived through . . . what he saw . . . Maarten wanted no part of religion. And he was so ashamed."

"Why ashamed?" Tyler threw his hands in the air. "Opa was a victim."

"Ashamed of surviving, when so many didn't." Liesbeth smiled distantly. "Maarten never set out to hide his Jewish heritage. Just Auschwitz. He never wanted to discuss his experience or what had happened to his family. To that end, he found it easier not to tell people he was Jewish."

Tyler was still digesting the news of his Jewish roots and tragic family secret when his belt vibrated. Distractedly, he reached down and grabbed for his pager. He glanced at the screen. The phone number for the SFU appeared with the numbers "911" added afterward.

He hopped to his feet. "Liesbeth, there's an emergency on the ward."

"Go, go," she said, unfazed by the abrupt interruption like the consummate doctor's wife she had been.

Tyler leaned forward and kissed his grandmother on the cheek. "I want to hear more about this."

"Next time."

Tyler turned for the door. He squeezed his cell phone between his shoulder and his ear as he hurried out to his car. The SFU's receptionist told him that one of his patients, Paige Newcomb, had developed "a major allergy" but she knew few details, only that the nurses told her to page him "stat" and the girl "was going down the tube."

As Tyler raced into the hospital, he thought about the anxious teenager with leukemia who had been more worried about the cosmetic impact of her rash and impending baldness than her cancer. Little had gone right for Paige since her admission. Her allergies to the chemotherapy drugs continued to worsen. Tyler had changed her treatment protocol three times and premedicated her with numerous drugs to try to prevent the allergic reactions but nothing seemed to help.

His car screeched into the Alfredson parking garage seven minutes after leaving Le Bistro. Abandoning his car in one of the emergency on-call parking spaces, he ran down the stairs and along the tunnel leading to the children's hospital. By the time he reached the SFU, the main corridor was deserted. In front of Paige Newcomb's room, he spotted a cart loaded with equipment and machinery and recognized it, ominously, as the "crash cart" or mobile resuscitation unit.

Heart in his throat, he sprinted down the hallway.

The room was packed. Respiratory therapists, lab technicians, and nurses milled around the room, some purposefully, others just watching. Few words were spoken, but the air was electrified. Tyler spotted Nikki Salazar at the far side of the bed, adjusting the flow rate on an intravenous bag. Their eyes locked for a moment. Something seemed different about her, but Tyler didn't have a moment to even consider what might have accounted for the change. Her quick nod conveyed the gravity of the situation better than words.

Dr. Randall Gratton, the baby-faced senior resident, stood above the head of the bed, his complexion blotchy and brow sweaty. He was holding a triangular mask to Paige's face, fiercely pumping oxygen into her mouth with the attached Ambu bag.

Tyler wove hurriedly through the crowd to reach the bedside. "What have you got, Randall?"

Gratton glanced over at him without slowing the rhythm of his pumping hand. "Worst allergic reaction I've ever seen. Broke out right after her A.M. dose of chemo," he said in a grim but calm voice. "Her blood pressure has dropped to nothing from the anaphylaxis." He used the term for critical allergic shock. "And look at this angioedema."

Gratton lifted the mask from Paige's mouth to reveal her face. Tyler was shocked by the distorted anatomy. Her normally thin neck and face were so swollen that he wasn't clear where one ended and the other began. Her frightened eyes bulged out of their sockets from swelling. Her lips were so puffed up that they resembled two grotesque pink slugs. The end of her ballooning tongue protruded between them.

Tyler reached down and squeezed Paige's shoulder. He looked into her panicky eyes. "We're going to make this better, Paige," he said, hoping the promise wasn't an empty one.

Gratton eyed him doubtfully. "I can barely pump oxygen into her with the bag," he said, speaking in a quiet, urgent tone. "There's no way I can stick a tube down her airway through this much swelling."

The young doctor was right. Paige's airway anatomy must have been as distorted as her face. "Have you notified ENT and Anesthesia?" Tyler asked.

Gratton wiped his brow with his forearm and nodded. "They're on their way."

"Good." Tyler knew that even the best anesthesiologist or ear, nose, and throat surgeon might not be able to establish an airway, even with a tracheotomy, through so much swollen tissue. "What drugs have you given her?"

Gratton listed off the standard medications they had poured into Paige's veins.

Sweat streaming under his arms, Tyler looked over and caught Nikki's attention. "I want an epinephrine bolus of one milligram, followed by a steady infusion at thirty micrograms," he said, calling for the heaviest artillery of antiallergy drug at a dose that had the potential to cause a cardiac arrest. It was a risk he would have to take. If her swelling worsened, Paige's airway might close over, in which case she would suffocate in front of their eyes.

Gratton gaped at him questioningly. With a crisp nod, Nikki reached for a syringe, plugged it directly into the intravenous tubing, and squeezed the plunger down.

"Give her forty milligrams of dexamethasone," Tyler added, realizing that he was exceeding the maximum dose of the steroid. "And I want her to have two more liters of fluid, stat."

Within seconds after Paige received the drugs, her eyes clouded over and slowly rolled upward in their sockets. The young nurse holding her wrist snapped, "I've lost her pulse!"

*Not again!*

Tyler's eyes darted to the monitor, which showed a rapid heart tracing. His hand shot up to Paige's neck to feel for a carotid pulse. He had to run his fingers up and down the swollen mass of tissue before he finally detected the faintest sensation.

The same nurse who had sounded the alarm was now leaning over Paige's chest with her interlocking hands pressing down on her breastbone, poised to begin cardiopulmonary resuscitation.

"Stop!" Tyler barked. "She still has a pulse." He swiveled his head to look at Nikki. "Give her another milligram of epinephrine."

"It's too soon, Tyler," Gratton cried.

Nikki wavered.

"There's no other option," Tyler said with an encouraging nod.

The doubt left Nikki's eyes as she plugged another syringeful of epi-nephrine into the intravenous tubing. She squirted it into the line without hesitation.

Gratton struggled harder than ever to force air into Paige's mouth. Tyler reached down with both hands and dug his fingertips into the en-gorged folds of skin at the angles of the patient's jaw. He yanked up and forward.

"Better!" Gratton grunted, able to squeeze larger volumes of oxygen into Paige's mouth.

Tyler tasted salt, as more sweat dripped into his eyes. *Hang in there, Paige . . .*

Nikki reached a slender hand up to Paige's bloated neck. Two of her fin-gers came to rest against the skin. "The pulse is strong," she said.

No sooner had she spoken the words when Paige's eyelids fluttered open. Her glassy eyes peered up at Tyler, still brimming with helpless anxiety.

Tyler forced a smile for her. "Paige, you've turned the corner," he said.

Nikki gently ran the back of her hand over Paige's cheek. "The swelling has come down, too," she reassured.

The rest of her engorgement dissipated like a tire slowly deflating. Ten minutes later, Paige's neck and chin reappeared. Since the girl was breath-ing easily on her own, Gratton pulled the mask away from her face. He looked over to Tyler and offered him a hangdog smile. "Thanks for coming in, boss."

Concerned that Paige's allergy might rebound unexpectedly, Tyler stayed by her bedside while waiting for the arrival of her parents, who were racing back to the Alfredson from their workplaces in Seattle.

Paige seemed shell-shocked. Tears streamed steadily from her puffy eyes, and she whimpered like an abandoned puppy. She offered only short yes or no answers to all questions and avoided eye contact with everyone.

An hour later, when Nikki and Tyler were the only two left in the room with her, Paige finally spoke up. "I thought I was going to die, Nikki," she said in a voice barely above a whisper.

"We weren't going to let that happen," Nikki said.

Paige's brow crumpled and her bloodshot eyes focused on Tyler. "Dr. McGrath, I don't want to die." Her voice cracked. "*Please* don't let me."

The words stabbed at his heart. "I won't, Paige."

"Thank you." Her eyes closed again and she drifted back to sleep.

Tyler turned to Nikki. "A little better, huh?"

Brown eyes sparkling, Nikki smiled at him with warmth he had not felt since their night at O'Doole's.

Turning back to the sleeping teenager, Tyler felt a wave of satisfaction wash over him. For the first time since Nate's death, he remembered why he loved his job.

## 24

Jill leaned against the bathroom countertop, the little white stick dangling between her fingers. She had seen the plus sign at first glance; it had not disappeared in the following three confirmatory checks. She stared at the mirror, overwhelmed with surprise and denial.

*How did this happen?* she thought, feeling as helpless as a pregnant fourteen-year-old who has barely connected 'cause and effect.'

She had only bothered to "waste" another pregnancy test because she was seven days late, but, as her periods were often irregular, she had been through the same situation several times before without being pregnant. After eighteen months of fertility treatment and countless pregnancy tests, she never expected this one to finally reveal the elusive plus sign.

Knowing she was supposed to feel elated didn't help Jill conjure the emotion. She stared blankly at her reflection, aware of the irony. Up until last fall, Tyler and she had worked so hard to become pregnant: the fertility-enhancing drugs, the regimented sex, and even the adherence to the old wives' tales on positions and times of day. Now, when they were no longer actively trying—arguably, with their near-dormant sex life and strained relationship, passively avoiding pregnancy—Jill found herself knocked up.

"Perfect!" she grumbled. She wondered if she experienced a moment of queasiness but decided the sensation had to be psychosomatic.

Jill was insightful enough to realize that no time would have ever been convenient for a pregnancy, but she had trouble imagining a worse one. So much had happened in the past week. She had already heard, unofficially, from inside sources that her major research grant was about to be renewed in the wake of the preliminary data on her stem cell study. The day before, news of her results had somehow found its way onto a popular academic blog. Ever since, she'd been bombarded with e-mails and voice mails from colleagues. She had also received numerous interview requests from journals and newspapers as far away as Sydney and Tokyo, all of which she had either ignored or refused. She had expected the attention to come sooner than later, but she was annoyed with the breach in confidentiality and felt unprepared to go public yet with her results.

Life had become a blur around her. She had no idea how she was going to balance all the directions in which she was being pulled. And she had felt like that even before she saw the little red plus sign on the stick.

*Why now, when I'm so close?*

Jill knew she should tell Tyler, but aware that a third of all early pregnancies ended in miscarriage, she saw no point in getting his hopes up prematurely. At least, that was how she rationalized it to herself.

Her ambivalence stemmed from more than just her once-in-a-lifetime academic opportunity. The timing on the personal front wasn't much better, either. Since moving to Oakdale, she and Tyler had hit a rut in their relationship. Based on the disastrous experiences of some friends and colleagues, Jill realized a new baby was not the savior for a troubled marriage.

Jill had a flashback of walking onto the oncology floor and seeing that dark-haired, exotic nurse with her hand clasped around Tyler's elbow. Though jealousy was not one of her prevailing traits, Jill recognized something deeply intimate in that moment. She doubted her husband was capable of having an affair, but the memory continued to gnaw.

Collecting the box and the stick, she tucked the evidence of her positive pregnancy test into an unmarked white plastic bag, tied it up, and tossed it into the garbage can. She decided to take a wait-and-see approach over the next few days before informing Tyler.

Downstairs, she grabbed a bite of breakfast, remembering only as she was putting the dish away to swallow a folate vitamin supplement with it. Imagined or not, her belly did not feel right after eating.

Arriving at the hospital, Jill considered stopping by to visit Senator Wilder, whom she had not seen since his drastic deterioration and transfer to the ICU. She wondered if Wilder had even survived the previous night. If he was still alive, Jill had nothing to offer the poor man except her pity. Out of a sense of duty, she started in the direction of the Henley Building. Then she thought of her pregnancy and the risk of exposing the fetus to

*C. diff* or any other microorganisms that might be floating around the ICU. Changing her mind, she turned around and headed straight to her office.

Jill arrived on the ninth floor of the neurosciences center, pleased to discover that she had the lab to herself. She experienced another wave of queasiness and began to doubt that the nausea really was all in her head.

She sat down at her computer but did not open any of the more than a hundred e-mails that had poured in overnight. The sudden attention her lab was drawing among the academic community again stirred the contradictory mix of apprehension and excitement.

Instead, Jill clicked open Andrew Pinter's spreadsheet. She had studied it so long and hard that she could see the table almost as well with her eyes closed, but she still wasn't satisfied. As the recognition of and interest in her study flooded in, her concern over the data's accuracy only deepened.

"Boss, if I showed you a photo of your house, would you even recognize it?" Pinter said through a yawn.

She looked up with a start. Pinter stood in the doorway, his thick hair disheveled and matted on the right side. Jill wondered if he might have been sleeping in the lab. It was not such a far-fetched idea. Pinter seemed to bounce between girlfriends' apartments, and the volatility of his relationships was legendary. The most recent flavor-of-the-month could have easily tossed him to the curb. But Jill did not want to tread those waters, so she did not ask.

Pinter sauntered up to her desk, wearing a black concert T-shirt with the name and logo of some band Jill had never heard of. "You're all aglow this morning," he said.

Nauseous, pregnant, and on edge, she was in no mood for his juvenile flirtatiousness. "Andrew, I want to see the raw data scores," she said tersely.

Pinter lazily nodded at her computer. "It's all on that spreadsheet you keep trying to stare down."

"No, I mean I want to see the individual forms on each enrollee," she said, referring to the original paper copies her research assistants would have filled out on each of the subjects.

"Why, Jill?" Pinter stifled another yawn. "You don't think I can transcribe a form onto a spreadsheet?"

She folded her arms across her chest. "Last time I checked, Andrew, I was still the principal investigator on this study."

"Whoa." Pinter gestured as though trying to calm a startled horse. "Easy there. I'll get you the pages." Then he viewed her with one of his frozen-lipped smiles. "Everything okay, Jill? You seem kind of . . . frustrated this morning?"

Jill ignored the innuendo in his remark. "You saw that blog about our study?"

Pinter shrugged. "It was going to get out one way or another. This is big stuff."

"How did it get out *this* way, though?"

"Don't look at me," he said, appearing amused rather than defensive. "I don't go for that blogging crap. It's kind of like deliberately leaving your diary on a bus for people to paw through."

She viewed him, stone-faced. "*The Sydney Morning Herald* wants to interview me."

"Way to go, boss!" Pinter nodded, impressed. "If they're noticing you down under, you've truly gone global."

"It's too early, Andrew."

He waved her concern away as he dropped sideways onto the seat across from her and threw a leg over the armrest. "The protocol is well on its way. The results are there."

"We *think* they are there."

He shook his head and snorted. "What's gotten you so spooked?"

"What if we can't validate the study?"

Pinter managed to smile again without moving his lips. "You can play that 'what if' game forever, boss. What if the Arctic melts away tomorrow?" He shrugged. "You learn to row in a hurry."

"Grow up, Andrew." She waved a hand up and down, indicating his slovenly appearance. "This carefree, grunge bohemian act of yours won't cut it anymore. Our study is getting international attention now. And that always attracts world-class scrutiny."

Pinter scratched his beard, unperturbed. "International attention. I thought that was the point of doing the fucking thing."

"I didn't know we would be judged this early." She sighed. "What if the results are wrong? It's one thing to have egg on your face for a grant re-application. Kind of another to wear it on the cover of an Australian daily."

"The data will stand. You're just getting a bit overwhelmed by the attention. That's all." He interlocked his fingers and cracked his knuckles. "A little neck massage might do you wonders."

Jill rolled her eyes. "The raw data would do me wonders."

"Your loss." Pinter stretched and rose from the chair. "These hands have been described as lethal."

As Pinter was heading for the door, Jill called after him. "Oh, and Andrew, I want to see the sheets on all the exclusions, too." She referred to the subjects who were initially enrolled in the study, but later excluded because they did not meet one or another of the criteria.

Pinter stopped and turned slowly. "Why do you want those?"

"Because they're part of the data, too."

"That's a lot of useless paper, Jill."

"Let me be the judge of that."

Pinter hesitated a moment before he walked back to the desk. He folded his arms across the chest. The laissez-faire indifference normally chiseled into his features gave way to a suspicious frown. "I thought I was your statistician on this project."

"What's your point, Andrew?"

"All this second-guessing my work." His eyes narrowed. "You make me feel like a kid whose parents don't trust him to finish his homework on his own."

She shrugged unapologetically. "This is the biggest study of my life, Andrew." She cracked a slight smile and tapped the center of her chest with a finger. "And like everyone around here says: This bitch is one major control freak."

Pinter didn't appear amused or mollified. He stared at her for a long moment before he turned abruptly for the door. "Okay, Dr. Laidlaw. I'll go get you every last page of it. Knock yourself out."

Watching Pinter stomp out of the room, Jill felt a pang of remorse. She wondered if she had been too hard on him. She had no reason to doubt his ability to run data; in fact, he had repeatedly proved that he was a whiz with statistics. She wondered if her shortness with him was related to the pregnancy. And if so, was it merely her reaction to the news or a genuine hormonal fluctuation? *I don't have time for this*, she thought again.

Distracted for the rest of the morning, she practically sleepwalked through her clinical rounds on the ward and her academic departmental meeting. With varying degrees of politeness, she brushed off all attempts by her excited colleagues to discuss the rumors of her stem cell breakthrough. Just before noon, Andrew Pinter walked into her office and dropped a box full of files on her desk. It landed with a solid thud. He didn't even make eye contact with Jill, but she had neither the time nor energy to address their rift. She merely nodded her thanks.

After he'd left, Jill decided she needed a break from the Alfredson. She hoisted the weighty box and lugged it out to her car. In the fresh air, she wondered if paranoia was getting the better of her.

Once home, she resisted the urge to brew a pot of coffee, resenting the deprivation her pregnancy was already imposing on her. Instead, she steeped a pot of decaf Earl Grey tea and then headed into her home office with a full mug.

Jill emptied the box of files onto her desk and organized them into neat stacks. Each of the files represented one study patient. Reaching for the first folder, she knew she was in for a long afternoon. The initial survey on each patient was ten pages long with five-page follow-ups performed at three-month intervals following enrollment. The subjects were kept strictly anonymous (to "blind" the assessors and data collectors) and identified only by unique eight-digit numbers. With the spreadsheet open on her computer screen, Jill found the patient identifier and began to compare the answers on the pages to the columns on the screen.

Three hours later, Jill had sorted through close to a hundred files from both the treatment and control groups of the study without finding a single discrepancy between the paper copies and the electronic spreadsheet. Tired, but relieved, she felt even more remorseful for having grilled Pinter about the results.

The last group of file folders she reached for contained the excluded patients—those people disqualified from the study after they had already been enrolled. There were over thirty such rejected patients. Though it was a large number, Jill wasn't surprised. In a study as complex as hers, it was natural people would be disqualified or change their mind and drop out of the study after enrolling.

Jill separated the exclusions into two piles: eighteen from the treatment arm and fourteen from the control group. A few patients had been dropped early on, but most had made it to at least the initial three-month reassessment phase. At the front of each file, a thick red stamp read EXCLUSION. Underneath, scrawled in pen, was an explanation why a particular subject had been disqualified. Though she found some of the explanations flimsy, most patients appeared to have legitimate reasons for being dropped from the study.

She began flipping through the pages. After the first few files, Jill wondered if this review was the best use of her limited time but, a perfectionist by nature, she read on. After about fifteen files, she began to notice a trend in the data. The excluded patients did not seem to have the same outcomes as the included subjects.

Jill stacked the pile of excluded files back on her desk and turned to her computer. She reformatted the tables on the spreadsheet, inserting extra rows. Her mouth dry, Jill reached for the first file in the stack. She painstakingly transcribed all the data she had on that patient into her spreadsheet. Then she reached for the next file and repeated the step.

By the time she had typed in the data on the last of the thirty-two excluded patients, the daylight outside her window had faded to dusk and her stomach grumbled violently. Jill sat in the near dark, enshrouded by a sense of doom. The mouse's pointer hovered over the icon, waiting to redraw the graph to now include the disqualified subjects. But Jill resisted tapping the button, already certain of what the new graph would reveal.

Time stood still.

Finger shaking, finally Jill clicked the button and watched as the graph popped onto the screen. While the two lines (the control and treatment group) still diverged over six months, they split from one another much more gradually; the statistical difference between them much less significant than it was before. Jill stared in horror at the newly calculated P value below the graph.

*It's all over!*

Light from the overhead fixture suddenly flooded the room. Jill looked behind her to see Tyler standing by the light switch, eyeing his wife with concern. "Jill? You okay?"

She shook her head.

Tyler hurried across the room and knelt at her side. "What is it? Your parents?"

Jill pointed to the screen. "That."

Tyler glanced from the screen back to her. "What is *that*?"

"It's my ruin, Tyler."

"What?"

"My study," she choked out. "It's a fraud."

"What are you talking about?"

"The excluded patients! Once I put them back into the spreadsheet, my numbers don't hold up. Look at the P value! I've lost the statistical significance between the two groups."

Tyler squeezed her shoulder. "Slow down, Jill. You're losing me."

"There were thirty-two patients excluded after the fact from my study!" she said. "That's a fair number, but not beyond expectation. But when I include the data I have on those subjects, my results don't hold up."

"So? They're excluded patients. They shouldn't be in the study."

"That's not the point. There is a trend here that is *anything* but random."

Tyler shrugged. "I still don't see it."

"It's right there in the graph!" Jill tapped the screen impatiently. "The subjects who were excluded from my study did not respond like the patients who were kept in. In the excluded group, the control subjects all did better than expected and the treated ones did worse."

Tyler's eyes widened and his jaw dropped a fraction. "Hold on, are you suggesting—"

She swallowed. "I think someone excluded subjects in order to make the study results look better." She felt tears running down her cheeks. "I think I've just committed research fraud."

"Jill, that's ridiculous! How could you have? You obviously didn't know about the exclusions until now," he said. "It must be someone else inside—"

"It's my lab, Tyler! My study. And I've already published the preliminary data in my grant renewal application. I swore to the validity of the results. Therefore, *I* am responsible."

Tyler wrapped an arm around her and held her tightly against his chest. "But you're the one who discovered it. There was no intent on your part. Now you just have to tell them."

She buried her head in his shoulder. "Oh, Tyler. It's too late."

"No."

"It's over. I'm finished," she said in a whisper.

"Come on, Jill. It just seems that way."

"It *is* that way."

He rubbed her back. "This is going to work out all right."

The stifling dread began to relent, and she felt a glimmer of comfort in his arms.

Jill wanted to tell Tyler that she loved him. She wanted to tell him she was pregnant with his child. But her voice failed her. So she just clung tightly to him and buried her head deeper in his shoulder, wishing none of it was happening.

## 25

Lorna didn't know whether the alcohol or the continuous storytelling was to blame, but Dot hit the wall during lunch. She had barely swallowed two bites of her frittata when her chin slumped to her chest and she dozed off in her seat, fork still in hand. Juanita had to practically carry the tiny woman off to her bedroom, which she did with an effortlessness that suggested she had done the same countless times before.

Pleasantly buzzed from her three prelunch drinks, Lorna worked the afternoon away on her laptop, typing new notes and reorganizing old ones. Everything had changed since her arrival at the Alfredson mansion. It now was a completely different story with more usable elements than Lorna had ever anticipated. The narrative was writing itself in her head, but she was desperate to tease out the rest of the family history from her great-aunt.

Consumed by her work, Lorna didn't notice that the sun had lowered and the afternoon had given way to evening until she heard Dot's clipped voice calling from downstairs. "Darling, dinner is on the table. And the wine has breathed so well that it's *positively* panting now."

"Damn it," Lorna muttered to herself. She had hoped to speak to Juanita and convince her to keep the dinner as dry an affair as possible so that she didn't lose Dot for another whole evening.

"Coming," Lorna called, as she finished bulleting two quick notes. She saved the file, closed her laptop, and tucked it deep under the bed.

She began down the stairs, but stopped on the landing to study the oil portraits that lined the wall. Marshall Alfredson stared down at her from the largest of the canvases at the top of the staircase. He wore a three-piece navy suit with his beloved pocket watch hanging prominently from his vest. Framed by a mop of red hair and muttonchops, his suspicious eyes and taut expression seemed to challenge her from the wall. Accentuated by the sheer size of the canvas, Marshall struck Lorna as a larger-than-life character. She felt a real pang of empathy for Evan McGrath, imagining how daunting it must have been for him to have to confront her great-great-grandfather.

Lorna turned her attention to the smaller portrait of Olivia, hanging adjacent and just below Marshall's. Though her complexion and hair color mirrored her father's, she exuded gentle warmth that transcended her unsmiling pose. Her youthful face possessed timeless beauty. Lorna understood how easy it would have been for Evan to have fallen head over heels for the girl.

"*Dar*ling?" Dot called in a singsong voice from downstairs.

Lorna peeled her eyes from the portraits and headed down the rest of the stairs and into the dining room with its elegant wainscoting and coved ceiling.

Glass of red wine in hand, Dot again wore tiger-striped leggings, this time with a black blouse that was long enough to be a dress. She gave Lorna's outfit—jeans with a gray sweatshirt—a quick once-over. "No need to dress up for dinner, darling." She chortled. "We're *hopelessly* informal here."

Unperturbed, Lorna sat down across from her great-aunt.

"We really should have seafood after last night's lamb." Dot raised her glass. "But I felt like red again tonight, so I'm afraid you will have to make do with Juanita's pot roast."

"It smells delicious."

"It's generally edible," Dot said louder than necessary, likely for Juanita's benefit.

Lorna reached for her wineglass and took a small sip, enjoying the slight bite but determined not to let the alcohol impede her progress. "So did Evan marry that schoolteacher, Grace Hathaway?"

Dot sighed. "What say we let the nineteenth century rest in peace tonight?"

"You must find me exhausting." Lorna laughed, feigning contrition. "It's just that I have to leave early tomorrow to get back to teach a class in the afternoon. And you've left me on tenterhooks. It's a real cliff-hanger. I just have to know how it all ends."

Dot waved the compliment away as she took another sip of her wine. "We did spring from some *wonderfully* memorable ancestors. I'm merely a cipher."

"Nonsense," Lorna cooed. "Without you, this would be forgettable minutiae. You bring the Alfredsons and McGraths back to life."

Dot lowered her glass. The vanity slid from her expression, and her eyelids narrowed warily. "I still don't quite see why this matters so much to you."

"It doesn't really," Lorna said lightly as she fingered the stem of her glass.

"Darling, am I *really* to understand that how Evan and Marshall managed their differences will impact your vote at the board meeting?"

Lorna pulled the glass from her lips and met her great-aunt's stare. It was a precarious moment. She knew better than to overdo her answer; Dot was too sharp to be taken in. "I've already heard enough to make up my mind. At this point, I just want to know how it ended between these two men . . . and Olivia, of course."

Dot viewed Lorna for several more seconds before her face relaxed. She lifted her glass again. "You asked me earlier how my father was related to Olivia."

Lorna nodded.

"To be precise, Olivia wasn't really my aunt."

"No? What is the relation then?"

"Let's not get ahead of our story." Dot's eyes lit mischievously. "On the tenth of August, 1896, Olivia gave birth to a boy—Arthur Marshall Grovenor Jr. Though from the day he was born, everyone came to know him as simply Junior."

"Hold on." Lorna sat up straighter. "Your father—Marshall's son—was called Junior, too. Were there two of them in the family?"

Dot shook her head.

Lorna clutched the table in front of her. "Are you saying Junior was Marshall's *and* Olivia's son?" she said, aghast.

"*Please!*" Dot rolled her eyes. "You can safely accuse us Alfredsons of more than a few unsavory acts, but not *that*."

"I don't understand," Lorna muttered.

Dot ignored her great-niece's exasperation. "As was Junior's lifelong tendency, he arrived early. Almost two months, apparently. But premature or not, he was born with the same solid constitution that would carry him through the next eighty-two years." She sighed. "And how they fawned over him! Not only was he the apple of his parents' eyes, but Junior was Marshall's only grandchild."

"But I thought you just said he was—"

"Ah, ah, ah." Dot wagged a bony finger. "In good time."

Aware that her great-aunt would not be rushed into her disclosure, Lorna folded her arms over her chest and leaned back in her seat. *Out with it, you old snake!*

"Evan McGrath, of course, was still heartbroken over Olivia's marriage." Dot sighed. "But 1896 was a hectic year for the young surgeon, too. By early that autumn, the Alfredson Clinic was nearing completion. He was still the only doctor for the town of Oakdale. And yes, darling, he did marry Grace Hathaway."

---

In those early days, Marshall and Evan faced daunting obstacles while establishing their new clinic. Together, they managed to overcome them all. But neither ever imagined how violently the winds of change would upend Marshall's life in the spring of 1897.
—*The Alfredson: The First Hundred Years* by Gerald Fenton Naylor

Evan felt as though he had lived a second lifetime in the ten months since Virginia's death. The clinic had risen rapidly from the muddy pit he had watched the crew dig. Despite his many differences with Marshall, Evan had to concede the lumber baron had erected a noble building that surpassed even his expectations.

The three-story redbrick building had a grand columned entrance with an esthetically pleasing façade that still conveyed a sense of healing and comfort. The spacious floors were flooded with natural light, providing ample room and privacy for staff and patients. The two operating theaters were the most modern and well designed Evan had ever seen. He considered the clinic's layout superior to even the Morgan Clinic in San Francisco.

Evan's life had changed almost as dramatically as the construction site. Renowned specialists—who had only existed for him in their writings in textbooks, journals, and correspondences—arrived in the flesh. Evan was starstruck; he could not have been more thrilled had he met his childhood heroes from his favorite Wild West stories.

Evan finally sold his house in Seattle. And after Grace and he wed in August, they moved into a house of their own in Oakdale. By the end of October, Grace had begun to show the first glow of pregnancy. Evan was so excited by the prospect of fatherhood that even the news that Olivia had given birth to another man's son did not dampen his newfound contentment.

The Alfredson Clinic opened on the morning of the first of November, 1896, to far more fanfare than Evan had anticipated. Marshall had lured the recently elected third governor of Washington State, John Rogers, out to the site along with a slew of Seattle's prominent civic, social, and business leaders. The photo of a beaming Marshall standing beside Governor Rogers as he cut the opening ribbon made the front page of both *The Seattle Times* and the *Post-Intelligencer*.

The last few months of the year passed in a blur for Evan. He was frantically busy in the weeks after the Alfredson opened. Despite the painted walls, ornate stonework, and modern interior, the clinic was largely a skeleton. Equipment had yet to arrive or be installed. The new staff, many of whom were unskilled laborers, needed to be trained. And the nine specialists who had already relocated to the Alfredson had yet to set up their offices.

Evan was so consumed with organizing his new clinic that almost a month passed before he recognized its most glaring challenge and greatest threat: aside from the denizens of Oakdale and the outlying areas, how was the clinic to attract patients from larger centers such as Seattle, Spokane, and beyond?

The Alfredson had drawn a unique collection of medical talent in the Pacific Northwest and it boasted one of the first diagnostic laboratories in western America. Evan had naïvely assumed that as soon as the doors opened, patients would find their way to the clinic. But by early January, the realities of geography had begun to set in. The clinic was located sixty miles outside of Seattle, and the long, meandering train trip was an arduous journey for ill patients to make.

By the end of January, the physicians at the Alfredson Clinic were collectively seeing fewer than ten new patients per day, most of whom lived in Oakdale or the scattering of towns in the vicinity. The large wards housed only a handful of patients, sometimes fewer.

While the camaraderie and spirit of intellectual collaboration still ran high among the Alfredson's specialists, unrest was growing. They had come to Oakdale expecting to step into a center of medical excellence but instead found themselves manning a largely empty rural hospital. They were not ac-customed to having time on their hands. Eventually, even the collegiality be-gan to wear thin, especially when the clinic's most renowned physician, an intestinal specialist named Dr. Nicholas Ames, resigned with only a day's notice. Other physicians threatened to follow suit.

The doctors were not the only ones threatening. Marshall Alfredson, who had bankrolled the underutilized clinic and idle doctors, vented his ire to Evan in a series of letters with escalating rhetoric. By the end of Febru-ary, Evan feared that his dream clinic might close before the spring had even arrived.

But March blew the winds of change in the Alfredson's favor. Word of the clinic's medically superior care—free of charge to those who did not have the means to pay for it—had spread beyond Oakdale. New patients began to trickle in via train, horse, and carriage from towns and centers far-ther away, including Seattle. Then, on March 12, the Alfredson's fortunes took a dramatic turn for the better when the brilliant but temperamental eye surgeon, Howard Nilsson (who had already informed Evan of his in-tent to leave this "ghost town hospital"), performed groundbreaking surgery on Miss Gertrude Iles. The sixty-year-old Seattle heiress had been prema-turely blinded by cataracts. Using a technique he had perfected for excising the cataract from within the lens, Nilsson was able to salvage the woman's eyesight. Iles was so grateful to Nilsson that she presented the Alfredson with its first donation.

Her substantial twenty-five-thousand-dollar endowment eased the imme-diate financial burden facing the clinic and Marshall Alfredson. More sig-nificantly, the news of the gift, and the reason for it, hit the pages of the Seattle newspapers. The publicity was better advertising than Evan could have imagined. He was delighted, and desperately relieved, when the dribble of patients turned into a steady flow, some of whom came from Oregon, Idaho, and even beyond.

By the beginning of April, Evan was feeling more optimistic than ever. His wife had ballooned with an uncomplicated pregnancy, and Evan antici-pated the birth of their baby with childlike enthusiasm. His marriage to Grace had evolved into a comfortable relationship, though it lacked the deep affection he had shared with Virginia or the consuming passion he had experienced with Olivia. Still, Evan was content with the prospect of raising a family and growing old with Grace.

However, he could not suppress the memories of Olivia. They came with unexpected frequency, often tormenting his nights. With all that had happened in the sixteen months since he had last laid eyes on her, the recollection of their stolen time together, while still deliciously vivid in detail, had assumed a dreamlike quality.

Evan never expected to see Olivia again, so he was shocked one gloomy overcast April morning to step out the front door of the clinic and find her standing at the bottom of the steps. Wearing a long-sleeved navy jacket with a flowing skirt, she leaned on a closed umbrella as though it were a cane. Her red hair was pinned up underneath her feathered bonnet. She stood studying the facility with an awed expression. His heart skipped a beat. She looked as radiant as she had the last time they were together at the Sherman Hotel.

After a moment, Olivia's gaze turned to him. Their eyes locked. Evan felt immobilized by the contradictory mix of affection, self-consciousness, and desire. After a faltering moment, Olivia stepped forward and climbed the stairs toward him.

When she reached the landing, Evan saw that her face was flushed. She offered him her gloved hand and a tentative smile. He took her hand in his and bowed his head, partly to hide his own embarrassment. "Good day, Mrs. Grovenor. A pleasure to see you again."

"Likewise, Dr. McGrath," she murmured.

He let go of her hand, but his heart ached at the brief contact and her unexpected proximity. "I hear congratulations are in order on the birth of your son. I trust he is well."

"He is wonderful." Olivia's green eyes lit, but she looked away. "Junior is eight months old and growing like a stalk of corn. He was born early, you know." In profile, her face reddened deeper and she cleared her throat. "Thankfully, he has shown no ill effects."

Evan nodded. "I am so very glad. As it happens, my wife and I are expecting a child next month."

"Oh?" Olivia's shoulders twitched with surprise. "I did not . . . um . . ." She sighed. "I meant to tell you how very sorry I was to hear of Mrs. McGrath's passing. And, of course, to congratulate you on your recent marriage."

A ripple of melancholy swept through him. "Thank you," he murmured.

They stood in awkward silence for a moment before Olivia spoke up. "Dr. McGrath, I do apologize for arriving without advance notice."

He smiled. "Really, Mrs. Grovenor, there is no need."

"You see, we were off to visit close friends in Spokane," she sputtered to explain. "And Oakdale was not far out of our way. I had heard and read so much about your clinic. Honestly, I did not expect to run into you. I so wanted to see the clinic for myself. I left Junior with Arthur and the nursemaid and I caught a train—"

"Olivia." Evan laughed, resisting the urge to touch her again. "You do not need to explain. I am delighted you have come."

"I did so want to see the clinic. I would have liked to have come for the opening ceremony, but the timing . . . um . . . with the baby and . . ."

"Of course."

Olivia swallowed again. "Ever since you first described the idea, I have always felt a part—an absolutely minuscule part, mind you—of this place. Your clinic."

Evan shook his head. "It's your father's clinic, not mine. And your role could not have been further from minuscule."

Olivia adjusted her hat as her eyes scanned the front of the building again. "I still remember every word of your description." She turned back to Evan. "Did it turn out as you envisioned?"

Evan broke off the eye contact, concerned he would lose himself in those eyes. "It is still very early of course, but the clinic is taking shape. Your father has built us a wonderful facility. And we have been fortunate to attract such brilliant and talented physicians. And now that the patients are showing a willingness to travel here . . ."

Olivia's smile broadened. "You have realized your dream, haven't you?"

"It is premature to say, but—" He chuckled. "Oh, bother, Olivia. I truly have!"

Beaming, she gazed at him with unconcealed affection. "I am really so happy for you, Evan."

The look sent his spirits soaring. "May I offer you a tour of the facility?" he asked.

"Thank you. I would like that very much."

"Please." He held his hand out toward the door.

Bursting with pride, Evan led Olivia into the marble-floored foyer. He guided her down the main floor hallway and through the large ward, of which over half the beds were full. He toured her through one of the operating theaters but could not show the other as it was in use. On the second floor Evan introduced Olivia to a few of the specialists, including the eye specialist, Howard Nilsson. She hardly said a word, but Evan could tell from her wide-eyed expression that she was starstruck.

Excited as a child showing off his favorite toy, Evan rushed Olivia down the hallway to the room at the end. She was bowled over by what was waiting inside the small dark room. The Alfredson boasted the first and only medical X-ray machine in Washington. Evan tried to explain how the bulky machine and its complex series of vacuum tubes worked, but he barely grasped the principles himself. The theory didn't matter to Olivia once he showed her the series of plated X-rays. Most of them were images of human hands, revealing the bones underneath the skin, which were covered only by the outline of rings worn over them.

"I have never even heard of this X-ray before," she sputtered, overawed.

"The German physicist Roentgen invented it only two years ago."

"It is like magic, Evan," she breathed as she ran a finger over the plate.

"Can you imagine how much this technology will help us for setting fractured bones or visualizing internal organs without having to cut the patients open?"

Olivia glanced at him with an impish grin. "It might just put you out of work, Dr. McGrath."

He chuckled. "It will only create more work for me. Better work, too."

Examining the plates together, their heads were so close that Evan could feel Olivia's breath on his cheek. His nostrils filled with her familiar lavender perfume. Closing his eyes for a moment, he fantasized that they were back in the Sherman Hotel.

Olivia looked up from the plates. Evan was not certain in the dimly lit room, but he thought he read invitation in her expression. His breath caught in his throat, but he fought off the impulse to grab her shoulders and pull her lips to his. Too much had happened in both of their lives in the past year. The stakes went so far beyond them now. It would no longer simply be about romantic betrayal; there were the children to consider, hers and his soon-to-be.

Holding her gaze, Evan still relished the moment of intimacy he never expected to experience again. Then, reluctantly, he straightened up. "Perhaps we should finish the rest of our tour?" he said.

She pulled back and lowered the X-ray plate to the table. "Yes, of course. I . . . um . . . need to return to Junior soon."

Heavyhearted, Evan led Olivia through the rest of the hospital, deliberately stretching the tour as long as he possibly could. Reaching the foyer again, he walked her out the front door and down the steps. They stood in front of the expanse where the newly laid grass had only begun to sprout through the soil that had been sown six weeks before.

"Thank you, Olivia, for taking the time to come visit our clinic," he said awkwardly. "It was an honor and a privilege."

"The honor and privilege were all mine, Dr. McGrath," she said with a distant smile. "However, I really must be going."

"Of course." He bowed his head again. "Good-bye, then."

Olivia nodded, turned away, and headed briskly down the pathway.

Evan watched her take a few strides and then called out: "Mrs. Grovenor, I will be in Seattle at the end of May on business. Perhaps our paths might cross again in the city?"

She answered without turning back to face him. "Oh, I think not. Arthur has planned a sailing trip for us in May. He does so love to sail."

The memory of Olivia's unexpected visit haunted Evan for weeks. He threw himself even more deeply into his work, but it didn't help. Even when Grace reached the ninth month of her pregnancy, he had trouble shedding the thoughts of those few intimate minutes spent with Olivia in the dark room. The regret for his inaction—for letting reason prevail over emotion—was so strong that he ached inside.

A week before Grace's expected delivery date, Evan received another unannounced visitor. That morning a windstorm had blown out of nowhere and battered Oakdale. Evan was sitting at his desk in his office and reading through the hospital's latest inventory report as the remnants of the storm continued to rattle his window. A loud throat-clearing drew his attention. He glanced up to see the massive frame of Marshall Alfredson filling his doorway.

"May I have a moment of your time?" Marshall grunted without a word of greeting.

Evan rose from his seat and indicated the chair across from him. "Please."

With his hat tucked under his arm and leaning heavily on his cane, Marshall limped into the room. Evan recognized that Marshall's chronic gout must have flared up, but he did not comment as the giant squeezed himself into the chair on the other side of the desk. "I think I was very clear when I told you that I am not Andrew Carnegie," Marshall said.

"I do not believe I have ever confused you for him."

"Is that so? And yet you expect me to provide this clinic with a seemingly bottomless source of charitable funding."

Evan shuffled the pages on his desk. "Mr. Alfredson, I thought you understood the initial expense of establishing this clinic—"

"I was here for the ribbon-cutting seven months ago. The clinic *is* established!"

"In the next few years, it will only become more entrenched and self-sufficient. In the meantime, we have Miss Iles's endowment—"

Marshall slapped the desktop irritably. "That woman's donation represents a fraction of my investment. Also, it was merely a onetime gift. Meanwhile, every month you are incurring more costs than I dreamed imaginable."

Evan pointed toward the still-shaking window. "But look how the clinic has grown in stature in just a few short months. The Alfredson is drawing patients from all over the state and beyond. It is becoming known as the premier—"

Marshall interrupted with a dismissive wave of his hairy knuckles. "As best as I can tell, you are primarily attracting idlers and indigent opportunists who recognize a handout when they see one."

Evan clenched his fist under his desk as he struggled to control his tone. "We have an agreement, Mr. Alfredson. One of this clinic's founding principles was that we would never turn away patients because they were unable to pay."

"Maybe so, but I was not aware that you intended to actively solicit such patients." Marshall shook his head gravely. "It must be quite easy to hold such lofty principles when you are not the person who has to pay for them."

Evan fought to remain calm. "You are the businessman, Mr. Alfredson," he said evenly. "Do you have suggestions for improving our situation?"

"In fact, I do." Marshall interlocked his fingers and extended them with a series of loud cracks. "We need to attract more of the right sort of people to the Alfredson for treatment."

"The 'right sort of people.' Who would that be, Mr. Alfredson? The aristocracy?"

Marshall nodded as though the doctor were serious. "More members of society like Miss Iles. The donations will surely follow them. And, of course, the word of mouth will spread among the proper circles. To that end, you should employ more people like that eye man, Dr. Nilsson."

"There is no other eye surgeon as good as Howard Nilsson."

Marshall shrugged. "Then you need to find the leading people in other areas. The right fields, of course."

Evan grimaced. "The *right* fields?"

"As I understand it, you have here a women's specialist, a laboratory scientist, and another man who focuses on disorders of the brain."

Evan didn't bother attaching the correct names to those specialties. "Among others, yes."

"The Alfredson doesn't need those kinds of doctors. They will never bring in decent income." Marshall blew out his lips with rumbling disdain. "What we want is a good bone man or two who can help with rheumatism and joint problems. Perhaps someone who is capable of treating consumption. Or shingles. The sorts of afflictions that might be of interest to the desirable class of Seattleites."

Evan folded his arms across his chest. "That is not what the clinic is about."

"This clinic has *my* family name on it, not yours. Only my money has made it possible. So please do not try to tell me what it is or is not about."

Realizing it was futile to argue with the pigheaded man, Evan said nothing.

Marshall smiled and his tone took on a sudden conciliatory note. "Besides, Dr. McGrath, I have not come to squabble with you. I am here to help find solutions."

Evan stiffened, more wary of Marshall's uncharacteristic friendliness than his wrath. "What else do you have in mind?" he asked.

"There is a doctor in Seattle who has done quite well for himself. I believe he is the right person to elevate the Alfredson's reputation among certain circles. I have already approached him about coming to the clinic. He has expressed interest."

Evan felt uneasy. "Which doctor?"

"His name is Sibley. Garth Sibley."

*Sibley!* Evan's stomach turned. The same man who had drawn the Mc-Graths to Seattle with his empty promises and then ended up nearly poisoning Virginia with his vile elixir. Evan shot up from his chair. "*Never!* The man is a dangerous quack."

Marshall shrugged in his chair. "I am not seeking your permission, Dr. McGrath."

"I will never work with Sibley."

Marshall's smile assumed a malicious quality. "Then perhaps you will need to look for work elsewhere."

As Evan gaped at Marshall, he suddenly realized that none of this was a coincidence. He distinctly remembered telling the lumber baron about Sibley and his contempt for the snake oil salesman. Marshall must have sought out Sibley for that very reason. "Why are you doing this?" Evan demanded.

The smile left Marshall's lips. His face darkened as he rose to his towering height. He pointed a finger accusingly at Evan's chest. "Did you or did you not promise to never see my daughter again?"

Suddenly, Evan understood. "It was a chance encounter."

"A chance encounter?" Marshall's voice rose. "*Here?* In the middle of nowhere?"

Evan was not about to incriminate Olivia to her father by pointing out that he did not know of her plans to visit. "I wanted her to see the Alfredson," he lied. "She has worked hard to see it realized."

"She did, indeed," Marshall grumbled, almost under his breath. He shook his finger harder at Evan. "You, sir, swore a promise to me—"

"Mr. Alfredson!" a voice called frantically from the doorway.

Evan and Marshall looked over simultaneously to see the squat private detective, Wellsby, fidgeting to the point of writhing where he stood just inside the door. He still wore his bowler hat, but he was panting heavily and sweat dripped along his brow and over his ghostly pale face. He looked around in every direction but avoided eye contact with his boss.

"What is it, Wellsby?" Marshall demanded.

"It is . . . ," Wellsby stammered. "Out in Puget Sound. This morning . . . in the storm."

"Out with it!"

Wellsby pulled off his hat and clutched it to his chest. His gaze dropped to the floor. Sudden foreboding flooded Evan. "Mr. and Mrs. Grovenor," Wellsby said. "They were out sailing . . ."

Marshall's face blanched and his eyes dilated widely. "My Olivia! *No!*"

"Sir, their boat capsized." Wellsby swallowed. "No one made it to shore."

"No, no, no!" The words tumbled from Evan's lips almost in unison with Marshall's.

## 26

By 6:45, the sun had crested over the peak of the mountain and bathed the trail below in a golden-orange glow. Birds chirped noisily in the trees above Erin and Tyler, and the air was thick with the scent of pine and fir. Only the slight chill at the base of the trail reminded Erin that fall had already arrived, but by the time she had hiked up a half mile even that was a distant memory and she was drenched in sweat from the demanding climb. She glanced over to Tyler and saw that he'd stripped down to a T-shirt and shorts, his sweater tied around his waist.

As children, Erin and Tyler had hiked the same trail with their grandfather, Maarten Vanderhof. Erin cherished those memories. Nothing was as refreshing as the swims in the glacier-fed lake at the top of the hike. And little could compare to the picnic lunches Liesbeth used to pack with mouth-watering roast beef and turkey sandwiches along with the kind of sugary snacks and drinks that their mother never allowed at home. The path was known locally as the Ravine, but Erin still thought of it as Opa's Trail.

For the past few summers, Erin and Steve had taken the twins up Opa's Trail—even allowing them junky snack food that never graced their cupboards at home—but she had not climbed it with her brother in over twenty years. Erin had suggested the excursion as a chance for them to catch up, but they had hardly spoken a word since launching into the hike.

Erin was still mentally grappling with the article in the newspaper that had waylaid her over her morning coffee. It concerned the family of a deceased patient who was suing the Alfredson and her brother. Erin had not yet broached the topic with Tyler, and nothing in his demeanor suggested he had even seen it. On the contrary, he was in a brighter mood than she had seen in a while. And, though she considered herself to be in relatively good shape, she huffed and puffed struggling to keep up with him as he bounded up the trail.

Two-thirds of the way up, they stopped near a cluster of towering trees for a drink of water. Pulling the bottle from his lips, Tyler wiped the sweat off his brow with a sweep of his wrist. "Was this hike always so damn steep?"

Erin chuckled. "Opa never had any trouble with it. And he was well into his sixties when he used to take us."

Tyler leaned back against a tree. "Opa's personal trainer must have been better than mine."

"No doubt," Erin said as she sprayed him with a stream from her water bottle.

"Feels good," he said, shaking the water out of his hair. The grin vacated his lips. "Speaking of Maarten, Liesbeth let me in on an incredible family secret last week."

"About Opa and the camps?"

Tyler squinted at her. "You knew, too?"

"Liesbeth called me after your lunch. She wanted me to hear it directly from her."

"Amazing, huh?"

"Remember that funny blocklike tattoo Opa had on his forearm? I once asked him about it. He laughed it off saying he always wanted to be a sailor, but I bet it covered up those numbers the Nazis used to tattoo on the inmates."

Tyler shook his head. "I remember him as so upbeat. And yet he endured a Nazi extermination camp and then treated kids with cancer at a time when few of them survived."

"God, he must have had some kind of inner strength."

"Superhuman, I'd say."

Erin nodded. "It's kind of weird to find out you have a whole heritage you never knew about. It's amazing to think we're part Jewish."

"I know. I'm completely off bacon."

Erin rolled her eyes.

He thumbed at the trail. "How about we race the rest of the way up, like old times?"

He began moving toward the trail, but Erin stayed put. "Tyler, did you see the paper this morning?"

He stopped in his tracks. With his back still to her, he nodded.

"I'm sorry," she said.

He turned slowly back to face her. "I knew it was coming."

"What they said in the article . . ."

"Most of it is true." Tyler went on to summarize the Stafford case for her.

"I don't dwell on every single potential complication to my preop cardiac patients, either." Erin shook her head. "Your case still sounds like informed consent to me."

"Nate was dying." Tyler's gaze drifted to the trees above her. "That drug was the very last thing I had to offer him, but it's no excuse. I should have told his parents that the spinal fluid route carried a higher risk."

"Easy to say now."

His eyes found hers again. "Erin, I was arrogant. I downplayed the side effects because I didn't want to give them a chance to back out."

She viewed him for a long moment. "Don't think I would have done it any differently, Pip."

"Not sure if that testimony will help much in court." He ran a hand through his damp hair and grinned. "Still, thank you."

She cocked her head. "Tyler, are you as . . . okay with this as you seem?"

"Probably not." He looked down and ran the toe of his hiking boot over an exposed tree root. "But I have to be."

"For the other kids you treat?"

"Them. And Jill."

"Jill?" Erin frowned. "Is this publicity an inconvenience to her?"

"Jill has her own publicity disaster to worry about."

"She does?"

He told her about Jill's tainted study data. "She's convinced she will be ruined when the truth gets out," he said.

"Oh, crap! Poor Jill. Those academics can be the worst cutthroats of all, huh? So much professional jealousy among them."

Tyler dropped to the ground, sat on his sweater, and hugged his knees. "Ironic part is that her new treatment seems to really work. They just haven't had enough cases or time to prove it yet."

"What's she going to do?"

Tyler dropped his chin to his knees and shook his head.

Erin sat down on the lumpy dirt beside him. They sat without speaking for a long while. "Poor Dad," Tyler finally said.

"You mean his back pain?" Erin asked, confused.

"No." He frowned. "The motion before the Alfredson's board. He's worried sick about that vote."

"Can't blame him. If some private interest takes over the Alfredson, he'll lose the one thing that matters most to him."

Tyler sighed heavily. "And Jill and I are only hurting his cause with our public debacles."

"Me, too."

"You? How?"

Erin stared affectionately at Tyler. The naked angst swam in his eyes, and she realized he had been mounting a brave face for her all morning. Suddenly, she had second thoughts about adding her problems to his already full load.

"What is it, Erin?" he pressed.

"Nothing."

"Come on. It's just me." He held out a hand. "How are you hurting Dad's cause?"

"I've had to take a leave of absence from the OR." She was prepared to recycle the lie about carpal tunnel syndrome, but something in her little brother's gaze moved her to the truth. "Ty, I've been having panic attacks."

"*Panic*?" Tyler did a double take. "You're the fearless one, Erin. Remember those late nights when we were home alone? I was the one cowering behind the couch. You used to laugh through those slasher films."

"I'm not laughing now."

"Wow." He shook his head. "When do they hit you?"

"That's the problem. I can't predict. They can happen anywhere, anytime. Last week I had one as I was starting a transplant. I was lucky I didn't wind up killing my patient."

He laid a hand on her shoulder. "How long has this been going on?"

"Two months or so."

"Never before?"

Erin shook her head.

"Why now, Erin? What's changed?"

"Africa."

Tyler didn't look surprised. "What happened to you over there?"

"It wasn't so much what happened to me . . ."

"Come on, Erin. Tell me."

"The hospitals in Nakuru don't have heart-lung machines, but there's no shortage of people who need coronary bypasses. I went there to perform off-the-pump bypasses."

Tyler nodded. A year before, she had walked him through the tricky procedure of operating on a still-beating heart.

"The off-the-pump surgery is a real technical challenge," Erin went on. "I'm always refining my technique. This was an opportunity for me, too. But my timing really sucked. I showed up days after the contested general election. All hell was breaking loose in the Rift Valley. Political and tribal unrest, that kind of thing. Especially between the two main tribes, the Kikuyus and the Kalenjins."

"I thought you didn't get caught up in any of that."

Erin looked down and spoke to the dusty trail. "I had only been there two days. People warned me not to go to the hospital that afternoon. They said it wasn't safe." She swallowed. "But some patients had been waiting a year for me to come operate on them. I couldn't just abandon them."

"Erin," Tyler said. "What happened?"

"I was supposed to do a bypass on a sixty-five-year-old man with bad coronary disease. Turns out he was one of the elders of the Kalenjins. But all I knew when they wheeled him into the operating room was that, with his plugged arteries, his heart was a time bomb. The hospital had no central air-conditioning. It was so damn hot in the OR that afternoon." As she spoke the scene drifted through her head as though she were watching it on a reel of film.

There were six of them in the operating room, including the patient. The anesthesiologist, Jomo Karanja, was handsome and fairer-skinned than the others. Roughly the same age as Erin, he lived and worked in Nairobi but had come to the Rift Valley as part of Erin's surgical outreach team. Even though they had only known each other for three days, with Jomo's congenial attitude and easy laugh, Erin found him impossible not to like.

Erin had met the three nurses in the OR only a few minutes earlier, but she quickly recognized them as capable scrub nurses. In their mid-twenties, Ayanna and Ita were both petite, by Kenyan standards, and had matching large almond eyes. More solidly built and at least twenty years older, Sesi was clearly in charge. Aside from her Kenyan accent, she could have passed for a head nurse in any American hospital with her no-nonsense attitude and seamless efficiency. Erin soon fell into a comfortable collegial rapport with the entire staff.

Even Kipruto Mugenya, the patient lying on the operating table, couldn't stop flashing his golden-toothed grin, despite being moments away from open-heart surgery. Tall and skinny to the point of skeletal, Mugenya had coal-black skin that contrasted with his whitish hair. His gratitude seemed to be bottomless, as he kept interrupting Erin to thank her while she tried to walk him through the steps of his impending surgery.

Ita had scrounged a second electrical fan to supplement the minimal cooling from the first one. Erin was concerned that the steady stream of sweat dripping into her eyes might hamper her surgical technique. But Ayanna always seemed to be nearby at the perfect moment with a sponge to dab her brow.

Sitting at the head of the OR table, Jomo reached forward with the flat of his hand and patted the patient on his chest. "Well, my friend." The anesthesiologist laughed. "Are you ready to have your heart fixed, good as new?"

"Yes. Yes," Mugenya answered eagerly.

"Good." Jomo reached for a syringe. He laughed again as he squeezed out an air bubble in the tip. "You're lucky, Kipruto. You are the only one who gets to sleep through this heat."

Mugenya chuckled. "I hope I am the only one."

Erin laughed, too. She barely even noticed the steady shuffling sound coming from outside the door of the OR, until she saw Ita and Ayanna exchange wary glances. Even Sesi put down the surgical tray she was holding to stop and listen with obvious concern.

Erin eyed Jomo with a wordless question. He grimaced and shrugged back, looking as bewildered as she felt.

Suddenly, Mugenya sat bolt upright, accidentally yanking out the intravenous line that ran into his elbow. Fresh blood oozed down his forearm, but he didn't even notice. His pupils seemed to fill his entire eye sockets. "The Kikuyu," he whispered.

"Who?" Erin asked, as the pounding footsteps grew louder.

"Mr. Mugenya is a Kalenjin," Sesi hurried to explain in a low voice. She pointed to the other nurses. "We all are. But Mr. Mugenya is an elder, a leader, in our community. Since the election, Kikuyu militia have been on the rampage in Nakuru. They want—"

The door to the OR burst open, cutting off Sesi's explanation. Eight or nine men stormed inside. Ranging in age from their late teens to their mid-twenties, they wore an array of outfits from old jeans and T-shirts to what appeared to be tattered soccer uniforms. Two of them had on mismatched combat fatigues. The only unifying features were the red berets they wore, and the weapons they all brandished. Each of them carried either a club or a long machete.

One of the men in fatigues, who looked to be the oldest, marched the group toward the table. Before they reached the patient, Mugenya jumped to his feet. He leaned back against the operating table and pointed a shaky finger at the leader. "You have no right—"

With his weapon-free hand, the leader silenced Mugenya with a quick slap to his face and a punch to his gut.

As Mugenya doubled over, Sesi rushed toward the aggressor. "What is the meaning of this?" she demanded.

The man spat something in what sounded like Swahili and shoved her roughly away.

Erin stepped closer to them. "What the hell are you doing here?"

The leader turned to her, eyes ablaze. "Shut up!" he snapped in clear English. "This is none of your business. This is about our home, not yours."

The leader's head whipped back to Mugenya. He berated the old man in a stream of rapid Swahili accompanied by a steady spray of spit. In spite of the fierce tirade, the fear seemed to seep from Mugenya's eyes. He stood up straighter and folded his arms across his chest. A look of intense pride crossed his face. He even flashed the leader a golden smile. "I do not accept any of what you say," he said in English. "I have done nothing but serve my people well."

The militia leader shook his head slowly, as though terribly disappointed.

Jomo leapt off his chair and hurried over to Mugenya's side. "This is a hospital! A place of healing. Not a place to settle tribal disputes."

The leader glanced at Jomo and laughed. Then, without warning, he suddenly swung his machete like an ax at Mugenya. It whizzed through the air and buried itself into the old man's chest with a horrific whoosh. The older man cried out as he crumpled back against the table.

Shrieks of terror and hoots of encouragement erupted simultaneously and filled the room.

The leader jerked the blade free and swung again, slashing deep into Mugenya's neck. A fountain of blood burst from the slashed carotid, splattering Erin's gown.

"You can't," Erin screamed, instinctively lurching toward her patient.

A pair of strong hands wrapped around her upper arms and yanked her away from the fallen man. Then the same hands tightened around her neck. The smell of stale sweat and rum filled her nose as the young man began to choke her. Her eyes darted around the room, desperately seeking help. She saw Jomo struggling against two men. He managed to pin one of the men against the wall, but with his back turned to the other he didn't notice the bat cocked over his head, ready to swing.

Erin tried to call out to Jomo, but only a weak croak emerged past the choking grip. She watched in horror as the bat came down full force on the top of his scalp. He dropped to the ground. The two youths jumped on him and swung wildly at his unconscious body as though trying to crack a stubborn piñata.

Suffocating from the grip, Erin thrashed wildly against her captor but she could not free herself. She heard another bloodcurdling shriek. It was Sesi. Out of the corner of her eye, Erin saw the blur of the blade as it dug into the nurse's abdomen and drove the woman backward.

"*No!*" Erin gasped.

Erin scanned the carnage around her. Sesi lay dead on the floor. They were still beating Jomo's lifeless body with clubs. And two other youths were dragging Ayanna and Ita by their hair toward a man in the corner of the room who waited with a bloody machete.

Suddenly, Erin's view was obscured by a tall man in military fatigues. His broad face hovered over her. His eyes were filled with bloodlust and his thick lips curved in a malicious grin. He cocked the machete. Just as the blade rose over his head, another hand wrapped around his wrist and yanked it back roughly.

Erin saw that it was the militia leader who had intervened to stop her execution. "No!" he snapped. "Leave the American."

Fuming, William McGrath sat in his chair with the newspaper spread open on his desk and the phone to his ear. It took every iota of restraint not to explode into the receiver as he listened to the high-pitched self-important voice of the reporter who had written the article about his son.

Because of the Alfredson's size, scope, and international standing, including the celebrity and VIP status of some patients, the administration building's entire sixth floor was dedicated to the communications and media relations department. The staff numbered more than twenty. They were supposed to screen media inquiries and intercept them before they reached William's line. *How did this parasite, of all people, slip through?*

William knew the reporter, Denny Rymer, only by reputation. Rymer was the self-appointed watchdog of the region's professional community. Physicians were his favorite prey. He hounded them with the zeal of the McCarthy-era Communist witch-hunts. Rymer had a knack for digging up sympathetic "victims" (often children or the disabled) who had suffered from questionable medical care. Sometimes he uncovered acts of true negligence or incompetence, but more often Rymer torpedoed the reputation of physicians who were guiltless. Once Rymer got his teeth into a story, he rarely let go, often drawing out his inquisition for days or weeks across the front pages of the paper.

"Do you agree that Dr. McGrath—the *other* Dr. McGrath—performed a potentially lethal procedure without getting fully informed consent from the family?" Rymer demanded in his self-righteous nasal tone.

William took a slow breath while he mentally vetted his reply. "That is an issue of patient-doctor confidentiality on which I simply cannot comment," he said, unconcerned by how trite the answer sounded.

"Hmmm," Rymer grunted. "Perhaps if we weren't discussing your son . . ."

William's grip tightened on the receiver until his fingers ached. "My response would be the same."

"I wonder," Rymer grunted again. "The parents swear that your son did not fully explain the risks—"

"No procedure occurs at the Alfredson without a signed consent. We ensure everyone adheres to that policy."

"Yes, but according to Mr. and Mrs. Stafford, your son deliberately misrepresented the risks of the procedure in order to get them to sign the consent."

William's face burned. "Mr. Rymer, you sound more like some kind of personal injury attorney than an impartial reporter."

"I don't have much choice, do I?" Rymer said petulantly. "Your son has refused to talk to me, so I cannot present his side of the story. That's why I was hoping you *might* be a little more forthcoming."

"It would be highly irresponsible for a physician to comment publicly on medical care provided to a patient," William said pointedly. "Since the Stafford family has stated their intent to file suit, *no one*—including the family—should be discussing this case."

"Now who sounds like a lawyer?"

"If you have no further questions—"

"Listen, Dr. McGrath." Rymer's tone suddenly softened to the point of sounding sympathetic. "I realize we're talking about your son, and that can't be easy. But try to see this from the Staffords' point of view for just a moment. They've lost their only son to a treatment they agreed to without being fully aware of its risks. The guilt is killing them."

"It must be extremely difficult for the family. And I am sorry for their loss." Despite his strong bias, he believed Tyler was at least partly in the wrong for his approach to the consent. However, he knew better than to share that with anyone, especially a reporter who made a career out of disgracing physicians.

"So you agree that Dr. *Tyler* McGrath bears some responsibility for the outcome?" Rymer demanded.

The resurging anger swept away William's empathy. "You're putting words in my mouth, Mr. Rymer. I did not even remotely suggest that."

"You can't, can you? Not with your son facing a lawsuit."

"Mr. Rymer, do you have any idea how many malpractice suits are launched every single day in this country?"

"I don't see what that—"

"Thousands. The vast majority are dropped, dismissed, or proven frivolous. Very, very few of them reach the newspaper. I do not understand why you are choosing to pursue this case. This is not a newsworthy story."

"A child died, Dr. McGrath."

"And there is no sadder loss," William said. "However, that does not mean anyone is responsible for what happened."

"His parents think otherwise." With a slight snicker, Rymer added, "And you *clearly* know how strong the urge is for a parent to protect his son."

"Mr. Rymer, I think it would be best if you directed future questions directly to our media relations department."

After hanging up, William sat and stared at the phone. Without thinking, he let his hand drift to his lower back and began to rub the spot where the cancer had eaten into his vertebrae. As frustrated as he was with Denny Rymer and his inflammatory article, William had bigger worries. An e-mail he had received moments before the phone call threatened to set off a media storm around the Alfredson that would make Rymer's story pale in comparison. Marked "For Your Eyes Only," the director of communications' e-mail warned William that a TV news producer had caught wind of Senator Wilder's critical illness and the superbug rampaging through the hospital.

William was pulled from his thoughts when the office door flew open and Normie Chow marched up to his desk. He stopped and mock-saluted. "Chicken Little, reporting for duty, sir!"

In spite of himself, William chuckled at the comic sight of the balding, fiftyish microbiologist standing with his back over-arched and his hand glued to his forehead, palm outward. "I'm afraid to ask, Normie."

Chow relaxed and pulled back a chair. "Believe it or not, Bill, my old man, this doomsday prophet actually bears some good news."

William sighed. "I don't even know what that means anymore."

"A doomsday prophet is someone who—"

"Not that! I meant about the good news."

Chow shrugged. "It means a few things."

"Such as?"

"For starters, you don't need to run out and find yourself a new former presidential front-runner to replace the last one."

William sat up straighter. "Senator Wilder is better?"

"Much. He surprised the pants off the folks in the ICU. He's off the ventilator. He's even taking fluids by mouth this morning."

"That's wonderful," William murmured, feeling his first flicker of hopefulness in days. "What else?"

"Last two days, we've had a drop in the number of new *C. diff* infections reported."

"How big?"

"Five cases yesterday. Only two so far today."

William smiled. "Two days ago, we had thirteen cases in a single day. This is a promising trend."

"Before you go planning your parade route, don't forget the day is young, Bill, my boy."

William laughed out of relief.

"There's more," Chow said. "Our index case from the kitchen has recovered. She was touch and go for a good while. Her poor priest deserves air miles for all the false-alarm trips he made in to offer her last rites."

William chuckled, enjoying Chow's eccentricity more than he had in a long time. "Sounds like you're finally getting your job done, Normie."

"Don't go crazy over the top with your praise, Bill. Makes me uncomfortable to see you gush." Chow threw up his hand, feigning embarrassment. "And speaking of the kitchen, it's been seventy-two hours without any new *C. diff* detected on our surface swabs."

"So we can open the kitchen again?"

"Don't see why not."

A weight rose off William's shoulders. His backache even subsided. "This is all good, Normie. Very good. But I keep expecting to hear a catch."

"Bill, Bill, Bill . . . you know me. There's *always* a catch." Chow's expression darkened momentarily with a hint of uncharacteristic concern. "All the new cases in the last twenty-four hours have come from the Henley Building. Specifically, the surgical ICU."

"I see." The ominous implication wiped away William's smile. The Henley Building, home to the Alfredson's most critically ill, was the deadliest spot for the superbug to strike. The fatality rate could be catastrophic among those patients.

"The latest case is a post–heart transplant patient. Matter of fact, your daughter performed her operation. The girl is only twenty-something." Chow blew out his cheeks. "She ain't doing well, Bill. Not well at all."

William massaged his temple. "What do you propose we do?"

"We don't have a heckuva lot of choice," Chow said matter-of-factly. "It's kind of like having a hungry shark loose in the tots' pool. We have to shut the surgical ICU down."

"*Shut it down?*" William grimaced. "That would paralyze the Alfredson. We would have to cancel all heart surgeries and most of the bigger cancer operations. Without the backup of critical care beds, we might have to abandon all surgery."

Normie tapped his bald pate and shrugged. "You got a better idea?"

William thought frantically. Shutting down the surgical program was tantamount to closing the hospital. *We can't*, he thought. *Not when the board meeting is so close.*

Then an idea hit him. "The medical ICU has not been touched by *C. diff*, has it, Normie?" William asked.

"Not so far."

"Then we'll have to double up."

"Hold the phone! You mean combine the medical and surgical ICUs?"

"Yes. We'll leave the patients who are already infected in isolation in the surgical ICU. Use it as a quarantine space. All new postoperative patients will have to go to the medical ICU."

Chow pursed his lips. "Yeah . . . I guess that could work."

"It has to."

"I'm on it." He saluted again with a quick tap to his forehead. "Like butter on toast."

As Chow hurried from the room, William considered the mixed update the microbiologist had delivered. The decline in the new cases of *C. diff* and Wilder's recovery both boded well for the Alfredson, but all those gains would be more than erased by the impact of having to close the operating rooms.

In his twenty-five years in senior leadership, William had never endured a more tumultuous few weeks. He wondered if he was too old, and too physically frail, to helm the Alfredson at this critical juncture in its history. *Have I outlasted my usefulness here?*

William stared out the window into the courtyard below. Lately, he reflected more and more on the history of the institution. Now it was all he could think about. No threat, including the devastation wrought by the Spanish flu, had ever shut the Alfredson's operating rooms. If the *C. diff* outbreak closed them now, the damage might be undoable. Gloom enveloped him as he wondered whether this heinous superbug was destined to negate a hundred years' worth of the McGrath family legacy.

William's phone buzzed twice, indicating Eileen Hutchins had arrived for her appointment. Forcing the bleak thoughts out of his mind, he folded the newspaper and slid it into the desk's top drawer and then rose to his feet. Suddenly self-conscious, he adjusted his loose-fitting jacket before he limped to the door. He picked up the scent of lilacs the moment he reached Eileen, where she stood at the door.

Instead of the usual welcoming smile, she offered only a restrained nod. "Hello, William."

"Hello, Eileen." He smiled. "Please come in. Have a seat."

Eileen walked briskly into the room, her expression and body language more businesslike than before. Still standing, she asked, "Do you have an update on Senator Wilder's condition?"

William was surprised by how much he missed the warm familiarity that usually accompanied their meetings. "The senator is much improved. He's in stable condition now."

Eileen uttered a soft sigh and sat down in the chair across from William. "That's a huge relief," she said, but her expression remained distant.

"Eileen . . . something else is bothering you."

She opened her purse and extracted a piece of newsprint. William recognized the article on Tyler even before she had fully unfolded the paper. "I've seen it," he said.

"And?"

"It's unfortunate."

"It's a bit more than unfortunate, William." She shook her head. "And the timing . . ."

"It couldn't be worse. I know." He rubbed his eyes. "The reporter just phoned me."

She shuddered slightly in her seat. "Rymer, I assume. What did the man have to say?"

"This whole business is not about malpractice." He sighed. "The parents are devastated after losing their only son to an incurable cancer. They are lashing out any way they can."

Eileen pushed back the bracelet on her wrist. "I'm in no position to judge the validity of their allegation, but I do know that their timing is disastrous. And whether the accusation is grounded or not, it looks bad, William. Very bad. Especially considering your role."

He squinted. "My role?"

"As the father of the accused physician." She cleared her throat. "It raises the appearance of conflict of interest."

"What conflict? *Whose interest?*" he said. "It's a newspaper story. No one, not even the parents, has raised a concern directly with the hospital about the child's medical care. Besides which, we have already launched an internal review of the case."

Eileen looked up to the ceiling as if searching for heavenly guidance. "My family is just about to meet to decide the fate of this hospital. And now a very public accusation of malpractice has been leveled at one McGrath, who happens to be the son of the hospital's CEO. Most of those attending the board meeting are very aware of the long, at times rocky history our two families have shared. I can't see this helping our cause."

"I see." William swallowed away the lump that had formed in his throat. He sat up straighter, a streak of pain searing through him as he did so. "Eileen, perhaps it would be best for everyone if I submitted my resignation—"

She waved her hand to interrupt. "I am not suggesting that." Her expression softened and a more familiar glow returned to her green eyes. "I am sorry, William. I know you are not responsible. I am just so very frustrated with the way events keep conspiring against us."

Bittersweet relief washed over him. "I share your frustration, Eileen." A moment of quiet passed between them. William held out an open hand. "In spite of the setbacks, you have done an admirable job rallying support for the status quo."

She touched her cheek. "I am not so convinced."

"Well, I am. You have done wonders."

Eileen smiled gratefully. "Yet it still might not be enough."

"I realize that," he said quietly. "Eileen, I hate to add insult to injury, but we have another potential publicity crisis brewing."

Her face blanched. "Regarding?"

"Senator Wilder and the infectious outbreak." He quickly updated her about the alarming e-mail from the communications director. "Of course, now that the senator has improved, maybe the media will lose interest in the story."

"I'm not so sure." She laughed mirthlessly. "William, I think our job security might be in jeopardy."

"I'm not worried about job security."

"No?"

"I'm more worried about posterity."

Eileen tilted her head inquisitively.

William had already said more than he intended, but somehow he wanted, even needed, Eileen to understand. "My children don't see what the fuss is about. To them, the Alfredson is just another hospital. They could resume their medical careers somewhere else tomorrow without much of a sneeze."

Eileen smiled sadly. "Not quite as easy for you?"

He swept his hand through the air. "I have no desire for a career outside of here, but that has nothing to do with it."

"What then?"

"Except for college, I've spent all my years in Oakdale. At the Alfredson. This is not just my job, Eileen. It's my life. Has been since I was a child. I remember coming here with my uncles. Even then, all those years ago, it felt like . . . home."

Eileen offered an understanding nod, but said nothing.

"Lately, I've taken more and more comfort from my modest contribution to the Alfredson. And not just mine, personally, but the role my ancestors played in shaping this hospital into a world-class facility. One with a heart and a soul. Perhaps the McGrath legacy doesn't matter to anyone else, but it means so much to me." He paused. "Probably too much."

"Surely not too much, William."

Embarrassed, he broke off the eye contact and looked down at the polished surface of his desk. "My family has always paid the price for my blind dedication. My wife played second fiddle to this hospital. Jeannette accepted it without ever complaining. I promised her that in our later years, I would make up for some of our lost time. But Jeannette didn't live to see those years. Besides, I probably wouldn't have kept my word anyway."

"William—"

"And my children . . ." He cleared his throat. "I've been an absentee father. Luckily for them, Jeannette's father usually filled the role for me." He looked up at her again. "Maarten Vanderhof. Now there was a great man. He never had to choose career or family. He did it all."

She wrinkled her nose. "You're being too hard on yourself."

"Am I?" He laughed bitterly. "My son and daughter view me—and fear me—more as a chief of staff than a dad. I don't blame them, either. It's what I deserve, really."

"William," Eileen said gently, "your children's reputation precedes them both. I am sure they could have worked anywhere they wanted. And yet they both chose to come back to Oakdale and the Alfredson." She smiled. "To be near you."

"I doubt that," he said, but her words brought him some solace.

"Besides, it's never too late to reconnect with family."

The malignant throb in his back reminded him that it might be getting too late to accomplish much of anything.

Eileen leaned forward and grabbed the back of his hand, squeezing tenderly. "I haven't sacrificed nearly as much as you have, William, but I understand what this hospital means to you."

He merely nodded, enjoying the feeling of her hand on his.

"I feel it, too, William," she continued. "It's more than just pride in my family's association with the Alfredson. For me, it's like a bridge to my past." Her face creased with melancholy and her voice cracked. She let go of his hand and looked away. "It's hard to imagine that we might not be a part of its future, isn't it?"

## 28

The sight of Paige Newcomb stopped Tyler at the doorway to her room. Sitting up in the bed, the young teen was moving her head to and fro and studying herself at various angles in her handheld mirror.

Tyler broke into a chuckle. She dropped the mirror on the bed and flushed with embarrassment. "What?" she asked coyly.

"You took my advice, after all." He pointed to the bright pink wig she wore over her natural hair. "That's wild."

"I'm just trying this one out." She shrugged as she chomped noisily on a wad of bubble gum. "Agnes said I could see how I liked it."

"Well, I love it," Tyler said as he approached her bed. "Very punk. Makes a real statement."

With a giggle, she ran her hand over the wig's short-cropped hair. "I figure everyone's going to know it's a fake, so I might as well go over the top with it."

The gum's fruity scent hit Tyler as he reached her bed. "Go for it," he said.

Paige pulled off the wig. Numerous strands of her hair stuck to the liner. She straightened her thinning hair with great care, clearly attempting to avoid any more hair loss. But the effort was futile, as clumps came out with each pass. "I'm not totally sold, Dr. McGrath," she said. "Agnes has an okay wig in a brown that's kind of like my natural color. I might go with that one . . ."

"Why not both?"

"Yeah. I guess."

Tyler sat down on the edge of her bed. He glanced at her exposed skin, pleased not to see any blotches or rashes apart from the few small pimples across her cheeks and forehead. "Day two of the new treatment and no sign of another allergic reaction," he said.

"Could I still break out later?"

Tyler knew a delayed reaction was still a remote possibility, but he didn't want to spook her. He was about to dismiss the concern when he thought of the Staffords and the repercussions of his decision to withhold information. "You can develop an allergy to any medicine at any time."

Her face paled.

"*But*, Paige, you have already had four doses," he soothed. "If you were going to have a serious reaction, it probably would have happened by now. You're tolerating it well."

"I hope so." She swallowed and some of the color returned to her cheeks. "I never want go through that angio . . ."

"Angioedema." Tyler helped her with the pronunciation. "Me, neither."

"They said you saved my life."

He shook his head. "I'm the one who ordered the medicine that caused your reaction in the first place."

She shrugged again. "And the new stuff is just as good as the drugs I was supposed to get?"

Tyler hesitated. A week before he would have answered with a simple "yes," but Nate's outcome had affected his approach. "About ninety-eight or ninety-nine percent as good."

"I guess that's pretty close."

Tyler told Paige about her latest lab results, specifically the drop in her circulating white blood cells that was expected after starting chemotherapy. He explained how she would have to be watched even more closely for fever or other signs of infection and kept isolated from the outside world, since her depleted immune system would have trouble fighting off previously harmless microorganisms. Paige raised several concerns of her own—including the question that most teens asked first: "Can my friends still visit?"—but overall she seemed far calmer, showing little, if any, of the fatalistic angst that she used to ooze.

Upbeat, Tyler left Paige to her wig-fitting. He made it only a few steps down the hallway when a hand grabbed him by the elbow. He looked over to find Maya Berry standing beside him. She brought a finger to her lips. "Will you meet me in the courtyard in five minutes?" she whispered.

Her pained expression stopped him from questioning her secretive approach. "Okay."

Ten minutes later, he walked out the sliding glass door of the cafeteria and into the courtyard beyond. Maya was already outside, pacing back and forth in the shade of two large maple trees when Tyler reached her. Without a word, she began to walk toward the pathway that led to the administrative building, and he followed her. She stopped near the entrance of the building and had a glance around, ensuring no one was within earshot. "Dr. McGrath, I read that newspaper story about Nate and you."

Her cloak-and-dagger behavior suddenly made sense. "I see."

"Is any of it true?"

He looked her in the eyes. "Most of it."

"Honestly?"

"Maya, I won't make that mistake again."

"Do you mean about the consent?" She paused. "Or never using Vintazomab again?"

"The consent. I won't ever downplay the risk again."

Maya's eyes filled with insight. "What happened to that boy . . . that's why you're reluctant to give Keisha the medicine, isn't it?"

Tyler nodded. "I'm a little gun-shy, yeah."

Her voice cracked. "There are no other drugs that can fight Keisha's cancer, are there?"

"I don't think so, Maya."

She sniffed a few times, but when she spoke her voice was strong. "I hid the newspaper from my husband."

"Why?"

She sighed. "Jonah doesn't think we need to take drastic steps for Keisha. He is still convinced the Lord will intervene."

At a loss for words, Tyler just nodded.

"He won't, at least not how Jonah thinks He will. I don't know how I know, but I know it in my bones." She gaped at him. "I don't care what Craig Stafford or that reporter said. I trust you with my baby's life. If God is going to help us, it will be through *you*, Dr. McGrath."

"Maya, my department head has banned any further use of the drug until—"

She waved a hand to stop him. "We both know Keisha needs that medicine. You just have to give it to her. *Please*. Just give my baby another chance. That's all I ask."

They stared at each other for a long moment. "Okay," he said softly. "I'll order everything up this afternoon. We should be able to start Keisha on the Vintazomab tomorrow."

Tears suddenly welled in her eyes and flowed down her cheeks. "Oh, thank you, Dr. McGrath. Thank you."

"I have to tell Jonah everything. You understand?"

She nodded. "He doesn't have to know about Nate, does he?"

"I won't lie to him, Maya."

Her round face creased with purpose. "I would never ask you to. I want Jonah to know about the risks and all. I just don't think he needs to hear what happened to that poor boy. Besides, isn't there some kind of doctor-patient confidentiality that would stop you from talking about it?"

"But it's in the newspaper. And I think it's a story 'with legs' as the expression goes."

She wiped away the last of her tears. "Let me worry about that, Dr. Mc-Grath."

Tyler left Maya on the pathway and headed back to the children's hospital. Despite Keisha's temporary improvement on steroids, the medicine had only been stalling the inevitable. Her mother was right. Vintazomab was Keisha's last real hope. But the dread rose with each step nearer at the thought of infusing the same experimental medication into Keisha's spine that had pushed Nate over the edge.

Tyler cut off the pathway and onto the lawn. Focused on his thoughts, he walked past a tree without even noticing the person sitting at its base until she called out to him. "Well hello, Tyler."

He stopped and looked down to see Nikki. In her mauve scrubs, she sat on a small blanket with her back to the tree trunk. She held a bagel in her hand.

"Not a bad spot for lunch," he said.

"There are worse." She sheltered her eyes from the sun and grinned. "Want to pull up a tree?"

"Okay," he said. "I'm just going to grab a sandwich. You need anything?"

She dabbed at her lip with a finger. "I'd look a lot less trailer-trashy with a napkin."

"Done."

A few minutes later, he wandered back out with a chicken breast sandwich, a bottle of water, and several extra napkins. He sat down across from her and unwrapped his sandwich.

"So?" she said, stretching out the word. "How are you?"

"Better."

"Me, too."

With her brown hair falling loosely around her shoulders and her cheeks flushed with a healthy golden glow, Nikki did look better. And more attractive than ever. But as he raised his eyes to hers, he saw that the pupils of her brown eyes were tightly constricted. He had noticed the same small pupils the last time they were together, sitting in Paige's room after her life-threatening reaction. Tyler wondered if her eyes were simply reacting to the bright sunlight, but the doctor in him did not accept the explanation. Her pupils were the size of pinholes. He had seen the same response many times in his patients, but only the ones on narcotic painkillers.

The state of her pupils, combined with the dreamy quality of her features, reminded him of her confession about her hydromorphone addiction. *Is she using again?*

"What's the matter, Tyler?" She dabbed at her cheeks. "Am I still wearing cream cheese?"

"It's just . . ." He cleared his throat. "You don't usually let your hair down at work."

"Are you being funny, Doctor?"

"Apparently not," he said, eager to change the subject. "I am going to start Keisha on Vintazomab tomorrow."

Nikki smiled broadly. "About time," she said.

"It is, isn't it?"

She squinted at him and her front teeth dug into her lower lip. "You nervous?"

He nodded. "Once bitten . . . and all that."

"It's going to be okay, Tyler," she said softly. "You'll see."

"Will you be around to help me?"

Her hand swam through the air in a florid gesture. "I'm your humble servant. Always."

"Nikki, are you all right?"

"We've been through this. About five minutes ago. Remember? We established we were both better." She giggled. "You want me to read the transcript back to you?"

"It's just that . . ."

"Out with it."

"You're acting a little . . . different."

She dismissed the idea with a small wave. "It's all this fresh air and sunlight. Does wonders for me. Sometimes it makes me a little silly, too."

He did not intend to pursue it, so he almost surprised himself when he said, "And your pupils . . ."

Her smile drained away, and she shifted uneasily. "What about them?"

"They're so constricted."

"So? I forgot my sunglasses," she snapped, and quickly looked away. "I'm not sure you've noticed, but it's damn bright out here."

"Of course—"

She hastily gathered up the remains of her lunch, stuffed it back into her nylon bag, and jumped to her feet. "I'm already over my break. I better run." She turned to go.

He stood up and caught her arm. "Nikki, listen, if you want to talk, anytime, I'm—"

She pulled her wrist free of his hand. Without looking at him, she said, "Remember the last time we talked? *At O'Doole's?* That didn't work out so good for either one of us."

"That was my fault," he said. "I meant that if you had anything you wanted to get off your chest—"

"I don't need your sympathy, Tyler." She glanced at him briefly, her eyes bloodshot and her expression pained, and then looked away. "And I certainly don't need any more of your mixed fucking signals."

"Nikki . . ."

But she lurched away from him and broke into a jog toward the children's hospital. He stood and watched her go. Her sudden defensiveness only hardened his suspicion.

Squinting to read his watch in the sunlight he realized he was already late for his afternoon in the outpatient clinic, and his appointment slate was crowded.

Dodging between examining rooms, he ran a minimum of two patients behind all afternoon. His load was compounded by the phone calls he had to make between appointments to organize Keisha's Vintazomab infusion for the following day.

It was after eight P.M. when he pulled into his driveway. Kramer met him outside the front door, meowing to be let in.

"Jill?" he called out as he stepped inside.

"I'm in the kitchen," she replied weakly.

He walked into the kitchen to find her sitting at the counter with the newspaper spread out in front of her. She cradled a mug of tea in her hands. He was surprised to see that she was dressed in the same pink dressing gown she was wearing when he had left for work in the morning. She wasn't wearing any makeup. Her face looked pale and drawn, but her lips cracked into a slight smile. "Hi," she said.

Tyler headed over to her chair. He bent to kiss her, but she moved her mouth away and his lips brushed against her cheek. Uncharacteristically, she shot out her arms and pulled him into a tight hug.

"Tyler, I'm so sorry," she said as she released him.

He detected the faint odor of vomit underneath her toothpaste. "Sorry? For what?"

With a worried frown, Jill turned the pages of the newspaper over to reveal the article featuring him.

He nodded. "It's okay. I'm dealing with it."

"Really?"

"Yes." He pointed at her dressing gown. "Did you leave work early?"

"I never went." She ruffled the lapels on her robe.

In their ten years together, he had never known her to miss a single day of work. "Jill, what's wrong?"

She shook her head. "My stomach is a little upset. It's just stress."

His concern rose. "You sure that's all it is?"

"Yeah. I'm better now." She waved her hand. "I even ate a banana and a few crackers."

"Is that why you didn't go to work?"

"I couldn't, Tyler." Her eyes dropped to the countertop. "All those people in my lab, all the phone calls and the e-mails, my colleagues . . . I just couldn't face any of them today." She pushed back her hair. "I just don't know what to say to any of them."

Tyler had rarely before seen his wife look so vulnerable. The sight moved him. He reached out and tenderly ran a hand over her cheek. "Jill, they'll understand."

"No," she said hoarsely.

"How do you know?"

She swallowed loudly. "Because if this kind of research fraud happened to anyone else, I wouldn't understand . . . or excuse them . . . for it."

He wanted to say something reassuring but everything he thought of struck him as trite and empty. Instead, he wrapped his arms around her and pulled her head against his chest.

"Thank you," she said.

"For what?"

"Understanding."

"If only I were one of your colleagues."

She chuckled into his chest and then pulled her head far enough back to look up to him. "Tyler, I need to show you something."

He released her from his grip but she didn't rise from her chair. Instead, she dug a hand into the pocket of her robe and pulled out a small clear Baggie. At first, Tyler was bewildered by its content, but then he recognized the butter knife–shaped home pregnancy kit. "Jill . . ."

She stared at him stone-faced. "I'm pregnant, Ty."

Tyler was too stunned to reply.

Jill waved the test in front of him. "There's no doubt."

A huge involuntary smile crossed his lips as the excitement swelled inside him. He folded his arms around her and lifted her off her seat. He rocked her gently from side to side before finally letting go. "You're pregnant, Jill!"

Her pained expression gave way to a small smile. "Who else but me could time it so badly?"

"Don't say that!" He held her by the shoulders. "Don't even think it."

"It's true, Tyler. I've committed research fraud and I'm on the brink of academic ruin. And you, you're dealing with a malpractice suit on the front pages of the—"

He put his fingers to her lips to cut her off. "Jill, none of that matters right now. We're going to have a baby." With his other hand, he reached down and rubbed her belly through her gown. "*Our* baby, Jill."

## 29

Jill had never heard pregnant women complain of being too cold, only too warm. But as she pulled the comforter tighter around herself, she fought off another chill. Her pregnancy was no longer free of symptoms. Her intestines rumbled constantly, and the nausea worsened by the hour.

Jill glanced at the alarm clock on her nightstand: 3:05 A.M. Still far from sleep, she rolled onto her side to face Tyler. He was only partly covered by the comforter. She wasn't hogging the covers; he always slept warm. Unlike the past few nights when he had practically thrashed the night away through restless nightmares, Tyler was still and his expression placid. She resisted the urge to touch or kiss his face. Instead, she tucked in as close as possible without waking him. In one week, Jill had plummeted from finger's-length reach of her lifelong dream to the depths of academic disgrace. Her ambition had been so single-minded that she had tuned out much of the rest of her life, including friends and family. Staring at her husband's peaceful face, Jill realized she had risked—and maybe still did—losing him, too. She almost grimaced at the memory of Nikki clasping Tyler's arm, her gorgeous face aglow with adulation.

Jill ran her fingers over her belly. It was as flat as ever, but she could imagine her fetus growing beneath. With a tinge of shame, she remembered her ambivalence at discovering she was pregnant. "I do want this baby, Ty," she whispered to her husband. "*Our* baby."

A flicker of optimism comforted Jill. Maybe her career couldn't survive the news of her research irregularities, but she was no longer convinced her world would end with its disclosure, either. Professional successes had never fully brought the fulfillment she had thought they would. Perhaps she had a better chance of finding it in parenthood.

Jill thought of her parents. The guilt of neglecting them gnawed at her. She was overdue for a return trip to San Diego to help out her mother and spend time with her father. With her lab suddenly in limbo, she contemplated going down for longer than a weekend—possibly even a month—to really reconnect with her parents. At the rate her dad was deteriorating, there would not be many opportunities left. Tyler would understand. Maybe he would even come along. After all, a break from Oakdale—away from the Alfredson—was what they both desperately needed.

With those hopeful thoughts and schemes rattling around her head, she drifted off into a dreamless sleep.

Jill didn't wake until after nine o'clock. Tyler was gone. But she had no time to think about anything except the knots seizing her stomach. She bolted out of the bed to the bathroom. Her head just made it to the edge of the open toilet bowl before she vomited violently. Kneeling in front of the bowl, she threw up three more times until she had nothing left to spit out. Her intestines twisted and gurgled noisily at the acrid smell of her own vomit.

She leaned back against the wall and spoke to her abdomen. "You're not going to make this easy, are you, kid?"

Jill sat on the edge of the bathtub and waited until the waves of nausea and cramping settled enough that she felt safe moving away from the toilet. She took a long hot shower but still had trouble warming herself against the chills that followed in the wake of her violent nausea.

Jill waited another fifteen minutes before she felt safe to leave the house. On the drive in to the Alfredson, she had to pull over to the side of the road twice to throw up again. She didn't reach the hospital until a few minutes before ten A.M.

Head down and sunglasses on, Jill trudged for the neurosciences building, praying she wouldn't be spotted by a colleague or anyone else who might want to discuss her study. Halfway there, she remembered the earlier phone call from one of the residents informing her of Senator Wilder's improved condition. Jill felt obliged to visit him, though she dreaded the prospect. It wasn't his illness—Infection Control had deemed him no longer contagious—so much as her embarrassment and shame over the tainted study that made her feel so uncomfortable. After all, not only had Wilder volunteered to be a subject, but he was prepared to be a spokesperson on her behalf.

Inside the Henley Building, Jill followed the signs to the surgical ICU where Wilder had been moved. The unit had been closed to postoperative patients and now housed only patients who were recovering from *C. diff* or quarantined after exposure to the superbug.

Outside the unit, Jill donned two pairs of gloves and double-checked the snugness of her mask and eye shield before she slipped into the protective gown. She paused to let a wave of nausea and cramping pass and then, satisfied with her protective gear, stepped past the gowned Secret Service agent guarding Wilder's door and into his private room.

Propped up by a pillow, the senator looked even thinner since her last visit and his color was paler. But his lopsided grin was as wide as ever and his eyes still possessed their usual sparkle. "Hello, Dr. Laidlaw!" he said, recognizing her through her mask. "I bet you thought I was one patient you didn't have to worry about any . . . m-more."

She stopped at the foot of his bed, conscious not to get too close. "I was very worried about you, Senator."

"Takes more than a s-stomach flu to finish me off."

"You scared us."

He chuckled. "Scared myself a tad, too."

Jill smiled behind her mask. "I'm glad you're doing better, Senator."

"My guts are better. The rest of me . . . not so much." His tone assumed a more businesslike edge. "Dr. Laidlaw, I'm eager to get started on your new treatment."

Jill glanced down at her hands.

"What is it?" he asked, his expression clouding with concern. "Am I too late to en-enroll?"

Jill wavered a moment and then said, "There's a problem with the study."

"What kind of problem?"

Jill looked up at him. "The data was, um, manipulated."

His jaw fell open. "You mean someone c-cooked the results?"

She swallowed. "It appears that way."

"Who?"

"I am not entirely sure, Senator, though I have my suspicions."

"So you didn't know about this tam-tampering beforehand?" His slightly uneven gaze still penetrated.

"Not until a few days ago. No."

His forehead wrinkled and his eyes narrowed. "Dr. Laidlaw, does your st-stem cell therapy actually work?"

"I think so." She nodded. "But now that I've used more *accurate* data, the results aren't as dramatic as I'd first thought."

"Oh. I s-see."

Watching the hope drain from Wilder's eyes, Jill felt the guilt soar anew. She wondered how many other patients were already counting on the rumored promise of her treatment.

"Dr. Laidlaw, what if I wanted to pro-proceed anyway?" Wilder rasped.

Jill grimaced. "You'd want to go ahead in light of what I just told you?"

"Yes."

"I don't think the hospital would allow it, Senator." She sighed. "Once the Research Ethics Committee learns of the irregularities, they'll suspend the study. They have to."

"I see."

Having trouble meeting his eyes again, Jill began to backpedal for the door. "I'm sure you're still exhausted from your ordeal. I'll come back tomorrow and—"

"Dr. Laidlaw, those ICU doctors never asked me if I wanted . . . treatment."

"You mean for the *C. diff* infection?"

He nodded. "I don't blame them. I got sick so quickly. They worked so hard just to keep me alive." He paused. "Maybe t-too hard."

"Senator, do you really mean that?"

Wilder viewed her for a long moment. "A few years ago, people said I was going to be the next president. Now, I can barely walk across a room. And without a miracle, we both know I'm only going to det-deteriorate." He shook his head slowly. "I know there are MS victims far worse off than me, but I am not cut out for the life of an in-invalid, Dr. Laidlaw."

A lump formed in her throat, but she could think of nothing to say.

"I want to try your stem cell treatment," he went on. "I'm w-willing to face the risks, whatever they are. Even if it's a long shot, I want one more chance to reclaim my life and my career. I want a chance to finish the race I started. Can you un-understand?"

"Yes, Senator, I can," she said, filling with empathy. "I will do what I can to proceed with your stem cell transplant."

He flashed a crooked grin. "Thank you," he said hoarsely.

Outside the unit, she shed her protective clothing and dumped it into a biohazard container. She was pulled from the verge of tears by the cramp that tore at her belly. She clutched a hand over her mouth and sprinted for the washroom down the hallway, relieved to find it empty. She arrived just in time to throw up in the sink.

*How can I go from feeling nothing to this in just a few days?* she wondered as she studied her gaunt face in the mirror.

After fifteen minutes, the cramps settled. She hurried across the complex and into the neurosciences building. She was relieved to reach the door without being stopped by anyone. The people inside her lab—none of whom had yet heard about the taint of research fraud—were all smiles as she entered. Two of the young male research assistants even hooted and pumped their fists in the air as though Jill were a rock star taking the stage.

Jill mumbled an embarrassed hello and rushed to her office. In the hallway, she almost bumped into Carla Julian, another grad student in biostatistics. The cute, though emotionally frail, brunette nodded once to Jill but appeared equally eager not to chat. Carla had never been the same since her breakup with Andrew Pinter. Jill had heard rumors Pinter had broken Carla's heart by sleeping with her best friend, but she never broached the subject with the girl, always steering clear of her staff's personal lives.

As soon as Jill crossed the threshold of her office, she locked the door behind her. Gripped by another wave of nausea, she pressed her forehead against the cold door. Breathing slowly, she tried to decide on the best way to break the bad news to the rest of her lab, realizing that many of them would take it as hard as she had.

A laugh came from somewhere behind her. "Paparazzi causing you grief?"

Jill spun to see Andrew Pinter at her desk, leaning back in the chair with his hands clasped behind his head. The remnants of another muffin overflowed a torn paper bag lying on the desk beside his coffee cup.

The sight of him ignited her ire. "Can you please leave my office, Andrew?" she muttered tersely.

"Nice greeting." He offered a rakish grin. "I'm not sure sleeping in agrees with you."

"I'm not in the mood."

"I'd say."

"*Out*, Andrew!"

"I'm already gone." Pinter stretched and yawned noisily before rising from the chair. He swept up the coffee cup, paper bag, and most of the crumbs and tossed them into the wastepaper basket. He ambled around the desk and toward her. "You still sick, Jill?"

For a moment, she thought he knew about her pregnancy and nausea but then she remembered her alibi for not coming to work the previous day was that she had picked up a virus. "I'm doing better, thanks," she muttered.

"You look kind of peaked, as my grandma used to say."

"I'm okay."

He stopped a few feet from her. "What about those data files?" he asked.

Jill resisted the impulse to grab her abdomen as another cramp stabbed her. She intended to confront the statistician, but not until after she had let the rest of the team know about the data tampering. "What about them?" she asked.

"Are you done with them yet? I need to reorganize the files for the next go-round of data collection."

She tasted acid. "I didn't think researchers were supposed to reorganize data," she blurted.

He rolled his eyes and grunted. "I didn't say anything about reorganizing the data."

"Maybe not, but I did."

The self-satisfied smile slid off his lips. "What's your point, Jill?"

"Who excluded all those patients?"

Pinter shrugged impatiently. "We all did. You, me, and most of the others here working on the study."

Jill's face heated and her heart pounded against her rib cage. "I saw your name on most of those exclusions."

"No shit!" he snapped. "I'm the gopher who gathers and keeps the data forms, remember? Every one of those exclusions had a reason for it spelled out on the front page."

"You found some pretty flimsy reasons."

"Your opinion. I ran every one of those exclusions past at least one of the other research assistants."

"You didn't run them by me."

"Here we go again." Pinter heaved a sigh. "I didn't think I needed to bother you. What am I, eight? I know how to do my job. I could—"

"I plugged them back in," she said, cutting him off.

His eyes narrowed. "The exclusions?"

She nodded.

"You can't do that," he scoffed. "That's changing endpoints in the middle of a study. It's meaningless."

Knives tore through her stomach as she fought off a scowl. "Well, I did. And guess what?"

Pinter's cheeks had flushed red. "The results changed," he grunted.

"The variance between control and treatment groups dropped substantially. It sank the P value, Andrew. We lost the statistical significance of the original results."

"I see that all the time in statistics." His tone warmed as he mustered a contrite grin. "We go back, add a few raw scores that weren't there in the first go-round, and presto—you get a whole new playing field." He reached out and laid his hand on her shoulder. His thumb and fingers dug into her skin and began to massage the ball of her shoulder.

Jill recoiled from his touch. The nausea intensified. She backed away, concerned she might vomit on the spot.

"Those patients were excluded for a reason," he soothed. "You can't just go and plug them back in. It screws up everything."

"Which is exactly why I think they were excluded!"

His smile vanished and his eyes narrowed to slits. "Are you accusing me of doctoring the data?"

She could feel her intestines coiling. "Yes."

"This is so fucked up." He shook his head and sighed again. "Okay. Yes. I knew what happened to the graphs if you plugged that exclusion data back in. That's why I didn't want to show you those raw scores." Then he hurried to add, "I'm a statistician. All I do is run and rerun the permutations. It doesn't mean I cooked anything."

"It means you lied to me, Andrew."

"No. It means I withheld a hypothetical outcome from you. There's a big difference. Besides, I don't know why we're arguing about this." He held out his palm as if offering an olive branch. "Aside from you and me, no one is ever going to see how the exclusions affect the results. We're not obligated to publish the subjects' scores after they've been excluded, right? For all anyone else knows, we don't even have follow-up data on those people."

Jill understood Pinter's point. They probably could bury the data so that even the study's auditors never knew how the exclusions might have altered the results. But it didn't change anything for her. "Problem is, I know, Andrew," she said.

"And guess what? I'm relieved you do. I didn't like hiding it from you." He ran a finger along his goatee, and showed her another small smile. "At the end of the day, it's just a statistical anomaly. It doesn't invalidate all the mind-blowing work you've done so far. Now, if you were to go public with this . . ."

A series of spasms twisted Jill's intestines. She was having trouble focusing on Pinter's words. A new fear was beginning to take root in her head.

"Look how far we've come. You, especially!" He pinched his fingers together. "You're this far from stardom. The *Prize*, Jill!"

"I've never been further," she choked out through her pain.

"Don't you get it? If this gets out, people will assume your whole treatment protocol was a giant fraud. Think about *that*, Jill. All your work. All the potential benefit to those poor sons of bitches with advanced multiple sclerosis. Your whole future . . ." He snapped his finger crisply. "Up in smoke! All for the sake of a stupid little statistical anomaly?"

"It's bad enough that I unintentionally abetted research fraud," she said through gritted teeth. "I'm sure as hell not going to cover up your crime to try to save my ass."

He lunged toward her. Jill shot her arms up to protect herself, but he stopped a foot away from her. His lip curled in a malicious sneer. His eyes burned with hostility. "You fucking self-righteous bitch. I'm not letting you make me your scapegoat."

Despite the cramps and Pinter's threatening stance, Jill stood her ground. "*Scapegoat*? You did this to yourself. To all of us! You doctored the data! You gambled with the future of everyone involved in this lab."

"I *saved* your fucking study! Your career!" he spat. "And this is how you thank me?"

His stale breath turned her stomach yet again. "All you've done is disgrace me and the rest of our team," she cried. "The whole damn Alfredson."

"You'll be just fine, princess." He shook a finger at the end of her nose.

"Unlike you, I didn't marry into the Alfredson royalty. My future's not guaranteed. I've had to work for every inch I've ever . . ."

His words faded away. Jill shot her hand to her mouth, but it was too late. The bilious green vomit sprayed between her fingers. At the same time, she felt as though she were going to explode from the other end.

*Oh my God, it's not the pregnancy, is it? I've got it, don't I?* Her insides turned to ice. *I have* C. diff!

*30*

Lorna reached for the coffee cup that rested inches from a phallic African carving. She didn't notice how close her fingers came to brushing against the sizable upright sculpture. The erotic artwork surrounding her no longer registered; neither did the oppressive darkness or the room's heavy wood-work. She wasn't even conscious of how the stale air, trapped inside by the permanently closed windows, irritated her dry throat. She was focused ex-clusively on 1897, desperate to find out what happened in the wake of Olivia and Arthur Grovenor's drowning.

Coffee was Lorna's idea. She was running out of time. Extending her stay at the Alfredson manor was not an option, even if she could stomach more nights in the stuffy room where Dot had romped with her Beat poets. Lorna hoped to keep her great-aunt alert and on track well into the evening to finish the tale.

After a while, Lorna wondered if the caffeine was even necessary. The old crone showed no signs of slowing. And the bottle and a half of red wine that Dot had almost single-handedly drained over dinner had no no-ticeable impact on her speech or manner.

"Their bodies didn't wash ashore for two days," Dot said matter-of-factly about the morbid aftermath of the boating accident. "No one—not even I—will care when *I* finally go, but it's *tragic* when people die in their prime. Imagine the grief, darling."

"Marshall's?"

"Marshall. Evan. The Grovenors. Theodora." She shook her head. "Only my father—still a baby—was oblivious to his parents' death."

"So Marshall adopted Junior right after the accident?"

"Arthur's parents didn't try to stop him. Arthur had several older siblings, and the Grovenors already had a brood of grandchildren." Dot fingered her cup without raising it. "My grandfather—technically, of course, he really was my great-grandfather—finally had the Alfredson heir he always wanted." She sighed heavily. "Though I don't think even vain old Marshall would have made that trade-off. Those who knew him from before said he never recovered from Olivia's death."

"And Evan?"

"I doubt he fared much better," Dot said. "Of course, McGrath had more than a few preoccupations in the spring of 1897. The Alfredson was still in its infancy, and suffering from all nature of growing pains. And speaking of infants, Evan's first son, George, was born the very same day Olivia was laid to rest. Otherwise Evan might have been among the more than four hundred people who did show up for her funeral." She wagged her finger toward the ceiling. "I still have all the clippings upstairs of the newspaper stories and obituaries. Marshall kept every word relating to the tragedy—right down to the invoice from the funeral parlor—in a lovely hand-crafted teak box with her photograph inlaid on the cover."

"Could I see it?" Lorna asked, trying not to appear too eager.

"Tomorrow, perhaps." Dot sighed as she patted the armrest beside her. "I'm *absolutely* planted for the evening. It would take several well-placed sticks of dynamite to move me."

Lorna knew there was no point in arguing. If necessary, she could always find the same articles in the archives of the Seattle library. Instead, she said, "Dot, the Alfredson came into being as a payoff—of sorts—from Marshall to Olivia so she would marry a man she didn't love."

Dot tilted her head from side to side. "I suppose."

"So with Olivia gone, how did Marshall view his ongoing commitment to the hospital?"

"Clearly, *darling*, history tells us that he didn't just up and walk away from it."

*I guess not, you old bitch!* Lorna thought, but she merely nodded. "Of course."

Dot took a quick sip of her coffee that Lorna had seen her spike with a healthy shot of whisky. "In many ways, Olivia's death only solidified Marshall's connection to the Alfredson."

"*Solidified?* Why?"

"To begin with, Junior now carried *his* surname," Dot said. "Suddenly, Marshall could look forward to the prospect of a continued Alfredson lineage in the Pacific Northwest. He saw a new relevance, in terms of posterity, to the family-named hospital." She ran her hand absently down the back of the copulating ceramic samurai on the table beside her. "Though I believe the real reason Marshall threw himself more fully behind the clinic was because he knew what it had meant to his daughter."

Lorna nodded. "Olivia sacrificed a lot for that hospital, didn't she?"

"She sacrificed *everything* for the place, darling." Dot sighed a slight whistle. "Olivia had no interest in sailing. If not for her foolish husband, she would have never been caught at sea in the middle of a squall. In effect, by striking that bargain with her father—agreeing to marry Arthur Grovenor—Olivia forfeited her life for the Alfredson. My grandfather must have realized it, too."

Lorna nodded, trying to decide if this information was helpful to her cause. "Did Olivia's death affect Marshall and Evan's relationship?"

"Only for the worse, darling." Dot chortled. "Marshall blamed Evan as much as Arthur for everything that happened to his daughter."

"Did he try to push Evan out of the Alfredson?"

Dot ran a hand over her shorn white hair. "They continued to butt heads as much as, or perhaps more than, before. Marshall still insisted that the clinic was being run far too much like a charity hospital. 'Like something the Catholics might operate,' he would rail in disgust. However, Marshall didn't try to wrestle control of the hospital away from McGrath—at least not right away. Perhaps out of respect for his daughter's memory."

*How do you know all this?* Lorna wondered again. For days, she had tried to work out who might have been her great-aunt's source for the intimate historical detail. Curiosity finally got the better of her. "Dot, the way you recount these stories . . . it's as though you were there."

"Darling, I might be an absolute *dinosaur*, but even I am not *that* old."

Lorna held her palms up. "Then how do you know the specifics so well?"

"To begin with, I read Olivia's journal."

Lorna's heart sped at the prospect. "Olivia kept a journal?"

Dot nodded. "As a child, I used to love exploring this old mansion. One day, I found it hidden under the wood beams in the attic. Of course, we are talking about the *nineteenth* century. Her writing was far more like self-indulgent teen poetry than a proper diary. But Olivia had a gift for prose. At the time, I wasn't much younger than Olivia would have been when she wrote it. Once I read about the mysterious doctor she had fallen in love with, I just had to learn more."

"But how did you?"

Dot's eyes twinkled again. "I had someone on the inside, you see. Someone who lived through it all."

"Who?"

"You're the historian, darling." Dot winked. "I am sure you can figure it out."

Lorna's mind raced through the list of candidates. She imagined her great-aunt would have been too young to have known Evan McGrath well enough to discuss Olivia with him, let alone be privy to his most private thoughts and memories. And even though Marshall had lived through part of Dot's childhood, Lorna was beyond certain that the fiercely proud man would never have told his granddaughter about the scandal involving his only daughter. Only one possible name popped to mind. "Theodora Douglas."

Dot clapped her hands together. "Well done, darling."

"You knew her, then?"

"Very well," Dot said. "Mother died of cervical cancer when I was only seven. My father, Junior, always wanted to conquer the world and make a name for himself bigger than even Marshall's. Growing up, I spent as much time with Theodora as anyone. She worked for our family until the day she died, you know. She helped raise three generations of Alfredsons—Olivia, Junior, and then me. Of course, she was already positively *ancient* when I was a child." She waved her hand around the room. "Despite her age, Marshall, and then later Junior, always found some small role for her. To be honest, I think the men were too terrified of her to ever try to get rid of her."

Lorna reached for her cup and took a sip. The coffee was cold, but she had no intention of interrupting Dot to get it heated up. "Still, it seems odd to me that in the twenties, a maid would share such . . . explicit details . . . with her employer's daughter."

"Not the twenties, darling," Dot said. "The thirties. I was already a teenager, and pestered Theodora relentlessly for the details. Eventually, I wore the old relic down." Dot glanced sidelong at Lorna. "Much in the same way you've done to me, darling."

Lorna laughed uncomfortably, again sensing insight in Dot's catty remark. She shifted in her seat. "Dot, you were meant to tell this story."

Her great-aunt smiled enigmatically before continuing. "Old as she was—in her nineties at the time—Theodora's memory was ironclad."

Lorna put her cup down. "Okay, but how about Evan McGrath? How did Theodora know so much about his side of the story?"

Dot flashed another sly grin. "Theodora might have worked for us *forever*, but she did have a life outside the Alfredsons, you know."

Lorna suddenly made the connection. "Moses Brown!"

"Though they lived apart—Theodora continuing to work for the Alfredsons in Seattle, and Moses for Evan in Oakdale—they stayed together until Moses died in 1918."

Lorna nodded. It all made sense. "And Moses had been Evan's confidant throughout his affair with Olivia."

"Moses became McGrath's lifelong friend." Dot nodded. "He ended up as the Alfredson's first building engineer."

Now that she had uncovered Dot's source, Lorna was eager to get back to the boating accident. "So Olivia's death left both Marshall and Evan heartbroken . . ."

"Life went on as it tends to do." Dot cracked her knuckles. "My grandfather dedicated his time and energy to his new son. Before Junior could even walk, Marshall began to groom him for his *ascendancy* to the Alfredson throne. Meanwhile, Evan was extremely busy with his young family and his other baby, the Alfredson. After George was born, Grace and Evan had two more children in quick succession. Olivia in 1898 and then Nicholas in 1900."

"*Olivia?*" Lorna grunted. "I still cannot believe Evan named his daughter after Marshall's."

"Why not? I doubt Grace knew any better. And how could Marshall stop them?" Dot shook her head. "Besides, no one ever called her Olivia. She was always simply Liv. And she was the absolute apple of her father's eye."

"And what about Junior? Did Evan ever discover that he might have actually been Junior's real father?"

"That was one secret Theodora kept even from Moses." Dot touched her temple conspiratorially. "But Grandfather knew, of course. And it was to become quite an issue for the old man."

---

With a world at war and outdated colonial attitudes falling by the wayside, Marshall and Evan championed the idea of integration and racial harmony at the Alfredson, long before the concept would be embraced by most other hospitals in America.
—*The Alfredson: The First Hundred Years* by Gerald Fenton Naylor

Evan sat at his desk staring out his second-floor window. He loved looking down on the rolling lawn and the colorfully landscaped gardens. They were never more beautiful than in the early spring months when the cherry blossoms seemed to flower overnight. He enjoyed the view even more now that two more brick buildings—the second one almost completed—had sprung up on either side of the original clinic. He loved to watch the automobiles and trucks rolling in and out of the paved driveway leading up to the main entrance. The loud chugging motors and the smell of the burning petroleum filled him with a sense of vitality, progress, and even hope.

Evan still remembered, as though it were yesterday, standing with Moses at the mouth of the muddy pit and watching Marshall's men excavate the site. He could not believe the Alfredson had already marked its twentieth anniversary or that he had turned fifty the previous winter. Though Evan had put on a few pounds around the waist and suffered from intermittent bouts of sciatica, which he tamed with aspirin, he felt otherwise as spry and energetic as he had at thirty. Time had numbed the sense of loss that had plagued him through the clinic's early years. He thought of Olivia, and Virginia, as often as ever, but the memories were easier now, retaining their joy without the piercing loneliness they had once conjured.

Evan and Grace's marriage had evolved into a comfortable businesslike relationship that suited them both, though at times they had little to say to each other. Evan took more and more satisfaction in watching his three children, each so different from the other, bloom into such decent adults. He had high hopes that George or Nicholas would someday step into his medical leadership role at the Alfredson.

*If Liv does not beat them to it!* He laughed to himself.

His daughter had no interest in following her mother into teaching school. The eighteen-year-old had made it clear since she was ten that she intended to become a doctor like her father. There was already precedent for it, too. Evan had only recently accepted the application of a female physician who specialized in pediatric care.

With a deep sense of contentment, Evan watched the bricklayers put the finishing touches to the roofline of the new building. He was incredibly proud of what had been accomplished at the clinic. It boasted sixty-seven physicians, many of them internationally renowned, who worked in over twenty different specialties. The radiology and laboratory departments were among the best in the country. And access to the Alfredson had been steadily improved as its name grew in stature. Instead of the original meandering five-hour train ride, people could now drive by automobile from Seattle to Oakdale on the new road in less than two hours.

Every day new patients poured in from all across Washington and well beyond, seeking the exemplary and humane care on which the Alfredson had built its reputation. And not only people of means. Despite ongoing battles with Marshall and even some of his own medical staff, Evan had tenaciously stuck to the clinic's founding principle that no patient in need, regardless of financial or social standing, would be turned away.

A rap on the door drew Evan's attention, and he reluctantly turned from the window. "Come in," he called, expecting his secretary, Mrs. Corley, to arrive for dictations.

Instead, his eldest son, George, strode in. A month away from his twentieth birthday, the boy was already taller than Evan. George shared his father's dark handsome features, but he had yet to shed his teenaged scrawniness. Still, George had always carried himself with a somber deportment far beyond his years. Now, as a third-year medical student at the University of Washington, he was serious to the point of grave. Evan sometimes jokingly referred to him as "my old son."

As George approached the desk with a newspaper tucked under his arm, his expression was particularly grim. "What is it, Son?" Evan asked.

"Have you not heard, Father?" George pulled the newspaper from under his arm and laid out the front page on the desk facing Evan.

Evan glanced down at the page, dated April 3, 1917. The headline's three letters consumed most of the page. "*WAR!*" it screamed.

"President Wilson has asked Congress to declare war on Germany," George said in a voice resonating with patriotism.

Evan sighed heavily. He had heard the saber-rattling for months, but he had hoped that America would stay out of the conflict that had been ravaging Europe for almost three years. "This is not good, George. Not good at all."

"What do you mean, Father?" George asked with surprised indignation. "The Germans are sinking all ships in European waters, regardless of the flags they fly or the innocent lives lost. German spies even tried to convince our Mexican neighbors to attack us." He pointed to the paper. "This is exactly what those Huns deserve."

Evan shook his head sadly. "Have you not heard how the fields of France are littered with the graves of young soldiers? Too many to count, I hear."

George brought a hand to his chest. "There are things worth dying for, Father."

"I agree, George." An ominous gloom descended on Evan as he recognized the fervor in his son's eyes. "However, I do not believe a few square miles of farmland in France qualifies as such."

"Germany and Austria-Hungary represent the forces of tyranny and oppression." George pounded his fist into his open palm. "The French and the British are fighting for democracy. This is a war about justice and freedom of people everywhere. It's a noble cause. President Wilson said as much in his speech."

"What did old Woody say?" asked a female voice.

Evan looked over to see his eighteen-year-old daughter bounding into the room. Liv wore a blue dress and stockings, and her auburn hair was tied back in pigtails. She was as vivacious as George was solemn. And she had an irrepressible brazen streak that was always leading her into trouble. But ever since she was a baby, her huge smile could always melt Evan's heart. Now was no exception, as Liv flashed a broad grin to her father and her older brother. "Hello, George, old boy," she said in a mock English accent as she rushed past him. She reached Evan and kissed him on the cheek. "Hi, Papa."

The sweet scent of soap and talcum powder drifted to him as her soft cheek brushed his. "Hello, Liv," he said.

Liv returned to a spot beside her brother. "What's new, soon-to-be-Dr. McGrath?" she asked playfully.

"We're going to war, Liv!" George said.

Liv frowned. "Why, for goodness' sake?"

"For the sake of democracy. It's the Great War, Liv!" George looked from his sister to his father with disappointment. "Have you not been following the newspaper accounts?"

Liv rested a hand on her brother's shoulder. "A little, George. I have heard old Woodrow's attempts to justify dragging us into this mess."

"*Drag* us?" George shook off his sister's hand. "I believe we are duty-bound to participate." He turned to Evan questioningly. "Father?"

Evan folded his arms across his chest. "At its core, this war is about historical European grievances. Little more." He shook his head. "I have read ghastly reports. Both sides using poisonous gas, enormous mortar cannons, and other unthinkable weapons. So many maimed and dead. As a doctor, I simply cannot in good conscience support such slaughter."

"Father's right, George," Liv said gently. "This is not our war."

"It is now!" George snapped. "And I intend to enlist and fight for my country."

Since the moment his son marched into his office, Evan had suspected the declaration was coming, but the words still pierced like a lance. He sprang out of his chair. "You will do no such thing, George!"

George dropped his gaze to the floor but his expression remained resolute. "Father, I have to do this," he said steadily. "For my country and for myself."

"No, Son." Evan struggled to control his tone. "What you have to do is stay here and complete the final year of your medical education."

"I will, Father. When I return."

"If you return," Evan said quietly.

"George, you really do not have to go," Liv said in a faltering voice.

He looked over to her with a self-conscious smile. "Liv, I do. It's my duty."

"And what of your duty to your family?" Evan demanded. "And to your patients? Or to the Alfredson?"

George nodded solemnly. "I will come back and fulfill those, too, Father. I promise."

A sense of foreboding welled inside Evan. He racked his brain for something to dissuade George's patriotic impulses, but nothing came to mind.

Besides, Evan knew his son well enough to know that George would enlist, no matter what he said.

George cleared his throat. "Father, I have to go back to report my intentions to the dean of medicine."

Evan nodded. "You'll come back, before . . ."

George nodded. "Of course."

Liv also seemed to recognize the finality of her brother's decision. "You're terribly brave, George. I am so proud of you. Promise you will be careful. All right?"

He showed her another bashful smile and then hurried out of the room. As soon as he was gone, a glum silence fell between Evan and his daughter.

"George has many talents, Papa, but he is no soldier," Liv finally said.

Evan nodded.

"What will become of him?"

Before Evan could answer, there was another loud knock at the door. *Who now?* "Yes," he snapped without even glancing over to the door.

Marshall Alfredson stood in the doorway. "Dr. McGrath, may we have a moment of your time?" he asked in a cool expectant tone.

"Of course," Evan said, rising from his seat.

Leaning heavily on his cane, Marshall limped into the room. He had lost little of his imposing stature over the past twenty years but, at seventy-two, his back was slightly stooped and the gout had reduced his gait to a slow hobble. His reddish hair and sideburns had grayed and his face had developed the wrinkles and blotches of his age. But his glare was as commanding as ever. "Good day, Miss McGrath," he said frostily to Liv.

Dressed in a natty gray three-piece suit with a high collar and blue tie, Junior Alfredson strode in behind his father, careful not to overtake the old man. Junior oozed confidence that Evan thought more fitting for someone twice his age. At twenty, he was good-looking with a Romanesque nose, dimples, and curly dark brown hair. He bore little resemblance to his mother, except around the eyes. Junior had Olivia's green irises and the same shape of brow. Consequently, Evan found it impossible not to like Junior despite how they disagreed on nearly every issue facing the Alfredson.

"Good day, Liv," Junior said with a slightly theatrical bow.

"Hello, Junior," Liv said curtly, but with a trace of unmistakable playfulness.

Marshall's lip curled into a brief sneer as he watched the exchange be-tween Liv and his son. The old man rested his hands on the carved handle of his cane. "Dr. McGrath, we have some pressing business to discuss." He harrumphed.

Evan turned to his daughter. "Liv, could you please give us—"

"Do you mean the war, Mr. Alfredson?" Liv indicated the newspaper still spread over Evan's desk.

"No, I do not, Miss McGrath," Marshall said pointedly.

"George intends to enlist," Liv informed the other two.

Marshall nodded approvingly. "We will need plenty of good men fight-ing for us over there."

"We don't need to be over there at all!" Evan snapped.

Marshall tut-tutted his disapproval.

"The United States Congress believes otherwise, Dr. McGrath," Junior pointed out.

Evan looked up at the young man. "Do you intend to go, Junior?" He regretted the question as soon as it left his lips. He didn't want to see Olivia's son put in harm's way any more than he wished it for his own son.

"I would love to, but—"

Marshall held up his large hand in front of his son's chest. "I am too old to run our lumber business on my own. Junior needs to stay at home to help me. No doubt timber and other building supplies will be in great de-mand to fuel our war effort. And he can do far more good for his country *here* in the Pacific Northwest than on the fields of France."

"I feel the same way about George," Evan muttered, more to himself than Alfredson.

"Medics," Marshall grunted. "You cannot have enough of them on a battlefield."

Evan's bitterness surged. His eyes shot daggers at the old man who, while protecting his own child, seemed perfectly willing to sacrifice the sons of others.

Before Evan could reply, Liv spoke up. "George is a man of science, not war, Mr. Alfredson." She placed her hands on her hips. "We think it would be of far more use for George to finish his medical studies, here."

Unperturbed, Marshall shrugged. "Obviously, the boy feels otherwise."

Fighting back a scowl, Evan looked from Marshall to his daughter. "Liv, will you please give me a moment with these gentlemen?"

Liv viewed her father defiantly for a moment before she turned to the visitors. "If you will excuse me, Mr. Alfredson." She turned to his son. "Junior."

Evan noticed how she held the young man's gaze for a moment longer than necessary. Out of the corner of his eye, Evan spotted another disapproving glower from Marshall.

After Liv had left, Evan held out a hand to the chairs in front of the desk. "Please."

They sat down at the desk. Evan folded up the newspaper and slipped it into the top drawer. "If not the war, what have you come to discuss?" he asked.

Junior looked at his father. The old man nodded his approval. "Dr. Mc-Grath, we would like to discuss the admission policy here at the Alfredson."

Evan almost rolled his eyes. "We have waded these waters too many times before. The foundation is bringing in a healthy stream of income now. Enough to cover the expenses of those patients who cannot pay their charges."

"Hardly," Marshall grumbled. He thumbed out the window at the new building. "And where do you think the money is coming from to pay for the third building? Not the foundation, I can assure you."

Junior's smile only widened. "Besides, Dr. McGrath, we are here to specifically discuss the clinic's policy concerning colored patients."

Evan sat up straighter in his seat. He was never happy with his original compromise to establish a separate ward for the black patients. He'd had little choice at the time, as he was facing a potential revolt, not only from the Alfredsons and his own staff but from the other patients, as well. Close friendship with Moses Brown aside, Evan had no time for small-minded bigotry. He had witnessed too many autopsies to think there could be any fundamental difference between the races. He still hoped to one day see the wards integrated, but in the meantime consoled himself with the knowledge that despite the segregation, the blacks were still receiving reasonable care. However, he sensed a renewed threat behind Junior's benign smile.

"What about them?" Evan asked warily.

Junior shrugged. "I happen to be fond of a number of colored people.

I am particularly attached to our old maid, who has been with us so long that she is almost a part of our family."

Evan knew Junior was referring to Theodora. He still saw her from time to time when she came to Oakdale to visit Moses.

Junior held out a hand, helplessly. "However, more and more coloreds are arriving at the door of the Alfredson seeking free medical care."

"As our reputation grows, we attract more patients," Evan said flatly. "I thought we agreed that was the goal."

"Some people in Seattle," Marshall began—and Evan immediately appreciated he was referring to the city's upper crust—"are beginning to refer to the Alfredson as a 'nigger hospital.'"

Evan folded his arms across his chest. "Mr. Alfredson, I do not appreciate the use of that term in my office," he said.

"Your office!" Marshall scoffed. "After all the time, money, and sweat I have invested in this site . . ." He banged his cane loudly onto the hardwood floor. "I will tell you what I do not appreciate, Dr. McGrath. Being ridiculed by people who matter the most to me! That is what. Do you understand me?"

"No, sir, I do not." Evan rose to his feet.

Marshall looked up at him as though viewing a cockroach that had crawled out from a crack between floorboards. "Perhaps the time is long overdue to find a doctor who *does* understand the wishes of the owner of this hospital."

Evan held the older man's stare, but doubt began to stir. He had heard many threats over the years from Marshall but none struck him as more heartfelt. The dream of passing on the reins of the Alfredson Clinic to one of his children seemed in real peril, but the alternative—banning people on the grounds of their race—was unconscionable. "If you are suggesting that we stop offering treatment to the Negroes, then—"

Junior held up a palm as he stood to his feet. He glanced quickly from Marshall to Evan. "Dr. McGrath, my father is not suggesting that at all."

Marshall said nothing.

"What are you suggesting, then?" Evan asked.

Junior offered a conciliatory smile. "We think it is best to avoid the impression that the Alfredson is pandering to a particular . . . ethnicity. Perhaps the approach would be to keep a reasonable ratio of white to nonwhite patients. Say, in the neighborhood of ten to one."

"A quota?" Evan shook his head. "That is what you are suggesting, Junior, is it not?"

"I prefer to think of it as a compromise, Dr. McGrath. One that will allow—"

Marshall cut his son off with a quick glance. "Junior, I need a moment alone with Dr. McGrath."

Junior's smile dissipated. "Father, I think—"

"A moment!"

Junior nodded. His shoulders slumped slightly as he turned and walked out of the room, closing the door behind him.

Marshall stared Evan back into his chair. When he spoke, Alfredson sounded more tired than belligerent. "This liberal policy of yours—toward the needy, the drifters, and the colored—is a mistake, Dr. McGrath. Mark my words. It will undermine the reputation of this hospital."

"Mr. Alfredson, you were well aware of the principle when we began—"

"Yes. Yes." Marshall waved his big hand impatiently. "I did not believe in it then. I certainly do not believe in it now. But a long time ago, I gave my word that I would support you in this endeavor, and I do not intend to break it now."

Evan had no recollection of Marshall making such a promise to him. He wondered if the old man was showing the first signs of senility.

"Dr. McGrath, I will entrust you to abide by some ratio or balance—however the bother you choose to view it—whereby this hospital does not appear to be overrun by Negroes. In turn, I will continue to support the new construction and whatever operating costs are not paid for by the foundation. Am I clear?"

From the man's cold hard eyes, Evan realized the offer was nonnegotiable. Appreciating that he would have some leeway in his interpretation of the "quota," he decided it was another compromise he would have to live with. "Mr. Alfredson, I will see that the hospital is not overrun by Negroes." As the words left his lips, he felt as though he were betraying Moses.

"Good." Marshall made no attempt to rise from his seat. "There is one other matter I wish to discuss with you."

"Oh?"

"Your daughter."

Evan's voice rose defensively. "What about Liv?"

"I have seen the way she eyes my son."

Evan gripped the desk in front of him. "I beg your pardon."

Marshall shook his head. "I am familiar with that look, Dr. McGrath. I saw it on my daughter's face, too." He looked up at the ceiling and cleared his throat. "When you came to call on Olivia after her surgery." His eyes found Evan's again. "I only wish I had interceded sooner. Maybe then . . ."

In all the years since Olivia's death, Evan had never heard Marshall mention her name. "They are young, Mr. Alfredson," Evan said.

"There can be no friendship of any nature between our children, Dr. McGrath."

Evan felt his cheeks burning. "Because of something that happened to their parents a lifetime ago?"

"The reason is of no concern to you."

Evan shook his head, feeling an unexpected pang of empathy for the man who had been his lifelong nemesis. Marshall was clearly trapped in the past, still enslaved by his love for Olivia. In many ways, Evan felt the same. But he was not going to let history dictate his daughter's future. "Mr. Alfredson, whatever you feel about me, and vice versa, it has nothing whatsoever to do with Liv and Junior."

Using his cane as a vault, Marshall leapt to his feet with an agility that stunned Evan. The old man took two steps until he reached the desk and then leaned across it. "Understand this, McGrath!" He shook a thick finger a few inches from Evan's face. "If your daughter so much as shares another affectionate conversation with my son, I will banish your entire family immediately and forever from the grounds of my clinic!"

## 31

Erin McGrath leaned against the far wall of the room, wishing she could dissolve into it.

*That fucking storm,* she thought again as she fought back the tears.

The head of Kristen Hill's bed was tilted upward. Moisturized oxygen hissed out of the bowl-shaped reservoir under her chin and swirled around her face forming an otherworldly veil of vapor. Kristen's two small children stood beside the bed, looking like trick-or-treaters in their oversized yellow gowns and full face shields (which Erin had borrowed from Tyler at the children's hospital).

Erin suspected Katie and Alex might already know they were seeing their mother for the last time. They never said a word to justify her hunch, but something in their quiet demeanor and sorrowful stares transcended the usual separation sadness she had seen in them before.

The children would not have even had any chance to see their mother again without Erin's intervention. She had appealed to almost everyone within Infection Control to make an exception, on compassionate grounds, to the stringent no-visitor policy for patients quarantined with *C. diff.* They wouldn't budge, so Erin finally took matters in her own hands. After outfitting the kids with pediatric biohazard suits, she led the children and Kristen's aunt up to the ICU, effectively daring the staff to prevent them from visiting their dying mother. No one tried to stop them.

Kristen had already outlived expectations. She had refused to go back on a mechanical heart pump, and Erin supported her decision since it would only stall the inevitable for days at most. Kristen's transplanted heart was essentially nonfunctional. The rest of her organs, including her kidney and her liver, had also begun to shut down. She was surviving on will alone.

Erin's tears started to flow behind her mask again as she watched the visitors begin their good-byes. Shaking her head nonstop, Kristen's elderly aunt mumbled a few empty words of encouragement and then shuffled to the door to wait for the children there.

Somehow Kristen mustered the strength to lift her arms off the bed and hold them out to Katie and Alex. The children threw themselves into their mother's outstretched arms, each leaning against opposite sides of the bed.

"Promise . . . you'll be . . . good for Auntie Kay," Kristen gasped through the mist enveloping her face.

"We will, Mommy," Katie cried softly.

Alex buried his head in her chest. "Can we come again tomorrow?"

"We'll . . . see," Kristen said, stroking his head.

Katie and Alex leaned against their mom for a long time. Only the hissing oxygen and her labored respirations filled the mournful silence. Then Kristen broke into a harsh wet cough that shook her entire body. Frightened, both children straightened up and backed away a step.

Erin saw that, behind the vapor, Kristen's face had gone blue from the cough racking her. Finally, Kristen managed to fight it off and somehow catch her breath again. "Mommy . . . needs to . . . sleep . . . a little." She conjured a smile to her blue lips. "You better . . . go."

"Come on, children. Alex, bring your sister . . . ," the aunt called in a hushed voice from the doorway.

Kristen looked from Katie to Alex. She began to raise a hand again but it dropped to the bed, powerless. "I love . . . you two . . . more than anything," she said.

Katie rushed back and threw her arms around her mom again. "I love you, Mommy."

"Come on, Katie," Alex croaked. "Mommy wants to sleep."

Katie straightened up and walked with her brother toward the doorway. As she passed, she said, "Bye, Dr. Erin," without looking at her.

"See you, Katie. Bye, Alex," Erin said as lightly as possible.

As soon as they left, Erin hurried over to the bedside. Kristen's face was still a grayish blue and behind the mist tears now ran down her cheeks. Her eyes were half shut when she looked over at Erin.

"They won't . . . get sick . . . right?" Kristen asked anxiously.

Erin shook her head. "Those were sealed biohazard masks they had on. They're safe."

Kristen nodded slightly and then looked away.

"Do you want a few moments to yourself?"

Kristen's eyes opened wider and she turned back to Erin. "I was . . . hoping . . . you'd stay . . . a bit."

"Of course." Erin nodded. "I will stay as long as you want me to."

Another series of coughs shook Kristen and her face darkened again. Erin knew that she could not continue much longer like this. "Listen, Kristen. Are you *certain* you don't want us to put you back on the respirator? It might give your body a chance to rest, and even—"

"No," Kristen choked out as the cough subsided. "We've . . . tried . . . everything."

Erin reached down and took hold of Kristen's hand. She squeezed it gently but felt only the slightest flicker in response. "Yeah. We have."

Erin stood at the bedside holding her patient's hand for a few minutes, while Kristen panted as she tried to recover enough breath to speak again. "Dr. McGrath . . . ," she finally croaked. "Alex and Katie . . . you remember . . ."

Erin squeezed her hand tighter. "Of course, I remember. You don't have to ever worry about that." Her voice cracked. "They're going to be okay. Better than okay. Those two are special."

A weak smile crossed Kristen's lips and then her eyes drifted shut and her hand went totally limp. Erin heard the rattling respirations and saw her chest moving, but she knew the end was near.

The nurse pulled up a rolling stool. Without releasing Kristen's hand, Erin sat down beside her patient. The moisturized oxygen continued to fizzle around Kristen's face, intermittently drowned out by her wet wheezes. With nothing left to say or do, Erin hummed the same Joni Mitchell tunes she used to sing to her toddlers at bedtime. Kristen's eyes stayed shut, but she murmured incoherently every so often. Erin was relieved to see that her patient was not suffering.

After about fifteen minutes, Kristen's breathing began to slow. Within five minutes, she stopped breathing altogether.

Fresh tears rolling under her mask, Erin released Kristen's limp hand and stood up. She reached for the valve on the wall and shut off the blowing oxygen. She leaned forward and ran her fingers over the young woman's cool brow. "Good-bye," she whispered, and then turned for the door.

Erin had seen other patients die. She had witnessed an entire surgical team massacred in Africa. But no death had touched her in quite the same ways as Kristen's. She felt as though she had just lost a close friend.

As she walked toward the cardiac sciences building, Erin reflected on her promise to Kristen. She would stay as involved as the family would allow, but she had also decided to honor her word with a financial commitment. The day before, she had phoned her accountant to set the wheels in motion to create a trust fund for Katie and Alex.

Her cell phone rang. She reached down and dug it out of her pocket.

"Rin?" Steve said. "You still at the hospital, hon?"

"Yeah."

"How's Kristen?"

Normally, her husband maintained a deliberate and healthy distance from Erin's professional life, but he had taken a deep interest in the single mother of twins from the moment Erin had mentioned the woman's plight. Steve had followed Kristen's progress closely and wanted to actively assist his wife in her promise to watch out for the two children.

"She just died," Erin said hoarsely.

"Ah, Rin!" he groaned. "I'm so sorry."

"I was with her at the end, Steve."

"I bet that meant a lot to her."

Erin ran a hand over her misting eyes. "I hope so."

"Rin, you did more than most doctors—most people—would have. I'm proud of you."

"I liked her. A lot. You would have, too, Steve."

"What's going to happen to the kids now?"

"They're going to live with Kristen's aunt for the short term," Erin said. "But apparently, their dad is moving back to Oakdale so Katie and Alex don't have to change schools and start over."

"It's the least the son of a bitch can do," he grumbled.

"Kristen once told me that he's an okay guy. Just very immature." She sighed again, realizing that no matter how life with their father panned out,

Katie and Alex would have been so much better off with Kristen. "At least the kids will have one parent around. And I promised Kristen I would keep an eye on him and them."

"I'm your muscle if you need it." He chuckled quietly. "You coming home? I've got a bottle of wine chilled. And if that ain't enough, there's vodka in the freezer."

"Soon." She smiled to herself. "I just have to drop by my office."

"Are you going to be okay, Rin?"

"Yeah."

"No more of those . . . um—"

"No panic attacks, Steve. I swear."

"Good. Someone's got to be strong in this family."

"I love you, hon."

"Right back at you," he said.

After Erin hung up, she was shocked to realize she had not even thought about the anxiety attacks before her husband mentioned them. She had not experienced another attack since the day before her hike up Opa's Trail with Tyler. Erin knew what Tyler had told her was true. She did need professional help, and her brother was probably correct in suggesting that she suffered from post-traumatic stress disorder. She had always associated that diagnosis with Vietnam War vets and others who had been through hell and back, but after reading up on PTSD, she recognized that her symptoms were classic for the disorder.

She had already made an appointment to see Dr. Marie Genest, the psychiatrist who worked on the cardiac floor. Ever since opening up to Tyler, and allowing herself to relive that murderous afternoon in Nakuru, she had noticed her symptoms had begun to subside. She didn't fear sleep, and the nightmares it was guaranteed to bring, as much as before. Erin didn't know whether she had begun to heal or was simply too preoccupied with her patient's terminal illness to experience anything else.

Erin looked up and noticed a woman in scrubs cross the lawn in front of her. Recognizing her as the nurse who had come to her aid the week before, Erin broke into a jog to catch up with the woman.

"Nikki?" she called out as she closed the gap.

Nikki stopped and looked over her shoulder—leaving Erin no doubt she had called to the right person—but then began walking again.

"Hold on a sec," Erin said.

Nikki slowed, as though reluctant, and then turned to her. "Oh, hi, Erin," she said. "Are your migraines gone? You feeling better?"

It took a moment for Erin to remember her white lie about the headache. "Yeah. I'm much better."

The nurse looked flushed and beads of sweat ran from her hairline even though the temperature had cooled to a more usual fall range. *Has she been working out?* Erin wondered, but noticed that Nikki was still wearing purple Crocs along with her hospital scrubs.

"Good." Nikki shifted from foot to foot. "Glad you feel better."

"I wanted to thank you."

Her shoulders rose and fell rapidly. "I didn't do anything."

"You did. And it meant a lot to me."

Nikki smiled distantly. "You're welcome then, I guess."

A thought occurred to Erin. "You work on the sixth floor with Tyler, right?"

"Uh-huh."

"Did you see that . . . um . . . article on him?"

"We all did." Nikki shuffled on the spot. "Matter of fact, I was involved in that same case, too. The parents could just as easily have blamed me."

"Doesn't sound like anyone is to blame," Erin said. "I tried to talk to Tyler, but he put on a brave face. Very macho. Said he's all okay with it now."

Nikki swept back her hair and laughed nervously. "There isn't a rug too small for men to sweep their emotions under, huh?"

"Nikki, you've worked with my brother for a while, haven't you?"

"Yeah. Tyler is a good doctor. A great doctor, actually. And I . . . um . . . consider him a friend, too." Nikki ran the back of her wrist over her forehead and then glanced from side to side as though she were expecting someone else.

"Do you think he's as okay with this as he's making out?"

Nikki hesitated a moment. "No," she said softly. "I don't."

"Me neither."

Nikki's shoulders twitched again, and she made a show of glancing at her watch. "How about I give you my number?" she asked. "Maybe we could talk about this over a coffee sometime soon?"

"I'd like that," Erin said.

Nikki fumbled with the top pocket of her scrubs to find a pen and piece of paper. She scrawled her name and number on the narrow strip. She started to extend it to Erin with a shaky hand, but she fumbled and dropped the paper. In one frantic motion, she scooped it off the ground and handed it over.

Erin wondered why the nurse seemed so jumpy. "Are you feeling okay, Nikki?"

"I'm totally beat. Just finished a double shift." Nikki giggled nervously. "It's my Achilles' heel. I just can't say no to all that overtime dough."

Nikki looked anything but tired. Her agitation reminded Erin of how she felt during one of her panic attacks. She considered saying something, but decided she had no right to. Instead, she said, "How about tomorrow or the day after for coffee?"

"Sounds a lot better rested to me. Give me a call in the morning?" Nikki smiled, nodded, and then rushed off.

Erin watched as Nikki darted off in the opposite direction from where she had been originally heading. She wondered what might have spooked Nikki. *An incident at work? Or possibly a personal matter?* She noticed Nikki hadn't worn a wedding band. And the nurse had lit up, beyond professional admiration, at the mention of her brother's name. Erin intended to gently probe a little more over coffee.

She realized she had no business prying into the life of someone she barely knew, but the distraction was good for her. Anything was preferable to remembering Kristen Hill and those two motherless kids.

## 32

Nikki didn't stop until she reached the stall in the staff washroom and clicked the lock behind her. She sat down hard on the closed toilet lid, hugged her knees to her chest, and rocked back and forth on the seat. She could feel the little packet in her breast pocket almost burning into her skin. She'd nearly spilled its contents—those four precious pills—when she reached into the same pocket to find the pen and paper to scribble Erin's number down.

*I used to be a dancer, now I'm all thumbs*, she thought miserably. *What is wrong with me?*

But Nikki knew beyond a shadow of a doubt what was wrong. She had lived through the same clamminess, nausea, clumsiness, and irritability too many times before not to recognize it now—narcotic withdrawal, or "junk sick" as it was better known by addicts.

Despite her attempts to ration her supply, Nikki had polished off the last of her hydromorphone tablets the night before. It was the second bottle she had emptied in under a week. She knew that the walk-in clinic physician who had prescribed it to her would not refill it so soon. Having pushed her stubborn denial beyond the breaking point, she no longer even bothered to tell herself that she was seeking relief from the chronic back pain. What she craved was the warm woolly calm the hydromorphone had brought back into her life.

Now she ached all over. And it would only get worse. The vomiting and diarrhea would follow if she didn't find another source of pills. She wasn't certain she could suffer through another five minutes of the withdrawal, let alone the day or two the symptoms would take to pass without more narcotics.

Opportunity had presented itself unexpectedly right before lunch when her fifteen-year-old patient, Kerry Novak, refused his afternoon dose of painkillers. The two-hundred-pound teen was on massive doses of narcotics for his incapacitating hip pain ever since the steroids he had been prescribed had destroyed both his hip joints. The orthopedic surgeons would have implanted artificial hips, but Kerry was still too immunocompromised from his leukemia treatment to have his hips replaced. Instead, he relied on numerous painkillers. He hardly ever refused his "breakthrough" dose—those extra hydromorphone tablets he took when the long-acting pills weren't enough to control his pain. No one would expect Kerry to skip the lunchtime dose, so when he did, Nikki slipped the packet in her pocket and signed out the pills as administered.

The guilt hit her before the pills even reached her pocket. It was Arizona all over again, except there would be no second chances if she were caught this time. Her career would be ruined. Even worse, she was betraying the manager, Janice Halverson, who had gambled on her sobriety.

Desperately concerned about being spotted with the stolen pills, Nikki had been rushing out to her car to take them home when Erin intercepted her. After she managed to finally brush off Tyler's sister, Nikki panicked. Overexposed and not thinking clearly, she dashed toward the nearest private haven that came to mind: the staff washroom on her floor.

Nikki wiped the steady stream of sweat from her brow. She dipped her trembling fingers into her breast pocket, clasped the unmarked packet (a tiny envelope for loose pills) between her index and middle finger, and slid it out of her pocket. She dried her other palm against the sleeve of her scrubs and then emptied the contents into the same hand. Four pills rolled out and came to rest on their sides.

Nikki could almost taste the sweet release the pills would surely bring from the awful withdrawal, and she fought off the urge to swallow the whole handful.

An image of her dead fiancé popped into her head. As usual, Glen was smiling in the memory. She had no doubt that he would have understood her addiction. He would have seen her through it, regardless of the slips and setbacks. Of course, if not for that senseless head-on crash—caused by an overworked driver who had fallen asleep at the wheel of his van—her addiction would never have even been an issue. Glen would still be here for her. Life would be so very different, and so much better.

A ripple of shame racked Nikki. She understood that if she gave in now, it would only be that much harder the next time. Despite the craving and her nauseous restlessness, she decided to try to hold out another hour.

*Just make it home and then see.*

Nikki carefully poured the pills back into the open packet and stuffed it back into her pocket before leaving the stall. At the sink, she ran a paper towel over her damp hair and then washed her face and hands.

She had just stepped out of the bathroom and turned for the staircase when Tyler called to her. "Nikki!"

*Oh God, why now?* Nikki screamed inside her head as she turned to face him.

"Do you have a moment?" he asked.

"I—I'm just racing out. I have to meet someone at home."

"I just need five minutes, Nikki. One cup of coffee, that's all."

"How about tomorrow?"

"*Please*, Nikki."

She could tell from his expression that he wasn't going to relent. "Okay. Just a quick one though," she said, dreading the thought of trying to hold a serious conversation while she felt like crawling out of her own skin.

With the dinner rush still hours away, the cafeteria was quiet. Nikki grabbed an empty table in the corner and waited impatiently for Tyler to return.

Tyler came back with two mugs in hand. Nikki decided to preempt questions about her appearance. She ran her arm across her forehead, where the sweat had begun to bead again, and said, "I didn't have a chance to work out in days. So I just ran the set of stairs at the hospital a couple times for a little cardio." She forced a smile. "I wasn't expecting this."

"Sure," he said distractedly. "Nikki, about yesterday—"

She wrung her moist palms together. "No big deal. You caught me at a bad time."

"I owe you an apology. I was . . . um . . . out of line."

"Don't worry about it." She reached for her mug and raised it to her lips, but the scent of the java intensified her queasiness. She only pretended to sip it.

"I just jumped to conclusions. I had no right to."

Nikki didn't reply. Instead, she fought back the nausea and struggled to control her wriggling. Her urge to escape the cafeteria verged on claustrophobia.

"Not just for yesterday. I'm sorry for everything." His lips broke into a small, self-conscious grin. "The stops and starts. The mixed signals. And especially . . . um . . . what happened that night at O'Doole's."

She put her coffee down. "I get it, Tyler. But I was there, too, remember? I'm not a child. I played my part." She wiped her brow again. "We got swept up in the music and the drink. Happens to people all the time. At least, we—well, you, anyway—did stop in time. I'm not angry. I was just . . . embarrassed, is all."

"Still, it was a crappy way to treat you. You deserve better. A hell of a lot better."

"Thanks." She glanced at her watch again. "Tyler, I really have to—"

He reached out a hand but stopped short of touching her. "More than just how much I respect you, I like you. A lot. Too much, probably." He stared at her intently. "You're the best friend I have in this place."

A lump formed in her throat. "I feel the same way."

"I want to be . . . available for you. This isn't about yesterday. I had no business. Forget that conversation even happened. I just want you to know that if you want to talk . . . or if you need a shoulder . . . whatever. I'm your guy." His smile widened. "I'm sorry I ever messed with that."

More than his words, Nikki was deeply touched by the sincerity that burned in his blue eyes. Without stopping to consider the implications, she blurted out, "Tyler, you were right, yesterday."

"I was?"

"About my pupils."

"Oh," he said, and nodded gravely. "For how long, Nikki?"

She looked down and shrugged. "The past week or so," she said softly.

"Any particular . . . reason?"

She pushed her damp hair back with both hands. "Not really. My back was bugging me again. Ibuprofen wasn't helping." She shook her head. "I was a fool for hanging on to that last bottle of hydromorphone."

"Why did you?" he asked gently.

"My first day of sobriety—the last time around, anyway—started the day I filled that prescription," she said. "In a weird way, the bottle marked a milestone for me. Like a little trophy for what I'd overcome."

"I get it," he said unconvincingly.

"Bullshit. Even I don't believe that line anymore," Nikki muttered with a snort of laughter. "In the last three years I'd been tempted so many times to crack that bottle. Hanging on to it was really just a sign of weakness. It guaranteed my failure."

"Now what?"

She held out her arms, palms facing down, to show him the coarse tremor in her hands. "I haven't had a pill since last night."

"I thought you looked a little . . . on edge."

"So did your sister."

"Erin?"

"I just bumped into her outside." She thumbed at the window. "The poor woman must think I'm out of my freaking mind."

"I doubt that." He cocked his head. "Nikki, do you need something to help take the edge off? A few Valium or whatever?"

She hesitated but could not bring herself to mention the pills weighing in her pocket. "I have to do this cold turkey," she said. "I've done it before, Tyler."

"You want some company for a while?"

Viewing his kind face made her heart ache. He was such a decent guy. *If only our circumstances were different. . . .*

"You know what, Tyler? I really don't think I would be good company right now." She sighed a chuckle. "Kind of like Joseph Stalin, but more paranoid and less tolerant."

He laughed. "I've seen worse."

Nikki rose from her seat. "I need to do this alone. Really."

Without arguing, he nodded.

"But thank you," she said as she turned to leave.

"Nikki?"

She glanced over her shoulder at him.

He tapped his temple. "You're going to be okay."

With a quick smile, she hurried for the exit. She walked out of the building and started for the parking garage but stopped after a few steps and turned back. She entered the children's hospital and mounted the stairs up toward the SFU. She stopped at the nursing station and pretended to read through some charts while she waited for another nurse to clear out of the medication room. Then, with a quick glance over either shoulder, she skulked inside the room and closed the door behind her.

She walked over to the narcotic log where she had recorded the stolen dose of hydromorphone as given. She stared at the criminal entry for a long moment. Then she picked up the attached red pen and crossed it out. She wrote "returned" above the words and signed her initials.

She fished in her pocket and pulled out the small packet. Unlocking one of the narcotics drawers with her personal code on the keypad, she placed the contents back inside a bottle and then closed the drawer.

Despite the throb in her back, her shaking limbs, and the ravenous longing for one more pill, the little step brought her a glimmer of hope.

## 33

Tyler was eager to get home to his wife. Whether it was related to her pregnancy or not, he felt closer to Jill than he had in recent memory. With her newfound fragility and sudden need for support, he felt as though she had let him back into her heart for the first time in ages. Clearing the air with Nikki had helped untangle his emotions, too.

Despite the colorful bouquet of lilies at risk of wilting in the passenger seat of his car, Tyler couldn't get home to Jill any time soon. He had to stay at the children's hospital into the evening waiting for Keisha's prefilled doses of Vintazomab to be sent up from the pharmacy.

At 7:45, his phone rang. "Hello, Dr. McGrath," a young man said with somber professionalism. "I'm Devon Sinclair, the on-call pharmacist for chemotherapy meds."

"Yes, Devon. Any word on that Vintazomab?"

"That's the issue." Sinclair cleared his throat nervously. "You see after the, er, incident with the last Vintazomab patient, we sent most of the medication back to the supplier."

"I ordered it yesterday, Devon," Tyler said evenly.

"I realize that, Dr. McGrath," Sinclair said. "We were expecting to have more supply couriered to us this morning. It hasn't arrived yet. And as per policy, we do not dispense chemotherapeutic drugs after eight p.m. So even if it were—"

"Will you get it in by tomorrow?" Tyler cut him off impatiently.

"I hope so."

"So do my patient and her family, Devon."

Frustrated with the bureaucracy, he slammed the receiver into the cradle. But he couldn't deny his relief at having avoided the medication for at least one more day. He still dreaded the thought of walking Keisha through the same procedure that had proved fatal for Nate.

When he broke the news to the Berry family, Jonah was accepting while Keisha acted indifferent. Only Maya seemed to struggle with the word of the delay.

Tyler didn't reach home until 8:35, leaving him only a few minutes to catch up with Jill before he had to head out again. Liesbeth had phoned shortly before he left work requesting that he come over at nine o'clock. Though Tyler desperately wanted to spend the evening with his wife, he felt obliged to go and more than a little curious to know why his grandmother needed to see him so urgently.

Jill's car was already parked in the driveway, but she didn't answer when Tyler called her name from the entryway of their house. He bounded upstairs, bouquet in hand, hoping to surprise her in the bedroom, but she was nowhere to be seen. Mystified, he hurried back down to the main floor. Passing by the basement steps, he noticed the lights on downstairs.

"Jill?" he called. "Are you down there?"

No reply.

He raced down to investigate. Stopping in front of the door to the spare bedroom, Tyler heard the sound of water running from within. He tried the door handle, but it was locked.

*What the hell?*

He knocked on the door. "Jill?"

She didn't reply.

He heard a distant retching noise followed by the flush of a toilet. Concerned, he pounded harder. "Jill, are you in there?" he shouted.

After several seconds, she said, "Yeah. I was just . . . um . . . sleeping."

"Why in the spare room?"

"My stomach is so bad," she said. "I needed to be near the washroom. I didn't want to disturb you. Or make a mess of our room."

The spare room did have a small attached bathroom not far from the bed, but the explanation still struck Tyler as hollow. "What's with the locked door?" he asked.

"I didn't want you to walk in on me. Could have been a nasty surprise for us both." Her voice was louder as she neared the door, but it still sounded throaty and rough. And she had yet to unlock the door.

"You won't surprise me now," he said warily. "Can you please let me in?"

"I'm a mess," she said. "Worse than that girl from *The Exorcist*, you know? I really don't think anyone—including you—should see me right now."

Concerned, Tyler jiggled the handle of the door. Still locked. "Stop fooling around, Jill!"

The knob finally clicked and the door opened a crack. Inside, the spare room was lit only by a bedside lamp. Tyler could barely make out Jill's features through the small opening.

"Ty, I know you're worried, but I'm okay. I've got water and juice down here. I just need a couple hours to myself. I know this will pass."

Firmly, but gently, Tyler pushed the door open wider. "Think of me as an overprotective first-time dad-to-be," he said.

Jill leapt a few steps back from him. He tried to approach her but she shot out a palm to stop him. "No closer. I haven't been anywhere near a toothbrush since this started."

Tyler's hand fell to his side along with the bouquet he was holding. Even though the light was dim, he could see Jill better. She had not exaggerated. Her skin held a gray-greenish hue. Her bloodshot eyes were encircled by puffy folds. She still had flecks of regurgitated food at the corners of her cracked lips.

"Jill, you're sick."

She swallowed. "Bad morning sickness. That's all."

Despite the five or six feet separating them, the harsh scent of vomit wafted to him. "I need to get you to the hospital," he said.

She laughed weakly. "Now you really are being a neurotic dad-to-be. It's morning sickness. Comes with the territory. No need for flashing lights or ERs."

"Plenty of women require intravenous rehydration during the first trimester. You know that. It's safer for the fetus to have a well-hydrated mom."

"I'm not at that point yet. I'm keeping some fluid down." She waved her hand to indicate the half-empty bottles of juice and water lined up on the nightstand. "Besides, I don't want to expose myself and the baby to whatever's floating around the ER."

"Jill, you look pretty . . ."

She fluffed her hair and pretended to misinterpret his unfinished comment.

"Aw, too sweet. I don't even have my makeup on." She pointed to his hand holding the flowers. "For me?"

Tyler raised them to her.

"Thank you, Ty. They're gorgeous!" Her cheeks suddenly puffed up as she visibly fought back nausea. She breathed through her nose for several moments until her mouth relaxed. "Will you put them in a vase for me?"

"Jill, we really should go to the hospital."

"Give me a few more hours. If I can't keep the fluids down, then I'll go in for an IV. I swear."

Though dubious, Tyler saw the determination in her stance and realized it was futile to try to force her.

"I am so dog tired from this pregnancy and morning sickness. What I really need is a little more sleep." Moving like an old woman, she hobbled back to the bed and sat down stiffly. She hoisted her legs up onto the bed, crawled under the sheets, and then covered herself up to her neck with the gray comforter.

"Go put the flowers in a vase for me, please, Ty."

"All right." He shrugged. "Liesbeth asked me to come over to her place tonight. She said it was important."

"That doesn't sound like your grandmother."

Tyler nodded absently. "I know."

"Is she unwell?"

"She didn't sound it."

"You better go."

Tyler shook his head. "I don't want to leave you alone like this."

"I'm okay." A smile crossed her puffy face. "You'd help me by going. I need some peace and quiet. Honest."

Tyler stood his ground. "I can see her tomorrow."

"Liesbeth wouldn't call if it wasn't important. You know that."

"Yeah . . ."

Jill reached for the cordless phone receiver beside the lamp and laid it by her pillow. "Keep your phone on. I'll call if I get worse. I promise."

Tyler hesitated.

Jill shooed him weakly with her fingers. "Please, Ty, just give me a few hours. Okay?"

Defeated, he turned for the door. "I'm going to call you in an hour. If you don't pick up, it won't be me pounding on the door . . . it'll be firemen with axes and the Jaws of Life."

She offered a faint laugh. "Make it two hours. I need a bit more sleep before that kind of excitement."

Tyler closed the door behind him but stood outside and listened with his ear to it. If he had heard her throw up, or even rush back into the bathroom, he would have dragged her to the hospital kicking and screaming if necessary. But Jill was quiet on the other side for the five minutes that he waited by the door. Finally, he turned and headed for the stairs.

With no traffic on the road, Tyler reached Liesbeth's seniors' complex in less than ten minutes. The lobby was laid out like that of a hotel, except the Asian woman behind the desk wore a white nursing uniform. She buzzed upstairs for permission and then directed Tyler to the bank of elevators.

He was surprised when his sister answered the door. "Hi, Tyler," she said, and turned quickly from him.

In the brief glimpse, he recognized that her eyes were red from crying. "Erin?" he said, as he followed her into the living room.

Liesbeth was sitting on the rust leather couch in front of a coffee table, where two snifters of brandy rested on coasters. In front of her, a weathered photo album lay closed. Liesbeth straightened her skirt with gnarled fingers and rose to greet Tyler. She held a few tissues in her knobby hand, and it was obvious that she had been crying, too.

He bent forward and hugged her lightly. The peppermint scent of her favorite mints drifted to him. "Hello, Liesbeth."

"Thank you for coming, Tyler."

Tyler glanced from his grandmother to his sister. "What's going on, you two?"

The women shared a quick look, and then Erin said, "I was telling Liesbeth about Africa."

Tyler nodded, relieved to hear his sister had shared her hellish experience with others. And he could think of few better people than Liesbeth to open up to. "How's it going?" he asked.

Erin seesawed her head from side to side. "Remember that young mother who had the heart transplant?"

He nodded.

"She didn't make it."

"I'm sorry, Erin."

She shrugged. "Otherwise, I'm a little better. No panic attacks recently. I finally told Steve what really happened in Nakuru. I don't know why I ever kept it from him. So stupid. Trying to stick my head in the sand and pretend it never happened." She sighed heavily. "I've booked an appointment with Dr. Genest."

"Sounds like you're on the right track," he said.

"How about you?" She tilted her head down and looked at him as though peering over reading glasses. "How's it going with that . . . you know . . . reporter?"

"No article today," he said. "Hopefully my fifteen minutes of fame are up."

"And Jill? Any word on her study?"

"Day by day." Tyler was tempted to let Erin and Liesbeth in on the news of his wife's pregnancy, but he bit his tongue. It was too early to tell anyone. Besides, he knew the announcement needed to come from both of them. His concern for Jill stirred again, and he pulled out his cell phone and double-checked that he had not missed a call. Nothing.

While the two siblings caught up with each other, Liesbeth headed over to the small bar trolley in the corner of the room and poured a third snifter of brandy. She walked back to Tyler and, without asking, passed him the glass.

Erin sat beside Liesbeth on the couch, while Tyler took the chair on the other side of his grandmother.

"I'm sure you're wondering why this old woman was in such a hurry to see you both," Liesbeth said with a soft laugh.

Erin rubbed her grandmother's arm. "It is a little unlike you, Liesbeth."

"To put your mind at ease, I'm not dying, as far as I know." She smiled. "And, even better, I haven't changed my will."

Both grandchildren chuckled politely.

Her smile vanished. "I wanted to tell you something about your grandfather."

Tyler glanced at his sister. Erin turned to her grandmother. "What about Opa?" she asked.

Liesbeth looked from Erin to Tyler and then reached for the photo album in front of her and pulled it closer. Using the side of her disfigured forefinger, she awkwardly opened the front cover and flipped through the first few pages before she stopped on a page.

In the yellowing color photograph, a young man in a swimsuit smiled widely. The backdrop of a beach with the corner of a cabin visible looked vaguely familiar to Tyler but he couldn't place the location.

"Ha!" Erin laughed. "Opa looked just like you back then, Pip. Only skinnier."

Tyler saw the strong resemblance to himself in Maarten's wavy brown hair, strong jaw, and slightly crooked grin, but Erin wasn't exaggerating about the gauntness. Even in the faded old photograph, Maarten's ribs were completely visible and his legs looked like sticks.

Erin tapped a finger on Maarten's turned-out forearm where a blockish black tattoo ran. "Opa covered up the numbers the Nazis tattooed on him, right?"

Liesbeth nodded. She ran her swollen finger along the edge of the photograph. "Maarten and I met this same summer, 1946. More than a year after he had been liberated from the camps."

Erin shook her head. "I can't imagine what he must have looked like then."

Instead of answering, Liesbeth flipped the book over so that it rested on its front cover. She opened the back cover and, with obvious difficulty, dug her swollen fingers inside the attached small pouch, withdrawing a wallet-size black-and-white photograph.

"Oh my God," Erin said as soon as she saw it.

In the photo, Maarten wore a striped prisoner's shirt. Unsmiling, his face was wasted to the point of skeletal. His neck wasn't much thicker than a drainage pipe.

"The American troops took this the day he was freed," Liesbeth said. "By then he had spent over a year in Auschwitz and seven more months in the Mauthausen concentration camp in Austria."

"How did he survive like that?" Tyler muttered, unable to tear his eyes off the disturbing snapshot.

"He didn't," Liesbeth said. "Not completely, anyway."

Confused, both grandchildren turned to Liesbeth for an explanation.

"What you are both going through now . . . Erin, that terrible senseless attack in Africa. And Tyler, the shame you feel about the poor little boy's outcome . . ." Liesbeth looked tenderly from one grandchild to the other. "I'm so pleased that both of you are speaking about your experiences. Maarten never would."

"Never?" Erin said.

"We were married for three years before he let me know he was ever in Auschwitz. I had known all along, of course. You saw the photographs. One look in those kind eyes of his told you immediately that he had survived something unimaginable. But Maarten never wanted anyone to know. And it was many years before he told me what he really went through."

Liesbeth appeared on the verge of tears again. A painful silence fell over the room. Erin and Tyler looked to one another, both at a loss for words.

"Maarten wanted to take it all to his grave with him." Liesbeth cleared her throat. "But I think these terrible secrets drove him to his grave. The poor man couldn't sleep afterwards." She shook her head adamantly. Her eyes were burning when they locked onto Tyler. "And I will not take his secrets to *my* grave. You are family. You need to know. I only wish I had told you sooner."

"Told us what?" Erin demanded.

"Yeah, Liesbeth," Tyler agreed. "Why the secrecy? It wasn't Opa's fault that the Nazis committed genocide. Millions of Jews were sent to the concentration camps. I thought a number of the young men like him, who were strong enough to work as slave laborers, did survive."

"Not exactly like him," Liesbeth said in a hushed tone, as she looked down and slowly stroked the inside cover of the album. "You asked earlier how Maarten survived . . ." She steadied her voice. "You see, your grandfather was forced to work for Josef Mengele."

"*Mengele?*" Tyler felt as though he had been punched. "The Angel of Death?"

Erin's face fell. "That doctor who used to do all those horrific human experiments? Opa worked for *him?*"

"He had no choice." Liesbeth sighed. "Mengele or one of his cronies met every new prisoner as the transport trains arrived at the station. He would walk down the lineup assessing each new arrival on sight, and divide them into a line to his left or right. Those on the right would go to the slave labor camp, where many were worked to death anyway. And those on the left—the elderly, the infirm, and the younger children *along* with their mothers—were immediately murdered in the gas chambers."

Tyler had already learned this from a documentary he had seen on Auschwitz, but he had grown up unaware of his Jewish ancestry and had never heard any direct eyewitness accounts of the atrocities. It was so much more viscerally chilling to hear the crimes described by his own grandmother.

"Maarten had dust allergies and asthma," Liesbeth went on. "He would not have survived a week in the labor camp. So when Mengele asked the group of new Dutch arrivals if there were any doctors with experience in surgery or pathology, his older brother, Fritz, shoved him forward." She shook her head. "Poor Fritz died of cholera only days before the Nazis abandoned Auschwitz."

"Did Opa have any experience in surgery or pathology?" Tyler asked, confused.

"Nonsense," Liesbeth said. "He was only twenty-eight. He had barely finished medical school in Amsterdam when the Nazis invaded. He was never allowed to work as a doctor. He had to pretend." She sighed again. "I think some of the other Jewish doctors helped him. Maarten once told me that Mengele recognized his inexperience. But apparently the monster took a bit of a shine to him and gave him a little more leeway than most. In other words, he didn't murder Maarten."

"Poor, poor Opa," Erin muttered.

"Maarten assumed he was going to work as a doctor for his fellow inmates," Liesbeth said. "And at first, he did."

Tyler remembered from the documentary how Mengele had forced Jewish doctors to help in his ghastly research on human guinea pigs. "Did Opa have to work on Mengele's experiments?"

Liesbeth tucked the concentration camp shot of her husband back into the pouch and gently shut the album. She looked over at Tyler, and her eyes clouded with tears. "You remember I said all the children in Auschwitz were gassed on arrival? That wasn't quite true. Mengele selected out the identical twins. He saved them to experiment on."

"Oh, God, I remember when I first told him I was having twins." Erin brought her fingers to her lips. "He cried when I told him . . . ," she croaked. "I thought he was overjoyed. I had no idea."

"How could you know?" Liesbeth said. "I'm so sorry he never lived to meet Martin and Simon. He would have loved those boys so much."

"And Opa . . . ," Erin gasped.

Liesbeth nodded. "Those savages forced Maarten and another Jewish doctor—a Czech—to perform many of the autopsies after their ghastly experiments. No! That's not the right word! It was not experimentation. It was sadism and torture. Absolutely inhuman. Evil." She squeezed her gnarled hand into a ball. "Maarten worked and slept in Block Ten. So he saw the poor little darlings before, during . . . and after. He once told me that Mengele could be quite charming when he wanted. He sometimes gave the children candy. Many of them even called him Uncle. But the things he did to those children. You wouldn't do them to an insect . . ."

Erin leaned forward and buried her head in Liesbeth's shoulder. The smaller woman wrapped an arm around her granddaughter. The sight of his robust sister being comforted by his frail grandmother moved Tyler beyond words. He had an involuntary memory of the Mengele documentary that described how the sadistic doctor had once tried to re-create Siamese twins by sewing two young twins together, back to back. Tyler winced at the thought.

"Maarten did nothing wrong," Liesbeth murmured. "He was as much a victim as the children themselves. He came close to suicide, but he never could do it. Do you know why?"

Erin and Tyler shared a blank stare.

"He was desperate to help those children. And he risked his life to do just that." She stopped to get her voice to cooperate. "He helped them the only way he could."

"What do you mean, Liesbeth?" Erin asked.

"Many of those children went through such hell before they died," Liesbeth said. "Often, when one twin died during an 'experiment,' Mengele killed the other immediately. Just so he could do the autopsies at the same time." She looked down at her knees. "Maarten used to steal extra doses of morphine, potassium, and any other drugs he could get his hands on." She paused. "He could not bear to watch the children suffer to death. When no one was watching him, he helped to end the agony sooner for the ones who were already dying."

Erin sat up straighter and looked at her grandmother. "Oh my God . . . ," she whispered.

"What he did was noble!" Liesbeth said in a stronger voice, and folded her arms across her chest. "He risked his life to ease their pain."

Erin reached out and ran her hand over her grandmother's wrinkled cheek. "That sounds like Opa."

Numb, Tyler shook his head. "And later, after he came to America? Opa's work with the children with cancer . . ."

Liesbeth nodded. "He dedicated his life to those children. He would have done anything for them. He could never stomach the thought of a child suffering needlessly. Nothing in the world was more important to him."

Suddenly, it all made horrible sense to Tyler. A tide of pity rose inside him for his grandfather and the awful things he must have seen and had to live with. His feelings of guilt must have been immeasurable.

"He was such an amazing man, your grandfather," Liesbeth went on. "He worked himself beyond exhaustion. Giving everything for those poor cancer-stricken children. Until his heart broke a hundred times over. And he still had enough love to be a wonderful husband, father, and opa." She uttered a shaky sigh. "But he could never sleep. The poor man tried everything and every pill. It never worked. In our fifty-two years together, he never once slept a whole night through. If I woke up in the middle of the night, I would find him tossing and turning in bed beside me or pacing at the window." She laughed sadly. "It's funny, you know. Maarten once told me that before the war he slept like a lamb. His mother used to have to shake him awake in the morning for school."

Erin wrapped her arms around Liesbeth and pulled her into a hug. Tyler took her other hand and gently squeezed it in his.

After a few moments, Liesbeth shook free of both of them. She looked sternly from one to the other. "I wanted you both to know about your family history. I needed to tell you what terrible damage secrets can do. If Maarten had only shared his story like so many other Holocaust survivors did . . . maybe then he wouldn't have stayed up every night of his life with the ghosts."

Liesbeth shook a crooked finger at each of them. "But promise me you will not remember Opa that way." She patted the photo album with the flat of her other hand. "Maarten was a wonderful man who rose above this terrible, terrible thing."

Erin smiled warmly at Liesbeth. "Opa was the best grandfather any kid could want. That's how I will always remember him."

Tyler reached out and stroked Liesbeth's arm. "Now I have even more respect for him, if that's possible."

Liesbeth dabbed at her eyes and smiled. "You know? I don't think Maarten would be angry with me for telling you."

"I am so glad you—," Tyler began when the phone jangled in his pocket. *Jill!*

Frantically, he dug it free and brought it to his ear. "Jill? What is it?"

"Ty," she rasped, and stopped for several breaths. "Come home."

## 34

Jill lay sprawled on the carpet in the same spot where she had collapsed minutes earlier. The spasms in her abdomen were more intense now, gripping her in wrenching waves. Her head lay only inches from a small pool of her own drool and vomit. The rank odor made her retch again, but there was nothing left to throw up. Her light-headedness had lessened since she'd crumpled to the ground, but even in her fog, she recognized that she must have been severely dehydrated to have fainted for the first time in her life.

The *C. diff* infection was leaching every drop of fluid from her. She could not believe how much had poured out already. But all she could think of was how badly the circulation to her uterus—and to her fetus—must have been compromised in her dehydrated state.

*Our baby! Why did I send you away, damn it, Tyler?*

Jill now realized how feeble her plan had been. She had hoped to ride out her infection at home and treat it with oral metronidazole, an old-fashioned antibiotic that was safe in pregnancy and used to be universally effective against *C. difficile*. But the medication wasn't working. Besides, she could no longer keep the pills, or anything else by mouth, down. She needed intravenous rehydration. It was a risk Jill had hoped to avoid. If the doctors got wind of her *C. diff* infection, they would insist on treating her with the newest, most potent antibiotics to tame the superbug. She shuddered at the prospect. Those drugs were well known to cause miscarriages and birth defects.

In her mind, her whole future rode on this pregnancy. She considered it a miracle that she ever conceived in the first place. It probably would never happen again.

*How can I take a medicine that might destroy or mutilate our baby?*

Jill heard a door slam on the main floor. The rumbling thuds of running feet vibrated on the ceiling above her. A few seconds later, the bedroom door burst open and Tyler rushed in.

"*Jill!* God, Jill." As he knelt down beside her, the sole of one foot sank into the collection of her bodily fluids, but he didn't seem to notice or care.

Jill tried to smile but wasn't sure if her lips even cooperated. "It's not as bad as it looks, Ty. I just need an IV. A few bags of saline. That's all."

He shot his hand to her brow. "You're burning up."

With all her strength, she arched back from his hand. "I know. I've picked up a bug. Don't get too close."

The warning didn't deter him. He reached out and stroked her cheek tenderly. "What bug?"

"There's a stomach flu going around my lab," she lied. "We think it's the Norwalk virus. Whatever it is, I've got more than just morning sickness."

Tyler pulled his cell phone from his pocket. "I'm calling an ambulance."

"No." Jill shook her head. "You drive me. Please, Ty."

"Can you even stand up?"

She swallowed. "I'll try." She buried her hands in the rough carpet and pushed herself up, but her elbows began to buckle as soon as her chest lifted off the ground.

"Let me." Tyler slipped his hands underneath her waist and then hoisted her up, cradling her in his arms.

She turned her head from his face, desperate not to expose him to the superbug she carried. The deceit gnawed like a toothache, but Jill saw no other option; if he knew she had *C. diff*, he would force her to take those antibiotics that would be toxic to her baby.

"Ty, Norwalk virus is ultracontagious," she said. "You need to get me a mask. Both of us."

He carried her through the doorway and toward the staircase. "Don't worry about that now, honey."

She squeezed his arm as hard as she could. "You're no help to me if you're sick, too!"

His pace didn't slow as he rushed her up the stairs through the main floor, but he muttered, "I have a mask in my briefcase."

She wriggled in his arms. "Go get it now, Ty. Please," she implored.

He hesitated and then stopped and laid her down on a couch in the family room. "I'll just go grab it." He turned for the stairs.

"It was so . . . messy . . . down there. Wash your hands!" she called after him.

He disappeared for a few moments. The rush of running tap water from upstairs eased her conscience slightly.

*I don't deserve him.* Again, she had an unwelcome flashback of stumbling onto that intimate moment between Tyler and Nikki at the nursing station on the SFU. *But I can't lose him now.*

When Tyler reached her again, he was clutching a surgical mask. He leaned toward her and tried to slip it over her head, but she drew back from his touch. "I'll do it."

He nodded and held out the mask for her. She took it from him, careful not to touch his hand, though she longed for the reassuring contact. With trembling fingers, she fitted it over her face.

Jill looked up into Tyler's worried eyes. "Where's yours?" she asked.

"Don't need one." He pointed to the surgical mask that now covered most of her face. "That's an N-ninety-five particle mask, Dr. Laidlaw. No bugs can penetrate it."

"Right," she said, but still turned her head when he hoisted her back up into his arms.

Tyler carried her out to his car. He laid her down across the backseat. Before he left, he reached out and squeezed her arm lovingly. "It'll be okay, honey."

Despite the coarse chills and fever raging through her, Jill felt so much safer in Tyler's presence. She mustered a smile for him.

Eyes closed on the ride to the Alfredson, Jill could tell from the engine's high-pitched whine and the way she was pulled into each corner that Tyler was driving well over the speed limit. It reminded her of a worried father racing a wife in labor to the hospital. A lump formed in her throat at the thought. If she had any fluid left in her, the tears would have poured.

*When did I become such a sentimental marshmallow? Damn these hormones!*

Tyler abandoned the car across two of the ambulance bays in front of the emergency room. He raced around to Jill's side of the car and reached in to lift her from the seat, but she waved him back.

"Let me try." She pushed herself up to sitting and swung her feet out of the car. She clutched the headrest in front of her and managed to pull herself upright. The ground swayed violently beneath her. Her legs buckled. She expected to collapse again at any second. Just before she dropped, Tyler's hands slipped under her armpits and steadied her weight.

"It's going to be okay, Jill," he repeated, as he ushered her twenty or thirty long steps toward the sliding doors.

*Everything will be okay*, she repeated to herself, despite the cramps racking her abdomen and the violent chills shaking her. *Our baby will be okay. She has to be.*

Inside the brightly lit modern entrance to the emergency room, Tyler led Jill toward the triage check-in desk. She stumbled several times but, as he was basically holding up her weight, they made it to the triage desk without a fall.

Several patients sat in the waiting room while others lined up at the registration desk, but no one was waiting at the triage desk. The gray-haired, motherly triage nurse rose to her feet as soon as she saw them approaching. Tyler lowered Jill into the wire-framed wheelchair stationed at the desk in front of the tall pane of glass with the inset microphone and speaker.

The nurse—Helen, according to her name tag—possessed that same welcoming, but slightly wary expression that Jill remembered all too well from her medical school rotation through the emergency room. She had hated the experience. The chaos and unpredictability of the ER conflicted with her need-to-control personality.

"What's the problem, hon?" Helen asked in a friendly Southern accent.

Before either of them said a word, a stocky security guard with a Marine-style crew cut hurried toward them waving wildly toward the ambulance bays. "Sir, you can't park there," he hollered.

"My wife is sick!" Tyler snapped.

"She's in good hands now," Helen said to him. "Why don't you go let those poor paramedics back into the parking lot again?"

Though her head swam and she felt as if she might fall out of the chair at any moment, Jill nodded her encouragement. "I'm okay, Ty. Go."

He hesitated a moment and then turned for the door.

Helen rose from her seat. She slipped on a pair of gloves as she came around the desk wheeling a machine toward Jill for measuring vital signs.

She pointed to Jill's mask. "What's that all about? Are you concerned about catching something here?"

"I work here," Jill said. "Dr. Jill Laidlaw. I'm a neurologist. I have gastroenteritis. I think it might be Norwalk. We've had a few cases in my lab."

"I appreciate your precautions, Dr. Laidlaw. Thanks. That Norwalk is one contagious little critter." Helen winked. "And in one hour I'm off for vacation. Don't need to take it home to my daughter and grandkids in Florida."

"Helen, I'm six weeks pregnant, too."

Picking up on the worry in Jill's tone, Helen smiled kindly. "Don't worry, we'll take extra good care of you," she said as she unhooked the blood pressure cuff from the machine and wrapped it around Jill's upper arm. She pressed a button and the cuff instantly began to squeeze tighter. As it measured the blood pressure, Helen pulled out an electric thermometer and sheathed it in a disposable cover. "Open up, hon."

The nurse stuck the thermometer under Jill's tongue. A moment later, the blood pressure machine uttered three long worrisome beeps. Helen's eyes darted to the reading and the reassuring smile slid off her lips. Then the thermometer offered a lower-pitched long single beep. Helen glanced at it and shook her head ever so slightly. She whipped the cuff off Jill's arm and dropped the thermometer on top of the machine. Stepping in behind the wheelchair, Helen shoved it so hard that Jill jerked forward as she flew toward the sliding frosted doors that led to the inner treatment area of the ER.

"What is it?" Jill asked.

"Your blood pressure is low. Too low. And your temperature is over forty degrees Celsius. I need to get you onto a stretcher. Get some fluids in you."

"Am I in shock?"

"That's for the doctors to decide, hon." They passed through the doorway and into a room abuzz with noises and activity. "I just want to get you into a stretcher right away."

The lights began to swirl around Jill until they coalesced into one bright blur. She was vaguely aware of her head falling toward her knees but could do nothing to prevent it. She heard Helen yell something, but it sounded as though the nurse was speaking underwater.

The bright white light tunneled into a single point.

Jill's forehead slammed against something hard.

Her world went dark.

## 35

Tyler raced around the emergency room's parking lot without finding a nearby spot. Giving up, he ditched his car in the on-call doctors' lot behind the ER and then sprinted back to the entrance. As he squeezed through the sliding doors without waiting for them to fully open, his shoulder caught and dislodged one of the doors off its track with a crunch, but he didn't stop to assess the damage.

The security guard jumped up from his desk at the noise and called to Tyler to stop. Tyler could not see his wife or the triage nurse anywhere in the waiting room. Ignoring the shouts from the guard, he flew straight for the next set of frosted doors and ducked sideways through them as soon as they parted.

While very familiar with the children's hospital ER, Tyler had never stepped foot inside the Alfredson's adult emergency room before. He stopped a moment to gain his bearings. The nursing station sat in the middle of the open room, with bays and beds circling it like spokes on a wheel. People, equipment, and stretchers were everywhere, most of them in motion.

Tyler turned to the short young man in scrubs who passed right in front of him. "Hey," he called out. "I'm Dr. McGrath. My wife, Jill Laidlaw, just came in. You know where she went?"

Without stopping, the man shrugged and said, "Not a clue. I'm just the ortho resident."

"Dr. McGrath!" A large woman in a lab coat beckoned to him from a few feet away.

He recognized the woman holding the basketful of test tubes as one of the lab techs who occasionally came to the SFU to draw blood from his cancer patients.

She pointed her arm straight down toward the far wall. "They just placed her in Resusc Two, Dr. McGrath."

"Thanks!" Tyler nodded his gratitude and started for the resuscitation room, but he was halted by a voice from behind.

"Hey, sir!" the panting security guard called out. "You can't just run in here like that—"

The lab tech waved the security guard off. "It's cool, Charlie. His wife just went to Resusc Two."

Tyler's stomach sank as he realized that the room alone was enough to convey the gravity of Jill's condition. He ran to the glassed-in room the woman had pointed to. The door was open but covered by a curtain. He pushed the curtain out of the way and bounded in.

Still wearing the same mask, Jill lay flat on the stretcher in the room's center. Helen was on her right side, squeezing an intravenous bag on the pole above her with both hands to increase the speed of fluids running into Jill's arm. Another nurse, about half Helen's age, squatted on the other side attempting to insert a second IV in his wife's left arm.

Jill's head flopped back on the bed, her eyes were unfocused and her eyelids half shut. She didn't even look up at Tyler as he reached the foot of her bed. Above her, the monitor showed that her heart was galloping at over 150 beats per minute. Her blood pressure hovered at sixty over forty. Tyler recognized that the reading was barely compatible with consciousness.

He reached out and clutched his wife's leg through the blanket. "Sweetheart, I'm here."

At the sound of his voice, Jill's gaze drifted toward him. He could not tell if she was focusing on his face or the curtain behind. Her lips moved slightly but only garbled sounds emerged.

"It's okay, sweetheart. These fluids will make you feel better," Tyler said in a calm voice, but his own heart fluttered with worry. He had an ominous feeling that, with Jill's profound shock from dehydration, their unborn baby might already be beyond help.

"She's bone dry and burning up," Helen commented without looking over her shoulder as she inflated a blood pressure cuff around the intravenous bag to speed up the flow of fluids. "She'll perk up with some saline. You'll see, hon."

Tyler felt desperately grateful to Helen. Aside from his mother's sudden death—and she had not even reached the hospital alive—he had been sheltered his whole life from the "patient experience" on the other end of the stethoscope. He ached to do something useful for Jill but felt desperately impotent and largely in the way.

He sidled around the younger nurse to an open spot near the head of the bed. He reached a hand toward his wife's brow. Helen stopped his hand with a quick shake of her head. "Remember the Norwalk?" she cautioned. "You best wear some gloves."

Helen reached behind her, grabbed a pair of disposable gloves off a cart, and tossed them to Tyler. Though the precaution made sense, he hated the barrier the rubbery layer created. The gloved contact with his wife struck him as cold and clinical.

When his hand reached her brow, her eyelids opened a fraction wider. "Ty? That you?" she mumbled through her mask.

"I'm right here, Jill."

Her eyelids lowered again. "Whatever happens, don't let them . . ." Her words drifted into incoherence.

Tyler mopped her brow with the back of his gloved hand. He turned his head and lowered his ear nearer to her mouth. "Don't let them what, Jill?"

"Our baby, Ty . . . ," she said. "Don't let them give me anything that will harm her."

*Her.* The word moved Tyler deeply. His wife couldn't actually know the fetus's sex yet, but with a single mumbled word the life inside her seemed so much more real to him. So did the risk of losing their baby.

"They know you're pregnant, sweetheart. They'll be careful."

"Please, Ty," she insisted. "Nothing to harm the baby. It's so . . ." Her words petered out.

Jill's eyelids shut and she appeared to drift off to sleep. Tyler glanced over to Helen, who nodded reassuringly. "It's the Dramamine," she said. "For the nausea. It's knocked her out, hon. It's totally kosher in pregnancy." She pointed to the monitor above Jill. "Look at that blood pressure. I told you."

Her blood pressure now read seventy on forty-five. Though still critically low, it had at least moved in the right direction. Jill's heart continued to race at almost 150 beats per minute. And she still looked as pale as the moment he had swept her up off the carpet.

Helen finished adjusting the intravenous lines and then turned to Tyler. "You're in good hands with Angela over there." She nodded toward the younger nurse whose flaming red hair was tousled from all the activity. "I have to get back to the triage desk now."

"Helen, you've been wonderful," Tyler said. "Thank you."

Without responding directly to him, Helen leaned closer to Jill. "When I get back from Florida, I want to see you back at the Alfredson. As a doctor, not as a patient. You understand me, hon?"

Jill muttered something unintelligible, and Helen turned for the curtain.

Tyler had never faced Norwalk virus in his practice. He reflected on the little he had learned about the virus from training. He did remember that, while highly contagious, it was not supposed to make its victims particularly ill, even if in the early stages of pregnancy. Clearly, Jill was an exception. Something gnawed at him. Pregnant or not, her story did not fit.

*What if Jill is wrong about her own diagnosis?*

The curtain pulled open again and a middle-aged, balding Indian man walked in. He wore green scrubs under his lab coat. His hound-dog eyes suggested he had already been on shift for a long time. "Dr. McGrath? I am Bal Dhillon," he said in a refined accent that sounded British, tinged with a trace of Punjabi. "I am afraid your wife is stuck with me for her attending physician." He showed a tired grin. "It is a pleasure to meet you."

"Likewise, Dr. Dhillon." They shook hands.

"I saw Dr. Laidlaw briefly when she arrived." Dhillon gripped his chin with his thumb and index finger. "Helen has kept me abreast of the events. As you know, your wife shows all the signs of hypovolemic shock. However, we do not know whether she is also manifesting a form of septic shock."

"That would be unusual for Norwalk virus."

"*Most* unusual." Dhillon frowned. "Perhaps the pregnancy combined with her very advanced dehydration explains her condition."

"Maybe."

Dhillon grabbed a pair of gloves from the wall-mounted box beside him and then moved closer to the bed as he pulled them on. "Dr. Laidlaw, I am going to examine your belly, if that is all right?"

Eyes still closed, Jill murmured her consent.

After Dhillon applied the buds of the stethoscope to his ears, he gently folded down the sheet covering Jill. With equal care, he lifted her gown up to the level of her bra line. He placed the stethoscope's bell on the center of her abdomen and let it rest freely as he listened for a few moments. Next, starting at her left upper abdomen, he palpated her belly with one hand pressing down on the other. As soon as he reached the left side, Jill emitted a small moan of discomfort. Dhillon appeared to ease up on the pressure of his probing fingers as he continued to move them clockwise around her entire belly.

He pulled the stethoscope from his ears. "Dr. Laidlaw, we have to run a full battery of blood tests, of course, but we will also need stool samples to test for the exact microorganism you have acquired." He smiled at her shyly. "The good news is that your blood pressure has responded to the fluids. I am hopeful you will continue to improve now." He paused. "Do you have any questions, Dr. Laidlaw?"

"My baby?" Jill croaked.

Dhillon glanced at Tyler with a quick frown and then turned back to Jill. "I have asked the obstetrical team for an opinion," he said. "They will be here very soon." He turned for the curtain. "I will return shortly. I need to place the orders now."

"Of course," Tyler said as he watched him leave.

Dhillon's comment about the "exact microorganism" resonated with Tyler. His concerns suddenly crystallized into a new theory. Worry coursed through his veins. He could not believe he had not thought of it earlier. He grabbed hold of Jill's shoulder and shook it gently. "Jill, are you awake? Can you hear me?"

Her eyes opened a little wider than before.

"This isn't Norwalk, is it?" he asked.

She just stared at him.

"It has to be *C. diff*," he said. "Christ, Jill! The senator exposed you to the superbug, didn't he?"

"Tyler . . . ," she breathed.

"That's what you meant by the harmful drugs. You're worried about those drugs they're using to treat *C. diff*, right?"

"Tyler, our baby," she croaked.

"Damn it, Jill!" he snapped. "You're so sick. We don't even know if the fetus is still alive! Besides, there is no baby without a live mother!" He regretted the words as soon as they left his lips.

Jill rolled her head away. Her shoulders began to undulate, and she made a raspy grunting noise through her mask.

Tyler reached out and caressed her cheek with his glove. "Babe, I'm so sorry. I didn't mean it like that. I'm just so worried about you."

Jill looked back to Tyler. "I should have told you . . ."

A mechanical rattling noise broke the moment. Tyler looked over his shoulder to see a skinny young man with prominent cheekbones rolling a machine toward them that looked like a large laptop computer secured to a trolley. Tyler was relieved to see that the man was already wearing a gown and gloves and had a mask dangling loosely around his neck.

"I'm Darren, one of the ultrasound technologists," the man announced in a nasal tone. "The ob-gyn team sent me down. Okay if I perform an obstetrical ultrasound now?"

Jill glanced nervously at Tyler. He nodded to her. "Sure, Darren," he said. "Go ahead, please. But you should put your mask on. She's got a GI bug."

Darren nodded and pulled the mask over his mouth. As he set up his equipment on the other side of the stretcher, Tyler reached for Jill's free hand and squeezed it tenderly. "Whatever happens, Jill, it's going to be okay. You understand me?"

Her eyes reddened, but they were still too dry to produce tears.

Darren positioned the machine on the other side of the bed, giving Tyler and Jill a clear view of the flipped-open ultrasound screen. He lifted back the sheet and gown covering Jill below mid-belly. With a noisy squirt, he squeezed a large blob of jelly onto a long thin ultrasound probe. "Let me know if this hurts," he said as he lowered the probe between Jill's legs and gently slid it inside her vagina.

The screen filled with varying degrees of gray ultrasonographic shadows as Darren expertly slid, rotated, and tilted the probe inside Jill. Finally, he brought it to rest in one position. He reached his free hand out and adjusted a few dials on the machine.

Suddenly, the screen zoomed in on the shadowy shape of Jill's uterus. Inside, Tyler saw a round sac that was about the size of a dime. Despite the magnification, he could not make out much more detail of its shape. As his eyes adjusted to the grayscale image, he thought he saw movement near the center of the dime. Something was definitely flickering inside it.

Darren tapped a few buttons and the object of Tyler's attention began to strobe in a fluctuating blue and red pattern.

Tyler flushed with excitement at the sight.

Jill raised her head off the stretcher. Her eyes went wide and her scaly lips cracked into a trace of a smile. "Ty! That's her heartbeat, isn't it?"

## 36

"George did come back from World War One, didn't he?" Lorna asked, though she already knew the answer.

They had been sitting in the same spot since finishing dinner hours before. She had never seen Dot go so long without having a drink, but Lorna wasn't complaining. She had a critical meeting in the morning in Portland, which meant leaving the Alfredson mansion before dawn.

"Yes, he did," Dot said. "Or at least part of him did, darling."

"Oh?"

"George lost his right arm and most of his leg when the Germans shelled his trench. Liv was right, of course. Her brother was no soldier. He lasted less than twenty-four hours on the front. He was back at the Alfredson by January of 1918."

"As a patient?"

"Hardly." Dot chuckled. "You have to give the boy *oodles* of credit for his pluck, darling. With only one arm and a leg and a half, he resumed his medical training as though he had been on nothing more than a European sojourn. When the time came, he stepped—or perhaps hopped would be more apt"—she tapped her own leg for effect—"straight into his father's role as the medical administrator. Of course, his wounds had a *huge* impact on his father and therefore on the Alfredson."

Lorna knew the Alfredson had become one of the leading world centers in prosthetics and limb reconstruction. "The prosthetics program?"

"Exactly, darling. Being a turn-of-the-century surgeon, Evan had created more than a few amputees in his day. That alone had stoked his interest in their rehabilitation. When his son and numerous other veterans returned from the Great War missing limbs, Evan was terribly dissatisfied with their primitive prosthetics. He recruited one of the leading designers in the country, Oliver Goodman, to improve the field. And George, being George, threw himself *wholeheartedly* into championing the cause."

Lorna nodded. "How about Liv and Junior? What became of their attraction?"

Without looking over her shoulder, Dot pointed at a painting on the wall behind her. It wasn't particularly large compared to the others, but Lorna had spotted it earlier. Vietnamese or perhaps Thai, Lorna guessed, the picture depicted three naked Asian girls frolicking under a waterfall, their hands exploring each other's bodies. "Ah, the forbidden fruit is always the *most* appealing, isn't it?"

"But Junior and Liv were half siblings!"

"Yes, but they didn't know that, darling. All they had heard was their fathers constantly warning them to stay away from one another. And of course that made the attraction between them *absolutely* irresistible."

"It's still incest."

Dot rolled her eyes. "Don't get your bourgeoisie sensibilities twisted in a knot, darling. It was all terribly innocent. A few furtive meetings with a kiss here and there, at most."

"Did they get caught?"

Dot smiled enigmatically. "In October of 1918, they had larger worries than being caught by their fathers for a stolen kiss."

Lorna knew what Dot was alluding to but, as before, she didn't want to give the appearance of knowing any more than she needed to. "What other worries? I thought World War One ended that autumn."

"The war was winding down, all right, but the decommissioned soldiers were bringing home something more than just wounds and battle stories." She nodded to herself. "Something far deadlier."

---

More than twenty years after saving Olivia's life, Evan would be present to repeat the feat for another Alfredson: this time, his good friend and partner, Marshall.
—*The Alfredson: The First Hundred Years* by Gerald Fenton Naylor

Even when Virginia was at her most disabled and Marshall Alfredson was threatening to kill him, Evan had never felt the cumulative weight of so many troubles as he did in early October of 1918.

His eldest son had returned from the Great War maimed. Despite the vehemence with which George had thrown himself back into the medical training, Evan worried for the boy's future. With only one arm, George would never be the surgeon his father had hoped. Evan told himself that George of all people would triumph over his injuries, but the memories of Virginia's final years gnawed at him. He knew only too well how limiting physical disability could prove to an able-minded person.

Evan's paternal worries were not confined to George. At seventeen, his youngest, Nicholas, showed no interest in following his father or brother into medicine. The boy, who had always been particularly sensitive and somewhat effete, had become obsessed with acting. He had even sought his father's permission to travel to a place in Southern California called Hollywood. Nicholas enlisted his mother's help to lobby his father. While Evan loved to indulge his children, he could see no future for his son in acting, especially in moving pictures. He was convinced the allure of those ridiculous films was merely a passing fad that would soon be replaced by something better. Believing he was looking out for Nicholas's best interest, Evan forbade the boy to go. Nicholas sulked for the next two months and then, in early September, disappeared without a word of warning. His parents found out that he had gone to Hollywood only after they received a letter from him with a California postmark.

But of all Evan's progeny, the one nearest to his heart was causing him the most dismay. Headstrong as ever, Liv was still hell-bent on becoming a doctor. Impressed by her determination and pioneering spirit, Evan intended to help her realize the goal any way he could. But Liv was never one to wait. Without her father's consent, she had begun to shadow the consultants and volunteer with the nurses on the wards, creating her own informal medical apprenticeship. Evan was astonished by how quickly the girl had learned. Two months earlier, he had walked onto the ward to see her expertly applying a full-length plaster cast to a patient who had a shattered tibia. Though he pretended to disapprove, inside Evan was bursting with pride at his daughter's aptitude. However, the next time Evan had happened across Liv unawares, he was deeply troubled by what he witnessed.

Ten days earlier, Evan had been out on one of his daily walks that took him around the Alfredson complex and, time permitting, sometimes miles beyond. Approaching the back of the new building along a dirt path, he slowed when he saw two figures tucked away in the shadows under the second-floor balcony. From the alignment of their bodies, Evan appreciated the intimacy of their interaction. Intending to leave the couple to their privacy, he stepped off the path and ducked behind a nearby oak tree. He was about to slip away when the sound of the girl's voice froze him. Though she spoke softly, the breeze carried it to him.

*Liv!*

Hugging the tree with his back, he peeked around its edge. Neither one of them looked in his direction, but Evan recognized Liv leaning against Junior Alfredson.

Marshall did not usually allow his son to come to the clinic unsupervised. However, Evan remembered that the old man had come to see a rheumatic specialist regarding his gout. Junior must have accompanied his father on the visit and slipped away with Liv during his father's appointment.

Liv stood inches from Junior. They spoke in hushed tones. Evan could only make out snippets of their conversation, but from the laughter and their proximity, the nature of their encounter was unmistakable. After a few moments, Junior reached out and drew Liv into his embrace. They kissed for several long moments. Transfixed, Evan watched in dismay as Marshall's threat to throw him and his family out of the Alfredson rang in his ears.

Now, as he sat at his desk and stared out at the same building where Junior and Liv had shared their illicit kiss, Evan's heart sank at the vivid memory of it. Desperately conflicted and still undecided as to how best to respond, he had yet to confront Liv. Though his daughter was gambling with the future of the family business, Evan still believed she had a right to pursue her own happiness. His heartbreak at having been forcibly parted from Olivia had never fully healed. And he had learned from his difficult experience with his youngest, Nicholas, that it was better not to meddle in his children's lives.

Besides, a worry far greater than any personal or family trouble had been amassing like storm clouds over the clinic. And it threatened not only the Alfredson, but everyone in the civilized world.

Evan's apprehension had begun to rise in the summer after he first received a letter from a colleague in Philadelphia warning of an unusually virulent strain of influenza. Evan had heard rumors already, but it was his friend who first used the term "the Spanish flu." All summer, Evan followed the reports with growing alarm as the Spanish flu jumped from its origins at military bases into the civilian population in cities such as Philadelphia, Boston, Chicago, and New York with a death toll previously unheard of for influenza. For months, Evan had expected the Spanish flu to find its way to the Pacific Northwest. He had worked diligently to prepare the Alfredson and its staff. He made them separate the beds on the wards, so all the patients were at least ten feet apart. He asked Moses Brown to construct makeshift partitions out of wooden poles and bedsheets. He instructed the nurses to sew stacks upon stacks of six-ply-thick masks. He mounted posters with simple instructions on infection control, including advice on hand-washing frequency and technique. He even set out draconian rules, banning such benign contact as handshaking.

After reading promising research papers on the benefits of oxygen for soldiers whose lungs had been decimated by poison gas, Evan stockpiled oxygen tanks for the Alfredson, hoping that it might help with the severe pneumonia known to be associated with the Spanish flu. Working with Moses, Evan fashioned rubber tubing and face masks for delivering oxygen to the patients.

The Spanish flu finally reached Seattle on a rainy fall day—October 2, 1918. People were panicked. They had heard the grisly stories and rumors of hundreds of dead in a single day in many cities. Tales abounded of people going to bed well and never waking up. Gymnasiums were piled to the ceiling with the bodies. Evan knew from colleagues across the country that these stories were not exaggerated. Unlike in previous influenza outbreaks, the ones dying were not the infirm or the old. The young and healthy were perishing at a catastrophic rate.

The Alfredson admitted its first case of Spanish flu three days after the virus reached Seattle. From the moment the young sailor, Harry Stone, was carried into the clinic by his family on a makeshift stretcher, his diagnosis was never in doubt. Evan immediately mobilized his staff. He oversaw the relocation of the black patients onto the wards in the other buildings with the white patients, clearing out the entire main-floor wards of the original building exclusively for flu victims. Within forty-eight hours, forty-two more Spanish flu sufferers had joined Harry Stone at the Alfredson.

Nothing in the written accounts or the newspaper photographs prepared Evan for the deadliness of the epidemic. A day before, he had assessed a young victim, Philip Enders, who had presented with relatively mild symptoms typical of the grippe. The young man had protested, claiming he was too well to waste a hospital bed. Evan almost agreed. However, within two hours of admission, the head nurse urgently summoned Evan to the bedside where Enders was coughing up bright-red blood. He was bathed in sweat, and his complexion had turned navy. Enders was racked by ceaseless paroxysms of coughing, and the skin between his ribs puckered with each breath, his body desperate for better ventilation. Trousers soaked with urine, Enders was so delirious from the fever that he called out to imaginary visitors and dead relatives.

Evan had tried to treat the young man with everything at his disposal, including oxygen, morphine, digitalis, atropine, and camphor. None of the interventions helped. Enders died less than four hours after proclaiming his healthiness. In that moment, Evan realized there were no preparations sufficient for this monstrous disease.

Now, as he secured the mask tightly around his face and walked onto what had already been dubbed the "flu ward," there were thirty-three patients inside. Stone, Enders, and seven others—all young and previously healthy—had already died. Moses's partitions only separated the patients from one another, so from Evan's vantage point in the center of the room, he could see most of the patients with a turn of his head.

A number of reasonably well-looking patients lay in bed reading, sleeping, or just staring back at him with varying degrees of wariness or fear. Almost an equal number of sufferers appeared to be in distress; some of their faces had turned as blue as Enders's. No one spoke, but the room was filled with harsh sounds of coughing, retching, and hacking. Unintelligible moans rose intermittently. The smell of sweat and death hung heavily in the air.

Three masked nurses, wearing long white aprons over full-length dresses, scurried from bed to bed, carrying buckets of cold water. Evan watched a nurse stop by an ill patient and try to ladle water into his mouth. The same quantity dribbled right back out. Using the same bucket, she wet a cloth and applied it across the man's brow in an attempt to lower his raging fever.

Outraged, Evan watched the nurses use the same ladles over and over on different patients. Sometimes, they even dipped the contaminated cloths back in the water bucket two or three times and then gave a drink to the next patient. These practices inflamed Evan; he had been so clear to the staff about attention to hygiene and infection control.

Evan suspected that the sloppy infection-control practices had already exacted a terrible toll. He had come to the flu ward specifically to see Cecilia McClellan, the first nurse to contract the Spanish flu. Evan had desperately hoped his precautionary measures would prevent such cross-contamination to the staff. He was devastated to find out that, within two days of the virus reaching the clinic, one of his nurses had already taken ill.

Evan spotted McClellan on the far side of the room where the six female patients were clustered. The waiflike girl was on a bed in the far corner with the blanket drawn up to her neck. She lay very still with her eyes wide open. From thirty feet away, Evan saw the ominous bluish tinge that suffused her cheeks.

Approaching her bed, he heard McClellan's raspy breathing before he even reached her. McClellan looked up at Evan with a stoic grin. "I'm so sorry, Dr. McGrath," she panted.

Evan touched his chest. "I am the one who is sorry, Miss McClellan." He shook his head. "I feel responsible."

"No . . . Dr. McGrath," she gasped. "You have done . . . what you could . . . to prevent this."

Evan reached for his stethoscope in his jacket pocket. He slipped the buds in his ears, leaned forward, and then applied the bell to the blanket over her chest. He moved the stethoscope around. In every zone he heard the same crackling wet sounds of overwhelming pneumonia. Disheartened, he pulled his stethoscope from his ears.

"How . . . do I . . . sound?"

Evan saw how hard the poor girl tried to mount a brave face, but he could almost smell her fear. It made his heart ache. He nodded as encouragingly as he could. "The air is moving well," he lied. "You have a lot of mucus to expectorate. That will help. Meantime, we will start oxygen therapy."

Evan looked over his shoulder and saw the head nurse, Gertrude Flanders, glide into the room from the hallway. He turned back to McClellan. "I will go arrange it now." He held her gaze for a brief moment. "You can still overcome this flu, Miss McClellan."

"I believe I can, too." But her voice bore little conviction.

"I must speak to Mrs. Flanders now, but I will be back to check on you soon."

"Thank you."

Evan hurried over to the newly installed sink on the near wall. He scrubbed his stethoscope with soap under the running water and then washed his own hands. After drying them, he hurried over to where Flanders stood talking to one of the younger nurses.

The head nurse was a tall heavyset woman of around his age, but she moved with an effortless grace that made her appear to almost float at times. He respected Flanders for her ability and her kind manner with the younger nurses, who uniformly looked up to her. But at this moment he was as upset with her as he had ever been. "Mrs. Flanders, may I have a word, please?" he said in a low voice.

"Of course, Dr. McGrath."

Flanders led him out to the corridor. Neither of them removed their masks. From where they stood, they could see only the nearer half of the ward. "Miss McClellan is not well at all, is she?" Flanders said.

Evan shook his head. "We need to administer oxygen to her."

"Of course." She nodded. "I have taken the liberty of already requesting a tank."

"Mrs. Flanders, if we do not immediately change our practices, I am most concerned that Cecilia will not be the only nurse to fall ill."

Flanders folded her arms across her chest. "How so, Dr. McGrath?"

Out of the corner of his eye, Evan saw another young woman pass by him heading toward the flu ward, but she disappeared inside the room before he could make out her face. Evan focused back on Flanders. "The nurses are moving from patient to patient without washing their hands," he said gravely.

"My nurses are doing the absolute best they can," she said with cool defiance. "They have no time. You see how sick their patients are."

"They need to make the time!" he snapped. "Look at poor Cecilia. The one simple measure of proper hand-washing could make the difference between sickness and health—life and death—you understand?"

She eyed him for a moment and then nodded contritely.

"Also, we need to stop this practice of sharing contaminated water between the patients," he said.

"All these patients already have the flu." She waved back to the door to the ward. "What is the danger of using the same bucket for those who are already infected?"

"We do not know what else the patients are harboring. Only some patients develop the pneumonia and it is worse than any I have seen. Perhaps a share of patients also carries a bacterium along with the influenza."

"I see."

He pointed back in the room to the one visible window that was wide open. "And we must shut those blasted windows!"

"But what of the draft? The ventilation. Is that not helpful?"

"The breeze is blowing the influenza particles all around the room! It is potentially exposing the rest of us to the Spanish flu."

"I see, Dr. McGrath." Flanders's chin dropped and her shoulders dipped in defeat. "My nurses are only following my instructions. I take full responsibilities for all these breaches of conduct."

Evan shook his head. "Mrs. Flanders, you and your nurses are trying your best under unimaginable circumstances," he said in a much gentler tone. "I admire them for their selflessness, but we must do everything in our powers to prevent another nurse or doctor from falling ill."

"I could not agree more. I will go right this very—"

The young woman who had passed him earlier suddenly drifted into Evan's field of view. His heart leapt in his throat. Without a word of explanation to Flanders, he dashed back into the room and caught the girl by the upper arm.

"Papa?" Liv gasped in surprise.

Maintaining his grip on her arm, he dragged her over to the sink. "Wash your hands, Liv!"

She scrubbed her hands under the water, and he did the same again. Then, with only a slightly lighter grip, he led her out of the ward, down the corridor, and through the front entrance. He stopped only when they reached the steps outside the building. He tugged at his mask and let it fall to his chest, as did Liv.

"What the devil are you doing in there?" he demanded.

"The nurses need help, Papa. They are so overwhelmed."

"You are neither a doctor nor a nurse!" he cried. "You have no business on the flu ward. I specifically told you to stay away from the hospital during this epidemic."

She placed her hands on her hips. "Please do not treat me like a child. I am perfectly capable of helping out."

"You most certainly will not!"

Liv held out a palm to Evan. "Papa, there are not enough of them. It's so awful. The patients are suffering so. I only want to help."

"By exposing yourself to the Spanish flu?"

"I am following your precautions."

"Easier said than done," he said. "I witnessed experienced nurses blatantly ignoring my instructions this morning. We already have one gravely ill staff member because of it."

"Poor Cecilia." Liv's face fell. "She has always been so kind to me, so welcoming and happy to answer my many questions." Her voice cracked. "Will she . . . survive, Papa?"

Her angelic expression melted the last of Evan's ire. He sighed heavily. "I do not believe so, Liv."

Unfazed, Liv nodded. "Papa, Cecilia is alone there. Her family is not allowed to visit. I think she finds a little comfort in my presence."

He shook his head adamantly. "No, Liv. You will not go back there. I will not permit it."

Liv reached out and touched his shoulder so lightly that he barely felt her fingers. "No one should die alone."

"She will not be alone. Her colleagues—her friends—are with her." He patted her hand. "Liv, I admire your compassion. One day, you will be a wonderfully humane doctor. But right now, you must leave this flu to the fully qualified professionals. Do you understand me?"

"Yes."

He looked away. "If anything were to happen to you . . ."

She squeezed his arm and laughed freely. "Oh, Father. You are such a dear sweet man."

"Promise me, Liv," he said, turning back to her. "Promise me you will not go back there."

Before Liv could reply, Moses Brown suddenly appeared around the corner and jogged up to them. In his early sixties, he was still an imposing figure. However, the years of dust from his carpentry work had taken a toll on his lungs, leaving him with severe asthma. He wheezed audibly from his run. "Mr. Alfredson is in your office," Moses said. "He wants to see you right away."

"Did his son come too, Moses?" Liv asked with nonchalance that Evan knew was feigned.

"No, ma'am," Moses said. "Just Senior, today."

"I wonder what the old man wants today of all days," Evan grumbled. He looked at Liv sternly. "You stay away from the wards, Liv."

She nodded but Evan recognized a spark of rebelliousness in her eyes. He turned to his old friend. "Moses, please keep an eye on Liv. Do not let her anywhere near the wards."

"Papa!"

But Evan waved off Liv's protest and hurried up the path toward the building.

He walked into his office to find Marshall Alfredson leaning back in the chair facing the desk and window. His gold-handled cane rested against the chair and a waft of blue cigar smoke floated above him. Marshall did not turn at the sound of Evan's approaching footsteps. "Are you aware that Mr. Wellsby is still in my employ?" he said in lieu of a greeting.

Evan tensed at the mention of the name. He associated Marshall's squat private investigator with some of the worst moments of his life, like the beating he received at the Alfredson coach house or the news of Olivia's drowning. "That does not surprise me, Mr. Alfredson."

"Wellsby is as good at his job now as he was twenty years ago. Possibly better."

Evan circled the desk and dropped down into the chair across from Marshall. Seated, he suddenly realized how exhausted he was. He had hardly slept a minute since the first influenza case arrived. And now Liv's reckless visits to the flu ward preoccupied him. Evan had no energy left to verbally spar with Marshall.

"For example," Marshall went on, "Mr. Wellsby brought back a rather detailed report of a stroll your daughter took with my son last week."

Evan's stomach somersaulted. He sat up straighter in his seat but still did not say a word.

"According to Mr. Wellsby, they hid themselves behind one of the buildings that *I built and paid for*." A sense of cold inevitability ran through Evan. Marshall took a drag of his cigar and blew the smoke at the doctor. "They were not there to discuss the war or politics, Dr. McGrath. But I think you know that already, do you not?" He grunted. "According to Mr. Wellsby, you saw them kissing behind the building as clearly as he did!"

Evan felt like a convict whose sentence had just been pronounced. "They are hardly more than children," he mumbled to himself.

"Perhaps I could have overlooked this flagrant disregard of my most specific instructions," Marshall growled. "But to hear that you witnessed this abomination and did nothing to stop it . . ." Saliva flew from his lips as his voice grew to a shout. "Why, it is beyond the pale!"

Evan stared at the old man, neither intimidated nor afraid. "Abomination, is it? Because it happens to be *my* daughter that your son has feelings for."

"You will never understand!" Marshall snapped. "You cannot understand."

"And you will never stop living in the past!"

Leaning on his cane, Marshall hoisted himself to his feet. "I warned you, sir." He shook the still-lit cigar at him. "I explained the consequences were this to ever happen. And I intend to see them realized. I will remove you from this office *and* my hospital! You have until the end of this month to get your affairs in order here."

Evan felt remarkably numb to his own dismissal. "All of this because I fell in love with your daughter?"

Marshall's lip curled into a sneer. "Don't you dare mention my daughter, McGrath!" He waved the cigar at him like it was a knife. "You have no idea what it feels like to lose what is most precious to you."

Evan snorted a laugh. "Do not be so sure of that, Mr. Alfredson."

"The end of the month!" Marshall repeated, and then pivoted and hobbled for the door, leaning heavily on his cane. He stopped at the door. "In the meantime, while we are searching for your successor, I want you to close the Alfredson to any more cases of this ghastly influenza."

Anger suddenly jolted Evan into action. He leapt to his feet. "I will do no such thing."

"What?"

"I am not closing our doors to victims of the Spanish flu," Evan said as he walked around his desk. "No one needs us more than those patients. It would be morally negligent to turn them away."

Marshall limped back toward him. "I did not ask for your opinion."

"Nor did I yours," Evan snapped. "This is a hospital. We offer comfort and help to the sick and the needy. It is our guiding principle."

"Yours maybe. Not mine." Marshall kept approaching until he stood a few feet away. He dropped his cigar into the ashtray. "I did not build this hospital to watch it be brought down by an influenza epidemic."

"*You*? You didn't build this hospital!" Evan cried. "I did."

Marshall's eyes narrowed to slits. "How dare you!"

"On paper, you might own the building and the land, Mr. Alfredson." Evan leaned closer. "You might even legally be able to replace me." He brought his fist to his chest with a thump. "But make no mistake. I built this hospital. From its origins to the modern center it has grown into. And every step in between. I am the backbone and the soul of this clinic. You are just the bank, Mr. Alfredson. Nothing more."

Marshall's face went pale with rage. Hand shaking, he suddenly raised his walking stick and swung it wildly at the doctor.

Reacting out of instinct, Evan dodged a step and arched backward at the waist. He felt the breeze of the cane as it zipped past his head. He had barely regained his footing when Marshall cocked his arm again. Before the blow came down again, Evan launched himself forward and grabbed the old man's arm, catching it between his hands.

Marshall fought back with surprising strength for his age. "You snake!" he cried, as he swung his free arm and clubbed Evan on the side of the head with a closed fist.

Twenty years of frustration and hatred erupted inside Evan. He yanked the walking stick free of Marshall's hand and hopped back. He raised the weapon up over his own head. "You miserable old man," he growled. "You won't rest until you've destroyed everything. Will you?"

Marshall glared at Evan with a loathing as intense as any he had ever seen. Then suddenly, before Evan's hand had even flinched, Marshall's expression went blank. His legs buckled and he dropped to the ground as though shot. He landed on his side and seemed to involuntarily roll onto his back.

Marshall lay staring up at Evan with eyes wide open, but the left side of his lip drooped noticeably. He was moving his right arm, but his left lay like a discarded rope. The old man was clearly conscious, as Evan saw the right side of his mouth moving and he heard garbled sounds.

Evan was so distraught that it took him a moment to realize Marshall was having a stroke. He dropped the cane and knelt down beside him. Marshall raised his right arm shakily to Evan and muttered something incoherent out of the right side of his mouth.

"What?" Evan asked, as he leaned his ear closer to the other man's lips.

"Junior . . . and Liv . . . ," Marshall muttered.

"What about them?"

"You have to . . . stop them. It's not . . . natural."

Evan shook his head, dumbfounded. Even while suffering a massive stroke, the old man still obsessed over petty family grievances.

"They are . . . ," Marshall stuttered. "*They are . . . brother and sister.*"

# 37

Sitting on the leather couch with her feet tucked beneath her, Erin rested her head on Steve's shoulder. The twins were finally asleep judging from the quiet floorboards above. Despite the warm autumn night, the wood-burning fireplace crackled beside them. Diana Krall crooned softly through the ceiling speakers. Two glasses of red wine stood on the coffee table, though Erin had hardly touched hers. She had been too busy talking.

Finished now, she inhaled the soapy scent of her husband's shampoo. He'd been using the same generic brand since before they met. That was Steve—consistent, reliable, and comforting. All her recent emotional upheaval felt so much further removed by his side. Steve was her refuge. And she loved him deeply.

He mussed her hair and kissed her on the forehead. "Holy crap, Rin! It never ends for you," he said with the perfect touch of lightness. "Kristen Hill, Africa, panic attacks, and now Auschwitz . . . Man, you're overdue for a little slice of calm and happy. Why don't you let me take you to Hawaii?"

She kissed him on the neck. "Might be safest if we moved into a bomb shelter for a while."

Steve pulled his head back and studied her with his kind hazel eyes. "Poor Maarten. I would have never guessed. He always seemed like a guy without a care in the world." He paused. "A slave laborer for Josef Mengele? Can you imagine living with *that* your whole life?"

She shook her head and shuddered at the suggestion.

"At least something good came out of his experience." Steve hurried to add, "I mean, in the way he dedicated the rest of his life to kids with cancer. All the good things—great things—he did at the Alfredson after the war."

She kissed him again on the lips. "I have to believe—at least I desperately want to—that his work after the war was some consolation to him."

Steve touched her cheek gently. "Rin, how are you coping with all this? Has it made the panic attacks worse?"

She stroked the back of his hand with hers. "I love how you worry over me. But I haven't had a panic attack in almost three days."

"Good."

She locked eyes with him. "I'm so sorry, babe."

"For?"

"Not telling you sooner . . ." She cleared her throat. "About what really happened in Nakuru."

He swept her apology away with a backhanded gesture. "I told you, Rin, I understand. I really do. I probably would have done the same. Out of sight, out of mind . . . and all that."

"It doesn't work, though."

"Probably not, but you're on the right track now." He pursed his lips quizzically. "How do you feel about going back to the OR?"

"Operating again?" She shook her head vehemently. "I don't think I'm ready."

"I'm cool with that." He grinned. "I kind of like going to bed with you and knowing you'll still be there in the morning."

Erin leaned forward and planted a long inviting kiss on his lips. She stood up and took his hand in hers. "Speaking of bed . . ." She pulled him upright and began leading him toward the staircase.

He heaved an exaggerated sigh. "I hate it when you drag me to bed. Makes me feel so cheap and tawdry."

She fluttered her eyelids. "Cheap and tawdry are underrated emotions."

He laughed. "The things I do to sustain this marriage."

The phone rang. Steve moved closer and wrapped an arm around her waist. "Let it go to voice mail," he said.

"Tyler McGrath." The audio caller identifier's robotic voice droned from the nearby wall phone.

"Tyler?" She grimaced at her husband. "At this time of night?"

"You better take it."

She broke away from her husband and grabbed the cordless receiver off the wall-mounted cradle. "Tyler, what's up?"

"Jill," Tyler croaked. "She's sick."

"What's the matter?"

"Severe gastroenteritis. She's in shock from the dehydration. She might even be septic, too."

"*What?*"

Tyler updated his sister on Jill's condition. At the mention of *C. diff*, Erin instinctively thought of Kristen Hill. She swallowed hard. "Where is Jill now, Tyler?"

"Still in the ER."

"I'm on my way."

"Erin, you don't have to come tonight. Why don't—"

But she hung up the phone before Tyler even finished.

Though there was no love lost between Jill and Steve, Erin's husband valued family over everything else. His face crinkled with concern. "What's wrong with Jill?" he demanded.

"*C. diff.*"

He nodded. It was explanation enough for someone who had followed Kristen's illness so closely. "I'm coming, too."

"Who will stay with the boys?"

"Oh, crap. I guess it's too late to call over and see if Hannah can watch them?"

"She's only in eleventh grade. It's a school night for her, too."

"Yeah." He sighed. "Drive safe. Call me from the hospital as soon as you know anything."

Erin wrapped her arms around her husband and planted a kiss on his lips. "I will."

She hurried out to her car. Despite the potholes, twists, and poorly marked intersections on the country highway, Erin could have driven it blindfolded after making countless middle-of-the-night trips into the Alfredson while on call. As she drove, her head swirled with jumbled thoughts and images: her grandfather, Josef Mengele, Kristen Hill, those brutal youths in Nakuru, and now her sister-in-law, flattened by the superbug. Erin wondered whether the cumulative angst might trigger another panic attack, but she pulled into the driveway in front of the Alfredson's ER without experiencing any of the telltale symptoms.

She parked a few spots down from Tyler's car. Though worried about

Jill, Erin could not deny her relief that she was not arriving to perform heart surgery. The prospect still unsettled her.

Inside, the ER was hopping. The beds were crowded with men and women who ran the gamut in terms of age and race. A number of staff greeted her with friendly but distracted smiles. A few glanced around, trying to help locate a phantom cardiac surgical patient, until Erin explained she had come to see a relative. Across the room, she spotted her father standing beside Tyler, who wore a yellow gown and had a mask dangling loosely below his chin. Erin dashed over to where they stood in front of a room whose entrance was covered by a closed curtain. She tried to hug Tyler but he warned her off, pointing to his gown. She turned to her father and wrapped him in her arms. He felt as rigid as usual, but when she squeezed him she could feel his rib cage through his jacket, and realized he was thinner than ever.

Breaking off the embrace, she pointed to the room. "How's Jill doing?"

"She's sleeping now," William said.

"Stable?"

"Her blood pressure is better." Tyler sighed. "But she's still in rough shape."

Erin nodded. "What are they treating her with?"

William glanced over to Tyler—who shook his head helplessly—and then back to Erin. "Jill is refusing treatment," her father said.

"*Refusing*? What the hell? She can't be thinking clearly, Tyler!" Erin said. "We can get around this with a psychiatrist's opinion."

"Erin, there's a reason she doesn't want the antibiotics," Tyler said.

She threw her hands in the air. "What could that possibly be?"

"She's six weeks pregnant."

"She is?" Erin gaped.

Tyler showed her a grim smile. "We just saw the heartbeat."

"Even more reason for her to get proper treatment," Erin said.

William folded his hands together. "The antibiotics they are using to treat this *C. difficile* infection are potentially harmful to the fetus."

Digesting the news, Erin considered Jill and Tyler's long fertility struggles. She appreciated her sister-in-law's dilemma; this pregnancy had to be especially precious to her. "I really need to talk to Jill," she said.

"Okay," Tyler said. "I'll take you in now."

"No, Tyler. Alone."

He stared at her, bewildered. "Okay," he finally said.

Erin looked from her brother to her father. Uncharacteristically, William's shoulders were slumped. He looked so much older, and his downcast eyes suggested an air of defeat she had never seen in him before. She felt a deep pang of sympathy. "Another case of *C. diff* isn't going to help your cause with the Alfredson board, huh, Dad?"

William chuckled but only looked sadder for it. "I'm an old man who's a little slow on the uptake. But I am starting to realize that my 'cause' is totally insignificant relative to what our family is going through."

"That's not completely true," Erin said. "The Alfredson *is* part of this family."

"We'll see for how much longer." William pointed to a cart by the room's door with gowns, gloves, and masks. "You'll need those to see Jill."

Erin headed for the cart and quickly slipped into the mandatory protective gear. The steps reminded her of prepping for surgery, and her heart skipped a beat.

She pulled open the door and stepped into the room. A gowned nurse, whose bright red hair peeked out from under her cap, sat a few feet from the bedside and wrote notes in the chart. Erin exchanged a nod with her as she approached the other side of the bed.

Jill's eyes opened and she recognized her sister-in-law immediately, despite the mask. "Erin . . . hey, thanks for coming," she said weakly. She struggled to push herself up on the bed.

Erin grabbed hold of Jill's arm and helped slide her a few inches up the bed. "You feeling any better yet?"

Jill's shoulders twitched slightly. "Not my best day ever." She nodded to the two IV lines running into her. "The fluids are helping, though."

"I hear congratulations are in order."

Jill rolled her eyes. "That might be a tad premature."

"You've made it this far."

Jill's gaze dropped to her sheets, and she said nothing.

"You don't want to risk exposing the baby to the antibiotics, right?" Erin ventured.

Jill looked up at her plaintively. "Have you read the potential side effects to fetuses?"

Erin shook her head.

"In the first trimester, the risk of miscarriage increases more than ten-fold. If the baby does survive, she is at marked increased risk for heart and kidney defects, limb malformation, and even brain damage."

"Ah, crap, Jill. That's tough," Erin muttered.

"I just want to try to see if I can beat this *C. diff* without damaging my baby," Jill said, her eyes glistening. "She . . . survived my dehydration to the point of shock. If I can stay better hydrated and keep the metronida-zole down—"

"Metronidazole won't fight off this superbug. We both know that."

"It's almost a miracle that I ever became pregnant. It won't happen again."

"You feel that way now. I remember when I first got—"

"I'm not you, Erin!" Jill snapped. "Life doesn't always fall into place perfectly for me. I didn't get my instant two-child family as soon as I hit thirty." She snorted. "I wish."

Jill's jealous outburst only deepened Erin's sympathy. She reached out and touched her sister-in-law's shoulder. Jill tensed at the contact, but Erin left her hand in place. "I've been incredibly lucky. I don't deny that. But now is your chance. You and your baby."

"I can't risk exposing her." Jill shook her head. "I just can't."

"I'm not sure you have a choice."

Jill stared at Erin for a long moment. "If you were in this situation—this bed—instead of me, what would you do?"

Erin squeezed Jill's shoulder. "I just lost a patient to this miserable su-perbug. Her heart was shot, and she didn't stand a chance in the end. But she left two young children behind. It was so awful." She waited a moment for her voice to cooperate. "Kristen was one of the best moms I've ever seen. She would have done *anything* for those kids. No matter what."

Jill's eyes glistened. "You see!"

"Don't *you* see, Jill?" she said gently. "If you don't make it through this, neither does your baby. How is that possibly any better than taking the med-ication?"

Jill broke off the eye contact and turned her head away.

Erin could tell by the soft snuffling sound and gentle shake of Jill's shoulders that she was weeping. Her heart sank. She wondered if she had only made matters worse. "Get better soon, Jill, okay?" Erin whispered.

Erin removed her hand and was about to turn away when Jill reached up and caught her wrist in a tremulous grip. "I'll think about it, Erin. I will." She paused. "Thank you."

Erin smiled. "Can I come see you tomorrow?"

"Please." Jill released her grip.

Erin headed for the door, stopping only to tear off her soiled gown, mask, and gloves and toss them in the biohazard waste bin. Outside the room, Tyler and William stood at the nursing station talking to a short woman with a dated bob cut, whom Erin recognized as one of the infectious disease specialists.

"Erin?" someone called to her in an English accent.

She looked over to see Dr. Bal Dhillon nearing. His stiff smile complemented his starched white lab coat. "Bal, hi. Are you looking after my sister-in-law, Jill Laidlaw?"

"I am. Or at least I was, until I passed her care over to the very able Dr. Hansen." Dhillon pointed to the woman with Tyler and William. He shuffled on the spot. "Erin, I hate to bother you while you are with family, but it is important."

"What, Bal?"

"There has been a stabbing. A nasty one."

"In Oakdale?" she said in disbelief. Violent crimes were so rare in the sleepy well-to-do town that assaults or car thefts made the local paper; a murder would mandate the entire front page.

"A domestic dispute," Dhillon said. "A man stabbed his common-law wife twice in the chest. The paramedics just phoned. They are on the way."

*Stabbing.* Erin's mouth went dry. An image of Sesi, the lovely Kenyan nurse, popped into her head. She could almost hear the woman's mournful scream the moment before the machete blade tore through her abdomen.

"ETA is less than five minutes," Dhillon went on. "The victim's pulse is very thready. I was hoping—"

Erin waved her hand to interrupt. "Bal . . . I . . . you better page the on-call team. I don't know if you've heard, but I'm on a medical leave right now."

"Yes, yes. Of course." He bowed his head apologetically. "Dr. Fujimora and his fellow are scrubbed in on an urgent bypass. The backup surgeon is at least forty-five minutes away."

Erin's heart thumped in her throat. The victim would surely require surgery, and she was not convinced that she would be able to operate if overcome by another anxiety attack. She tried desperately to conjure up a better excuse to avoid getting involved.

"Trauma ETA two minutes!" a voice bellowed on the overhead speaker.

A nurse called out to Dhillon from the desk. "Bal, they've lost the pulse in the field!"

"Traumatic cardiac arrest. The poor woman." Dhillon sighed. His head hung a little lower. "I am sorry, Erin. I had no right to ask."

Erin looked over his shoulder and called out to the charge nurse at the central desk. "I'll need a thoracotomy tray!" she said, referring to the chest-cracking kit.

"Already waiting," the nurse called back almost nonchalantly.

Bal smiled his gratitude as he turned for the large resuscitation room, Trauma One, beside Jill's room. Erin trudged after him, her feet heavy.

She could not shake the looping mental image of Sesi being repeatedly stabbed in the chest and abdomen. Erin looked down and saw that her fingers had begun to tremble. The invisible hands, which she had kept at bay for days, encircled her neck again. Her breathing grew more difficult with each step nearer to the room.

The ten-person trauma team—including residents, nurses, and respiratory and X-ray techs—assembled almost simultaneously inside the resuscitation room. People moved with silent purpose while preparing their own equipment.

Erin's hands shook noticeably as she slipped into the waterproof gown and secured her full facial shield. She panted under the mask, begging herself to slow her breathing before her fingers began to cramp up.

*Easy, chick. You can do this.*

A siren's wail rose in the distance. Erin's mouth went drier as her chest thumped harder. The latex on her gloves felt sticky against her damp palms.

*Keep it together*, she commanded herself, to no effect.

The siren suddenly cut off in mid-cry. A few moments of absolute silence fell on the room and then the doors of the ER burst open and a stretcher hurtled through the gap. A blur of activity joined the clamor of voices. A young female paramedic straddled the stretcher, as though riding a bronco, while she leaned forward and rapidly compressed the patient's chest, her palms flat and arms locked straight.

People in the room parted as the stretcher flew between them and halted beside the hospital bed. The paramedic hopped off the stretcher. Her partner and two nurses hoisted the young patient from the ambulance gurney onto the hospital bed. The female paramedic immediately slipped back to the right side of the bed and resumed chest compressions.

Dhillon stepped beside her. "What do we have?" he asked.

"Deana Roscoe," she grunted without slowing her pistonlike pumping motion. "Two half-inch stab wounds with a kitchen knife. Husband stabbed her thirty minutes ago. First wound under left nipple. Second lateral to left breast. One liter blood loss at scene. Cardiac arrest five minutes prior. CPR in progress ever since."

As Dhillon rapidly ran through the ABC's—airway, breathing, and circulation, the universal "cookbook" approach to assessing major trauma patients—Erin studied Deana Roscoe from the left side of the bed. Thinness aside, she looked nothing like Sesi, but the flashbacks of that Kenyan murder scene were so intense that Erin almost winced. The pressure across her windpipe intensified and her legs went rubbery as she fought off the urge to turn and flee.

Deana Roscoe had dyed blond hair and narrow cheeks studded with acne scars. Her face had the look of someone who had lived through a lot in her twenty-something years. Two IVs snaked into her tattooed right arm. An endotracheal tube was stuck between her prominent teeth and attached to the breathing bag that the second paramedic squeezed to pump oxygen in and out of her lungs. Her glazed eyes were open but her dilated pupils stared blankly at the ceiling. Roscoe's shirt had been cut wide open and now lay beneath her like a shed jacket. Caked blood obscured much of her small left breast. With each chest compression, blood leaked out of the puckering wound below her nipple and dripped onto the stretcher.

"Stop compressions," Dhillon instructed and the paramedic released her hands in mid-thrust. Dhillon palpated Roscoe's neck in vain for a carotid pulse. After five seconds, he said, "Resume compressions, please." He looked over to Erin and shook his head gravely.

She stepped forward on a shaky foot. "I am going to crack her chest now," she announced.

As the patient was technically dead without a measurable pulse or blood pressure, she required no anesthesia. Erin grabbed the open surgical tray beside her and wheeled it a foot closer to the bed. She shot her right hand out and grasped the handle of the largest of the three side-by-side scalpels. She used her left-hand fingers to walk along the skin over Roscoe's sternum, which was slippery with fresh blood. On the bony chest, Erin easily found the landmark she sought, where Roscoe's fifth rib met her sternum.

Erin applied the blade to the skin and pierced it. In one continuous swooping motion, she dug the blade through the skin and muscle, cutting all the way along, following the underside of the rib until her blade almost hit the bed. Dark red blood trailed after the expanding incision.

Erin was surprised to notice how steady her hand was as she tossed the scalpel back on the tray. Her hands felt less sticky, too. The squeezing at her throat lessened. A familiar sense of purpose nudged the panic and nightmarish Kenyan flashbacks from her consciousness.

She picked up a pair of oversized serrated scissors. She dug its teeth into the cartilaginous edge of the fifth rib right where it met the sternum. Squeezing the handles with full force, she felt the scissors gnaw through the rib with a loud pop, freeing it from the breastbone.

Erin grabbed for the rib spreaders, which resembled a long, flat car jack. Breathing easier, she maneuvered the device's blades into the space of the incision she had just created. As soon as the edges were securely positioned, she began turning the small crank dial. With a series of audible clunks the blades spread wider apart, exposing more and more of the inside of Roscoe's chest. Blood gushed out along the lower edge, but Erin kept spreading until she had exposed a ten-inch gap.

Spongy pink lung tissue poked out of the wound. She grabbed a retractor off the tray and stuck it inside, pushing the lung out of the way. She let go of the handle and gravity held the retractor in place for her.

"More light please," Erin ordered.

Someone adjusted the overhead light and Roscoe's chest cavity was bathed in brightness. Blood continued to well up from inside the chest and run over the edge of the wound, obscuring Erin's view of the heart. "Suction," she said, aware that every second lost would reduce the chances of getting the heart restarted.

A gloved nurse handed Erin sterile hoselike clear suction tubing that hissed in her hand. She stuck it into the back of the wound and threaded it behind the lung. On contact, it made a sloppy slurping noise and the tubing turned instantly red with blood.

With the blood cleared, Erin finally saw the shiny gray outline of the pericardium, the thin tissue that covered the heart. She reached for a pair of forceps with her left hand and fine scissors with her right. She slid the tools inside the chest and grabbed the edge of the pericardium with the forceps. She tented up the tissue, freeing it from the heart, and cut through it with the scissors.

The red muscle wall of the heart poked out as she peeled the pericardium away. Deflated like a torn wineskin, the heart twitched away ineffectively. Erin eyeballed the wall of the heart but could not spot the hole in the muscle that she knew had to be present. She put her hand in the wound and ran her fingers along the slippery side until she felt a small defect in the left ventricle, the biggest of the heart's four chambers. She poked her finger through the gash and slipped it inside the heart.

"Stapler!" she cried.

A nurse passed her an instrument that looked like a small white staple gun. With her right hand, Erin applied the nose of the stapler to the far edge of the one-inch gash. Using her left index finger to guide her, she ran the nose along, stapling the wound shut with click after click as though slowly closing a zipper.

Finished, she dropped the stapler on the tray and palpated the edges of the wound, satisfied she had closed the defect. She wrapped her palm around Roscoe's heart and felt it reinflate with blood. She squeezed the big muscle in her hand and then released it. She repeated the internal compressions every second for almost a minute. When she felt the heart contracting on its own in her hand, she let go.

She adjusted the light again and watched the big muscle. A wave of satisfaction overcame her as she saw how vigorously Roscoe's heart pumped.

Dhillon placed his fingers back on Roscoe's neck. "We have a very good pulse," he announced happily.

Erin wasn't surprised. What floored her was the blissful realization that she had just performed cardiac surgery again. And she had done so with a calm that, a week earlier, she despaired she would never again find.

## 38

The night was hell.

Nikki spent more than half of it on the toilet or throwing up into it. The cramps were unrelenting, but the craving was worse—so intense that she thought she would pluck out her own eyeballs in exchange for a single hydromorphone pill.

And between bouts of narcotic hunger came the recriminations that accompanied the shame of being an addict who had again stooped to stealing drugs from children with cancer. That she had returned the drugs to the dispensary without swallowing them brought her no solace.

*What have I become?*

Past ghosts visited throughout the night. Nikki saw little Nate's brave, sad face. Snippets of her intimate conversation with Tyler at O'Doole's looped in her head. The memories of her dead fiancé only intensified the guilt. Even Glen, with his boundless compassion, might have had a hard time forgiving her—the nurse who tried to seduce a married doctor and then stole painkillers from sick children.

Nikki was sitting at the kitchen table, sipping tepid tasteless tea, when the first light of dawn leaked through her window. She was so emotionally and physically beaten down that she hadn't even realized the symptoms of her withdrawal had abated. The cramps and cravings had subsided. Only the worthlessness and self-loathing remained.

*I've made it through the worst*, she tried to encourage herself, but her words were hollow. She felt like such a failure for having ever fallen off the wagon in the first place.

Tired as she was, she decided that the sunlight and some light exercise might perk her up. After a quick shower, she changed into a pair of shorts and a T-shirt, grabbed her Rollerblades, and headed out. She only skated half her normal route but, with her reduced speed and energy level, it took almost as long as the full loop.

By the time she returned to her apartment, she had begun to emerge from the fog of narcotic withdrawal. She saw the indicator light flashing on her phone. Even before she listened to the message, she knew it had to be the SFU calling to beg her to come in to work another overtime shift. With three of the specialized oncology nurses on maternity leave and five others out on disability—ranging from caregiver burnout to work-related back injuries—the ward was chronically short-staffed.

*Not today. I just can't.*

Still in her blading gear, Nikki lay down on top of the bedspread expecting sleep to come easily. But her mind raced faster than her skates had. An hour later, she heard the faint ringing of her phone, which she kept out of the bedroom so as not to be disturbed after night shifts. Giving up on sleep, she rolled off the bed and wandered out to answer it.

She found herself hoping that it was Erin McGrath calling to arrange the coffee they had discussed earlier. Nikki instinctively trusted Tyler's sister. She could imagine herself opening up to Erin, even about her addiction to painkillers and her feelings for Tyler. She knew it would be reckless to discuss either, especially with Tyler's sister of all people, but she felt the need to unload her secrets. Still relatively new to Oakdale, Nikki couldn't think of anyone else in whom she could readily confide, short of a public confession at a Narcotics Anonymous meeting, which did not appeal to her at all.

But it wasn't Erin on the phone. "Is this Nicola Salazar?" asked a man whose voice she didn't recognize.

"It's Nikki." Heart galloping, she immediately assumed someone at the Alfredson had discovered her aborted attempt at narcotics' theft.

"I am Denny Rymer with the *Times*."

A flood of relief washed over her but then she made the connection to the reporter who had written the vicious exposé on Tyler. She scowled at the receiver. "Where did you get my number?" she snapped.

"The phone book."

"Why are you calling?"

"I understand you were involved in the care of a young patient named

Nate Stafford?" Rymer's tone was obsequious. "His parents spoke incredibly highly of your professionalism and compassion. They said you shared a special bond with . . . little Nate."

She wasn't taken in by his flattery. "So?"

"They feel indebted to you." Rymer paused and his voice lowered. "However, they have serious concerns about Nate's medical care—"

"I am not going to comment on that!"

"Of course not," Rymer agreed quickly. "Wouldn't ask you to, either. I assume you know there is a lawsuit pending?"

"Yes."

"Dr. McGrath won't talk to me, Ms. Salazar. His father won't cooperate, either. It's making it really tough for me to report his side of the whole sad case."

"Why are you reporting this at all?"

"A family lost their child to a medication they would have never approved of, had they known its risks. It's tragic. If I can help prevent this from happening again to another patient—if for only *one* other patient or family—then don't you think it's worthwhile to let people know?"

*You self-righteous bastard!* Nikki calmed herself, before she fired back a knee-jerk response. That was probably what Rymer wanted.

"Ms. Salazar? Are you still there?"

"I don't buy your public service line," Nikki said evenly. "I think you are taking advantage of a very vulnerable family after they've gone through hell."

"You can believe whatever you want," Rymer said, unperturbed. "Besides, I didn't find them. The Staffords came to me. Regardless, I'm still trying to give our readers an unbiased—"

"You really think I'm that naïve?" she said. "You're hanging Ty— Dr. McGrath out as a scapegoat to sell papers and further your career."

"I'm doing my job, Ms. Salazar," he said with a hint of indignation.

"Let me tell you about Dr. McGrath," Nikki said through gritted teeth. "He is the most caring pediatric oncologist I have ever met. He would never choose to do anything that wasn't in a patient's best interest. Ever. Period."

"And I've heard others rave about him, too," Rymer encouraged. "Sometimes, doctors believe they're the best ones to make difficult decisions for patients and their families. I've seen it so many times." He sighed. "Sometimes even the very best of them wind up playing God. Wouldn't you agree?"

Nikki had the sudden sense that his comment was born from personal experience. She was tempted to ask but instead she merely said, "No, I do not."

"Are you saying Dr. McGrath explained all the potential risks to the Staffords?"

"I am saying that Nate was dying. There was only one drug left that might have helped him. And Dr. McGrath tried it."

"So he decided for them, then?"

She stopped herself from blurting a reply. "I don't want you to ever call me again, Mr. Rymer. Do you understand?" With that, she hung up the phone.

Nikki considered crawling back to bed, but she knew it would be hopeless. Instead, against her better judgment, she decided a shift on the SFU might provide a needed distraction from the turmoil raging inside her skull. She called the supervisor and agreed to come in for half the shift.

She arrived on the sixth floor in less than forty-five minutes. She had just finished taking her handover report at the nursing station when Tyler walked in. Spotting Nikki, he offered a slight wave and headed toward her.

Nikki was stunned by his appearance. In a stained, wrinkled T-shirt and jeans, he had at least two days' worth of stubble on his cheeks. His hair stuck out in unruly spears. Instead of his usual soapy freshness, she picked up a whiff of stale sweat. And the bags under his eyes were so deep that his eyeballs appeared sunken in their sockets. More than simply exhausted, he looked traumatized.

She immediately assumed his appearance had something to do with the weasel of a reporter, Rymer. Anger rippled through her. She felt the urge to comfort him. "Tyler, what is it?"

He rolled up a chair beside her and slumped into it. "It's Jill."

"What happened?" Nikki said, trying to push away the twinge of hopefulness that Tyler's marriage might be in deeper trouble.

"She's sick."

Nikki felt herself flushing, ashamed of her earlier selfish assumption. "It's serious, isn't it?"

He dropped his head and nodded. "She picked up *C. difficile.*"

"Oh, God, Tyler!" She reached her hand out to his shoulder, but something in his distant gaze stopped her. She let her hand drop to her lap. "I'm so sorry," she mumbled.

"I spent the whole night in the ER with her."

"Where is she now?"

"They moved her to the Henley Building. The surgical ICU."

"The ICU?" Nikki remembered hearing rumors of several patients who had already died from the superbug.

"For infection control." He sighed. "They're pooling all of the *C. diff* victims in the surgical ICU."

"Oh. Is she doing any better this morning?"

"The fluids have stabilized her blood pressure." He shook his head. "But the pregnancy hasn't helped at all."

The news hit Nikki like a kick to her stomach. "Jill . . . and you . . . are pregnant?" she stuttered.

Tyler grinned, almost apologetically, and then looked away in embarrassment. "We only found out a few days ago. It was a huge surprise to both of us." He shrugged minimally. "Jill assumed all her vomiting and GI symptoms were just part of her morning sickness. So the infection was really out of hand by the time we got her help."

"How awful . . . but . . . um . . . congratulations." Nikki had trouble focusing on his explanation. She had appreciated that there was little or no chance of a long-term romance between Tyler and her, but the fantasy had lingered. The news of Jill's pregnancy wiped it all out with cold, harsh finality.

"Jill has been through hell, Nikki." His voice was raw. "I'm not sure how much more she . . . or the baby . . . can stand."

Nikki tried to shake off her personal disappointment. In a way, she was happy for Tyler. She had seen how he lit up around kids, and she knew he would make a great dad. "Jill strikes me as a strong person," she said.

"Yeah, she is," he said. "But what she has been through recently . . ."

She touched him lightly on the shoulder. "It'll be okay, Tyler."

He stared into her eyes and smiled gratefully.

"Why aren't you with Jill now?" she asked.

"I've handed over all my patients to Alice Wright and Don Kitigawa. All except Keisha." He shook his head. "I can't abandon the Berrys now."

"You still plan to give her the Vintazomab today?" She thought of Denny Rymer again and the hair on her neck stood on end.

Tyler read the concern in her eyes. "Nikki, I promised them."

"But you're probably not in the best . . . um . . . headspace to start it, with what Jill and you are going through and what happened to . . ."

"Nate." There was no defensiveness in his tone. "I can't do anything about the past, but Keisha needs that drug. There's nothing else left for her."

"Tyler, you look as though you haven't slept in a week. You sure you're up to performing a spinal tap today? Can't someone else—"

"I have to do this, Nikki." He touched his chest. "Not just for the Berrys. For me, too."

She nodded. "Okay."

"Will you help me?"

She grinned. "Try stopping me."

"Thank you." He reached over and brushed his hand across the back of hers. "Nikki, how about you? Are you feeling okay? You were in rough shape yesterday."

She shrugged. "It was a tough night. Today is better."

"You did it, though." His lips cracked their first smile. "You made it over the hurdle."

His touch felt so good on her arm that her heart ached at the lost possibilities. Reluctantly, she pulled her hand from his and rose from her seat. "If it were only just one hurdle to get over."

## 39

As Tyler watched Nikki glide away from the nursing station, a pang of loss hit him. He knew that they would never share another evening like they'd had at O'Doole's. And judging from the trace of hurt that colored her words, she understood it, too.

Despite her composed appearance, Tyler realized Nikki had to be going through hell, physically and emotionally, after falling off the wagon. And she had to suffer through it without the support of a partner or family member in town. The thought evoked a mix of guilt, sympathy, and affection for her. He wished he could do more, but Nikki didn't seem to want that. Besides, Jill had to be his focus now.

It wasn't just the pregnancy, or even her illness. Jill's naked need for him had brought them closer than he would have thought possible a few weeks earlier.

In full mask, gown, and gloves, he had spent the night scrunched up in a chair by her bed. He dozed intermittently for short periods, but he was nowhere near comfortable or relaxed enough for real sleep. They went long stretches without sharing a word. However, they held hands throughout the night. Despite the latex, the minimal touch was as intimate as any contact in his memory.

He had opened his eyes at around two A.M. to find Jill staring at him. Although she looked pale, and still as fragile as a wounded fawn, she was smiling; her face more placid than he had seen in weeks. "I think I'm ready to start on them, Ty," she announced hoarsely.

After a bewildered moment, he understood. "You mean the antibiotics?" he asked.

"Yes."

"Good. Great, actually." Tyler squeezed her hand. His relief was intense. "It's the right decision, Jill."

"I know."

He viewed her for a moment. "What changed your mind?"

"The things you—and especially Erin—said touched a nerve." Her voice cracked. "And, of course, seeing that tiny beating heart . . ."

Tyler swallowed hard, but said nothing.

"I'm thinking clearer now, Ty. You guys were right. No matter what, the baby can't survive without me." She chuckled weakly. "And look how she's battled so far, surviving through the whole dehydration thing. Clearly, this is one little fighter."

"She gets that from her mom."

Jill touched his wrist gently. "Her dad, too."

"A little, I suppose."

"A lot. I figure if she can survive what we went through yesterday then she can hold her own with any antibiotic."

Tyler wanted to wrap his arms around her but had to settle for another squeeze of her hand.

Jill ran her thumb over his latex-covered knuckles. "I love you, Ty."

"I love you, too, Jill."

She cocked her head and viewed him with frail hopefulness. "Our baby is going to be okay, isn't she?"

"Remember? She's a fighter like her mom."

Jill laughed again. "Let's hope she inherits some of her Auntie Erin's persuasiveness."

The rolling rumble of a cart yanked Tyler from the poignant memory. Tyler looked up to see the chemotherapy cart being wheeled through the SFU's nursing station by one of the pharmacy techs. Similar carts rolled onto the sixth floor all day long, but the sight of this one—with the tinted bottles he recognized as Vintazomab hanging from the attached pole—launched his apprehension. Tyler had run out of excuses to delay Keisha's treatment another moment.

He took a few slow breaths, inhaling a faint whiff of his own body odor. Self-conscious and exhausted, he ached for a shower, a shave, and a nap. But he had no intention of leaving the hospital any time soon. Still, he decided he owed it to the Berrys to appear a little more presentable, so he had a quick shower in the staff lounge and then changed into a pair of scrubs. A glance in the mirror confirmed that, with sunken eyes and heavy stubble, he still looked like death warmed over, but at least he smelled better.

On his way out of the lounge, he stopped to phone the surgical ICU where Jill and all the other *C. diff* victims were clustered. "Your wife drifted off to sleep as soon as you left, Dr. McGrath," the nurse informed him.

"And her vital signs?" Tyler asked.

"Just fine," the nurse said compassionately. "The antibiotics are already making a real difference."

Jill's upgraded condition came as a massive relief, but the news did little to quell the dread that rose in the pit of his stomach with each step closer to Keisha's room. Inside, Jonah and Maya—both dressed as though attending a formal church function—sat in the chairs on each side of Keisha's bed. Despite her dark skin coloring, a noticeable pallor had overcome Keisha in the past days. But her demeanor was as unflappable as ever. Though minutes from her lumbar puncture and latest chemotherapy, she sat in her bed with her sketchbook wide open, absorbed in another picture.

"What are you drawing today, Keisha?" Tyler asked, fighting off his butterflies.

"Not you," she said.

"Oh?" Tyler frowned. "You mad at me?"

"No. You're hard to draw, is all."

"How come?"

"Your head is too big."

"Keisha!" Maya scolded.

Tyler laughed aloud. "So what is it then?" he asked.

"A self-photograph," she said proudly.

"You mean a self-portrait, honey," Jonah corrected.

Keisha shrugged. "It's gonna be better than a portrait, Dad."

"I bet." Tyler smiled. "Mind if I have a look?"

Keisha eyed him guardedly for a moment but then slowly turned the sketchbook around to show him. He was impressed by the eight-year-old's picture. Keisha had drawn herself riding a tall horse in a meadow with sunflowers reaching to the level of the horse's chest. "Awesome, Keisha. You're a real artist." He held out his palm to her, and she slapped it in a high five. "But I thought you preferred riding ponies."

She shrugged again. "Only 'cause my blood's too thin now. Once the medicine makes me better, I'll be able to ride horses," she said with certainty. "I'm not afraid of falling."

Her words tugged at his heart, and Tyler forced a smile. "Keisha, I'm going to talk boring grown-up-doctor stuff with your parents again. Okay?"

She sighed heavily. "And I'm gonna try not to listen."

"I'll make it even easier for you," he said. "I will take Mom and Dad out of the room."

"'Kay." With a single nod, she flipped the sketchbook around and returned her attention to the drawing.

Maya and Jonah followed Tyler out into the hallway. He closed the door behind him before he spoke. "We're going to move Keisha down the hall to our procedure room so we can start running the Vintazomab."

Maya's lip quivered. "Can we stay with our baby?"

"Of course," he said. "You do realize she will be heavily sedated?"

Jonah turned to his wife and grabbed her hand in his. He looked over to Tyler. "We still want to be there, Dr. McGrath."

"Understood." Tyler felt a new flutter of butterflies. "I know we've talked about this, but I want to walk you through all the steps again. All right?"

They nodded their consent, and Tyler launched into his explanation as though telling them for the first time. In lay terms, he described how Vintazomab worked. Then he turned to the potential side effects. "This is a very new drug. Most patients have done all right, but there have been a few very serious reactions in the early studies."

"How serious, Dr. McGrath?" Jonah asked.

"Very." Tyler cleared his throat. "Roughly one in a hundred patients died."

Jonah grimaced. "Died?"

"We don't know for sure if the medicine or the cancer was responsible in all the cases. Certainly the Vintazomab played a role."

"I see," Jonah said distantly.

Tyler looked from Maya to Jonah. "Only patients who received Vintazomab intrathecally, in other words through the spinal infusion, have died during treatment."

"Like you're going to do with our Keisha?" Jonah's tone dropped an octave.

"They have to, Jonah," Maya spat. "The cancer is around her brain and the medicine won't reach it any other way, right?"

Tyler nodded.

Jonah viewed Tyler solemnly. "What is your experience with Vinta-zomab, Dr. McGrath?"

Maya's eyes widened, silently begging Tyler to hold his tongue.

"Not good, Jonah." Tyler shook his head. "I've only used it once before. And the patient did not make it."

"I see," the minister said stonily.

Jonah turned to his wife, his expression dubious, but he did not say a word. Maya stared back without flinching. After a moment, Jonah exhaled heavily and then nodded. He looked over to Tyler. "God has sent us to you for a reason, Dr. McGrath." With that, the discussion was over.

Tyler hurried down the hallway to the SFU's procedure room, where the oncologists administered the intrathecal chemotherapy. Inside the scaled-down operating room, Nikki stood alone preparing the intravenous tubing and poles of medication.

They shared a shy smile when Tyler stepped inside. She nodded at his scrubs. "You actually look like a real doctor for once."

He chuckled. "Yeah, well, looks can be deceiving."

"Tyler, you sure you're okay with this?"

"Yes," he said without hesitating. "How about you?"

She pointed to the line of poles supporting bags and bottles of medication. "I think we're all ready."

"The CAT scan of Keisha's brain is normal, but just in case she seizes—"

Nikki reached into her pocket and pulled out two filled syringes that were marked with handwritten labels. "I've already drawn up lorazepam and diazepam," she said, referring to the two drugs most commonly used to abort seizures.

"I should have known you'd be ahead of me." He grinned. "Can you also prep Dilantin and phenobarb drips?" he asked, requesting two more backup antiseizure medications.

"Good as done," she said as she hurried for the door.

Standing alone in the room, Tyler had a flashback to the awful moment when he'd broken the news to the Staffords that their son died during the

Vintazomab infusion. He could still hear Laura's mournful wail and see the anguish in Craig's furious eyes.

*Keisha is not Nate!* he reminded himself as he wrestled the self-doubt out of mind.

Tyler headed to the table in the room's corner and slipped on his mask and hood before donning his sterile gown and gloves. He turned to the stand that held the lumbar puncture tray and unfolded the drapes covering it. As he was preparing his needles, Nikki rolled Keisha into the room on a stretcher flanked by her parents, who looked grave and uncomfortable in their procedural gowns. Tyler felt another brief bout of nerves when he saw Dr. Jane Lomas, the same anesthesiologist from Nate's ill-fated procedure, saunter into the room. But the heavyset anesthesiologist showed him a friendly smile, and he found her calm poise soothing.

Keisha was transferred from the stretcher to the bed. She was already sleepy from the sedative given to her before being transferred to the procedure room. Her gaze swam as she looked up from the table at the adults surrounding her. She did not say a word, but she offered her parents a heartrending gap-toothed grin and reached her hand out to her mother.

"Keisha, it's nap time now," Lomas said gently. She plunged the milky white anesthetic into the tubing that ran into the girl's arm. "Twenty, nineteen, eighteen . . . ," she counted down.

Lomas's count was still in the teens when Keisha's eyelids fluttered and then closed. Nikki glanced over to Tyler, who nodded his approval. She pressed a button on the electronic intravenous flow meter and turned the dials on the nearest of the lines. The yellow-tinted Vintazomab medication began to drip into the girl's intravenous line.

"I'm going to reposition Keisha now," Nikki explained to the Berrys as she rolled their anesthetized daughter onto her side and into the fetal position in preparation for her spinal tap.

Tyler moved closer to the tray. He felt slightly nauseous when he inhaled a whiff of the alcohol-based cleanser. As he sat down on the stool, his pulse pounded in his ears but his hand was steady. He reached for a pair of clamps and dabbed Keisha's back with a wet sponge.

After cleaning and draping the area, he walked his fingers along the backbone until he found the space between the third and fourth lumbar vertebrae. He froze the skin with a squirt of local anesthetic and then grabbed the spinal needle off the tray. Steadying the needle between his thumb and index finger, he poked it through the spot he had just frozen. He advanced the needle until he felt the familiar gentle pop as the tip entered the spinal canal. He removed the introducer from the needle and watched the clear spinal fluid drip slowly onto the sterile drape.

Tyler felt two sets of eyes upon him. He looked up at Keisha's wide-eyed parents and nodded reassuringly. "The needle is in the right spot now," he said. "We're going to start running the Vintazomab in now."

Nikki passed him the tubing. Through her mask, she showed him a small smile, but it didn't bolster his spirits. Tyler felt more on edge than ever as he connected the tubing to the needle.

He stood from his chair and walked to the foot of the bed, so he could watch Keisha's face. Eyes shut, her expression looked peaceful. "Okay, Nikki," Tyler said.

The nurse adjusted the roller dial on the IV bag and pressed two buttons on the machine. Yellowish fluid began to snake through the tubing toward Keisha's back. The room went very quiet as everyone watched the medication flow into her.

Tyler's stomach flip-flopped, but all was calm.

Twenty minutes ticked past without incident. Nikki calmly monitored the infusions like an air traffic controller tracking planes landing. Jonah looked his usual contemplative self. Only Maya was still taut with worry. Tyler pointed to the emptying bottle of Vintazomab, two-thirds of which had already run into the spine without complication. "We're getting there, Maya."

The words had just left his lips when, out of the corner of his eye, he noticed Keisha's chin bob. His gaze darted over to her just in time to see her whole head jerk up and down as though violently nodding. She shrieked a high-pitched moan. Suddenly her arms and legs began to flail, and she convulsed wildly. One of the intravenous lines flew free of her arm like a power line falling in a windstorm.

Tyler lunged forward to pin her thrashing body to the bed.

*Damn it! Not again!*

"*Keisha, no!*" Maya screamed.

"Oh, dear Lord, *please* show our daughter Your divine providence and mercy!" Jonah cried out in prayer.

As Tyler clamped Keisha's involuntarily bucking body to the bed, his eyes searched frantically for Nikki. "Lorazepam two milligrams IV stat!" he yelled.

"Already given," Nikki called from somewhere over his left shoulder.

Tyler glanced up at the head of the bed. Lomas studied him with quiet alarm. "She's still seizing," she said. "Do you want me to paralyze her?"

The anesthesiologist's offer to give Keisha a drug to temporarily block all muscular activity wouldn't stop the potentially lethal electrical storm from continuing to rage inside her brain. "No," Tyler said, as he struggled to hold the child through her fierce convulsions. "We won't be able to monitor the seizure if she's paralyzed."

"Another dose of lorazepam?" Nikki called to him.

"Yes. And start the Dilantin and phenobarb running!"

Keisha's moans evolved into gasps that sounded like someone trying to breathe through a chokehold. Then she stiffened as rigid as a log in Tyler's arms. A moment later, she stopped breathing altogether.

*Not again! Not Keisha, too.*

"Please, baby, *please!*" Maya wailed, as Jonah continued to mutter prayers.

Right as Lomas was shoving a breathing mask onto the girl's face, Keisha suddenly went limp as a rag doll in Tyler's arms. She grunted and then began to inhale in short whistling breaths. "Hold off," Tyler told the anesthesiologist, and Lomas pulled the mask away from Keisha's face.

Keisha's breathing quieted. Tyler felt her chest expand and contract in steadier respiration. Loosening his grip on her, he straightened up and turned to her anguished parents. "It's over now."

## 40

"They say the Spanish flu killed nearly fifty million people in the fall of 1918 *alone*," Dot said with an astounded shake of her head. "Over a half million Americans died. Almost all the victims were young and healthy."

"And the Alfredson?" Lorna asked.

"Thanks to Evan McGrath—who kept the doors open despite Grandfather's wishes—the hospital saw her share and then some," Dot said with another yawn.

Lorna had noticed the old woman's eyes start to glaze over the past hour, and she worried Dot might nod off at any moment. Lorna was hauling up unexpected payload now; like mining for copper and striking gold. She needed to keep the old crone focused. "So, as I understand it, Evan was responsible for Marshall's stroke?"

"That would *certainly* be the Alfredson family take on the whole mêlée." Dot sighed. "Of course, old Marshall was the one who attacked Evan with a cane, but why get hung up on the details?"

*Why, indeed?* "How bad was his stroke?"

"It's all relative, isn't it?" Dot said. "At the time, the morgue at the Alfredson was running out of space with the young bodies piling up so fast. An old man with left-sided weakness would not exactly have been a priority patient in October 1918. Then again, darling, that old man owned the place, so he was well taken care of."

"Did Marshall recover?"

"To a degree. He recovered much of the use of his left arm, but the old bugger would never walk again. I only ever knew him as wheelchair-bound."

Dot wiggled a finger at Lorna. "Make no mistake, darling, even from that *cumbersome* chair he could still strike fear into people's hearts."

"I guess so," Lorna said. "Did he follow through on his threat to chase Evan out of the hospital?"

Dot offered one of her now-familiar enigmatic smiles. "Marshall was preoccupied with his own infirmity. Evan was trying to cope with the worst natural disaster in recorded history. There was simply no time. *Besides*, before Marshall could do much of anything, Fate intervened and made his threat a moot one."

"How, Dot?" Lorna blurted out in her excitement.

Dot stared at Lorna for several seconds. "Despite all Evan's measures, poor Cecilia McClellan would not be the only member of staff to fall sick with the Spanish flu."

---

The Spanish flu wrought more heartache and tragedy than even the world war that preceded it. Though the hospital was overrun and its staff exhausted, Marshall insisted that the doors never be closed to the sorry victims of this dreaded disease.

—*The Alfredson: The First Hundred Years* by Gerald Fenton Naylor

Evan sat at his desk, holding the phone's earpiece in one hand and the mouthpiece in the other as he waited for the operator to connect his call to the military supplier who had last filled the hospital's oxygen tanks. He had been awake for almost three straight days and nights and could barely recall what sleep felt like. He had not left the grounds of the hospital during that time. The house was left empty since Grace had rushed off to Everett a week earlier to stay with her ailing mother.

Marshall's revelation that Evan had fathered a child with Olivia had so acutely evoked the memories of her that, despite the overwhelming demands on his time, his mind kept wandering back to those stolen hours spent joyously in a room at the Sherman Hotel. Evan felt like a fool for not having seen it earlier. The space between Olivia's wedding and Junior's birth was barely seven months, but he had never questioned the validity of the boy's premature birth.

Still shocked and numb from the news, Evan had yet to see Junior since learning he was the birth father. However, he knew Junior would be arriving soon to visit Marshall, even though the old man had banned him from the premises during the Spanish flu outbreak.

Evan winced again at the memory of Liv and Junior's clandestine kiss. Marshall was absolutely right—the young couple needed to sever all romantic ties immediately.

His thoughts turned to Marshall, who lay nearby recuperating from his stroke. Evan had assumed the old man's attitude regarding Liv and Junior was born from nothing more than sheer vindictiveness. Out of guilt, Evan had trudged over twice to visit him on the ward. Marshall was still in a stupor and didn't seem to recognize the doctor, let alone recall firing him. But he was already better than the day before, and Evan had little doubt his memory would improve as he continued to convalesce. He suspected the stroke would not shake Marshall's determination to banish the McGraths from the Alfredson.

The Alfredson had been Evan's life for over twenty years and yet, oddly, he fully accepted the inevitability of his departure. However, he intended to use every inch of leverage with Marshall and Junior to ensure that his disabled son could step into his role as the Alfredson's medical administrator. The Alfredson owed the McGraths that much. Besides, with George's wisdom, single-mindedness, and tenacity, he would make a very able leader for the clinic.

*Assuming, of course, the hospital survives the Spanish flu.*

The Alfredson was in the throes of a crisis worse than any Evan could have imagined. In three days, the clinic had admitted well over a hundred victims of the Spanish flu. As of last count—and the numbers were rising by the hour now—thirty-two patients had succumbed, including poor Cecilia McClellan, who died the day before her twenty-second birthday.

Evan had consulted frequently with the Alfredson's lung specialist and the clinic's other doctors who were most experienced in treating influenza and pneumonia. Between them, they tried every known remedy from silver to camphor, but nothing dented the lethality of this new flu. The only intervention that provided any measure of reprieve from death was the oxygen masks that Moses and Evan had fashioned out of rubber. Despite what Evan had considered a large stockpile, all the tanks were in use and patients were lined up threefold for their turn. Worse still, he knew that no matter how carefully they rationed the precious gas, the tanks would soon run dry.

Evan had sent two junior doctors to Seattle with a truck in search of more oxygen tanks, but the city wasn't coping any better than the Alfredson with its influenza catastrophe. Oxygen was as precious as rare gems. But Evan still had a few favors that he intended to call in. One of them was with the military supplier he was waiting for the operator to connect him to.

Evan was still holding on the line for the supplier when George hobbled into his room. As always, his son wore a suit with the empty right sleeve folded up to near shoulder level.

From the distress in his son's eyes, Evan immediately recognized that something disastrous had happened. Without waiting for the operator, he hung the earpiece up in the stand and set it on his desk. "George?" he demanded.

"Father, it's Liv."

The air left Evan as though a tree had fallen across his chest. "Oh, George, no. Please, God, no . . . ," he croaked.

George looked Evan squarely in the eye. "Liv has been moved to the flu ward. She has a high fever. And she is coughing up rust-colored sputum."

Evan grabbed his head in his hands and squeezed as hard as he could. "No, not Liv. *No, no, no . . .*"

With his only hand, George reached across the desk and grabbed Evan by the sleeve. "She needs you. Now, Father."

"Of course," Evan muttered as he leapt to his feet.

He raced around the desk and ran down the hallway and out of the building, without waiting for his lame son to keep up. Outside, the rain pelted down in sheets. Evan's shoes dug into the sodden grass and splashed the mud on his pants as he sprinted toward the building that housed the flu ward. He stormed inside, tracking the mud over the floor. The rainwater ran down from his hair into his eyes and mouth, but he did not stop to dry himself.

*Why can't it be me?* he thought over and over again.

Evan dug a mask out of his inner pocket and fixed it haphazardly to his face as he burst through the doors of the flu ward. "Where is she?" he cried to the stunned nurse who stood washing her hands at the sink.

"Miss McGrath?" the nurse asked stupidly.

"Yes!"

She pointed to the far corner of the room, but Evan could not spot his daughter among the haggard, pale faces in the beds he could see. A few of Moses's makeshift partitions still separated clusters of beds, though the ward had long since run out of curtains and poles. By now, the patients were all crowded close together, some lying on the floor with only a sheet or blanket between them and the floor. No one attempted to segregate white from black or men from women any longer. It was a small miracle just to find space to lay the next victim. Only death seemed to offer any new openings.

Evan rushed over to the corner of the room. He flung a partition out of his way and found Liv lying in a bed pushed tight against the wall.

Nothing he had seen in the past three days, or anytime in his life, prepared him for the sight of his daughter. Liv lay in her sweat-stained nightgown, covered from the waist down with a light blanket. Her face was wan; her lips bluish-tinged. An oxygen mask hung loosely around her face, hissing away almost uselessly. Panting heavily, she stared blankly at the ceiling and picked at imaginary objects floating above her.

The flu-induced delirium immediately told Evan how grave her illness was. His breath caught in his throat. He hopped over a patient lying on the floor and squeezed in beside her bed. "Liv, darling!" he said.

Liv's hands fell to the bed and her head swiveled to look up at him. "Papa?" she asked uncertainly.

"Yes, Liv. It is."

Her eyes came into focus and her discolored lips curved into the trace of an impish smile. "Oh, Papa," she said.

Evan felt his heart cracking. He reached out and cupped her slick face. "Darling," he murmured helplessly.

Liv lifted her hand and grabbed one of his, squeezing it weakly. "Papa, I am sorry."

"For what could you possibly be sorry?"

"Cecilia."

He patted her cheek softly. "There was nothing to be done for Cecilia."

Liv frowned slightly. "I came to see her, Papa."

"I know you did."

"After you told me not to." Liv squeezed his hand tighter. "I gave you my word, Papa, and I broke it." She stopped to gulp a few deep breaths of oxygen. "I could not let . . . Cecilia die alone. I just could not."

A swell of pride joined the grief mushrooming in his chest. He leaned forward and touched his forehead to hers. "Oh, Liv. You are a wonderful kind soul."

"I only want to be like you, Father," she murmured. "To try to be as good a doctor and a person."

Evan's cheeks flushed and his eyes misted over. "You are going to be better on both accounts, my love."

Suddenly, Liv's hand shot up, and she feebly pushed at Evan's chest. "Papa, not so close. You could become sick."

He resisted her shove. "I am wearing my mask, Liv."

The minimal force of her hands died away. For a long moment, their heads touched in silence. Each of Liv's raspy breaths tore at his heartstrings.

"I would give anything to change places with you," he muttered.

"What, Papa?" she asked, her eyes swimming again.

"Nothing."

She swallowed noisily. "Does Junior know?"

Evan grimaced. "I do not believe so. I only heard minutes ago from George."

"Will you tell him, Papa? Please."

Evan bristled at the thought of Liv pining for her own half brother, but he understood that she needed any and all support at this moment. "Yes, I will, Liv," he said, intending to send for Junior as soon as the boy arrived at the hospital.

"You do not approve." Liv panted. "You do not like his father."

*I am his father.* "It is not that, Liv."

"Junior is not like his father." Her eyes drifted shut. She appeared to be tiring from the effort of speaking. "He is not bitter like Mr. Alfredson. He wants . . . to do . . . grand things." Her voice trailed off to a hoarse croak. "I think I am in love."

"You are still so very young, Liv." He rubbed his forehead gently against hers.

She mumbled something unintelligible and lapsed into either sleep or unconsciousness. Evan wasn't sure which.

"Dr. McGrath!" a woman called out behind him.

Starting at the sound, Evan straightened up and looked over his shoulder. The head nurse, Gertrude Flanders, was staring wide-eyed and gesturing wildly from a few feet away. "This is reckless contact, indeed, Dr. McGrath!"

"You are correct, Mrs. Flanders," he said as he rubbed his eyes.

Flanders nodded with genuine sympathy. "I am so sorry for your daughter's illness. But, Dr. McGrath, you taught us how vital it is to take more care around . . . affected patients."

"You are absolutely right." He sighed.

Evan had just hovered within inches of a highly contagious patient, ignoring the most basic of infection-control measures, but he simply did not care. The most important person in his life was at the brink of death.

*Why, oh why, can it not be me instead?*

# 41

"You see this, Bill?" Normie Chow trooped into his office, waving the newspaper.

"I did," William sighed.

"And?"

"I am dealing with it, Normie."

Chow looked unimpressed as he dropped into the chair on the other side of William's desk. He unfolded the paper and held it up close to his face as though he had forgotten his reading glasses. " 'The McGraths are the medical family—arguably, the medical dynasty—who have controlled the Alfredson for more than a hundred years,' " Chow quoted. He lowered the paper momentarily and chuckled. "A *hundred* years? Bill, I thought you'd only been doing this job about eighty."

William wasn't in the mood. "Normie, I read the article."

Ignoring him, Chow raised the paper and read on. " 'The McGrath family has rallied behind one of their own, Dr. Tyler McGrath. His father, Dr. William McGrath, the Alfredson's president and CEO, has refused to answer questions regarding his son's alleged malpractice. However, according to sources within the hospital, he has stonewalled and blocked all attempts at an internal investigation of Dr. Tyler McGrath's actions that led to the untimely death of little Nathan Stafford . . .' Yada, yada, yada." His head popped up over the page.

Pain seared through William's lower back. "What is your point, Normie?"

Chow dropped the paper to his side as though it were an ax falling. "You know what people around here are calling this?"

William shook his head.

"*McGrath-gate.*"

"Who's calling it that?"

"Well, me." Chow chortled. "I'm just hoping it'll catch on."

"Glad you find this all so entertaining, Normie." William resisted the urge to rub his back. "Do you believe Mr. Rymer?"

"Nah. I got to give the guy some credit, though. Only person I know who hates doctors more than my grandpa did." Chow's face contorted into a grimace. "Besides, don't matter what I think."

William sighed. Chow was right. All that mattered was how the voting members of the Alfredson family viewed Rymer's inflammatory article.

"So?" Chow asked. "You going to take this lying down, Bill?"

"That's not my plan, no." William pointed to the newspaper dangling from Chow's hand. "In fact, the article has inspired me."

"Inspired by *this*, Bill? Really?" Chow's face scrunched again as he raised and dropped the newspaper. "You been reading self-help books again? 'Every setback is really an opportunity' and all that bull crap?"

William sat up straighter in his chair. "Between this board meeting, the *C. difficile* crisis, Denny Rymer, and so on, I've been too long on the defensive. And frankly, Normie, I am tired of it." He sighed. "Perhaps the Alfredson—at least, as my family has always known it—is beyond salvaging. But I am determined to go down swinging."

"That's the spirit, Bill." Chow made a supportive punch-to-the-chin gesture. "Won't do you a scrap of good, but I'm glad you're going to put up a fight."

William chuckled at Chow's fatalistic candor. "Might already be helping. Look at what has happened with Senator Wilder."

"Did you make him better?"

"No, but I enlisted his help. He's already spoken to the TV producer who was considering running the exposé on our superbug situation. Senator Wilder persuaded him not to run the story."

"*Persuaded?*" Chow laughed. "Like with a horse's head in the guy's bed?"

"No. On the contrary. They're spinning a positive story out of this. Senator Wilder is going public with his multiple sclerosis. He wants to endorse the experimental stem cell treatment my daughter-in-law, Jill Laidlaw, is pioneering."

Chow stretched his arms over his head and yawned. "Speaking of Dr.

Laidlaw, she's the last reported case of *C. diff* we've had in the past thirty-six hours."

"No one else since?"

"Nope."

"Good," William said with genuine satisfaction. "How is the surgical ICU coping?"

"We're treating the five remaining active cases, including your daughter-in-law. She's the sickest of the lot, but as you know she *finally* agreed to go on treatment." Chow rolled his eyes. "Holy smokes, you McGraths are stubborn sons of bitches. Who knew?" He shook his head. "You Scots make us Chinese look like an easygoing, laidback people. And that's saying plenty!"

"Laidlaw is an English name."

"Ah, she's a McGrath at heart." Chow waved away the difference with a backhanded flip of his wrist. "Point is, the *C. diff* outbreak appears to be contained for the time being."

"For the time being?" William muttered. "You don't think we're over the worst of it?"

"Who knows?" Chow shrugged, as though the question were academic. "This hospital is big enough to span two time zones and house its own weather system. Those tiny *C. difficile* spores could hide out almost anywhere. Could be years until we eradicate them all. If ever."

William nodded. "So, for the time being, we're in reasonable shape?"

"Better than last week." Chow heaved a sigh. "Then again, last week was not exactly a banner week for this joint."

"Your team has done a good job under trying circumstances," William said. "You've done well, Normie."

Chow reddened slightly as he stood. "Yeah, well, I'm eager to get back to normal times and my usual habit of just phoning the job in."

Chow left with a promise of another update in the morning. Moments later, the phone on William's desk buzzed. He reached for the receiver.

"Dr. McGrath, it's Denny Rymer," the caller said in a syrupy voice.

"Ah, Mr. Rymer. Thank you for returning my call."

"My pleasure," Rymer cooed. "Does this mean you're prepared to discuss the Stafford case?"

"No. No. Not at all."

The sweetness drained from Rymer's tone. "Then what's this about?"

"I wanted to discuss legal action with you."

"You mean the Staffords?"

"No, Mr. Rymer. The libel and antidefamation suit that the Alfredson Medical Center intends to launch against you and your newspaper."

Rymer sniggered. "If you think you can intimidate me for one second by threatening to sue, you're wasting your time, Dr. McGrath. Been there, done that."

"I wonder, Mr. Rymer." William paused. "What you wrote in today's paper was patently false and damaging to the Alfredson and myself, personally."

"I have sources that will back up everything I said," Rymer said defiantly.

"You might want to check your sources more diligently."

"I always do, Dr. McGrath." But a note of hesitation crept into his tone.

"You said that I 'stonewalled and blocked all attempts at an internal investigation.' In fact, once we heard of the unfortunate outcome, we deemed the Stafford case an extraordinary death and immediately designated it for a Section Fifty-nine review."

"Section Fifty-nine?" Rymer said nervously. "What is that?"

"It's when a group of senior physicians from the Medical Advisory Committee perform an internal audit on a morbidity or mortality case. It's as thorough as a coroner's inquest. The findings and recommendations are binding."

He paused. "I wasn't aware."

"Apparently not." William kept his tone as polite and cordial as ever. "Allow me to enlighten you about something else. Since the Alfredson has an international reputation to protect, we have an in-house legal department that deals extremely effectively with any and all unfounded accusations. As well, we keep the two best civil litigating law firms in the Pacific Northwest on permanent retainer. Our success rate under such circumstances is nothing short of extraordinary."

Rymer cleared his throat anxiously. "Listen, your threats might work on someone else, but I—"

"Mr. Rymer, what you reported today was inaccurate, defamatory, and libelous. We intend to bring the full weight of our legal resources down on you and your newspaper. You might think you are impervious to such actions, but I promise you that your editor and publisher will not."

Rymer didn't reply immediately, but William could hear him breathing steadily on the other end of the line. "What do you want from me?" he asked petulantly.

"Your paper will print a front-page retraction of today's story, apologizing for its inaccuracy."

"My editor won't—"

"And you will not write one more word about this hospital, my family, or the Stafford case ever again. Do you understand?"

"You can't be serious!"

"Never have I been more!" William snapped, raising his voice for the first time. "Today you handed us a smoking gun. And we will not hesitate to use it. Rymer, you have picked the wrong hospital to misrepresent and sensationalize!"

William put down the receiver without waiting for a response. Though his spiel included a healthy dose of bluster, William did believe the Alfredson's case against the reporter and his newspaper would be strong. From experience, he suspected either the reporter or one of his bosses would flinch sooner than later, but he intended to leave nothing to chance. He snatched the sticky note with the phone number for the newspaper's editor-in-chief off the edge of his computer screen. As he reached for the phone again, a voice called out from the doorway.

"Dad," Erin said. "You got a minute?"

"Of course." William rose from his chair with a stab of agony in his back, but he managed to hide the pain from his expression. He hobbled across the floor to meet her.

Erin put her arms around him and pulled him into a tight embrace. William broke free of the hug and led her to the seats at his desk. Though drawn, her face glowed with a familiar tranquility that he had not seen in a long while.

"I just saw Jill," she announced.

"How is she?"

Erin shrugged. "Her vitals are stable, and her spirits are a little higher. But she still doesn't look good. So weak and fragile."

He nodded. "It's going to take time."

"Dad, she is so worried about her baby and what those antibiotics might do."

"Can you blame her?"

"No. Not really." Erin chewed her lower lip. "She's not the only relative who has me worried, either."

"Tyler?"

"You, Dad!" She ran her hand up and down to indicate him from the waist up. "You're turning to skin and bones."

William laughed self-consciously. "You know me, I'm not much of a cook. I have never eaten well since your mother died."

"Are you eating at all?"

"I would be foolish not to. I get the wholesale price on everything in the cafeteria."

"Dad, I'm serious. The stress of this job of yours . . ." She shook her head. "I think it's killing you."

He shifted in his seat, aware of the cancerous ache in his spine. "Erin, no question it has been a hard few weeks. Maybe I have lost a few pounds over this, but this is as stressful a time as I have gone through in this role. However, the end is in sight. Next week is the board meeting."

"Are you still worried?"

He showed her a tired smile. "At this point, I just want it to be over."

"I want to come to the meeting, Dad."

William frowned. "It's a meeting for board members only—the Alfredson family."

"You're going, right?"

"Yes, but I am presenting to them."

Erin held her hands open in front of her. "Our family has been running their hospital for more than a hundred years," she said. "Don't you think more than one McGrath deserves to be present at the meeting that will decide its fate?"

William's heart warmed. He accepted that, as a father, he had not been nearly involved enough in her life, but no one could deny that his daughter had turned out exceptionally well. "You're absolutely right. I would like you to be there. Your brother, too, if he is interested."

"Count on it," she said. "By the way, Dad, I operated on a stabbing victim in the ER last night."

William smiled. "I heard you did well."

"She's doing all right." Erin shrugged modestly. "I think I'm going to be able to return to work sooner than I thought."

"And your carpal tunnel syndrome?"

Erin looked down at her hands. "Was never the issue."

He nodded understandingly. "Of course, Erin."

"It was Africa, Dad." Her voice cracked. "Or, at least, something that happened to me over there . . ."

He sat still as he listened to his daughter describe the hellish assault and massacre she had survived in Nakuru. As Erin described her anxiety attacks and post-traumatic stress disorder that followed, William realized his worries over the Alfredson's board meeting paled in comparison to what she had suffered. "Oh, Erin, how awful," he said.

She wiped her moist eyes with the back of her hand. "Now that I've stopped trying to pretend it never happened, I'm doing a lot better, Daddy."

Erin had not called him Daddy in years. William filled with even more affection for her. For a moment, he considered sharing his own secret about his bone cancer, but he held his tongue. It was not the right time.

Erin rose and headed for the door, but William stopped her. "You're such a caring person, Erin. A wonderful daughter, wife, and mother. And the very best kind of doctor." He paused and glanced down, embarrassed at his display of emotion. "I know I don't say this often enough, but I am so proud of you. I always have been." He nodded. "I always will be."

She reached out and wrapped him in another hug. "Oh, Dad."

As soon as she had gone, William checked his watch. He was late for his lunch meeting with Eileen Hutchins. He hurried out to the car, moving as fast as his damaged spine would allow.

By the time William reached the corner table at Le Bistro, Eileen Hutchins was already seated. She smiled politely as he sputtered an apology for his lateness.

"Glass of white?" she asked, holding up her own.

"Yes, thank you."

Eileen signaled to a waiter, who hurried over to fill William a glass from the bottle on ice by the table.

She raised her glass. "What shall we drink to?"

William smiled wryly. "How about the past?"

Eileen laughed. "You can't go wrong there, I suppose."

They clinked glasses. "To the Alfredson's storied past," she said.

"At least no one can sell *that*." William sighed. "Eileen, did you happen to see this morning's paper?"

She nodded noncommittally.

"I'm sorry."

"It's not your fault, William. Mr. Rymer is a parasite of the worst kind."

"His 'facts' were way off base. If it's any consolation, I spoke with him earlier. I do not believe we will be seeing any more articles on the Alfredson or the McGraths."

"That's something, I suppose."

"And we've managed to quash the *C. diff* story." He updated her on the improved status of the superbug and the senator's plans to publicly endorse his treatment at the Alfredson. She listened attentively, but her taut features showed little relief. "What is it, Eileen?"

Eileen reached in her pocket, extracted a piece of paper, and carefully unfolded it. William immediately recognized it as the one she had brought to his office that listed all the voting members on the Alfredson board. He saw that a few of the handwritten plus signs had been crossed out and replaced with minuses.

"We've lost some votes, have we?" he asked.

Eileen nodded. "I heard from one of my cousins in Seattle. He and his daughter have decided to vote in favor of the sale." She reached out and patted William's hand. "He said it has nothing to do with the recent publicity."

"I wonder." William glanced at her hand on his and smiled. "Where does that leave us?"

"Twenty-eight in favor, twenty-six against, and six unknowns."

The news was bleak but not unexpected. "So we need at least four of the unknowns to vote against the motion to block the sale," he said.

"Providing my count is accurate. Yes."

William stared at his glass for a long moment. So many events had conspired against their cause recently that it seemed as though the hospital was destined to be sold and the McGraths' ties to it severed. However, the growing inevitability no longer felt like the end of the world. He had come to see there were more important things in life.

He looked up and stared into her captivating eyes. "Eileen, after the board meeting is over—whatever the outcome—I wondered if maybe, sometime, you would consider having dinner with me?"

She flapped the page in her hand and laughed. "Not for more strategizing, I hope."

William reddened. "Just dinner."

"I would like that, William. I would like that very much."

## 42

Lorna awoke at five A.M. burning with impatience and curiosity. The night before, three-quarters of the way through the Alfredson's Spanish flu saga, Dot had suddenly arisen from the couch and announced she was going to bed, leaving Lorna in mid-story with Evan hovering by his gravely ill daughter's bedside.

Lorna had an appointment to see her lawyer at eleven. She had intended to leave the mansion by six, without waiting for the old crone to rise. But her lawyer would have to wait; Dot's information was too valuable.

Biding her time, Lorna sat at the desk of the guest room with her bag packed beside her. She stared at the screen of her laptop, reviewing the rapidly accumulating notes. Satisfied they were in order, she launched into a new chapter. Her fingers could barely keep up with the story as it unfolded on the screen.

Lorna smiled to herself as she reread the page she had just typed. She could not have invented better history. It possessed all the elements she had hoped to uncover and then some: secrets, life-and-death struggles, betrayal, and family conflict.

*Perfect.* She smiled to herself. The years of writing academic papers that no one read would be behind her soon. This was a story people could not ignore. All she needed now was the right ending.

Shortly before eight o'clock, Lorna heard shuffling sounds downstairs. She quickly stowed her laptop inside her bag and headed down. In a sheer leopard-print robe that exposed her thin legs and knobby knees, Dot sat at the kitchen table with a cup of coffee in one hand and a pen in the other. In front of her, *The New York Times* was opened to the crossword puzzle page. Dot finished inking in an answer before she even looked up at Lorna. "Good morning, darling. I thought I had already lost you *forever*."

"I wanted to say thank-you. And, of course, good-bye."

Dot studied Lorna with that amused twinkle in her eyes. "I am the one who should be thanking you."

"For what, Dot?"

"Taking the time to humor an ancient relative and listen to her rambling stories."

"I've been totally enthralled by those stories. You've completely changed my perspective on our family history and the Alfredson itself."

"Oh, I'm delighted," Dot said. "So you will be attending our little family gathering at the board meeting after all?"

"Absolutely."

"That's wonderful. All the family should be there to witness it."

"Witness what?"

"The end of an era, darling!"

"The *end*?" Lorna said. "You think the family will vote to sell the Alfredson?"

"Oh, it will be close, but of course we will." She chuckled. "We Alfredsons usually find a way to do the wrong thing."

"I thought you said it didn't matter to you one way or another how the family votes?"

"It doesn't." She looked back at her crossword puzzle and took the time to fill in a few more squares. "Besides, no one cares what this dotty old bird thinks. My opinion is completely irrelevant." She sighed. "Perhaps I have not had the good decency to die off like the rest of my ilk, but I realize this is a decision for the younger generations." She laughed again. "Still, I am *dying* to see how it all unfolds."

Lorna intuited there had to be to more to it. Something in Dot's devil-may-care attitude did not jibe with the passion with which she reveled in Marshall and Evan's story. But Lorna had no time to worry about her great-aunt's motives. "Dot, last night, you left Liv McGrath on her deathbed."

Dot tapped her chin with the pen. "Ah, so it seemed, darling. Didn't it?"

Only Fate conspired to prevent a marital union of the Alfredson
and McGrath families that would have legally enshrined the deep bond
the two families already shared.
—*The Alfredson: The First Hundred Years* by Gerald Fenton Naylor

Evan woke up with his forehead digging into the windowsill and drool
stuck to the inside of his mask. He would never have believed he had slept
at all, were it not for the dawn's thin light streaming through the uncovered
window.

Evan was gripped by a moment of sheer panic at the thought that his
daughter might have died while he slept. He sat up rigid and swiveled his
head over to look at his daughter. Liv lay perfectly still in the bed, the oxygen mask beneath her chin sputtering its last weak traces of gas from the
nearly empty tank. For one agonizing moment, Evan thought he was too
late. But then he realized Liv was staring at him, her eyes alert. The navy tinge
had left her features. Though still pale, she looked vastly improved from earlier in the night.

"Liv?" he said warily, fearing he might still be dreaming.

"Hello, Papa," she croaked.

"Are you . . . better?"

"I think so." She coughed, but the sound was drier. "The breathing is
easier now, Papa."

He leaned forward and took her hand in his. It was warm but nowhere
near as hot or clammy as it had been. "Oh, Liv!" he cried. "You *are* better!"

She tried to raise her head off the bed, but only made it a few inches
before she fell back against the mattress, panting heavily.

Evan's spirits soared. Nothing else in the world mattered but his daughter's almost miraculous improvement. "Liv, oh Liv," he murmured.

"Will I . . . survive, Papa?"

"Yes!" he cried joyously. "Oh, yes." He had seen enough of the killer flu
to know that those patients who did turn the corner seemed to recover as
rapidly as they had fallen ill.

Tears flooded down Liv's cheeks. "I thought it would be all over soon."

"We had reason to worry." Evan tasted his own tears before he realized
he was crying, too.

She reached out and clasped his hand between both of hers. "Don't cry, Father. It is going to be okay."

"Yes it will, Liv." And despite the tragedy and chaos encircling them, in his mind, his world no longer teetered on the brink of collapse.

"Where is Mother?"

"Still in Everett with your grandmother. The telephone lines have been clogged since this . . . catastrophe. We have not been able to make a connection. I have sent word with one of our interns, but I do not know if she has yet heard."

"I do not want her worrying needlessly," Liv murmured.

"Hardly needless, my love." Evan laughed as he wiped his tears away with the sleeve of his upper arm, careful to keep his potentially virus-contaminated hands away from his face.

Neither of them spoke. After a few minutes, Liv's eyes closed and she drifted back to sleep. Only then did Evan become conscious of the sounds of anguish and misery around him—harsh coughs and labored respirations intermingled with mournful and delirious cries. Though sympathetic to other victims, Evan was deliriously happy over Liv's unexpected improvement. And he swelled with pride as he glanced around and saw his tireless nurses moving from person to person, offering what little comfort they could in the form of compresses, ladles of water, or simply kind words. He felt guilty for having ever reprimanded Mrs. Flanders. Her nurses were nothing short of heroic, and Evan resolved to acknowledge them for it.

Evan realized, too, that despite his daughter's illness and his own imminent dismissal, he was still responsible for leading the Alfredson in this, its darkest hour. After convincing himself Liv was genuinely asleep, he gently freed his hand from hers and stood to his feet. He wove his way through the labyrinth of patients who filled almost every square inch of the ward, some of them now two to a bed. He stopped at the sink to scrub his hands with soap and then, with a final quick glance in Liv's direction, left the ward.

Out in the hallway as he was pulling the mask from his face, he saw Junior round the corner and come barreling toward him. The boy's face was taut with worry. At first Evan thought he was going to steam right past him and onto the ward. But Junior stopped abruptly and spun to face him. "How is she?" he demanded without a word of greeting.

"Better."

"Do you mean that, Dr. McGrath?"

Evan viewed the boy with deeper affection, appreciating that he was the embodiment of his own tryst with Olivia. "I do, Junior. She is much improved."

The anguish vanished from Junior's face. He beamed one of his open-mouthed smiles. "That is sensational news, Dr. McGrath! Just sensational."

Evan nodded. He could not get over Junior's likeness to George and Nicholas, and wondered how he had ever missed it before.

"I want to see her. Straight away." Junior's tone became as entitled as Marshall's.

"Liv is sleeping, Junior." Evan tried to discourage him. "She will need a long rest."

"I *need* to see her!"

"No visitors are permitted on the flu ward," Evan said. "It is far too risky."

"I am not afraid. And Liv could only benefit from the sight of a friendly face."

"Maybe so, but your father instructed you to keep away from the hospital during this calamity."

Junior thumbed in the direction of the other building. "My father is convalescing from a stroke." He puffed out his chest. "Until he regains his faculties—*if* he ever does—I am in charge of my family's affairs. And I will go where I choose."

Even the boy's resistance, bordering on arrogance, did not put Evan off. Much as he admired Junior's show of bravery, Evan had to put an end to the romance. "We must talk, Junior." He nodded toward the exit. "Alone."

Evan turned and began heading for the door, but Junior stood his ground.

"It concerns Liv," Evan said over his shoulder. "Please, Junior."

After another hesitant moment, Junior followed the doctor out of the building. They walked in silence along the same pathway where Evan had spied Junior kissing his daughter a week or two before. After three days with almost no food or sleep, Evan's legs felt rubbery. He breathed heavily as he followed the slight incline up and around the side of the building. Rather than show his exhaustion, he stopped halfway, pretending to have reached his chosen spot. "Junior, believe it or not, I am fond of you. I really am."

Junior eyed him warily. "What is this about, then, Dr. McGrath?"

"You cannot see Liv anymore."

Junior folded his arms across his chest in defiance. "You sound just like my father! And we will not listen to you any more than we did him!" He turned on his heel and began to march away.

"Do you know much about your mother, Junior?" Evan called after him.

The comment stopped the boy. "I have no memory of her, but I have seen photographs and heard stories." He sighed. "Father speaks of her often. He told me that she could be a real firebrand."

Evan chuckled. "Oh, she could be that. But your father loved her dearly."

Junior cocked his head in surprise. "You knew her, too, then?"

Evan nodded. "She was an amazing woman, Junior. So passionate. So caring." He swept his hand in the direction of the clinic. "There would have been no clinic without Olivia."

"No clinic without my mother? What does that mean?"

Evan considered his words. "She had a great deal of influence on your father. All I had was a youthful dream, but your mother recognized what was needed to see it realized."

Junior eyed him suspiciously. "Sounds as though you knew her quite well."

Evan looked down and nodded. "We were in love."

"*What!* You and my mother?" He grimaced.

"Junior, Arthur Grovenor was not your father."

"Now just hold on a minute—" Junior's eyes went wide as he backpedaled a few steps. "Are you suggesting . . ."

"I am your father."

"No!"

Evan brought a hand to his chest. "I only found out days ago myself."

"*That cannot be!*"

Evan shook his head. "Why do you suppose Marshall is so opposed to your relationship with Liv?"

Though he was desperately flustered, Junior's face creased with the ghastly realization. "Liv and I are . . ." His jaw fell open.

"I am sorry, Junior, it is true."

He shook his head wildly. "No, no, no . . ." Suddenly, Junior whirled and raced off up the hill.

Evan started after him but only made it a few strides before the shortness of breath stopped him. His head swam with light-headedness, and he reached a hand out for a nearby tree to prop himself up.

A chill hit him so hard that he shivered on the spot.

And then Evan began to cough.

## 43

The rubbery scrambled eggs and cold toast tasted better than anything Jill could remember. Once she finished the last crumb, she shoved the empty plate back onto the tray and then pushed the rolling table away from her bed. "Couple days ago, I would have never believed I'd get my appetite back."

"Oh, it's back, baby." Tyler eyed her with a mischievous grin. "The way you attacked that tray, I was even a little worried about my fingers when they got too close!"

"Give me a break." She laughed. "This was my first solid food in close to a week. I was ravenous. Besides, I'm eating for two now."

"You sure it's only two?" He chuckled. "I'm just so happy to see you eating again."

"Yeah. When else will I ever be able to get this excited about the prospect of gaining weight?"

Tyler held up two crossed fingers. "So far so good, huh?"

She nodded. Earlier in the morning, Jill—who had cried fewer than a half-dozen times in her adult life—wept again at the sight of her baby's thumping heart on the ultrasound machine's screen. They still did not know what the long-term consequences of her antibiotics use would be, but after four days of taking the medication, the risk of a drug-induced miscarriage was steadily decreasing.

"I'm so glad to be coming home today, Ty."

Jill's guts had quieted and she had not spiked a fever in more than two days. All the other *C. diff* victims had already been discharged from the surgical ICU, and she was the last known case of the superbug left at the Alfredson. Since she had been free of symptoms for forty-eight hours, her infectious disease specialist had declared her no longer contagious. And her obstetrician agreed that Jill was well enough to finish her antibiotics at home.

Jill stood up and stepped over to Tyler. She put her arms around him and leaned her head into his shoulder.

He ran his hand through her hair. "I've missed you, Jill."

She realized he was referring to more than just the past few days of quarantine. "Me, too." She spoke into his shoulder. "We get a do-over now though, right?"

He kissed her ear and whispered, "I like do-overs."

They stood like that for a few moments, before Jill pulled back. "Hey, how's Keisha doing?" She felt more invested in the little girl's outcome than she had in any of Tyler's previous patients.

"Pretty good," Tyler said. "She received her last dose of Vintazomab yesterday. No more seizures. Too soon to see any results, but her blood work is no worse. Justified or not, I'm a little more optimistic."

Jill would have liked to have kissed her husband on the lips but, even though she had been told she was no longer contagious, she did not want to take any chances. Instead, she pecked him on the cheek. "You did good, Ty."

"We'll see." He shrugged. "How about you? Thought any more about your research?"

Jill's mood deflated at the mention of her lab. "I drafted a letter to my funding agency last night."

"What did you say?"

"That the preliminary results I submitted were inaccurate, probably fraudulent."

"Jill, that's academic suicide!"

"What can I say?"

"That you made a mistake."

"A mistake?" She groaned. "Tyler, it's a multimillion-dollar grant application."

"But you haven't published anything yet. Nothing is written in stone."

"Might as well be."

Tyler reached out and stroked her cheek. "Tell them that the preliminary numbers were encouraging. That you might indeed have found a successful treatment for multiple sclerosis, but you haven't enrolled enough patients to know one way or the other yet."

Jill shook her head. "Tyler, they're not stupid. They've seen the initial numbers. They're going to know someone cooked the data."

"But *you* didn't."

She had been through this a thousand times in her head. "It's my lab. That means it's my responsibility."

"This affects more than just you."

"I realize that," she said, a little more curtly than intended. "I am not going to submit anything until after your father's board meeting."

"I wasn't talking about the impact on the Alfredson." He sighed. "Jill, while you're busy falling on your own sword, what about the patients who might actually benefit from your therapy? People like Senator Wilder."

He was right. If her study created a scandal, not only would it permanently taint her new treatment approach, but it could have a trickle-down effect on all ongoing stem cell research. She felt her resolve weakening. "Maybe I should run my letter past you before I send it to anyone?"

"Good plan," he agreed. "Why don't you finish getting ready, and I'll pull the car around the front?"

"Can you give me an hour, Ty?"

"Why?"

"I want to stop by my lab and pick up a few things to take home." She pantomimed inserting a key into a door. "The locks might be changed the next time I go back."

As soon as Tyler left, Jill brushed her hair and packed away the last of her belongings. Despite her recent professional and health crises, her spirit bordered on hopeful. She patted her belly. *We really do get a do-over.*

Jill slung her bag over her shoulder and headed out the door to the central nursing station. Tyler had already dropped off chocolates and flowers for the staff, but Jill stopped to individually thank each of the ICU nurses who had been involved in her care before she left. She slowly made her way toward the neurosciences building. She was surprised by how strong her legs felt after her ordeal and could have walked faster but, after having been shut in for almost a week, she was enjoying the temperate fall breeze and the scent of cut grass in the air.

As she stepped through the door into her lab, a hero's welcome greeted her. The research assistants and other staff lined up to share encouraging words and hugs. Jill was touched by the outpouring of support, but she felt sheepish. A phony. Aside from Andrew Pinter, no one else in the office knew of the impending disaster. They still believed their study was going to catapult them to glory, rather than cost most of them their jobs.

After ten minutes of small talk, she shook free of the crowd and escaped to her office. The sight of data files piled up on the desk set her nerves on end. Ignoring the pile, she walked over to the filing cabinet to find the hard copy of her grant reapplication. She was just pulling out the folder when the door clicked open behind her. She glanced over to see Andrew Pinter saunter into the room.

"Look at you, Jill," he said, as though he had completely forgotten their previous bitter encounter. "I knew that superbug would be no match for you."

"You're *still* here?" she said coolly.

Pinter shrugged. "The work goes on even when the boss is sick."

"That's not what I meant, Andrew, and you know it."

He held out an open hand in a conciliatory gesture. "Jill, it's been a week. Nothing happened. I know you've been sick, but I kind of assumed you were going to . . . you know . . . just forget about our stupid run-in."

She stared at him incredulously. "Just forget about research fraud in my own lab? That's what you thought?"

He rolled his eyes. "Guess not, then."

The sight of his smug smirk set off her anger. "You guessed right!" She slammed the file drawer shut. "Where do you get off pretending like nothing happened?"

"Where do you get off being all holier than thou?" he said without a hint of repentance. "A couple weeks ago, I'm your hero. Things don't work out, and suddenly I'm your fall guy."

"You can't be serious!"

He shrugged and then showed her another simpering grin. "I'm sensing you don't want me around anymore." She only glared in response. "Just as well, I guess. I have an offer from another lab. The pay is a bit better and the study more interesting." He smirked. "Best part, though? The principal investigator isn't a self-pitying, two-faced prima donna."

"Go then." She jabbed a finger toward the door. "What the hell are you waiting for?"

"A reference letter."

Jill squealed a laugh in surprise. "From me?"

His grin faded. "A formality, but I need one for the new lab."

"You're joking."

"Dead serious."

"Why the hell would I ever write you a reference, Andrew?"

"You should do it because I'm a fucking good statistician. But I'll tell you why you're going to do it." He eyed her threateningly. "Because if you don't, I'm going to go public about your study and how I uncovered your falsified result."

Jill's hand curled into a fist. She had never wanted to hit anyone as much in her life. "*My* results? You signed off on all those excluded patients. I never even saw them."

"Really?" Pinter flashed a look of pure malice. "You might want to look at those files again. You won't find my name on them anywhere. Yours, on the other hand . . ."

Jill suddenly understood. While she lay near death in the ICU, Pinter must have been erasing evidence and framing her for the fraud. "You miserable bastard!"

He turned for the door. "I'll need that reference within two days. Three signed copies."

As she watched Pinter swagger away, Jill reached an instant decision. "*No!*" she cried.

He wheeled around to face her. "I'm not fooling around, Jill."

"You think I am?" she shouted. "We would've been fine if you hadn't screwed me and everyone else on our team over by tampering with the data. Even worse, you might've taken the last hope away from the people who need it the most." Her voice quieted. "Now you want me to help infect someone else's research lab with the likes of you?" She shook her head. "I'd sooner rot in hell."

Pinter's face turned beet red. The muscles in his neck stuck out and he scowled at her, bug-eyed with hostility. Jill expected him to lunge at her. But, without another word, he whirled and stormed out of the room, slamming the door behind him so hard that the window rattled noisily.

*Will he really go through with it?*

Jill considered his threat and decided that the only way to protect herself, and her lab, was to preempt Pinter and go public with the truth before he twisted the facts irreparably. But if she did, Jill realized she might torpedo Wilder's hopes of starting on the stem cell treatment and undermine William's cause at his upcoming board meeting.

Feeling penned in by her own office, Jill gathered the folders she needed and rushed for the door. She dodged the well-wishers still congregated in the front of the lab and hurried to the elevator. She had already been on her feet longer than her doctors had recommended and would have gone straight to meet Tyler, but she felt compelled to make one stop on the way.

Jill stepped out of the elevator and headed straight to Senator Wilder's room. Outside, the same bald Secret Service agent stood guard. He nodded in friendly recognition as Jill rushed past him into the room.

She found the senator lying in his bed and staring at the wall-mounted TV across from him. At the sight of her, he broke into a friendly smile. "Dr. Laidlaw! Good to see you back on y-your feet," he stammered. "I owe you an ap-apology."

Jill realized that Wilder meant for spreading the superbug infection to her. "Not at all, Senator," she said as she pulled a chair up beside his bed. "Should be vice versa. You came here for our specialty care and ended up getting sick."

He nodded. "Let's call it even, then."

She nodded. "Deal."

Wilder brought a trembling hand to his chest. "The big Alfredson b-board meeting is in a couple days."

"What have you heard?"

"That the vote is going to be extremely close."

"Do you know which way it's going to go?"

He chuckled. "Only God knows. And I'm not entirely sure *She's* made up her mind yet."

Guilt rippled through Jill. She wondered if the premature news of the scandal surrounding her study might tip the vote in the wrong direction.

"What's wrong?"

"My study." She sighed.

"I take it things are not looking up any more for your lab since your last v-visit?"

"No, Senator. In fact, I need to talk to you about the treatment protocol."

His face fell. "Are you going to tell me that you can't start me on your ex-experimental treatment, after all?"

"It's not that." She reached out and touched his bony arm. "The news of the tainted results will become public soon. Very soon."

He frowned at her. "And?"

"All hell might break loose. There's no time to wait."

Wilder shook his head. "What are you s-suggesting?"

"We've already harvested your stem cells, right?"

"Yes."

"We need to implant them right away. Maybe today."

A huge smile lit his face. "Nothing on CNN but an-another boring election. Let's do it now."

# 44

It was supposed to be a dinner celebrating Jill's unexpected pregnancy and her triumphant return home.

Tyler rarely cooked anything aside from the basics, such as pastas or stir-fries, but for tonight he had dusted off one of his mother's recipes—slow-roasted short ribs, his childhood favorite. After returning from the local market with fresh produce, and a bottle of nonalcoholic wine for Jill, he tuned his satellite radio in to a world music station and happily hunkered down to whittle the afternoon away in the kitchen. Jill, who had been subdued since returning home, had told him she needed a rest and had gone up to their room.

She finally trudged down the stairs just before six o'clock, looking as downcast as she had on the ride home. She held several typed sheets in her hand.

"Did you even sleep?" Tyler asked, touching her cheek with balsamic vinegar–stained fingers.

Jill shook her head. "It took me a while to find an available neurosurgeon—Seth Warrington said he'd do it—and coordinate Wilder's stem cell transplant this afternoon."

Tyler grimaced. "It's already done?"

She glanced at her watch. "Should have happened by now."

"Good for him."

"God, let's hope so."

He pointed to the pages in her hand. "Is that the letter to your funding agency?" he asked.

She nodded.

"Oh. I thought you were going to wait until next week. Until *after* the Alfredson board meeting."

"I can't, Ty. I have to e-mail it tonight."

"*Tonight*? What's the urgency?"

"Andrew Pinter."

Tyler scowled. "What has that weasel done *now*?"

"He's extorting me, Ty." She explained Pinter's threat to set her up for research fraud. By the time she finished, her eyes had reddened and she was shaking her head repeatedly. "I was such an idiot, Ty. I should have just written his stupid reference. Let him be someone else's problem."

"That wouldn't be fair."

"Neither is blindsiding your father before his meeting."

Tyler was touched by her naked vulnerability. He draped an arm over her shoulders. "This is not your fault, hon."

She bit her lower lip. "I have to tell William."

Tyler nodded. "I'll call and see if we can drop over later."

But when he finally reached his father through his pager, William said he was on the road all evening and it would be easier for him to drop by their house than vice versa.

Tyler's effort to lighten Jill's mood over dinner fell flat, and the meal ended up tasting to him as bland as the nonalcoholic wine. She had just poured two cups of herbal tea when the doorbell rang. As soon as William stepped into the lit hallway, Tyler was struck by his father's frailty. He was limping noticeably as he entered, his gray suit floated on him, and his cheek-bones looked like ridges.

"Dad, you've really lost weight."

"Eating hasn't been my priority lately." He shrugged. "How is Jill?"

"Better." But Tyler could not shake his concern for his father. "Have you seen your doctor?"

"You didn't summon me here to discuss my weight, did you?" William sighed. "Because right now I'm more than a little preoccupied with the im-pending board meeting. Less than three days, Tyler. Everything else will just have to wait until after."

Tyler nodded. "Jill's in the kitchen. She needs to talk to you, Dad."

As soon as they stepped into the kitchen, Jill rushed over and kissed

William on the cheek, her hand resting on his shoulder. It was as warm a greeting as Tyler had seen them share in recent memory. She poured another cup of tea and they all sat down together in the living room.

They discussed her health, followed with a few minutes of forced small talk, before William said, "Jill, I understand there was something you wanted to discuss."

She glanced nervously at Tyler, who nodded his encouragement, and then turned back to her father-in-law. "There's a problem in my lab." She swallowed. "A big problem."

William viewed her evenly. "What is it?"

"My study data is not . . . entirely accurate." Without downplaying the significance, she went on to describe the falsified preliminary numbers as well as Pinter's intent to frame her for the fraud.

Bone straight, William sat entirely still through her entire explanation. When she finished, he said, "Jill, once you notify the funding agency, do you think these . . . irregularities will come to light straight away?"

"You mean before the board meeting?" Tyler clarified.

William nodded. He slid a hand behind his back and began to rub.

Jill sighed. "Blogs are incredibly popular among the research set right now. As a result, rumors like these spread like wildfire."

"I see."

Jill's chin lowered and her gaze fell to the floor. "William, I'm so sorry," she murmured.

William pulled his hand away from his back and showed her a stiff smile. "Jill, maybe it hasn't worked out as hoped, but I appreciate your efforts to try to stall this news from breaking until after the meeting."

Tyler expected his father's stoicism, but he was still touched by the man's restraint. "Dad, is there anything we can do?" he asked.

William shook his head. "Do you believe in fate?"

Tyler wasn't used to hearing his rigidly practical father pose such philosophical questions. "Not really. Why?"

"I never used to, either." He exhaled slowly. "So many factors seemed to have conspired against my—*our*—cause over the past few weeks. I think maybe the Alfredson is simply not meant to remain as it is."

"But what about the McGraths' role there?"

William interlocked his fingers. "When it comes to the Alfredson, maybe the McGraths' time has passed."

Jill sat up straighter. "You can't believe that!"

William viewed them with an expression more plaintive than any Tyler had ever seen from him. "I am no longer convinced our family's role in the Alfredson's past, present, or future matters to anyone other than myself."

Tyler reflected on his father's lifetime of commitment to the Alfredson; and the same for William's uncles and grandfather before him. Then he remembered how his other grandfather had brought his own hellish Holocaust experiences to the Alfredson and more than redeemed them by pioneering a better and more humane form of care for children suffering with cancer.

"It matters to me, Dad," Tyler said quietly.

William frowned. "Does it really, Tyler?"

"Yes."

"So . . . would you attend the board meeting with me?" he asked in a hedging tone.

"I should be there," Tyler said, nodding. "Matter of fact, Dad, I'd be honored to attend."

"Good." William chuckled, and his face shed a few years. "Now the Mc-Graths will only be outnumbered sixty to three by the Alfredsons."

"Three?"

"Your sister is coming, too."

After William left, Tyler joined Jill in the kitchen. He stood beside her and read through the final draft of her letter. He was impressed by the tone and tenor but frustrated by her insistence on assuming sole responsibility. "Why don't you name that lowlife, Pinter, in here?"

"Don't want to stoop to his level." She shrugged. "The truth is, from the start I suspected something wasn't right in the data, but I chose to ignore it. I was so blinded with ambition. Andrew probably thought he was doing me a big favor."

"He's still a weasel," Tyler muttered. He lowered the pages and fixed his gaze on her. "Jill, you sure you have to do this?"

"Yes." Her tired face broke into a small smile. "I want to. Whatever happens from now on, I already feel like a huge weight has been lifted off my shoulders."

Tyler leaned forward and kissed her on the lips. She turned her head away and said, "Ty, my infection."

"Has been treated."

"But what if—"

He gently turned her face back to his and then kissed her more deeply on the lips. She didn't resist. He laid his hand on the small of her back and pulled her closer. Their kisses grew moister as their tongues explored each other's mouths. Her teeth dug teasingly into his lower lip. Tyler hoisted her off the ground. She flexed her hips, wrapped her legs around his waist, and straddled him.

He broke off the kiss for a moment. "This okay for the baby?"

"She's a fighter, remember?" Jill nibbled at his ear. "Besides, I want to take care of *this* baby for a while."

Upstairs, they made love on top of the bedcovers. Afterwards, they lay murmuring contentedly in each other's arms. A rosy glow suffused Jill's cheeks, but she struggled to keep her eyes open and soon nodded off. Tyler had trouble sleeping. Despite other pending issues, his thoughts kept returning to the Staffords. The case had left a sour taste that he could not wash away, even after Keisha's more successful treatment.

Tyler looked over at Jill, who lay peacefully on her side. He respected his wife even more for taking a principled stand in her lab scandal, regardless of the personal cost. Her actions inspired him. He decided to take steps to ease his own conscience, despite his attorney's advice against it. Once he had made up his mind, he soon drifted off into a dreamless sleep.

Tyler awoke just before five A.M. and wandered downstairs to brew a pot of coffee. When he heard the thud of the morning paper hit the front door, he hurried out to pick it up. Inside, he leafed through the pages and saw that, for the fourth day in a row, there was still no mention of himself or the Stafford case. Denny Rymer had already turned his rancor to a judge in Olympia whom he considered overly lenient.

After downing two cups of coffee, Tyler tiptoed upstairs, showered, and changed. Heading out before Jill woke, he drove to the Alfredson. He reached Keisha's room just before seven A.M. She was sitting up in bed, her sketchbook open in her hands. "Hi, Keisha," he said.

"You think I'm ever gonna go home, Dr. M?" she asked without even looking up from her drawing.

"Sure," Tyler said, thrown off by the blunt question. "I think you'll be going in a few days. That's the plan. Though you might have to come back and visit me now and then. Otherwise I'm going to miss you too much."

Keisha sketched a few more lines and then flipped her book around to show him.

Tyler recognized the drawing by the wings and halo. "Pretty angel. What's her name?"

"He's a man angel, and I don't know his name." She shrugged. "But I dreamed about him."

Tyler sat down on the edge of the bed. "What happened in your dream?"

"The angel came to my room and told me God wanted me to sing in His choir in this big church on top of a cloud."

"He did?"

"Yup. I told him I didn't want to go without my mommy or daddy."

"Then what happened?"

"He said Mommy and Daddy would meet me there, but I might just have to wait a little for them."

Tyler squeezed her leg through the light blanket covering her. "What did you say?"

"I said I wouldn't go without my mommy," she said matter-of-factly. "And if he tried to make me, I'd scream for the police."

Tyler grinned. "Keisha, you don't have to go anywhere."

"Except I want to go home," she said in a smaller voice. "That's all."

"We'll get you there. I promise."

Feeling a little melancholic but cautiously hopeful after reviewing the results from Keisha's morning blood test, Tyler headed for the elevator.

Walking down the corridor, he slowed to admire the murals and donor plaques that lined the walls. His eyes focused on the plaque commemorating the new unit's opening fifteen years before. "That no child need ever suffer," the motto read at the bottom. Though the motto was not credited to anyone, Tyler knew the words and the spirit embodied his grandfather Maarten.

Steeling his resolve, he hurried out to his car. Driving toward the south end of Oakdale, he fished the sheet with the scrawled address out of his pocket. He turned onto a tree-lined street and, two in from the far end, found the sixties-style bungalow that mirrored the others on the block.

Tyler parked his hybrid out front and trudged up to the door. Several toy buckets and spades lay scattered on the lawn, which looked two or three weeks overdue for a mow. The flowers in the window box planter were dead and wilting. He could almost smell the air of neglect floating around the house. With a sweaty palm, he reached for the doorbell and rang it once. A long while passed. Tyler was reaching to ring the bell a second time when the door opened a crack.

"*Dr. McGrath?*" Laura Stafford gasped.

"Laura, may I come in?" he asked.

"You . . . you think you should?"

Tyler nodded.

"My daughter is still asleep, and Craig's still in the bedroom."

"I could come back another time."

Laura hesitated a moment and then opened the door wider for him, and Tyler saw that she wore a pink bathrobe. He stepped inside and followed her toward the warmly decorated kitchen. The interior was far tidier than he had expected based on what he had seen outside. The smell of brewed coffee grew stronger with each step nearer the kitchen.

The combination of weight loss and tragedy had aged Laura years in the days since he had last seen her. She mustered a smile for him and offered coffee, but he politely declined.

After they sat down at the kitchen table, Tyler asked, "How are you doing?"

She looked down and cupped her mug with both hands. "It's not that easy. Almost everything reminds me of him."

"Of course," he muttered. "How's Craig?"

"You know Craig," she said uncertainly. "He deals with stuff in his own way."

Tyler turned at the sound of heavy footsteps on the linoleum floor behind him and rose from his chair.

In a pair of pajama bottoms and a stained gray T-shirt, Craig Stafford trod into the room. His black hair was as messy as the last time Tyler had seen him, and he had grown a full beard that made him look even scruffier. He stopped on the other side of the room and folded his arms across his chest. "He doesn't know shit about me, Laura," Craig said in a scratchy morning voice.

Stafford's tone was neutral but Tyler tensed at the sight of him, feeling as though he had wandered into a bear's den just as the adult male had returned. "Hello, Craig."

Craig snorted. "Got to give you credit. Your family did a hell of a job on damage control. They shut up Denny Rymer pretty quick."

Tyler frowned. "My family?"

"Your father silenced Rymer and his paper with the Alfredson's legal machine." He scratched his beard. "As if you didn't already know."

Tyler didn't doubt Craig's theory for a moment. It explained the sudden absence of publicity. "I didn't know, Craig," he said.

"'Course not," he grunted. "But now you want me to drop our lawsuit, too, right?"

"That's not why I came."

Craig's eyes narrowed. "Then what the fuck are you doing in my house?"

Tyler glanced at Laura, who stared back in worried silence, and then over to Craig. "I wanted you to know about Keisha." The Staffords and the Berrys had bonded over their children who suffered from a similar cancer. Tyler had already asked for and received Maya's permission to update Craig and Laura.

"How is she?" Laura's voice cracked.

"We gave her Vintazomab, too," Tyler said.

Laura stiffened at the mention of the drug. "How did she do?"

"It was rough at first. Very." He paused, took a couple of breaths. "But she's doing better now. And the results—though very preliminary—are promising."

Laura relaxed in her chair. "Oh, thank God."

"I'm relieved for that family. I really am." Craig unfolded his arms and shook a finger angrily at Tyler. "But do you think that makes up in any way for what happened to Nate?"

"No," Tyler said.

"Damn right!"

Tyler sighed. "Craig, I think about him every day."

"*You* do?" he said. "What about us, huh?"

"I know it doesn't begin to compare."

"Not even close," Craig snapped.

Tyler took a deep breath. Despite the hostility that hung thick in the air,

Tyler's determination cemented. "You don't want me here. I understand that. And my own attorney warned me that it would be a huge mistake to talk to you."

"But?"

Tyler touched his chest. "For the rest of my life, I will regret how I handled Nate's case at the end. I should have been much clearer with you about the risks of Vintazomab. I had no right to conceal that from you."

Laura sniffled several times and then the tears began to pour from her eyes, but Craig only stared at Tyler with stony bitterness.

"I would give anything to go back in time and change what happened." Tyler swallowed. "I know it probably doesn't mean much, but all I can do is tell you how sorry I am."

Craig studied the floor for a moment. When he looked up the anger had left his features but his expression was far from accepting. "You might be sorry, but we still never got to say good-bye to our son. All your apologies in the world won't ever change that."

Tyler stared back at Craig, at a loss for words.

"We both know we would have agreed," Laura said in a voice no louder than a whisper.

Craig turned slowly to look at his wife. "Agreed to what, babe?"

"Nate was dying in front of our eyes," she said in a stronger voice. "We would have agreed to any treatment no matter what the risks."

"You don't know that we—," Craig started.

"I do!" she cried. "Dr. McGrath was trying to spare us from a brutal choice." Her voice calmed. "Maybe he never should have, but that's not the point. We would have tried anything. You know that. This is not his fault."

The Staffords shared a long anguished stare that stirred Tyler to the brink of tears. Then Craig turned to look at Tyler. His eyes had reddened, but his face was blank. He nodded once. "Maybe . . . maybe Laura has a point."

# 45

"So the Spanish flu caught up to Evan, too?" Lorna shook her head, feeling unexpected sorrow for the man.

"I doubt he was all that surprised, really," Dot said. "Evan was positively *reckless* about precautions when it came to contact with his own daughter. Part of me wonders if—when he thought Liv was dying—he did not *mean* to infect himself."

Lorna frowned. "Suicide by the Spanish flu?"

"Stranger things have happened, darling."

"Liv recovered, though," Lorna pointed out.

"Completely." Dot nodded. "She went on to become the first female surgeon at the Alfredson. One of the first in the entire state." She exhaled heavily. "She was a fireball, that one, but that's another story altogether."

"What ever happened to Junior and her?"

"He broke her heart, as men do." Dot sighed. "As soon as Junior found out the truth, he broke it off with Liv. My dear old headstrong father wound up dating a Seattle socialite named Lillian Dennison. They were married within six months." She laughed. "And *considerably* less than nine months later, I came along."

"Did Liv ever find out that she and Junior were related?"

Dot shook her head. "My father had the decency never to tell her, and Liv—being Liv—landed on her feet. Though she would wait ten more years before marrying. And she never did have children."

Lorna nodded. "What about Evan?" she asked.

Dot tilted her head and eyed Lorna quizzically for a moment. "You told me you read Naylor's laughable, official milquetoast version of the hospital's history. Surely you know what became of him?"

Lorna felt herself reddening. She had forgotten telling Dot that she had already read Naylor's book. She thought back on other details from the book, wondering if she had played too ignorant with her great-aunt. "Yes, well, I read the . . . um, bland textbook version," she blustered. "But as you pointed out, who knows how much, if any of it, is factual? Besides, I far prefer your account. You always add such a human element to the otherwise dry historical facts."

"Of course," Dot said with an accepting nod. "As it happens, in this case my version is not too much different from that horrid whitewash of a book. Although, there was *one* detail Naylor misinterpreted. . . ."

---

> Nothing, not even death, would deter Evan or Marshall's commitment to their shared dream. With his last breath, Evan beseeched his children, particularly his daughter, to perpetuate the legacy he had begun.
> —*The Alfredson: The First Hundred Years* by Gerald Fenton Naylor

Fifteen minutes passed before the coughing paroxysms settled and Evan had caught his breath enough to seek help. Dispassionately, he heard the rattling in his own chest with each breath and realized that pneumonia was taking grip. His rash conduct around his gravely ill daughter had caught up to him, as he had suspected it would all along. Evan was not afraid, though. He felt more ashamed than anything else, considering it a shoddy example for a doctor to set for his staff.

He reached in his pocket for his mask and secured it tightly around his face before taking another step. Whatever happened, he was determined not to spread his infection to anyone else.

Evan started down the slope toward the building housing the flu ward. Even downhill, he had to stop every few steps to get his breathing to cooperate or wait for another coughing fit to pass.

A chill gripped him so intensely that his whole body shook. He was so consumed with the sudden rigors that he didn't even notice Moses Brown had caught up to him from behind.

"Dr. McGrath?" Moses asked in his familiar deep timbre. "What is it?"

Still masked, Evan turned slowly toward the large man. Moses extended a hand to him, but Evan waved it away. "I have caught *it*, my friend!"

Sadness filled Moses's large brown eyes, but his face showed no surprise. "How bad?"

Evan shook his head once and then backed a few unsteady steps away from Moses. "One of us needs to stay healthy to keep this hospital afloat."

Moses pointed at his feet. "I reckon you could fill these boots in about five minutes." He shook his head. "But yours?"

"Maybe ten."

Moses chuckled in his low rumble. "Doubt they ever could."

"I need to admit myself to the flu ward," Evan said, aware that each word was becoming more of an effort.

Moses nodded. "You're in no shape to walk."

"I can make it, Moses."

Moses watched skeptically as Evan tried to take a few more steps. He stopped when another coughing fit racked him. "You stay right here, Dr. McGrath. I'm gonna go get a wheelchair."

"All right," Evan said, embarrassed by his own helplessness.

Moses hurried off in search of a chair.

Evan was burning up with fever, and his legs were too rubbery to support his own weight much longer. He spied a tree about ten feet away, and decided to use it to hold himself upright while waiting for Moses. He only made it three short steps toward the tree when he crumpled to the damp ground.

Evan was still lying on the lawn where he had fallen when Moses reached him with the wheelchair. The big man was wheezing loudly from his asthma, but he reached down and lifted Evan, as effortlessly as picking up a baby, and deposited him in the chair. Moses launched the chair into motion, and it rattled and shook Evan along the pathway toward the building.

Evan's world spun as Moses wheeled him onto the flu ward. Over the din of the overcrowded mayhem and the mournful sounds and smells of human suffering, Evan heard the murmurs and gasps of the staff members who recognized him. Two nurses rushed over to him.

"We need a bed for Dr. McGrath," Moses said.

"We will clear one straight away!" one of them replied.

"No. I do not require special treatment—" But Evan's words dissolved into another hacking fit.

By the time Evan caught his breath again, Moses had already transferred him to a cot against the far wall. Two of the makeshift dividers were placed on either side to give his bed a modicum of privacy. He looked down and watched helplessly as one of the nurses pulled off his shoes. A sheet was thrown over him and a cool wet compress applied to his forehead. He felt a band around his neck and then heard the hissing and spitting of the oxygen mask below his chin. When he looked up again, he saw Gertrude Flanders looking down kindly at him.

"How's Liv?" Evan croaked.

"Your daughter is resting, Dr. McGrath. She is improving by the minute, though. We will send her home soon, no doubt."

The relief was immense. He brought his hand up to his chin and tapped the oxygen mask. "Mrs. Flanders, others must need this . . . more than I . . ."

"Oh, you absolutely do—" She stopped. Pity filled her features. "Please, Dr. McGrath, allow us to worry over those decisions. You are the patient now."

He did not have the strength to argue. Flanders soaked the compress again and reapplied it to his brow. The cool moisture felt surprisingly soothing. Evan tried to thank her, but the words would not emerge. As he stared up at her, his eyes began to shut involuntarily.

Evan opened his eyes, assuming only moments had passed, but found that the room had darkened. A fire raged across his forehead, and he was drenched in sweat. His arms and legs ached as though someone had taken a club to them. Gertrude Flanders was gone, but George stood above him, staring down more earnestly than ever. "Father, can you hear me?"

Evan nodded.

"Papa, how is the breathing?" Liv asked urgently from somewhere nearby.

Evan turned his head and saw Liv resting in a wheelchair beside her brother. Her face had lost much of its fullness and she had deep bags under her eyes, but the color had returned to her lips and cheeks. The sight warmed Evan's heart and eased his body aches.

"I am all right . . . ," he gasped.

"Mother is on a train from Everett," George said urgently. "Nicholas is making his way up from California. He will be here by the morning."

"Why?" But Evan already knew the answer.

His two children shared a quick glance and then George said, "We believe the family needs to be together at this time of crisis."

Evan nodded slightly. He reached out for the oxygen mask, but his hand bumped directly into his chin.

A pained look crossed George's face. "Father, I am sorry. The clinic has run out of oxygen. We have not been able to locate another supplier."

"It was . . . inevitable, Son," Evan said. Over his own raspy respirations, he could hear the choking agonized pleas of a neighboring patient. He knew death was near.

A hand clasped his. "Oh, Papa," Liv said.

Evan trembled as another wave of chills swept over him. His limbs ached as though vises had tightened around them. And involuntarily, his panting steadily deepened.

Liv's features darkened with worry. "I was in this same condition, remember, Papa?" she murmured. "I got better, Papa. You can, too. *Please.*"

Evan tried to show Liv a reassuring smile, but he felt as though a sock had been stuffed down his throat. He knew time was running out. "This clinic . . ." He huffed. "It is needed . . . more than ever now."

"Absolutely, Father," George said.

"Promise me . . . ," Evan sputtered. "Promise me, you will see that it goes on . . . continues to offer the best care . . . to those in need . . ."

"We will, Father," George said. "I swear it."

"Of course, Papa," Liv added.

"It will be our legacy," Evan muttered under his breath.

"What was that, Father?" George asked.

Evan shook his head weakly. "And Nicholas . . . and Mother . . . You will always take care of each other . . ."

"Of course!" Liv said. "Always, Papa."

A sense of contentment descended on Evan, lessening the pain and breathlessness. "I am so . . . so very proud of you both."

His children's faces blurred until they were indistinguishable from the others around him. The colors of the walls bled into each other. And the clamor around him blended into a white noise that sounded like a seashell held to his ear. He raised his head off the bed. "Olivia!" he cried out. "Oh, Olivia."

"Father, she's right here!" George's words sounded as though they were shouted through a windstorm.

*No, Olivia. Olivia Alfredson!* Evan wanted to say, but he had no voice left.

The room faded away, and Evan could suddenly see her again. He stood on a beach with lovely warm sand between his toes. A pleasant light breeze blew in off the water. Olivia stood at the water's edge, wearing her familiar blue dress but no shoes or stockings. The water lapped around her ankles, and her red hair blew freely in the wind.

Olivia smiled broadly at Evan. Her green eyes sparkled with invitation as she waved for him to join her in the water. "Come, Evan," she cried happily. "Come with me now."

Evan didn't hesitate. Full of energy and breath, he sprinted for the surf.

## 46

The Alfredson's boardroom occupied most of the top floor of the administrative building. Erin had never before set foot inside, but the surroundings impressed her. Glassed in on three sides with floor-to-ceiling windows, the room provided a view of the rest of the complex and the Cascades to the east. The morning sun streamed through the translucent blinds on the east-facing windows and bathed the room in an ethereal light. A massive rectangular oak table, encircled by at least a hundred padded rolling chairs, sat in the center of the room. Ultramodern, with its integrated high-tech audio-visual system, the room struck Erin as more fitting to a major Wall Street corporation than a hospital.

More than half of the chairs around the table were already filled. Those seated ranged in age from early twenties to eighties. Erin suspected that one tiny woman, with shorn white hair and dressed in an outrageous saffron pantsuit, had to be pushing ninety. Most of the attendees were dressed formally in dark business suits, but a few were more casually attired, including a middle-aged man in jeans with a ponytail and hoop earrings. Scanning the room, Erin could not spot any discernible unifying feature, size, or coloring among the various Alfredson descendants. By the way the chairs were positioned and the people leaned, Erin saw that the family had naturally divided themselves into cliques and clusters. She wondered if they intended to vote in similar blocs.

*The vote.* A week earlier, Erin had been so consumed with her panic attacks that the thought of this meeting hardly registered. But in the past few days it had begun to sink in just how much the sale of the Alfredson would impact her program, her patients, and, most of all, her father. She had woken earlier in the morning on tenterhooks—as though on the verge of another panic attack that never materialized—over the meeting's possible outcome.

Since Erin, Tyler, and even William were invited only as guests and observers, they were not seated at the table. Instead, they sat in the row of chairs along the far wall with three other people Erin didn't recognize.

Despite the hushed conversations surrounding the table, an air of electrified tension ran through the room, which surged the moment Eileen called the meeting to order. As someone was closing the door, two stragglers—middle-aged women in bland suits—slipped through and muttered apologies before grabbing their seats.

On the screen above Eileen's head, an agenda appeared. Erin saw her father's name listed two-thirds of the way down the program with the subtitle CEO REPORT. She glanced over to her father. He sat as rigid as ever in his blue suit and dark tie. In profile, his face was a mask. Erin couldn't imagine his tumult of emotions, but from his impassive appearance, he could have passed for a commuter waiting for a scheduled train to arrive.

On the far side of William, Tyler leaned forward in his seat and turned to Erin with a little smile. "Victory," he mouthed, and she almost giggled out of nerves.

Eileen held up her hand, and the room quieted further. "Thank you for taking the time to convene for this extraordinary meeting of the Alfredson Medical Center's Board of Directors. I assume we have all seen the e-mails and letters pertaining to this meeting and the *sole* motion at hand." Eileen's tone was brusque and businesslike. "Though we only have one motion to address, as it is of an unprecedented magnitude and nature, we have set the entire day aside for presentations and discussion. All members who have requested to present have been allotted time to do so. As well, there will be time to open discussion from the floor. I hope we will commence the voting by the end of this afternoon." She paused and scanned the table with her eyes. "There will be no proxy voting. Only board members present will vote on the motion. It will require a simple majority, fifty percent plus one, to pass. I will begin now by reading the motion aloud."

A chill ran through Erin as she listened, for the first time, to the legalese wording of the motion that would decide the fate of the Alfredson. Again, she half expected those invisible fingers to creep around her neck, but they never touched her.

Erin had heard from her father that Hutchins was a staunch ally and supporter of the no-sale side, but Eileen kept her opinion to herself throughout her introduction. She concluded by saying, "We have sought three separate opinions on the legality of this motion, in terms of whether the Alfredson board has the right to sell the Alfredson Medical Center to a private-interest group or person. Unquestionably, the Alfredson family owns the land on which the hospital is built, but it is much less clear whether the board is entitled to sell the hospital itself." She indicated two of the people sitting in the chairs to the right of Tyler. "To that end, Mr. David Vogel and Ms. Jennifer Duluth from the Seattle firm of Hansen, Vogel, and Haworth have kindly attended to offer us a more informed opinion."

The two lawyers rose in unison. The younger woman followed the gray-haired senior partner to the front of the room. Vogel opened with a few general remarks and then deferred to his associate. The woman clicked a button and the screen above her filled with the first slide of her computerized presentation. As Duluth dryly outlined the legal precedents and citations of previous major hospital sales, Erin's mind wandered. She thought of Steve and her boys, who were taking Alex and Katie Hill to the zoo later today. She felt another flicker of pride at her sons' eagerness to help Erin keep the promise she had made to the dying mother.

By the time Duluth wrapped up her thirty-minute presentation, Erin didn't understand the ramifications of the vote any better than before she had begun. Judging from the bewildered expressions around the table, she was not alone. The man with the ponytail piped up. "Look, Ms. Duluth, that's a whole lot of mumbo jumbo to me. What's your gut tell you? Can we unload this albatross or not?"

A scattering of nervous laughter met the crass question. Duluth looked to Vogel, who nodded his permission. "Until it is tested in court, I do not believe there is a definitive answer to that," she hedged. "The Alfredson board is clearly within its right to negotiate a sale of the medical complex. However, certain interested parties—such as the hospital's foundation—have the right to contest any sales."

The ponytailed man threw up his hands. "For the love of God, jump off the fence and offer us your best guess. *Please!*"

Duluth opened her mouth to reply, but Vogel cut her off. "Undoubtedly it will be hotly contested in court, but at the end of the day, we do believe the Alfredson board can sell this hospital. Yes."

A buzz broke out among the attendees, with murmurs and comments circling the table. Eileen had to call the meeting back to order. After the lawyers were excused, she introduced Gregory Alfredson as the first board member to address the group. A skinny, stooped man in his early sixties, Gregory appeared nervous, speaking with notes and addressing only the podium in front of him. "The Alfredson hospital is synonymous the world over with excellence in medical care. My great-grandfather, Marshall Alfredson, always intended for our family to oversee this wonderful institution . . ."

While Erin appreciated Gregory's support, he was such an ineffectual speaker that she suspected the entire room had tuned him out after his first few sentences. After Gregory sat down, Eileen introduced Alison Baxter, a plump younger woman with curly red hair and a fiery demeanor to match. Baxter spoke without notes and made her perspective crystal clear from her opening sentence. "Listen, I might be distantly related to Marshall Alfredson, but I have no more connection to the Alfredson Medical Center than I do to the Mayo Clinic . . ."

For the next few hours, member after member rose to speak, almost equally divided for or against the motion. Some were eloquent and passionate; others droned on and on. But the longer Erin listened, the greater her unease became—she sensed that the tide had already turned in favor of the for-sale side.

Eileen adjourned the meeting by announcing the lunch break. Trolleys of food were wheeled into the room. After serving themselves, William, Tyler, and Erin sat down to eat. None of them had heaped much food on their plate, but William's looked barren with one roll and a few spoonfuls of pasta salad.

"What do you think, Dad?" Tyler asked, lowering his fork to his untouched plate.

William shrugged. "Very few surprises, so far."

Erin sighed. "A lot of the Alfredsons seem set on selling this place."

"It's bound to be close. There is a lot of money at stake for each member personally. Most have come here with their minds already firmly made up,"

William said. "It's going to come down to a small group of them whose votes are undecided, or at least unknown."

"You nervous about your speech, Dad?" Tyler asked.

William flashed a tired smile. "I can only do what I can do. Besides, I am not sure my words will make a drop of difference."

Erin reached out and squeezed his shoulder, feeling nothing but bone under his suit jacket. "You'll do good, Dad."

William looked at them for a long moment. "Regardless, I am glad you're both here." He cleared his throat. "Your mother would have been very proud."

A few minutes later, Eileen stood up at the front of the room. "In the interest of time, I think we can finish our coffee and dessert as we continue the meeting." She pointed to the back row of seats. "It's my honor now to introduce the CEO and president of the Alfredson, Dr. William McGrath."

William rose from his seat and, without a glance to either of his children, headed for the far end of the room where Eileen waited. He moved stiffly, as though in pain, but he kept his head high and back straight. By the time he reached Eileen, his first slide was already mounted on the screen above him.

"Thank you, Mrs. Hutchins. And to the rest of the board, too. I feel truly honored and privileged to have the opportunity to speak to you as the Alfredson's CEO."

On the large screen, a grainy black-and-white photograph of two men standing side by side at the bottom of the steps of the original brick building appeared. Erin had never seen the photograph before, but she recognized Marshall Alfredson and Evan McGrath from other photos she had seen. "I'm certainly not a historian," William began. "But I have to believe that Marshall Alfredson and Evan McGrath would be exceedingly pleased and proud of what their descendants have accomplished over the past hundred years." He pointed out the window to the nearby buildings. "The clinic that Evan dreamed of and Marshall Alfredson built in 1896 has truly become one of the world leaders in health care with one of the best research, teaching, and clinical programs in the nation. Arguably, the world." He swept a hand in front of him. "Just how special is the Alfredson? You might ask." He paused to scan the faces at the table around him. "Allow me to elaborate."

Though he spoke without notes, the slides changed above him in seamless continuity with his words. "This hospital has produced *three* separate Nobel Prize winners in medicine. Four major new classes of pharmaceuticals were born here. And numerous surgical techniques used the world over have been pioneered on these grounds. We have weathered two world wars, the Spanish flu, the population boom in the Pacific Northwest, and constant advances in technology and evolving health-care needs. The Alfredson has not only risen to every challenge, but emerged stronger for each.

"In the past year alone, the Alfredson has treated over two hundred thousand patients, who came from as near as Oakdale and as far as Madagascar. We house the third most successful organ transplant program in the country. Our cure rates for pediatric and adult cancers are as good or better than any other oncology program. We are widely acknowledged to have the leading neurological and spinal cord research program in the nation." He stopped to look at the others around him. "But such is the spirit of this hospital that we never rest on our laurels. I would now like to review some of the exciting, potentially earth-shattering research and innovations blossoming around us, literally, as I speak . . ."

Using a series of slides, some accompanied by video footage, William highlighted several of the major medical programs—from the joint replacement service to the diabetic care center. Even Erin, who had attended the medical staff meetings and heard some of this before, was floored by the amount of research and development taking place at the Alfredson. She found herself a little choked up when William turned his attention to the cardiac program, citing its phenomenal success rate with procedures such as angioplasty and heart transplants and expanding on the promise of experimental projects like the Alfredson pump—a new prototype for an artificial heart.

The screen above William ran through a series of financial slides and stopped on one with a steadily rising bar graph. "The work the Alfredson does is extremely expensive. As a nonprofit organization, our programs are supported almost entirely by the foundation through ongoing donations and existing endowments," he said. "However, no private company would ever, or *could* ever, afford to maintain or support the level of research and innovation we currently do. The sale of the Alfredson would paralyze, or more likely eliminate altogether, most, if not all, of the ongoing work in these areas."

The screen went blank above William. "I suppose at the end of the day, many of you have to ask yourself: So what?" He paused to shrug. "If not the Alfredson, then surely some other hospital will take up the slack and fill the void?" William shook his head. "Sadly, that will not happen. Do you want to know why?"

A few heads around the table nodded.

"Health care in this country has reached a state of crisis. With an aging population, increasingly complex care, and the spiraling cost of medicine and technology, we simply cannot afford to provide decent and accessible care to our citizens—often, to the ones who need it most. An entire segment of our population is suffering medical neglect. Arguably, criminal neglect. No private insurer or health-care company will look after these people, but in more than a hundred years the Alfredson has never ever turned its back on patients in need.

"Here at the Alfredson, yes, we have looked after movie stars, world leaders, and royalty, but we have also cared for the homeless and the poor. Children without insurance who need lifesaving subspecialized care. The frail elderly, psychiatric patients, substance abusers, and other disenfranchised patients have always found compassion and care within the walls of this hospital, just as Marshall Alfredson and Evan McGrath envisioned before the first brick was ever laid.

"If you choose to sell the hospital today, the Alfredson might live on in name." He paused for a long moment. "But I promise you, her spirit will not."

With that, William limped away from the screen and toward the back of the room. At first, the room fell into silence, but then someone at the far end of the table began to clap. Soon, others joined in until most of the people around the table were applauding. A number of people even rose to their feet.

William was still poker-faced when he reached Erin and Tyler. But Erin could not help herself. She hopped to her feet and wrapped him in a hug. "You did great, Dad." She swallowed. "You really did."

*47*

Aside from a smattering of unavoidable small talk with a few tedious cousins, Lorna Simpson had hardly spoken up to this point in the meeting. She sat halfway down the table, in a black skirt and a jacket a size too small, trying to appear as disinterested as possible. But her mind never stopped racing, and she was constantly tabulating a running tally in her head. The earlier anemic and hopelessly repetitive presentations from her distant relatives had helped Lorna compile her mental estimate of where the vote now stood.

For the most part, the meeting had progressed as Lorna anticipated. William McGrath's speech was undeniably heartfelt—some might have even considered it stirring—but his words were unlikely to sway any voters, especially once Lorna had the chance to refute them. The only real surprise, and a pleasant one, was that her great-aunt—whom Lorna considered a wild card—had remained silent throughout. The old bird had made eye contact with Lorna and waved a few times, but otherwise Dot had reclined back in her chair, seemingly content to just listen to the other board members.

Lorna had worked tirelessly in the two weeks since leaving Dot's mansion. She had gone to great effort to orchestrate events and leave as little as possible to chance. The master stroke, in her mind, was positioning herself on the agenda as the very last speaker with a bogus story of how she might be delayed having to care for her ill father.

Lorna was glowing with optimism when, after the afternoon's final coffee break, Eileen Hutchins announced, "We will close the formal addresses with a presentation from Dr. Lorna Simpson."

Tired and worn down by the long day of speakers, the others around the table showed little interest as Lorna strode up to the front with a thick folder tucked under her arm. Lorna didn't mind at all. After years of lecturing restless undergrads, public speaking no longer intimidated her. Though Lorna knew she lacked the charm and wit of the best lecturers, she possessed an innate sense of timing and enough of her great-aunt's flair for storytelling to hold an audience. Besides, she was certain there was no risk of losing her crowd today.

Lorna had a quick glance at the vaguely familiar faces around the table and then launched in. "Don't let the title fool you. I'm not a real doctor. I have a Ph.D. in history. And history is *exactly* what I would like to talk about today. But before I do, I need to touch on the present to help put the history in context."

Lorna looked down past the end of the table to where the McGraths sat at the far end of the room. She waved in a gesture of greeting. "We're fortunate to have three McGraths here today. Isn't it amazing that two families could intertwine so closely over multiple generations to produce something as special as the Alfredson?" She shook her head as though awed. "I was moved by Dr. McGrath's description of how far the institution has come and the incredible promise it still shows."

Lorna let the smile seep from her face. "But Dr. McGrath did gloss over a few details that I think are worth considering. For example, he mentioned that the Alfredson has treated numerous world leaders, but he did not point out that, only last week, our hospital almost killed a former presidential front-runner."

A few murmurs of surprise broke out around the table.

"It's true. It hasn't been discussed much publicly, but we've had a superbug—one of those multiresistant germs—raging inside the walls of the Alfredson. Several buildings, wards, the ICU, and the kitchen all had to be closed. More than ten people have died so far. And Senator Calvin Wilder, a patient of Dr. McGrath's daughter-in-law, came within a hair's breadth of joining them."

Lorna paused to allow the board members to absorb the news. She looked over at the three McGraths again. "As integral as the McGraths have been to the Alfredson, a history of unrest has followed the family throughout the generations. That might never have been more true than today." Lorna reached inside her folder and extracted the photocopies of Denny Rymer's articles about Nate Stafford. She divided the stack in half and handed each pile to the nearest person on either side of the table, who took one and passed the rest down the line. "Those of you who live in the Northwest might have already seen this story about Dr. Tyler McGrath." She pointed him out to the rest of the attendees.

Tyler folded his arms across his chest and shifted in his seat under the sudden focus, but he said nothing.

Lorna sighed. "Unfortunately for the young doctor—a very good childhood cancer specialist, by all accounts—he is embroiled in a nasty and very public accusation of malpractice and ethical misconduct." She went on to summarize the case, highlighting the lack of consent and the tragic outcome. "Aside from the potential for huge monetary damages, I think even Dr. McGrath Sr. would agree that it is not the kind of publicity the Alfredson would want. As you can see from the article, Dr. William McGrath has been more active in trying to clear his family name than in addressing the actual incident."

William rose to his feet. "Madame Chairperson, may I speak to this groundless allegation?" he asked in an even voice.

Lorna turned to Eileen. "If I've read our bylaws correctly, the floor is not open for discussion during a presentation."

Eileen shot her a look of distaste before turning more sympathetically to William. "Dr. McGrath, I'm afraid you'll have to wait until after this presentation when we will most *certainly* open the floor for discussion."

Lorna pulled out more pages from her file and passed them along to the board members. "Unfortunately, Tyler is not the only member of his family embroiled in a potentially disastrous controversy. So is his wife, Dr. Jill Laidlaw."

Tyler rose quickly to his feet. "Leave her out of this!" he spat.

"I wish I could, Dr. McGrath," Lorna said with feigned sympathy. "But the incident involving Dr. Laidlaw has the potential to have a massive impact on the Alfredson. The board has a right to know."

William tugged at his son's sleeve. Tyler glared at Lorna for a long moment and then lowered himself back into his chair.

"You might have heard that Dr. Laidlaw is performing important research using *stem cells*." Lorna stressed the term provocatively. She pointed to the pages she had just handed out. "Unfortunately for her—for all of us, really—this story broke on a major academic blog this morning. Apparently,

Dr. Laidlaw has been forced to withdraw her grant application as a result of data *irregularities*." She shook her head. "Having worked in academics my whole life, I know how serious research fraud can be. When this allegation comes to the attention of the media . . ." She sighed helplessly. "I'm afraid it will be a real blow to the Alfredson, not to mention a huge embarrassment to our family name."

As Lorna scanned the table, she recognized the rapt attention in the faces staring back. "But I'm a historian and I've come to discuss the past, not the present," she said. "These current-day controversies and crises are reflective of more than a hundred years of strained relationships between the McGraths and the Alfredsons."

She pointed to William again, who eyed her stonily. "I've heard Dr. Mc-Grath and others today allude to the noble beginnings of the Alfredson. Two men—a titan of industry and a medical visionary—working together to realize a lofty dream. It certainly makes for a fairy-tale beginning. But that is all it is, I'm afraid. A fairy tale."

A few seats down, Lorna noticed Dot smiling widely. The old woman even flashed her the thumbs-up sign.

"The truth is that Marshall Alfredson and Evan McGrath *despised* one another," Lorna went on. "In the end, they were largely responsible for one another's demise. And the Alfredson itself was never anything more than a 'devil's compromise,' as Marshall himself once referred to it."

A few mutters and catcalls broke out spontaneously around the table.

In no particular hurry, Lorna allowed the unrest to simmer before she finally continued. "Marshall Alfredson had no interest in philanthropy in general, least of all for a hospital sixty miles from his home run by a doctor he detested. However, his hand was forced when the married Dr. Evan McGrath seduced and *impregnated* his impressionable young daughter, Olivia."

Another noisy wave of protest and surprise burst from the table.

"When Marshall finally learned of the scandal, he almost beat the doctor to death with a fire log. Marshall vowed to kill Evan if he ever went near his daughter again." She shook her head sadly. "It didn't end there, though. No, no, no . . . Olivia was totally smitten by her older lover. So much so that she blackmailed her father." She stopped to utter a small laugh. "And can you guess what her demand was?"

"The Alfredson!" someone called out, as if on cue.

"Exactly. Olivia agreed to marry another man, Arthur Grovenor, and pretend her love child was Arthur's if, and *only* if, Marshall built the hospital for Evan McGrath." Lorna sighed. "So you see, the Alfredson was not exactly a hospital born from the altruistic dream of two great men." She tut-tutted. "In fact, after Olivia's fool of a stand-in husband killed them both in the boating accident, the blame and hatred between Evan and Marshall only intensified. For twenty bitter years, they locked horns over every issue facing the clinic. And then, in October 1918, while the Spanish flu was rampaging through the Alfredson, the two men had their final altercation over an illicit, potentially incestuous romance developing between Marshall's adopted son and Evan's daughter. Two half siblings!" Lorna paused a moment. "The old man tried to fire Evan and rid the Alfredson of the McGraths forever. Evan resisted. A fight broke out. And Marshall suffered a massive stroke that would imprison him in a wheelchair for the rest of his life."

Lorna took another quick visual survey of the attendees. Aside from the grinning Dot, most looked troubled. Some shook their heads, while others whispered urgently among themselves. Lorna fought back a smile.

"I keep asking myself: Why should our family cling to the ownership of this institution?" she asked of no one in particular. "It's a center plagued by crises and scandals, almost all of which are tied to the McGraths but have little to do with our family. And in terms of its 'noble' history, the Alfredson was in fact born out of deceit, treachery, and a shameful compromise." She paused, as though deeply disappointed. "Is that *really* a legacy worth keeping at any cost?"

Without another word, Lorna strode back to her chair.

Several voices erupted at once and soon turned into a cacophony. It took Eileen a minute or two of shouting, "Order! Order!" before the room finally quieted. The chairperson viewed Lorna with a look of unmitigated disgust as she announced, "I think *that* presentation will require a great deal of discussion. However, we need to keep the process orderly . . ."

Already seated, Lorna reveled in the turmoil surrounding her. She did not even notice that Dot had risen from her chair until her great-aunt was standing beside Eileen at the front of the room. "I would like to offer my perspective," Dot said.

"You are not on the agenda, and the bylaws . . . ," Eileen stammered, but then seemed to reconsider. "All right, fine . . . please." She stood out of the way for Dot.

The table came up to Dot's mid-abdomen but even without the aid of a microphone her voice was clear and strong. "I am neither a doctor nor a lawyer. Hell, I'm not even a historian." Dot grinned happily. "But darlings, I am the oldest person here and the last surviving member of my generation. The simple truth is that I *am* history."

The murmurs quieted as Dot continued. "I still live in the house my grandfather—well, to be technically accurate, great-grandfather—built. Marshall died when I was nine years old, but I remember the old bastard well. Oh, he was *something*, our patriarch." Dot held a friendly hand toward Lorna. "I actually had the pleasure of hosting our last and *highly* entertaining speaker in my home recently. We spent days together discussing this same fascinating history. And I have to tell you *everything* my great-niece told you just now is *absolutely* true."

Lorna relaxed in her seat, pleasantly astounded by her great-aunt's endorsement.

"If you view it the way she just laid it out for us, you would have to agree that the Alfredson did have an awfully shameful beginning." Dot paused and raised a bony finger. "Of course, you could look at it another way, too . . ."

Lorna sat up straighter. *What the hell is the old bag up to?*

"You could also see the Alfredson as the embodiment of a great love between Olivia Alfredson and Evan McGrath. One born from the ultimate sacrifice." She exhaled noisily. "What Dr. Simpson neglected to mention was that the two lovers met when Evan saved Olivia's life with a daring, last-ditch appendectomy. They never intended to fall in love, but they did—and not only with each other but with the concept of the Alfredson, even before there was such a place." She shook her head. "You have to understand that medical care at the end of the nineteenth century, particularly in hospitals, could be a sketchy proposition, to say the least. Evan experienced the worst of it firsthand with his ailing, crippled wife, Virginia. But he had the passion to imagine an innovative, better, and more humane way to deliver care to those in greatest need." She stopped and then added wistfully, "Essentially, Olivia and Evan forfeited their love—in fact, they both later laid down their lives—to see that vision realized."

Lorna glanced around nervously, recognizing the attentiveness in the faces. *That meddling old bitch!*

"My great-niece omitted one other small detail," Dot continued. "It concerned Marshall's son, Junior Alfredson, from whom you board members are *all* descended. You see, even though Marshall adopted Junior, the boy was in fact born his grandson. Junior was the illegitimate child of Olivia and Evan." She held out her weathered palms. "Which means, of course, that every single one of you at this table is not only an Alfredson, but you are *all* McGraths by blood as well! And your heritage is woven into the fabric of the Alfredson through *both* founding families."

The revelation palpably stirred the room again.

Dot squinted and pointed to the far end of the room where the three McGraths sat. "Of course, the converse isn't true. Evan McGrath's legitimate children were not descendants of Marshall." She paused and chuckled. "It's too bad, really. We could use the votes."

A sprinkling of laughter broke the room's rapt mood, but only momentarily. Lorna shifted uncomfortably in her seat. She desperately wanted to stop Dot but was helpless to intervene.

Dot dropped her hands to her sides. "In the end, does it matter today whether the Alfredson was conceived out of the devil's compromise or some grand romantic vision? Should we not judge the hospital on its hundred-plus-year record?" She shrugged. "I say we should. And I think, as Dr. McGrath ably pointed out earlier, the record is a good one. In fact, it is better than good. It is world renowned. A haven of hope for patients who would otherwise have none. And notwithstanding a few forgettable controversies . . ." Dot brushed off the current-day scandals Lorna had highlighted. "The Alfredson has done the name of our family exceedingly proud over the years."

Dot looked around the table. "If we are truly honest with ourselves, we would have to admit that we Alfredsons are a mediocre bunch, on the whole. This hospital is the *one* great thing we have done and continue to do. I personally think it would be an *unforgivable* shame to screw that up now." Dot laughed again to herself. "The Alfredsons have always had the capacity for pigheadedness and pettiness. We inherit that from Marshall, I'm afraid. However, I have never known our family to be especially deceitful. That is where my great-niece takes more after her father's side, I think."

All eyes turned to Lorna and she felt herself reddening with embarrassment. *You devious old hag!* she wanted to scream.

Dot stared directly at her. "Darling, while you were busy picking my brain, I was doing a little investigating of my own. Well, not so much me, per se, but I retained the services of my own Wellsby-like private investigator. Frankly, your excessive interest in the family history piqued my curiosity."

Dot broke off her eye contact and addressed the rest of the table. "As it turns out, our esteemed family historian has been writing a book about us. My investigator even learned that she has her own literary agent and is *shopping* the idea among New York publishers. She has a fabulous title, too." She stopped to laugh. "*The Rise and Fall of the Alfredson—A Hundred Years of Life, Death, Survival, and Greed.* Marvelous, darling! A vast improvement on Gerald Fenton Naylor's tepid title, and no doubt a far more gripping read, to boot." She feigned a dainty handclap. "Apparently, my great-niece plans to lay out on paper the darker underbelly of the Alfredson while airing all of our family's dirty laundry for the world to see."

*You can't, you tiny monster! I've worked too hard for this!* Lorna wanted to strangle the old woman. She wanted to melt into the floor. But she was too shocked to say or do anything.

"Of course, darling, with a title like yours, you do need the *right* ending for your story." Dot frowned. "One always has to be a tad suspicious of conflict of interest, though. If our family were to sell the Alfredson and embroil ourselves in a messy, well-publicized courtroom battle over its legality . . ." For the first time, Dot's voice assumed an accusatory edge. "Now *that* would be the ideal ending for a writer. The *perfect* launch pad for your new book to guarantee all the publicity in the world." She shook a finger at Lorna. "Is that not why you are so eager for us to sell the Alfredson, *darling?*"

Face heated with rage and embarrassment, Lorna glanced around the room. Some family members scowled while others looked away, too uncomfortable to meet her eyes. One group on the far side of the table, all of whom had publicly advocated for the sale of the Alfredson, ignored her entirely as they chatted urgently among themselves.

Eileen Hutchins opened the floor to discussion, but Lorna was too dismayed to concentrate on the speakers who followed. William McGrath stood first and calmly refuted her allegations about the Stafford malpractice case. A number of people rose after William to denounce Lorna, but she did not respond to her accusers, or even make eye contact with them.

*That old witch has ruined everything.*

After five or six speakers, one of her cousins stood up and coolly pointed out that Lorna's motives, regardless of their underhandedness, were irrelevant to the motion. Three others followed, arguing the same theme—the sale of the Alfredson was a business decision and should be viewed only as such.

Despite the mortification, Lorna felt a glimmer of hope that her cause was not yet lost.

After almost two hours of discussion, Hutchins halted further debate. "As per the bylaws, we will vote by ballots and then count each one aloud." She went on to read the motion again, as the ballots were distributed to each voting member.

Lorna checked off her ballot, folded it over, and passed it down. After all the lead-up and discussion, she was surprised by how quickly the voting process passed. Within five minutes, the ballots had been collected and the overhead screen filled with two columns and a one-word heading above each: FOR (those in favor of the sale) and AGAINST (those opposed).

Eileen sat at the front with the pile of sixty slips in front of her. Two other board members stood beside her as witnesses to the vote-counting. Without another word, Eileen reached for the first slip. "Against," she called out impassively and Lorna's stomach fell.

"For," Eileen said. She reached for another slip. "For." And then a third "for."

Lorna looked up to the big screen above the podium with growing optimism. The "for" side was leading three to one. *Could it be?*

"Against," the chairperson called out. "Against," she repeated.

Three to three. Lorna's expectations plummeted again.

Ignoring everyone and everything else around her, she kept her eyes glued to the two columns on the screen as Eileen continued to read out the slips. The numbers flip-flopped back and forth, and Lorna's hope rose and fell with them.

"For," Eileen called out as she read off the fifty-fourth vote. Someone across the table oohed. The numbers on the screen changed again to show that the pro-sale side had reclaimed the lead by two votes: twenty-eight to twenty-six.

*Three more votes in favor will be enough*, Lorna thought, barely able to breathe.

She stole a quick glance at the far end of the room. Erin shook her head disappointedly while Tyler clutched his temples between his thumb and forefinger and rocked in his chair. But William sat upright and very still, his hands folded in his lap and his face as much of a mask as ever.

"Against," Eileen called out.

*Damn it!*

"Against."

Lorna gripped the edge of the table.

The chairperson reached for the next of the only four remaining slips in front of her. "For," she called out, and Lorna's chest swelled with anticipation. *Only two more votes.*

The room was dead quiet except for the sound of the crisp paper unfolding. "Against," Eileen said.

Lorna dug her fingers into the tabletop until they throbbed. Twenty-nine to twenty-nine. *We need both of those last two votes.*

Eileen fumbled with the second-to-last slip. The room collectively held its breath and watched as she straightened out the paper in her hand and slowly unfolded it. "Against!"

Lorna dropped her head into her hands. *It's over.*

Whoops and groans broke out simultaneously as Eileen read off the last—and now meaningless—vote. "Against," she said. "So the final tally is twenty-nine for and thirty-one against. The motion to sell the Alfredson is defeated," Eileen shouted over the clamor.

"Darling. Darling. Oh, *darling!*"

It took Lorna a moment to register that Dot was calling out to her. Finally, she pulled her face from her hands and looked up at her great-aunt. The crafty woman was beaming with her most mischievous smile. She shrugged as though helpless to explain the recent turnabout. "Darling, it just wasn't meant to end yet."

Lorna simply gaped back at her great-aunt, speechless and agonizingly aware she had been utterly outmaneuvered.

## 48

Despite the cool chill that bit through his light jacket, Tyler stopped on the pathway as soon as he heard the thudding chopper blades above him. He craned his neck to stare into the drab November sky and admire the way the red bird swooped down toward the Henley Building as effortlessly as an eagle alighting. As he viewed the familiar buildings around him, it dawned on Tyler that, for better or worse, the Alfredson really was home.

He thought back to the dramatic board meeting a month earlier and remembered the moment—after the duplicitous Lorna Simpson had blindsided them by attacking the integrity of the hospital and the McGrath family—when it seemed inevitable the board would vote to sell off the hospital. As irate as he had been with her at the time, he had also experienced a sense of loss, as though a small part of his identity was being ripped away from him.

He still chuckled every time he thought of how that cagey little woman, Dot Alfredson, had torn apart her great-niece's case. The vote had still been uncomfortably close. The allure of the money must have been very strong for many family members.

The breeze picked up, and Tyler shuddered from the cold it brought. He glanced at his watch and realized it was time to head to the cafeteria.

Inside, Nikki was waiting for him at a corner table. She wore the same lavender scrubs and her hair was pulled back from her face as usual, but he noticed something different about her as soon as he sat down. It took him a moment to place it. Her dark expressive eyes were free of their recent angst, and she looked more at peace than he had ever seen her. "Nikki, you look great," he said. "So relaxed and rested."

"Five weeks clean and sober." She grinned. "Providing, of course, I don't have any slipups before dinner."

"Congratulations!"

"Other people climb mountains or run triathlons. I don't pop any pills for a month and it's an accomplishment." She laughed self-consciously. "How's Jill doing?"

"Better, thanks," he said, smiling. "We have another ultrasound today, but so far, so good."

She nodded. "Like I told you before, I have a good feeling about all this."

He wanted to reach out to touch her hand, but stopped himself. "Hey, I'm going to see Keisha again this afternoon in the clinic."

She smiled. "How's our little van Gogh doing?"

"Well. Really well. All the blood counts suggest her cancer has gone back into remission."

"Maybe even cured this time?"

"That would be amazing," Tyler said. "I have to give Vintazomab credit. If not for that drug . . ." He shook his head.

"Somehow it makes it a little easier to remember Nate and what he went through." She grimaced. "Know what I mean?"

"I know exactly. By the way, it looks like the hospital and my lawyers are going to settle the lawsuit out of court with the Staffords."

"Is that good for you?" she asked hesitantly.

"It's going to cost the insurance company a decent settlement and my premiums are going to go up." He shrugged. "But the point is, it's good for the Staffords. Even more important, I think it's going to help bring them some closure."

Nikki nodded. "That's exactly what they need."

"Yeah."

Nikki shifted in her seat and looked away. "Speaking of closure, Tyler, I wanted to tell you something."

"What's that?"

"I'm leaving," she said.

"Leaving? The Alfredson?"

"Oakdale. The Pacific Northwest." She looked away. "I'm going home to Arizona to be nearer my family."

"Oh." Tyler felt a twinge of loss. "When, Nikki?"

"Friday."

"So soon?"

"I have a job waiting at the children's hospital in Phoenix." She chuckled. "I'll make twenty-two cents less an hour, but the benefits are better."

A long, silent pause passed between them. "I'm going to miss you, Nikki."

She smiled warmly and for one millisecond Tyler felt the same rush as he did that evening at O'Doole's. But then it was gone. "I'll miss you, too," she said. "But I need to make this change. The time is right, you know?"

He nodded. "Of course."

They walked together out of the cafeteria. In the corridor they stopped and hugged for one long moment, and then she turned and hurried off.

Tyler headed directly to the outpatient ultrasound department. He arrived ten minutes early and was reading a magazine in the sprawling waiting room when Jill walked in. His wife had regained the weight from before her *C. diff* infection, and although she had yet to start adding any from her pregnancy, her skin's glow was unmistakable. Over the past month her raw vulnerability had subsided and her old self-assurance had rebounded, though not to quite the same extent as before; pregnancy had softened the edge.

"Hey," Tyler said as she sat down beside him. "Did you just come from your lab?"

"Indirectly." She gripped his hand. "I dropped in on Senator Wilder on the way here."

"How is he?" he asked.

"*He* thinks he's better." Jill shrugged. "The senator swears his hands are steadier. He thinks he's already on his way to reclaiming his political career. Maybe even another run at the presidency." She exhaled heavily. "But it's way too soon for him to notice any real difference."

Tyler ran a hand over her cheek. "Jill, even if his stem cells do nothing, you have given him fresh hope. Sounds like he needed that."

"Everyone needs that," she said with a little nod to herself. "I hope we can keep my study going."

"That's more than you would have thought possible four weeks ago."

"True enough."

A month before, neither of them would have dreamed that her lab was salvageable. Jill was convinced that she was facing permanent academic ruin. But Wilder's public endorsement combined with the surprise admission in her lab had strengthened her position. She had lost the funding of her previous agency, but she was guardedly optimistic that one of the other major multiple sclerosis societies might take up the slack and continue to fund her research.

"We're scrambling to get the new grant applications in," Jill said. "My staff has been so great, Ty. And Senator Wilder found backers who have donated the money to keep us afloat for the next few months."

"They all believe in you. So they should." He grinned. "Did you see Rymer's article this morning?"

Jill chuckled. "I almost feel sorry for Andrew."

"I don't. The weasel got exactly what he deserves." Tyler smiled, remembering the scandal. A few days after the board meeting, just as word of the cooked data in Jill's lab began to circulate, Carla Julian—the emotionally frail Ph.D. student whom Andrew Pinter had dumped for one of her friends—had stepped forward and publicly accused Pinter of tampering with the study data. The fallout had driven Pinter from the Alfredson, but it had not ended there. Somehow—Tyler still suspected someone in the Alfredson's communications department was involved—word reached Denny Rymer. The reporter jumped all over the case, holding Pinter up as the epitome of all that was corrupt and unethical in the world of academic research. The publicity had taken much of the heat off Jill, to the point where Tyler felt grudgingly grateful to Rymer.

"Ms. Laidlaw? Jill Laidlaw?" a tall blond-haired woman in white scrubs called out from across the waiting room.

Jill and Tyler rose and followed the ultrasound tech down a corridor and to a changing room. He waited outside for his wife to slip into a hospital gown and then they walked together across the hallway into the dark room, where the thin tech already sat on a stool between the empty stretcher and her ultrasound machine.

Jill climbed onto the stretcher, while Tyler sidled around the edge of it. He took her hand in his, and they shared a brief encouraging glance. The ultrasound tech draped Jill from the waist down with a sheet, pulled up her gown, and squirted the blue jelly onto her lower abdomen. The woman tapped a few buttons on her machine and then applied the ultrasound probe to Jill's belly. The screen filled instantly with a new sight. Instead of the tiny, ill-defined blob with the flickering heartbeat, they now saw a human fetus—with identifiable limbs, torso, and head—floating inside the gray shadow of Jill's uterus.

Tyler watched in awe as the baby's arm moved up toward its head while one of the legs suddenly bent as though doing hip thrusts.

Jill squeezed his hand tightly and stared up at him with unabashed joy. "Oh, Tyler!" Her voice cracked. She brought her other hand to her mouth. "She's got all her limbs and everything!"

Tyler leaned forward and kissed Jill on the cheek. "I count four, too," he said as a lump formed in his throat.

"Do you want to know the baby's sex?" the tech asked them.

"No need." Jill laughed. "We already do."

After a long congratulatory kiss outside the diagnostics building, Tyler parted ways with Jill and made his way to the outpatient clinic. The busy afternoon flew past, highlighted by a visit and another sketch from Keisha, who was continuing to thrive post-Vintazomab.

Tyler picked Jill up from home at 6:35 P.M., and they drove straight to his father's house.

Looking as thin as ever, but far more at ease, William greeted them at the front door and led them into the dining room. Tyler had expected Liesbeth and his sister and her family to be there, but he was surprised to see Eileen Hutchins standing by the table with them. The adults all exchanged warm hellos, while Simon and Martin raced each other—almost upending the end table holding the salad bowls in the process—to high-five their uncle, Tyler, and hug their aunt, Jill.

Tyler was impressed by the gourmet dinner, including the poached salmon and red wine–braised beef, which William had catered from Le Bistro. The guests attacked the food and downed four bottles of wine among the six people drinking. (Jill and the boys abstained, though the twins kept trying to steal sips of the other guests' wine.) The mood was celebratory, and the laughter frequent.

After dessert, Simon and Martin went upstairs to watch a movie, while the others gathered in the living room for coffee and port. William never explained Eileen's presence, but he sat beside her on the couch. Though there was no physical contact between the two of them, Tyler inferred a romantic spark and felt pleased for his father.

"I'd like to make a toast," William said as he stood from the couch, raised his glass of port, and waved it to each of the guests. "To family."

Everyone lifted their glass or cup and toasted.

Erin hoisted her glass again. "And here's to that kick-ass little broad, Dot Alfredson!"

They all laughed and shared another drink.

William stayed on his feet. "I also wanted to announce that I'm stepping down from my role."

"You're leaving the Alfredson, William? You got to be kidding!" Steve blurted out from where he sat beside Erin.

"But why now, Dad?" Tyler asked. "You just steered the Alfredson through one of its bleakest stretches."

William shrugged modestly and then nodded to Eileen. "I had the best kind of help imaginable. Besides, if it weren't for that"—he glanced at Erin—" 'kick-ass little broad,' I might well have run her aground." He chuckled. "However, I am pleased to tell you that we won't face a similar vote any time soon."

"How can you know that, William?" Steve asked.

"Because in the wake of our narrow victory, the board's chairperson acted decisively"—William glanced at Eileen with unconcealed admiration— "brilliantly, I would say, to amend the Alfredson's constitution and make it much harder—if not impossible—for the family to ever try to sell off the Alfredson in the future."

Eileen smiled awkwardly and reddened while everyone else applauded enthusiastically. Steve even hooted a couple times.

Erin hopped to her feet. "The Alfredson still needs you, Dad."

William broke into a contemplative smile. "Fool that I am, I used to think it did, too. Like there was some kind of divine-ordained reason for a McGrath to be in charge." He sighed. "The Alfredson is a hospital, not a kingdom. Tomorrow, Eileen will announce my resignation and launch the search for a new CEO." He glanced at her affectionately. "Meantime, she will act as the interim CEO."

"So the Alfredson will be run by an Alfredson for a change?" Jill mused aloud.

"What would poor old Evan McGrath make of that?" Tyler asked with a small laugh.

William looked from Erin to Tyler. "I have no idea what the future holds for the Alfredson, but I am proud and a little relieved to know that for now the McGrath presence continues on in the form of such consummate doctors as you two. In my heart, I have to believe that would have meant a lot more to Evan than who the CEO is." He paused. "It certainly does to me, now."

Liesbeth stood slowly to her feet. "Congratulations on your retirement, William." Her Dutch accent was more pronounced from the wine. She raised her coffee cup high. "And here's to all the years of dedicated service to the Alfredson and the wonderful job you have done. Well done! If my daughter and my husband were here today, they both would be very proud of you."

William flushed slightly as the others toasted him. His expression tightened and he lowered his glass. "On a less positive note, there is something else I need to share with you." He looked down at his feet. "I have been diagnosed with cancer . . . multiple myeloma."

A sudden silence descended as the elation was sucked from the room.

*Of course!* Tyler felt foolish for not having seen this coming. "When, Dad?" he asked.

"A few months ago."

Erin started to protest but William cut her off with a raised hand. "I am sorry. I had no right to conceal it from any of you. But I needed to see everything else through first. It was so important to me."

Without a word, Erin walked over and wrapped her arms around her father. Even after she released him from her embrace, she stood beside him with an arm around his back.

"What is the treatment, William?" Eileen asked.

"Painkillers, and of course I require blood transfusions from time to time."

"What about chemotherapy?" Tyler demanded. "They're doing great things combining new drugs with bone marrow transplants."

William stared at him for a long moment. "I never felt I could afford the time to go through chemo and a transplant. And to be blunt, I never used to think there was much point, really."

"And now, Daddy?" Erin asked.

William looked around the room at his collected loved ones. He cleared his throat. "I'm beginning to reconsider," he said softly.

They did not leave until almost midnight. Jill drove. Lost in his thoughts, Tyler stared out at the scattered few lights still lit in and around the town of Oakdale, while they drove home in intimate silence.

Jill pulled up into their driveway and turned off the engine. Before she could get out of the car, Tyler reached out and took hold of her wrist. "Jill?"

"Yeah?"

"I know you're convinced we're having a little girl."

"Mmmm," she murmured.

"But just on the outside chance little Angela Jeannette turns out to be a boy . . ."

"Not likely, but okay."

He paused. "You think we could call him William Maarten McGrath?"

She smiled and then leaned closer to kiss him softly on the lips. "How could we go wrong with wonderful names like those?"